Grigori

Written by Brandon Blake Varnell
Edited by Dominique Goodall
Illustrated by Lawrence Mann

Grigori – The Executioner Series
Copyright © 2019 Brandon Varnell
Illustration Copyright © 2019 Lawrence Mann
All rights reserved.

To see Brandon Varnell's other works, or to ask for permission to use his works, visit him at www.varnell-brandon.com, facebook at www.facebook.com/AmericanKitsune, twitter at www.twitter.com/BrandonbVarnell, https://www.patreon.com/BrandonVarnell, and instagram at www.instagram.com/brandonbvarnell.

ISBN: 978-0-9978028-9-4 (Paperback)
978-0-9989942-1-5 (Ebook)

CONTENT

Chapter 1..1
Chapter 2..13
Chapter 3..27
Chapter 4..37
Chapter 5..55
Chapter 6..73
Chapter 7..87
Chapter 8..105
Chapter 9..123
Chapter 10..141
Chapter 11..157
Chapter 12..171
Chapter 13..185
Chapter 14..213
Chapter 15..237
Chapter 16..249
Chapter 17..263
Chapter 18..283
Chapter 19..295
Epilogue...327

Chapter 1

Old Faithful Snow Lodge and Cabins looked astoundingly similar to Grant Lodge, except bigger. Much bigger. The building that housed the lobby was larger, more spacious, better furnished, and had a more luxurious appearance. The architecture outside of the main lobby was, similarly, much grander than those of Grant Lodge.

Consisting of what appeared to be a community, the lodge contained three structures that were enormous in size compared to the others, wider, lengthier, and more expansive in general; these constructs towered over the others. Several more medium-sized buildings, ones that, judging from a single glance, appeared to be three or four times the size of a large house, were scattered around, with dozens of smaller edifices in between these spaces.

Sitting in one of the several extensive parking lots were two vehicles. One, a bright yellow school bus, looked decidedly out of place. The many people who were visiting the hotel where Old Faithful was located—especially those who had children—were left wondering what a school bus was doing sitting in the parking lot of a lodge near Yellowstone National Park in the middle June. School wasn't even in session anymore.

The other vehicle at least appeared more normal—a Ford F-150. Well, it would have appeared more normal, except that the paint looked faded and peeled in some areas, and there were suspicious spots on it that looked almost like blood. Not to mention the front of the hood appeared to have been sat on by an elephant.

Everyone who saw the two vehicles sitting side by side decided it would be in their best interest to just ignore the unusual site and go about their business.

Ignorance truly was bliss.

***

Making for a sight that was even more unusual than the bright yellow bus next to the beaten-up Ford, Christian and Lilith, along with their mixed entourage of ex-Executioners, Succubi, and one incubus, walked through the streets that made up the small community known as Old Faithful Snow Lodge and Cabins.

It only took a short walk to reach their destination. However, during that time, the group became the subject of many looks.

Most of those looks were from the men.

They were drooling.

Some had even passed out.

"Clarissa," Lilith heard Christian speak from her side. She turned her head, looking at him as they walked, their conjoined hands lightly swinging between them. He had noticed the looks as well. "How many of these women know how to control their Aura of Allure?"

"Only myself and the Valkyries," Clarissa answered. "Celeste here knows how to as well, but she is an exceptional student." She gestured towards the redhead by her side. It was the girl Christian had saved during the first goblin attack. Celeste blushed, but she could not keep the pleased smile off her face.

It made sense that most of those with them did not know how to control their allure. The clear majority of women that made up the enclave were young, between the ages of fourteen and sixteen. The enclave had never been designed as a permanent place of residence, but as a shelter for succubus to remain safe while learning to control their Aura of Allure so they could eventually go out and find mates. Only the Valkyries and Clarissa actually remained in the enclave full time, except when they were mating.

"I guess it's a good thing you guys gave me this, then." Leon held up a medallion similar to the one Andrew had around his neck.

"Very. Without that, you would be a drooling idiot just like these people." Clarissa eyed the males, both old and young alike, in disgust. None of the men had tried to attack them. However, that didn't feel like much of a consolation. "At least the combined Aura of Allure of so many succubi has rendered them too stupid to move."

After looking at the men, noting the slack-jawed faces, the drool gushing from their mouths, and the glazed over eyes, Lilith found herself agreeing.

"So, has anyone here met this Azazel guy?" asked Kaylee. She marched alongside Clarissa, wearing a long cloak that hid the small armory she was packing on her person.

"None of my people have ever had dealings with Fallen Angels before now." Samantha cast both Tristin and Christian a bit of a glare. She had made her feelings on this subject perfectly known. Unfortunately, she had been outvoted, or so she had said. Lilith didn't understand why the woman hadn't just left if she didn't want to be with them, but she didn't feel the need to comment.

There was no need to start making brush fires with people.

"That said," Samantha continued, "Leon and Sif did have a run in with him when we were attacked by demons awhile back."

Everyone looked at Leon and Sif. Their reactions were interesting. Leon looked almost embarrassed as he ducked his head, while Sif had clenched her hands into fists as she glared straight ahead of them. It seemed neither of them wanted to talk about it.

"So, what is Azazel like?" asked Clarissa. "What should we expect?"

"I don't know." Sif shrugged. "We only met him for a brief moment. It wasn't enough time to really figure out what kind of person he was."

"I guess we're all in for something of a surprise, then."

"Looks like it."

Lilith didn't know what to expect upon meeting the Azazel, the Governor-General of the Grigori. Until Christian had informed her of just who and what the Grigori were, she had not even known about them, so she felt this was excusable on her part.

The building that was their destination looked to be made mostly of red wood with a thatched roof. It was about three stories high. Near the top of the building, just above a window, was a small logo that reminded her of a combination of sundial and compass. It looked weird.

The building itself seemed old, but she didn't know if it was actually old or made to have that rustic feel, and she guessed it didn't matter. They walked into the main lobby. It was fairly big. The floors were made of rock instead of wood or tile. Everything inside was mostly made of wood. Large wooden support beams jutted from the ground and traveled over their heads, though they didn't connect to the ceiling, which was even higher above them.

A lot of comfortable and expensive-looking couches and chairs were arranged around the room. A few people were sitting there. Some looked like they were reading the newspaper, while others chatted about whatever took their fancy. Most of them stopped and looked up when they entered.

Clarissa walked up to the front desk, where an unfortunate man stood. She made a disgusted face when he went slack-jawed the moment all of them entered.

While Clarissa went behind the desk and began searching for Azazel's whereabouts herself—seeing how the man wasn't going to be of much help—Christian and Lilith glanced around the lobby. Neither of them were sure what to expect. Lilith noticed the way Christian was slowly fingering his gun. He was probably wary of another attack.

"This is like what happens when men get near you—except on a much grander scale," Christian muttered as he looked at the mixed reaction they were getting. Men had become vegetables. Women were staring at them in loathing and disgust.

Lilith shivered. "It's creepy... but I'm at least glad I'm not alone."

Had she been alone, then Lilith would have been forced to endure these looks by herself, and she probably would have been attacked. With so many succubi there, the combined might of their Aura of Allure made it impossible for men to even think of attacking them. Of course, that just seemed to make the human women angrier.

"Have you found out where Azazel is staying?" asked Samantha.

"I'm working on it," Clarissa grunted. "Give me a minute."

"Maybe I should take a crack at it?" suggested Tristin.

"Absolutely not, vile fiend!" Clarissa hissed at him, causing the incubus to take a step back. Tristin raised his hands in silent surrender and muttered about how underappreciated he was. Christian felt a little bad for him.

Their group had spread out. Sif and Leon had moved as far from the main group as they could, and out of all those present, they seemed to garner the least amount of attention, which Christian found odd. Leon was a big guy. Standing at well over six feet, the only person who could match him in height was Andrew, the werewolf who had left along with Catherine. Leon was also carrying his massive warhammer, Sandalphon. It made their lack of presence even more shocking.

The rest of the succubus had gathered into a single group, with the older ones, the Valkyries, protecting the younger ones. Judging from the wary expressions on many of the succubus's faces, this was clearly their first time leaving the enclave—at least, their first time in a while. Many of those girls had been rescued by Clarissa and her group, so they had been outside before. However, it must have been many years since they'd left the sanctuary.

"Okay," Clarissa said at last. "I've found Azazel. It looks like he's booked a room on the third floor. Let's go—"

"There's no need to go and search for me. I'm right here."

At the words spoken by the unfamiliar voice, everyone turned their heads.

The man who stood before them could have passed off for a human—a really handsome human whose face was too symmetrical, too perfect for his own good. Dark hair with a spiky fringe shifted as he turned his head to study their group. His hair hovered over two purple eyes that glowed with an otherworldly luminescence. He was tall. While not taller than Leon, he was easily the second tallest person in that room.

He walked forward, his calm footsteps taking him toward the wary group. His dark leather boots tapped against the floor. Tight black jeans that fit him like a glove creased as he walked. A sleeveless shirt adorned his chest, though the large trench coat thrown over it hid a good deal of his body. Even so, it was clear from his broad shoulders and powerful legs that he was quite athletic.

"Well now." The man's grin was as wide as it was lecherous. "I must be one lucky man to have so many beautiful women coming here to see me. How unexpected."

There were moments in every person's life where they have something of an epiphany, a revelation so startling that it causes their entire world view to shift.

What Lilith had in that moment was *not* an epiphany. It was actually just a rather nasty chill that ran down her spine. She knew, in that moment, without a shred of doubt, that the man before her was quite possibly the most lecherous, perverted, lascivious creature in existence.

And that was not a good thing.

She was already beginning to regret coming here.

***

No one seemed to know what to make of Azazel, who had appeared before them and almost immediately began flirting with the various women present. He didn't flirt with just the succubus either. Samantha and Sif had both been subjected to his advances, though he did keep his lecherousness to a limit. It seemed he wouldn't touch a woman without her permission, as shown by how he kept his hands completely to himself.

Azazel had already booked several rooms for them to stay the night. In fact, the entire second floor was theirs, according to him, and they could choose any room they wanted. He also told them this lodge had a hot spring for anyone who wanted to relax. In fact, Azazel recommended they use the hot spring once the meeting was over.

Naturally, all the women were wary.

Clarissa had left Kaylee in charge of the younger succubus, telling her to get them set up in their rooms and to wash up. They hadn't been able to clean off since their battle against the goblins, trolls, and Faust the other day. Many of them probably appreciated having the chance to finally soak in a hot spring.

While the younger succubi were being led to their rooms, Azazel led everyone to a conference room, though Christian didn't know if it could truly be called a conference room. It was large and there was only one table. The table, longer than it was wide, could even fit around twenty people around it. However, the room held an appearance that made him think it had originally been meant as a dining room.

Two people were already present when they arrived.

One of them was a man wearing a black coat with icy blue eyes. He had pale skin, a pointed chin, and long hair the color of midnight. Christian almost mistook him for one of those Goths that he saw everywhere in Los Angeles, but when he blinked at the man, his red eye burned as he saw the strange power emanating from him. It looked like divine energy surrounding his body like a halo, though that energy was slightly tainted with darkness.

The other man was a blond whose hair had been cut short. Eyes a bright green, he studied the group that had arrived alongside Azazel with a studious expression, like something Christian would expect from a scholar. Unlike his dark counterpart, he wore all white clothing. His shirt, coat with high collar, and even his pants and gloves were all white. Like the other man, tainted divinity surrounded him, but it was a lot more muted, as if he was actively suppressing his power while the other let it flow freely and wildly.

"Feel free to sit anywhere you'd like," Azazel said as he wandered over to the two men, who stood and gave him a deferential bow. The fallen angel gestured for the two to reclaim their seats.

Christian tugged on Lilith's hand and sat in a chair near the center of the table. Lilith sat beside him, though it was clear from the way she squirmed that she wanted to claim his lap as her seat. That was her usual spot. She was probably restraining herself because of the situation.

Almost before anyone else could even move, Samantha had plopped down on his left. He glanced at her, but she appeared not to be paying him any attention, so he returned to looking at Azazel. Meanwhile, Clarissa sat on Samantha's left while Leon and Sif opted to stand. Leon had Sandalphon resting on his shoulder while Sif's claws were out.

It seems they don't trust these fallen angels.

Christian didn't blame them for not trusting this group, who had been banished from Heaven due to sins they'd committed. He was wary himself. However, given the circumstances, he didn't think this group wanted to kill them. In fact, he was pretty sure that if they had wanted them dead, they wouldn't have gone through all this trouble. They would have just done it. They had the power.

That one could kill all of us on his own.

He eyed the pale-skinned man with dark hair and thick eyelashes. The man, as if sensing his stare, turned to look at him. Christian felt a jolt travel down his spine when the man flashed him a grin. He had fangs. They weren't vampire fangs, but they were longer and sharper than the average human's.

"I wanted to sit by Christian," Tristin muttered.

"Too bad," Samantha shot back.

Christian almost rolled his eyes as the disheartened incubus stared longingly at Samantha's chair before, slowly, like a robot with unoiled joints, he trudged over to an empty seat further away from the numerous succubus present. He felt sorry for the young incubus.

"Allow me to introduce all of you to my two compatriots," Azazel began as he gestured to the two men sitting on either side of him. "The dark and moody-looking one is Kokabiel, and the one who looks like he belongs in a boyband is Shemhazai. They are my two seconds-in-command and help me deal with many of the day to day affairs."

"Though we usually end up doing most of the work ourselves while you go off gallivanting on your own," Kokabiel said. His voice was a deep baritone, but there was an icy chill to it that sent shivers down the spines of everyone present.

Shemhazai nodded. "You do enjoy foisting your work onto us."

Azazel merely chuckled at their remarks.

"I hate beating around the bush," Samantha began, a vein pulsing on her forehead. "And I do not wish to remain here any longer than necessary. Why don't you tell us why you asked us to come here so we can leave?"

Christian eyed the woman beside him. It seemed Samantha was reaching the limit of her patience. For as calm as she acted, there were some things she couldn't tolerate, and he guessed being in the presence of three angels who had fallen from grace was one of those things.

"Are you in that much of a hurry to die?" asked Azazel.

An icy chill swept through the gathered group.

"What?!" Samantha narrowed her eyes. "Are you... threatening me?"

"Is that what it sounded like? Forgive me. I meant no threat by it," Azazel replied easily enough. He didn't seem the least bit concerned by Samantha's hostile demeanor. "I just meant that if you continued going about things the way you have been, then you and the remaining Executioners will end up being killed by the people currently controlling the Catholic Church."

The words made Christian pay more attention. He sat up straighter, eying the man in charge. Azazel glanced at him, smiled, and then turned his attention back to Samantha.

What was that smile about?

"Let me make things clear for you," Azazel started again. "You Executioners have been played. The Catholic Church is no longer the force of good it once was, and it's duty is no longer spreading God's teachings. I don't think I need to tell you this, but the entire Church has become infested with demons."

Samantha grimaced. "No, you do not need to tell us this."

"Are you saying the Catholic Church has been infiltrated by demons?" asked Clarissa, leaning forward.

"Not infiltrated by," Azazel corrected, "taken over. The Catholic Church has currently been taken over by the Seven Demon Kings of Hell. Satan himself is currently possessing the Pope, and five of the other seven are possessing important members of the Bishopric. The only one who didn't possess a member of the Church was Asmodeus who, fortunately, these two managed to defeated."

Everyone turned to look at Christian and Lilith as Azazel gestured to them. Of course, it was already known that they had defeated Asmodeus. However, defeating a Demon King was an unheard-of feat. It was something that had never happened in the entire history of the Catholic Church. While Christian put up with the looks, Lilith reached over and grabbed his hand.

Samantha turned back to Azazel. "What you suggest is not possible. The Catholic Church is under the divine protection of God."

"It should have been impossible for them to infiltrate it as well, yet you and the others clearly saw several members of the bishopric summoning demons into your bases." Azazel shrugged. The nonchalance he displayed made Samantha scowl. Christian shook his head. "I know what you're talking about. Faith is a powerful deterrent. A place filled with the worshippers of Christ creates a unique divine energy that acts as a barrier to ward off demons. This is because God recognizes your faith and grants you his blessings."

Azazel paused long enough to let that sink in.

"However, Christianity and Catholicism have been waning within the last few decades." Placing his hands on the table, Azazel began tapping a steady rhythm against the surface with his index finger. "A lot of people are turning away from it, and even more people who call themselves Christian and Catholic are only calling themselves that to save face. They don't really believe in God anymore. It's like they're attending Church out of habit rather than a desire to worship Christ."

Christian, Leon, Sif, and even a reluctant Samantha, nodded at his words. It was true. A lot of younger people who belonged to religious homes had turned away from religion, and a lot of older people only went to Church because it was what their parents had forced them to do when they were younger. They did not believe in the teachings of God themselves. It was a habit born from attending Church as a kid.

"According to a survey taken last year, there are an estimated 1.2 billion Catholics in the world, but those numbers don't account for true faith," Azazel continued with a sigh. "It only accounts for the number of people who attend Church. I would say that of those 1.2 billion, only about a third of them actually have a strong belief and faith in God. With so few people no longer believing in the teachings of God, the blessings that God has bestowed upon the Catholic Church has naturally weakened over time."

"And this is what allowed the demons to infiltrate—no, what allowed them to take over the Catholic Church?" asked Samantha, eyes narrowed.

Azazel nodded. "Exactly. God's blessing is powered by the faith of His followers. The more followers God has, the stronger their faith in Him is, the more powerful His protection is. With people turning away from His teachings and less than half the Catholics truly believing in Him, His protection is at an all-time low, which is what gave Satan and his ilk the opportunity to possess members of the Bishopric and take over the Church."

No one spoke for the longest time. Christian glanced around the room, noting the pensive expressions worn by Samantha, Sif, and Leon. Of course, they were the ones this particular problem affected. Clarissa and the succubus with her didn't seem to care. They weren't religious.

Christian didn't know what to feel. As a devout Catholic, the knowledge that the Church had been taken over by demons was disheartening, but at the same time, the events with Lilith had given him a slight aversion to organized religion. The Catholic Church had been killing supernatural creatures for centuries now, regardless of whether they were evil or not, regardless of whether they were religious or not. It was something he could no longer abide by.

"If you've requested a meeting with us, I can only assume that you want our help to drive the demons out of the Catholic Church," Christian said into the silence.

Azazel smiled. "That's it exactly. You see, while we may be fallen angels, the reason most of us fell was because of our unhealthy love for humans. We loved them more than we should, helped them more than we were supposed to, and our actions ended up hurting humans more than it helped them. That's why we fell." He paused. "Except for Kokabiel here. He fell because he's a battle maniac."

Everyone chanced a glance at Kokabiel, who grinned at them. It was a vicious look. His fangs gleamed in the light, and his narrowed eyes radiated a strong bloodlust that even those who were not sensitive to such things could feel.

"If any of you would like to die by my hands, feel free to keep staring."

Everyone looked away.

"In any case, I believe that as the only angels present on Earth, we have a duty to help out the Church." Azazel flattened his palms against the table. "Besides, I don't particularly like the idea of the Demon Kings and their ilk roaming free on the Earth."

"Speaking of angels, why have Michael and the other archangels not been sent down here?" asked Samantha. "I know they have not appeared before man in many centuries, but I would have assumed that the Seven Demon Kings appearing on Earth and taking over the Church would be reason enough for them to come down and wage war."

The smile Azazel wore, had been wearing since the meeting began, shifted into something a lot more brittle and cynical. Christian didn't know why. However, seeing that expression sent a jolt down his spine.

Even the other two fallen angels looked uncomfortable. Kokabiel suddenly no longer appeared bloodthirsty and Shemhazai's shoulders were slumped as though a great weighed was pushing them down. Something was going on here. Christian was not sure he wanted to discover what that something was.

"I'm not surprised you don't know about what's happening up top." Azazel paused for a moment, his expression pensive, but then his eyes hardened, and he glanced at everyone in the room. "I only recently found out what was happening in Heaven myself. The truth is that Heaven has currently closed its gates. Michael and the other archangels are dealing with an unprecedented crisis and have refused to let anyone enter."

"A crisis?" Christian's tongue felt heavy and his throat dry. "What kind of crisis are we talking about?"

"The kind that could cause even more humans to lose faith in God if they found out." Azazel's smile was merciless. "God is currently not sitting on the Throne of Heaven. He has disappeared, and no one knows where he left for or why."

Chapter 2

The changing room was a lot bigger than Lilith would have expected from a hot spring. Lockers lined the walls and there were benches for people to sit down on in the middle. There were even a few couches, though they were made from a water-resistant fabric of some sort that wasn't as comfortable as the cushy leather couches in the lobby.

She frowned at how empty the room was, but then, maybe this place was normally a lot more crowded and required that much space? She didn't know. As she stood in front of a small locker and slipped out of her clothing, she imagined this place being filled with more women, all of them chatting as they lounged around. Then she berated herself. The image she had conjured was like something from one of her light novels.

Now bereft of clothes, Lilith grabbed a towel and wrapped it around her waist. She nodded to herself. Heading for the glass panel door, she slid it open and stepped onto the cool granite deck of the hot spring.

No one else was present yet. She imagined Clarissa was looking after the younger ones, informing them of what happened. Of course, the Valkyrie would also be by her side. She wasn't sure where Samantha and Sif were, but she also wasn't sure she wanted to know. Those two kind of scared her.

Wandering over to the largest of six pools that were spread across the decently-sized space, Lilith slipped out of her towel and stepped into the water. She hissed a bit. It was hot! However, slowly, inch by inch, she allowed her calf, then her thigh, and then her hips to sink below the surface. Once she was fully submerged, a sigh of relief escaped her mouth.

She leaned back against the lip of the tub, then frowned as she looked at her surroundings. The deck was made mostly of granite. There were a few tables and chairs to her left, sitting underneath a gazebo. Several of the hot spring pools were elevated. They required stairs to get to, and one of them created a waterfall that led into the large pool she was lounging in. This aesthetic wasn't quite what she had expected from a hot spring. Still, she guessed it was nice.

Just as this thought crossed her mind, the door to the hot spring slid open and in walked two other women. One of them had hair the color of raven feathers. It had a slight springiness to it, bouncing as she walked. Her body was lithe. Lilith couldn't see the slightest hint of fat anywhere, and what's more, while slender, the woman had incredible muscle definition.

The other woman was short—very short. Standing at a height that would reach Lilith's chest, the brunette walked beside the taller woman, her large breasts bouncing within the confines of a standard black and white bikini. Like the short woman, the taller one was also dressed in a bikini.

Lilith was so shocked that she stood up and spun around to face the two without thinking. Samantha and Sif paused as they saw her. There was a short moment of silence where Lilith suddenly felt oddly vulnerable despite those two being women, but maybe it had something to do with how Samantha and Sif were glaring at her body like their eyes were laser drills. That had to be it.

"Um…" Lilith began.

"Lilith," Samantha sighed.

"Why aren't you wearing a swimsuit?" asked Samantha at the same time that Lilith asked, "why are you two wearing swimsuits?"

There was another pause. Samantha rubbed her face.

"You know, Lilith, this hot spring isn't one where you get naked," she said at last. "Did you not read the sign before entering? It says swimsuits required."

"I-it does?" Lilith suddenly turned bright red.

Samantha studied her for a moment, and then sighed again. "You didn't read the sign, did you? I hope you realize that hot springs in America are nothing like the ones you read about in those weird light novels of yours."

Lilith said nothing but instead slowly sank back into the water as her body became a furnace of shame. She'd never felt this embarrassed in her life.

Another sigh. "You are very lucky this particular hot spring isn't co-ed."

Samantha wandered over to the hot spring that Lilith was in and stepped into the water. She sat down several feet away from Lilith. Meanwhile, Sif slipped into the hot spring at an even further distance. While she wouldn't say anything, Lilith had the distinct feeling that these two didn't like her.

Lilith wrapped her arms around her breasts and tried to ignore the two as they lounged in the pool. Samantha had leaned back against the hot spring's lip and Sif was sort of splashing around. She kind of reminded Lilith of a kid, though she would never say that out loud.

Scratch scratch scratch.

Lilith tilted her head as she heard a strange sound, but there didn't seem to be anything present aside from them. Outside of the pools and the gazebo, there was just the large wooden fence that separated the men's side from the women's.

"So you're the type of woman Christian likes, huh?" Samantha said so suddenly that Lilith whipped her head around so quickly she got a crick in her neck.

"E-excuse me?"

Samantha was studying her with keen eyes that seemed a touch... jealous? No. Well, maybe. That glare was no joke. The woman was frowning at her with narrowed eyes and a furrowed brow. Lilith covered her chest when she realized that Samantha was looking at her bare breasts.

The woman snorted. "I guess I can see why Christian would fall for someone like you. Blonde hair, big blue eyes, large breasts, and a completely innocent and endearing personality. That man may have abstained from entering a relationship or even having sex while he was an Executioner, but I doubt he would be able to resist someone like you —not with his hero complex."

"Uh…"

Scratch scratch scratch. Scratch scratch.

Samantha waved a hand through the air as if warding her off. "Never mind. I was just talking to myself."

Lilith bit her lip. She glanced over at Sif, but the woman wasn't paying them a whole lot of attention, or it didn't look like it at least. Frowning, she looked back at the woman who, despite only appearing a few years older than her, seemed so much more mature... or maybe sharp was a better word. There was a deadly quality to Samantha that set her on edge. This woman reminded her of a sword for reasons she couldn't immediately identify.

"Do you... um, that is... do you love... Christian?" Lilith asked hesitantly.

The look on Samantha's face was so shocked it was almost funny, but Lilith didn't laugh. She couldn't. With eyes that were practically bulging from their sockets, the raven-haired beauty, whose statuesque and powerful physique was imposing enough to make Lilith feel small, stared at her for several long seconds that felt like they stretched on for hours.

"You... don't really pull your punches, do you?" the woman said after a moment.

"S-sorry?"

Samantha scooted back against the bench that surrounded the pool, until her back was pressed straight against the wall. Her hands dove under the water. Presumably, she had placed them on her lap.

Scratch scratch scratch scratch scratch.

"I like to think I've done a better job of hiding my feelings, but I guess it's impossible to hide them from a succubus, isn't it?" she said at last.

"Um, no, that isn't it," Lilith began speaking in a hesitant voice. "It's just... ever since we first met, you've either been glaring at me or staring at Christian. I just, well, I sort of figured the only reason you would do that was if you had feelings for him."

"So I see." Samantha took a deep breath, held it, and then blew it out. This caused her bangs to sway out of her face. "I tried my best not to look at either of you, but it seems I was unsuccessful." She paused. Lilith had no idea what to say, so she kept silent. "Yes, it is true that I am in love with Christian. I do not know how much you know about our relationship, but I have known him ever since we were younger. He and I were trained together as members of the same caste."

The woman shifted, lifting one knee out of the water and placing her hands on it. She leaned over until her chin was resting against her hands and knee. Water gently rolled down her arms and shoulders, and a few small droplets of sweat had formed along her neck and face from the heat of the hot spring. A nostalgic expression crept across her face.

Scratch scratch scratch scratch scratch scratch scratch scratch scratch.

"I had always admired Christian's drive and desire to protect others," Samantha admitted. "At first, it was merely respect, but as we both grew older, and I continued to watch him do what others couldn't, my feelings for him slowly changed. I couldn't quite place them at first. I was raised by the Church at a young age, so I'm not well-versed in romance. It wasn't until Christian nearly died at the hands of Abaddon that I think I realized that what I felt for him was love."

"Oh…" Lilith didn't really know what to say. In truth, she felt slightly guilty. Samantha had known Christian longer, loved him longer, and then she had shown up, out of the blue, and stole Christian away.

"Does it bother you?" asked Samantha.

"What?"

"That I love Christian? Does it bother you?"

Lilith thought about that for a moment before shaking her head. "No-not really. You can't help who you love, and you've loved him longer than me. T-that said, I'm not giving him up, regardless of your feelings for him. Christian is mine."

Samantha's stare pierced through Lilith like a laser, but she tried not to let the woman know how unnerving she felt. She straightened her back and stared at the former Executioner commander. In a situation like this, showing weakness would only invite the woman to try something.

Finally, Samantha turned away.

"Even if I did fight you for him, I know it wouldn't change anything." The woman let out a slow breath. By this point, Sif had stopped splashing around and come over to sit by them. "Christian has never had feelings for me like he does you. I don't think that's going to change."

Lilith went silent again. She didn't really know what to say in a situation like this. It had never happened before.

Scratch scratch scratch!

Samantha suddenly frowned. "Just what is that noise?"

"So you noticed it too?" Lilith asked. "I thought I was just hearing things."

Sif cocked her head to the side, ears wiggling. The noise came back. *Scratch scratch scratch.* Glancing around some more, Sif finally lifted a hand from the water and pointed at the fence.

"It is coming from over there."

Samantha and Lilith looked at the fence, then at each other. Feeling the hairs on the back of her neck prickle, Lilith stood up, grabbed her towel, and, wrapping it around her body to keep her modesty intact, wandered over to the fence with Samantha.

Scratch scratch scratch scratch!

The noise was louder as they got closer, so it was definitely coming from over there. What was it? A bird pecking on wood? It sounded almost like a cat using a wood block as a scratching post. She and Samantha searched the fence to try and figure out where exactly the noise was coming from, but they found nothing.

Just as they were about to give up, a small object suddenly pierced one section of the wall. It was tiny. She couldn't figure out what it was at first, but then she realized as the object spun and shifted that what she was looking at was, in fact, a drill.

What?

As the drill suddenly disappeared, Lilith wandered over to where it had vanished with tentative steps. Her body was shaking. Her breathing had grown heavy. Feeling a sense of trepidation, she stopped in front of the newly furnished hole in the fence. She gulped. Then she knelt and looked into the hole.

"EEEK!!"

She stumbled back in shock as a bright eye appeared on the other side of the hole. She didn't recognize who the eye belonged to, though it looked vaguely familiar, but she now understood what was happening. A peeper! Someone was peeping on them!

"Damn..." a voice said as from the other side of the fence. "I think I was just spotted."

Lilith felt a tremor run through her body as fear and shock raced through her mind. Something inside of her surged like a swelling tide. She'd felt this way once or twice before, but it had never been this powerful. A loud click echoed inside of her. And then...

"N-NOOOO!!!!"

Her scream seemed to act as some kind of trigger because, without warning, all the water in the hot springs behind her suddenly swelled to life. She held a hand out in front of her, as if warding off the eye staring at her from beyond the hole. The water shot forward like it was being released by a fire hydrant. It slammed into the hole and, more important, the eye. A loud scream echoed from the other side of the fence.

Lilith was breathing heavily as she stared at the hole, which was now quite a bit bigger than before. She tried to calm down. However, it was hard to get her shudders under control.

"What… just happened?" asked Samantha. "What did you do to the hot spring?"

"W-what?" asked Lilith.

The woman studied her with a large frown, and then gestured to the pools. "Look at the hot spring."

Lilith didn't know what the woman was getting at, not until she did as suggested and saw the large hot spring, which had been filled with water but was now empty. She stared at the empty pool. Then she looked at the hole, now about the size of a basketball. After exactly .5 seconds of staring, she looked at Samantha.

"Did I… do that?"

"You did." Samantha confirmed with a nod.

"Oh…" Lilith looked around with an awkward hesitance, and then rubbed the back of her neck. "I think… I'm gonna get out."

"That's probably a good idea," Samantha admitted. "After all, you're still naked."

"Right."

Without a backward glance, Lilith, careful to keep the towel wrapped around her, walked back into the changing room.

She was so embarrassed.

***

The evening air was chilly. It buffeted Christian's hair as he leaned against the railing on the second floor. From up there, he had a perfect view of Yellowstone National Park, or at least a good portion of it. He gazed at the numerous forests, at the large rocks jutting from the earth, at the lakes and other natural land formations. That said, he could not see the lake that the succubus enclave had been under. It was too far away.

"I was wondering where you headed off to," a voice said behind him.

Christian sighed, and then turned just his head to watch the young man walking up to him. The pretty boy stopped beside the railing and grinned brightly.

"Not gonna join the other men in some good old-fashioned male bonding?" Tristin asked.

"I don't really feel like it right now," Christian muttered as he turned back to the view. "What about you?"

"I'm not really liked by men that much." Tristin shrugged his shoulders as he also looked at the expansive view below. "Even the fallen feel a bit awkward around me. Heh. It's tough being this sexy, you know? Every guy feels threatened by my hotness."

Christian snorted. "Hotness. Right."

Chuckling, Tristin turned around, set his elbows on the rail, and leaned back. "To be honest, you're the only male who has never once hated me because of what I am. You remember when we were kids, right? All the other boys at the orphanage used to pick on me. You were the only one who stood up for me. I really appreciated that."

Christian tried not to blush, but he wasn't sure he succeeded. Judging from the smile Tristin wore, which looked impossibly smug, he realized he definitely hadn't succeeded. He gave an irritated sigh and turned away to at least hide his blush. When his... his... well, he guessed Tristin was a friend. When his friend laughed, the blush merely grew as heat spread from just his cheeks to the rest of his face and even his ears.

"So..." A still somewhat amused Tristin settled down, "what do you make of what we learned in that meeting?"

"You mean about God being absent from the Throne of Heaven?" asked Christian, sighing as he ran a hand through his hair. "I don't know. It all seems unbelievable to me, but I mean, if God really has left the Throne of Heaven, it would certainly explain why more demons have been showing up. It would also explain why more people are turning away from Christ."

Tristin scratched the back of his head. "More demons have been slipping into our world. That could only happen if the barrier God created between the two realms has weakened." Tristin paused. "Do you think God's disappearance might have something to do with this?"

"What? Like maybe the demons somehow forced God to leave his Throne?" Christian shook his head. "I doubt it. More likely, God left because of some perceived threat that no one but he discovered, and he's gone off to confront it."

"You might be more right than you realize," someone said from the entrance.

Christian and Tristin turned to find Azazel walking onto the balcony, dressed in a white bathrobe, his hair falling around his shoulders like soft feathers. He looked completely relaxed with a small glass of wine in his hand. That said, his left eye was really red, and Christian didn't think it was from the alcohol.

"What do you mean?" asked Christian as Azazel came to stand beside them. It was easy to notice that he was as far from Tristin as possible without seeming rude.

"God is very protective over his creations," Azazel said, shrugging. "He loves them beyond what might be considered reasonable." A soft, almost nostalgic smile crossed his face. "I remembered one of the times I got hurt. It was... well, I got stupid and ended up in a fight with some Valkyries. I don't think I've ever seen God get so angry on my behalf. He went over to Asgard and literally tore the place apart to get justice. I hear Old Man Odin is still dealing with the fallout."

"Wait. Are you telling me other gods exist?" asked Christian.

"Forget that," Tristin exclaimed. "I want to hear more about these Valkyries!"

"Of course, other gods exist," Azazel said.

"Are you ignoring me?!" asked Tristin.

Taking a sip of his drink, Azazel continued, "Norse, Greek, Roman, Shinto, Hindu... all the gods are real. A god's power is generated by his believers. When more people believe in a god, when more people have faith, they become more powerful. God... our God, is a bit unique. He's kinda always been there. However, he chose not to interfere in the daily affairs of humans like most gods do. He simply loved watching over humans, though he has interfered on occasion when he felt the situation demanded it."

"I see."

Christian felt pensive as he listened to Azazel speak. He felt like he was hearing something potentially groundbreaking, something that could literally break the backbone of most religions. The fact that Azazel was telling him about it so casually, with such nonchalance, was kind of disturbing. Then again, things had already gone off the deep end. Demons had taken over the Church. Surely telling him about this couldn't cause something even worse to happen.

"Anyway," Azazel continued. "God has occasionally been known to leave the Throne of Heaven, but he usually comes back within a couple of months. This has been the longest time God has ever disappeared."

"How long has it been?" asked Christian.

Azazel made a face as he tilted his head. "Let's see... I'd say about... maybe forty years."

"That's an awfully long time."

"It is." Azazel nodded. "Which should tell you about the magnitude of whatever threat God is currently fighting."

A silence ensued as Christian absorbed this information, which was interesting but useless to their situation. Knowing that God had disappeared to possibly fight some unknown threat wouldn't help them right now. They didn't know what that threat was, whether or not it pertained to them, or even if they could even help. Still, it was interesting.

"By the way, why is your eye all red?" asked Tristin.

Azazel chuckled and finally looked at Tristin. "Let's just say that Christian's little succubus is more powerful than I thought."

Christian could only tilt his head.

***

Early the next morning, Azazel had asked everyone to gather for breakfast.

They were situated in the dining hall, a large space that featured numerous buffet tables filled with various breakfast foods. All the succubi were sitting around the tables. Each table was round and only had enough room for four or five people, so the over fifty succubi were spread out. The only ones who weren't forced to spread themselves out like that were the ones doing the decision making.

Christian sat at the only long table in the room with Lilith on one side and Tristin on the other. The table could seat about six on either side. On Lilith's left was Clarissa, and on Tristin's right was Samantha. On the other side of the table sat Kokabiel, Shemhazai, Leon, Sif, and Heather, the leader of the Valkyries. She had recovered enough from her fight against the trolls and goblins that she could move, but she still looked a bit like a mummy with all those bandages wrapped around her.

Azazel was sitting at the head of the table, which Christian didn't find too surprising. The man seemed to have recovered from whatever happened to him last night. His eye was no longer bloodshot.

The noise from the other tables was nearly overpowering as the succubi chatted. While there had been a lot of nervous energy coming from them the previous day, they seemed to have mostly recovered from the shocking situational altercations that led to their current circumstances. Many of them were smiling as they spoke with the other girls. That said, a few still glanced at Tristin like he was pond scum several times. The incubus did an admirable job of ignoring them.

"Hey, hey! This is pretty good. Wanna try a bite?" Tristin held up his spoon to Christian.

Looking at the other man in disgust, Christian said, "If you try to feed that to me, I am going to punch you in the face."

"Hey, Christian," Lilith said suddenly. "Have you tried the pastries yet?"

"Not yet."

Christian rarely ate food like pastries since they didn't have much in the way of nutritional value. They were just carbs and sugar, and they weren't even the complex carbs that helped his body function more smoothly.

That morning, Lilith was wearing a pair of tight jeans that fit her bottom snugly and a regular T-shirt. The pants weren't too small for her, but since her chest was a bit bigger than most, the shirt looked a little stretched.

"Here." Lilith held out a pastry to him. There was a chunk missing, showing that she'd already taken a bite out of it. "Try it. It's really good."

While Christian wasn't one for sweets, he leaned over and bit into the section where Lilith had already taken a bite. He thoughtfully chewed with his mouth closed as the sugary sweet taste of strawberries and a sugar glaze hit his tongue.

"It is good," he admitted. Lilith smiled at him, which caused him to smile back.

"Someone gag me," Leon muttered.

Christian frowned at the large man, but then Sif elbowed her partner in the side, getting him to shut up.

Breakfast continued for a bit longer without incident. The fallen angel, Azazel, spoke mostly with Clarissa about what her plans were. She and her enclave were out of a home, and she had a large number of succubus to take care of. Their only option was to find another place they could hide. However, that would be harder than ever now that their sanctuary, which had been built over several centuries, was gone.

"You can always come with us," Azazel said with a gesture. "Fallen angels are immune to a succubus's Aura of Allure, so you won't have to worry about anyone falling prey to your girls. Our base is also located far away from any human civilization that you won't have to worry about men accidentally stumbling on it. Once your girls master their Aura of Allure, I can have our people transport them back to human civilization, so they can go out and find mates."

"That does sound like a promising prospect," Clarissa admitted, though her eyes told everyone that she was still suspicious. "But what do you want in return for this kind gesture?"

"Nothing much." Azazel wore an easy-going smile as he spoke with the succubus. "Just intelligence. Once your girls go out into the world, I would appreciate it if they could send regular reports back to us about anything interesting that's happening wherever they end up."

"That's all?" Clarissa appeared skeptical.

Azazel nodded. "That's all."

"Hmm…" Clarissa cupped a hand to her chin while, sitting beside her, Heather frowned at her leader. "If you can offer my people a safe haven and only want information in exchange, it would be foolish of me to decline. I accept your offer."

"That's good. And what about the rest of you?" asked Azazel, looking at the Executioners first, and then at Christian and Lilith. "All of you are welcome to join us. In fact, my reason for calling you here was to ask if you would team up with us."

"You want The Executioners to team up with the Grigori?" asked Samantha, a skeptical expression suddenly crossing her face. "You do realize that we are not allies, right?"

"True, but we're not enemies either." Azazel's smile grew as a twinkle entered his eyes. "Besides, as things stand, the Executioners aren't going to last much longer. Without the Catholic Church's backing, you no longer have the power you once did. On the other hand, if you come with me, I will offer you funding, training, and a place where you can actually accomplish something good."

"And what do you ask for in exchange?" asked a narrow-eyed Samantha.

"That you help us defeat the Seven Demon Kings."

Leon and Sif sucked in a breath as Samantha's eyes went from narrow to wide. Christian would also admit to being surprised, but he'd already suspected that the Grigori's ultimate goal was the defeat of the Seven Demon Kings. The man had already intimated as much during their meeting the other day.

Christian glanced from Samantha to Azazel. His former commander appeared pensive, but the Grigori leader wore a calm smile as he leaned back in his seat.

"I do not know about anyone else," Christian suddenly said, calling attention to himself. "But Lilith and I spoke about this last night, and we would like to join you."

"I assumed you would," Azazel said with a nod. "You are, of course, welcome to come with us. Far be it for me to turn away the reincarnation of Lilith and the man who defeated Abaddon the Destroyer in single combat."

"Reincarnation?" Lilith tilted her head.

"You mean you don't know?" Azazel scratched his chin. "The other night, you created an illusion so powerful that it became real. Those powers you possess are something only those who have inherited the powers of the original four succubi can wield. Given your name, it is quite obvious that you inherited the powers of the original Lilith, which makes you her reincarnation."

"I… I had no idea," Lilith muttered.

"Haven't you noticed that strange things happen around you?" asked Azazel.

"Well, yes, there have been a few strange things that happened to me," Lilith admitted. "It just never occurred to me that I was creating illusions."

"Well, I'm sure Clarissa here can teach you more about your powers than I can." Azazel shrugged. "In any case, I would like to welcome you two aboard."

"Thank you," Christian said.

"I'm also going with Christian!" Tristin raised his hand and interjected suddenly. "I'm an excellent intelligence agent. I can gather and disseminate more information than an entire group of hackers! I can even hack into some of the most secure networks in the world."

"Well, we could always use more intelligence specialists," Azazel hedged. He didn't look very enthusiastic

"I only request that you let me bring my girls along with me!"

The words made Christian jump, but then he remembered that Tristin was actually an incubus and had a harem. He tried not to grimace. He liked to think he succeeded, but the two succubi sitting at their table didn't even bother. Their noses wrinkled in disgust as they glared at the former intelligence officer.

"I don't see a problem with that," Azazel admitted.

Shemhazai turned to Samantha. "I guess that just leaves you and your group. May I ask what it is you would like to do?"

Biting her lip, Samantha looked around in indecision. Christian had never seen such a conflicted expression on the woman's face. He guessed, though, that she'd never been stuck in this position before. The Executioners were all but destroyed, and her group were basically wanted fugitives on the run from the very organization they had served. She had to know they would be destroyed if they stayed on their own, but the idea of joining the fallen angels was probably equally unappealing.

"The enemy of my enemy is my friend." Samantha sighed as her shoulders slumped. "I suppose we don't have any other choice. You are right. Our group can't do anything on its own. We lack the manpower, the funding, and the equipment necessary to defeat the Seven Demon Kings. That being the case, we will join you, if only temporarily."

"Fair enough," Azazel replied lightly. It seemed he'd been expecting an answer like that. "Since everyone has made a decision on what they want to do, let's finish up breakfast and get moving. I have several vehicles on the way. They should arrive within an hour."

As everyone began eating again, Heather, who had been mostly silent, summed up her thoughts in a single sentence.

"An incubus, a succubus enclave, the Grigori, and the Executioners. We might be the oddest alliance ever created."

Christian couldn't disagree.

Chapter 3

After the decision to ally themselves with the Grigori was made, plans needed to be created. Of course, Christian, Lilith, and the succubus enclave were going to be traveling from the Old Faithful Snow Lodge to a shuttle that would transport them to the Grigori's stronghold. However, Samantha, Leon, and Sif needed to return to their hidden base and round up the other Executioners. Tristin also couldn't head right over. He was fairly adamant on traveling back to Los Angeles to round up his harem.

Kokabiel was going to travel with the Executioners to gather their members. The fallen angel had grumbled and complained about it, but he still did as ordered, leaving alongside Samantha, Sif, and Leon in their dinky little Ford F-150. Shemhazai left with Tristin. Apparently, the fallen angel second in command had his own personal car.

The succubus enclave was asked to leave their school bus behind, which no one had a problem with. The bus was something Clarissa had procured somehow. Leaving the bus in the parking lot, the group followed Azazel to a parking lot on the opposite side of the lodge.

It was a lot larger than the other one, or maybe it only looked that way because there weren't as many cars. In fact, there were only four vehicles parked there, and they weren't even cars. They were…

"Those are RVs," Christian muttered.

"Definitely RVs." Lilith nodded.

"Is that a Winnebago?"

"It is." Azazel stepped in front of the four RVs, all of which were large enough that they could probably comfortably fit at least 10 or 12 people each. He spread his arms wide and grinned. "I didn't know how many people to expect, so I decided to bring four of these bad boys. Each one has a maximum carrying capacity of thirty-thousand pounds. They might still be a tight fit, but I believe all of us can fit inside of them."

Clarissa, Heather, and the other succubus stared at the RVs with the same dumbfounded expressions that Christian was sure he had on. He didn't know why, but the idea of a fallen angel driving an RV didn't compute with him. It just seemed too surreal.

"Why did you decide to bring RVs and not something like a bus?" Clarissa couldn't help but ask.

Azazel shrugged. "These were already in storage and I didn't feel like buying another vehicle that I might not use."

"So… you use these?" Lilith asked.

"I like to go camping."

No one had a response to that.

Since there were no more questions, Azazel ushered everyone inside. The groups were divided into four. Since there were about 56 people present (Azazel, Christian, Lilith, plus the succubus enclave, which was comprised of 53 people), the groups divided into 14. Clarissa and Heather went into one, Azazel became the driver for another, and Celeste, the redhead he'd saved from goblins a while back, drove the last one.

Christian and Lilith boarded the one being driven by Azazel. The reason primarily had to do with how Azazel was a man and most of the succubus weren't comfortable around men. Making up the rest of the group were members of the Valkyries. As adult succubus who had already mastered their Aura of Allure and mated at least once, they were the only group who didn't get skittish around males.

The RV was big but lacked places to sit. There was one bench along one side that extended until it reached the hallway that led into a bathroom and a bedroom. On the opposite side was a bar with several stools. Two of the Valkyrie had already broken into Azazel's stash of alcohol and were drinking. The others had turned on the TV and were watching, of all things, a chick flick called The Notebook.

Neither he or Lilith were interested in the movie, so while the Valkyries began watching their flick with the most rapt attention, the two of them traveled into the bedroom, where they laid down to get some sleep.

"I can't sleep," Lilith said after several minutes of silence.

Christian sighed. "Me neither."

"I wanna have sex."

"We can't do that here."

"I know."

Their position was comfortable enough. Christian was lying on his back, and Lilith had burrowed into his side and was using his pecs as a pillow. She had wound her legs around one of his. Since they were wearing clothes, he couldn't feel her skin caressing his, but the warmth of her body was enough to lull him. Honestly, were it not for the Valkyrie making noise as they watched their movie, he was sure he'd have already fallen asleep.

"How long do you think it will take for us to reach the Grigori's stronghold?" asked Lilith.

"I don't know." Christian hummed as he ran his fingers through Lilith's hair. It felt like silk against his fingers. "I suppose that would depend on where the base is located."

"I suppose." Lilith yawned.

"Sounds like you really are tired."

"Not… really…"

A peaceful quiet settled upon them, broken only by the noise from the space beyond the bedroom. Christian must have fallen asleep at some point. He opened his eyes after what felt like several seconds later. He blinked several times as he fought the sense of grogginess that came from waking up so quickly. Looking around, he spotted his swords and the case carrying his guns leaning against a wall. Lilith was still asleep against him, her soft, even breathing making him tempted to go back to sleep. However, something had woken him up, and he wanted to know what—

Just then, a loud rumble shook the bus. Tires screeched as the bus swerved enough that he and Lilith were nearly thrown off the bed. Lilith woke up with a scream. Christian kept an arm around her and reached out to grab a handle jutting from the wall.

"What's going on?!" asked Lilith.

"I'm not sure," Christian muttered. "Let's find out."

When the vehicle evened out, Christian and Lilith hopped off the bed and went into the main room. All the Valkyrie members were standing on their feet. Some were grabbing onto something for support and others had merely bent their knees to keep stable. With Lilith's hand in his, Christian rushed to the front, where Azazel was swearing up a storm as he drove.

"What's going on?!" he asked.

"We're under attack!" Azazel shouted, cursing again as he swerved left. Christian and Lilith had to grab something to keep from falling.

As if to emphasize his point, a massive beam of energy tore through the space the RV had been driving through, continued on, and slammed into a vehicle several yards ahead of them. Christian felt horror wash over him as the small sedan that had been struck detonated in a brilliant flash of energy, but he quickly mastered himself. Something was attacking them. Now wasn't the time to mourn the pointless loss of life.

"Who is attacking us and how many are there?" he asked.

"Just one," came Azazel's grim response. "Hey, kid. You know how to drive one of these?"

"Don't call me kid, and no, I don't... I've never driven a day in my life."

"Damn!"

"I know how to drive," Lilith announced, raising her hand.

While Christian gawked at her, Azazel grinned in relief and vacated the chair.

"Then take the wheel! I need to drive this pest away!"

Azazel didn't even give time for Lilith to respond before he raced to the exit, opened the door, and leapt out. Not knowing what else to do, Lilith jumped into the driver's seat and slammed on the gas. The RV swerved a bit, but she cranked the wheel to bring them back in place and steadied it. Christian quickly shut the door to seal the room back up and keep the howling wind from bothering them.

"What do you think is after us?" asked Lilith as he placed a hand on the driver's seat.

"I don't know," Christian muttered, "but I imagine it's a powerful demon."

"Do you think it's one of the Demon Kings?"

"Could be, but I really hope not—"

Before he could finish, a powerful explosion rent the air and a shockwave slammed into them. The Valkyrie were surprisingly silent as they fiercely gripped the railings and seats with clenched teeth. Lilith was gnashing her teeth together as she tried to keep the vehicle from flying off the road.

Christian looked out the window and quickly spotted the other three RVs, which were miraculously still in one piece. He found one on their left and two on their right. One of them, a Freedom it looked like, was driving on ahead of everyone else. He thought that one had Clarissa in it.

More explosions rocked the RV, which shook as fierce gale winds struck it. Lilith did everything she could to keep on track, but on top of the explosions and winds, several vehicles were striking the sides of theirs. Perhaps the drivers had panicked. Maybe the explosions and aftershock had pushed them. Either way, Lilith was having trouble dealing with the numerous variables attacking them.

"Try and keep her steady!" Caspian shouted as he rushed back toward the bedroom. There was no way he could just stand there and let Lilith handle everything.

He heard Lilith shout behind him, but he ignored it and unlocked his case, grabbed his guns, and checked his ammunition. He had… two ammo clips. They were also regular bullets. He grimaced. These wouldn't make a dent in any demon, but perhaps he could provide Azazel with a distraction to capitalize on.

Racing out of the room, he stopped in front of the exit.

"Caspian!" Lilith shouted. "What are you doing?!"

"I'm going to help Azazel!" Caspian shouted, not giving Lilith any time to shout back.

He opened the door and grabbed the door frame. Then he leapt and latched onto the lip. Flexing his abdominal muscles, he lifted his legs and curled his body. Biceps bulged as he pulled himself up, slowly reversing his position. The wind howled around him as his body fully emerged from the RV. His thighs and shins hit the roof of the vehicle, and he ignored his rapidly beating heart as he slid himself across it, so he was on his chest and stomach.

Flipping onto his back, Christian pulled Phanuel from his holster, used his other hand to keep steady, and then looked around.

Azazel was fighting against someone. Christian had no idea who they were, but the other person was clearly a demon. While Azazel hadn't changed much. In fact, the only difference was he now had 12 wings sprouting from his back, the creature he was fighting looked nothing like a human.

Red leathery skin covered its body, which appeared several sizes bigger than Azazel. Thick arms and legs flexed with rippling muscles as massive wings flapped on its back. The wings on the demon's back reminded Christian of a fly's wings. Similarly, his head looked sort of like those of a locus. While the insect-like appearance seemed almost silly, the demon was not only huge, but its hands and feet had massive claws that looked like they could easily rend through steel.

Azazel launched several spears composed of divine energy. Those must have been the famous light spears. He aimed a few at the demon's face, but the demon, who Christian was going to assume was Beelzebub due to his appearance, swatted them out of the sky. However, those appeared to be distraction. Several more spears flew at the demon's wings, though all of them splashed against a red shield that sprang to life around Beelzebub.

For just a moment, Christian wondered if he could actually do anything. Could he really fight against something like this? Could he help against such a fearsome foe? As he was lost in indecision, a beam fired from Beelzebub's wings went wide, destroying an entire swath of road along with God only knew how many vehicles.

Red hot anger surged through Christian. What a callous disregard for life. This was why he hated demons. They didn't care about the humans they slaughtered. Humans were like gnats to them. No, they were even less than that. A gnat was something someone would actively go out of their way to kill, but this demon hadn't even been aiming for them. They died merely as a result of being around. Of course, mixed into the anger was guilt. Had they not been there, these people wouldn't have died.

Christian hissed as his red eye stung like someone had poked it with a needle, causing him to reach up and feel the wetness around his eye. It was bleeding. Frowning, he closed his green eye and looked at Beelzebub again.

Huh?

It was just like last time when he fought against Asmodeus. Christian could see a small mark on Beelzebub's body. It was located on his left armpit, the symbol of the sin of gluttony, glowing a bright red.

Christian took aim, but just before he could fire at the symbol, a massive beam shot from Beelzebub. It wasn't fired at Azazel, however. The beam launched from Beelzebub was aimed at one of the RVs. Having not been present for most of the fight, he couldn't know for sure, but it must have become obvious to the demon that the fallen angel was protecting those RVs.

A moment of silent horror raced through Christian. Everything seemed to be happening in slow motion. He watched the beam as it shot toward the RV, but then, just before it could reach, a barrier appeared behind the vehicle. The beam splashed against the barrier, a glowing white circle reminiscent of a buckler shield. Loud buzzing filled Christian's ears as the beam, which he realized was a horde of locust and not energy like he'd assumed, continued slamming against the barrier until the locus died out.

The RV was safe, so Christian turned his attention back to Beelzebub, only to realize there was more trouble. Azazel had obviously been the person responsible for that barrier. However, doing so must have taken his attention away from his enemy. Beelzebub slammed into Azazel and bit into him with his insectile-like mandibles. The fallen angel grimaced as he summoned a spear of light and jabbed it into the demon, which caused the beast to emit a loud shriek but not let go.

Christian gritted his teeth as he took aim, closing his green eye in favor of looking only through his red eye. The world around him slowed. Everything became shades of gray, all except the symbol on Beelzebub's armpit. He took a deep breath. He steadied his arm. And then he exhaled and pulled the trigger.

The sound of his gun firing was lost over the howling wind. However, Christian was still using his red eye's incredible vision to watch the bullet as it soared toward its target. He grimaced when the bullet didn't strike the symbol. Beelzebub moved at the last second. That said, while it didn't strike the symbol dead on, it did graze the symbol. A small gout of blood streamed from the wound.

Despite the bullet merely grazing the wound, Beelzebub shrieked and let go of Azazel, who used that opportunity to create a pair of light swords shaped like falchions. The fallen angel brought the blades down on the demon, slicing straight through its wings. Beelzebub shrieked again, louder this time, and fell to the street below. Christian closed his eyes when several cars slammed into the squirming demon.

Something hit the RV roof beside him. He opened his eyes to find Azazel staring down at him with a tiny grin.

"What are you looking at?" Christian asked in a yell.

Azazel shook his head. "Nothing. I was just thinking about how similar you are to—" a loud screeching of tires garbled whatever the fallen angel had said.

Christian frowned and shouted at him again. "What was that?!"

"… Never mind."

***

Azazel and Christian went back into the RV. Of course, since Christian would have been forced to climb down while it was still moving, Azazel merely picked him up and flew in through the door. Christian did not like the smirks the Valkyrie sent his way. Even Lilith giggled at him! He'd never felt so humiliated in his life, and that was saying something since he knew Tristin!

Since Azazel was back, Lilith allowed the fallen angel to take her place. However, rather than going back into the bedroom to sleep, Azazel requested they stay up there with him. He said he wanted to talk to them about something.

"It's been awhile since I've seen someone with an eye like that," Azazel said as Christian and Lilith stood near the driver's seat.

There was no seat for them, so Christian grabbed onto a railing and Lilith grabbed onto him. She was pressed into his side. The scent of her hair pervaded his nose, and the feel of her breasts pushing against his chest as she hugged him made him realize they hadn't had sex since the day they were attacked by Fauste.

"You've seen someone who has an eye like mine?" asked Christian.

"Not eye," Azazel corrected. "Eyes. The person I'm talking about had two Eyes of Belial." Azazel grinned over at him. "Your father. Back before Monica tamed him, your old man had been quite the demon."

"My dad? Demon? Eyes of… did you call them the Eyes of Belial?" asked Christian, unable to believe his ears. It felt like he'd just been hit by three rather important pieces of life changing information with the subtlety of a sledgehammer.

"Yup. Your old man was a powerful warrior with the blood of Belial in him. He made a living for centuries as a wandering mercenary. He'd go up against demons, monsters, or entire human armies. During the late fourteen-hundreds, your father had been called The Immortal by the King of France." Azazel paused to look at the shell-shocked Christian. "You didn't know that, did you?"

"No…" Christian shook his head. "Not really. I mean, Clarissa suggested I might have demon blood in me, but…"

"You didn't believe it." Azazel nodded as he turned back to face the road. By this point, the other three RVs had formed up behind him now. They were visible in the monitor that showed them a view of the back. "That's understandable. I mean, an Executioner working for the Catholic Church suddenly learns he's part demon? I wouldn't believe it if our positions were reversed."

Christian removed his hand from the small of Lilith's back and reached up to touch the flesh just below his crimson eye. A sudden, overwhelming urge to dig his fingers in and pluck the eye out surged through him, but he didn't. It wasn't fear that kept him from doing this. He knew that it was only thanks to this eye that he'd been able to protect Lilith. During his fight with Asmodeus, if he'd not possessed this eye, Lilith would have died. Also…

Even if I removed this eye, it's not like anything would change. If I really am a demon, if I really am a monster, then…

"Stop that right now." Before Christian had time to respond to the voice, a pair of hands grabbed his face and pulled his head down, until he was staring into Lilith's oceanic eyes. "Do you think I can't feel the self-loathing building inside of you, Christian? I do not understand why you would think any less of yourself after learning this. Does having demon blood change who you are? Did it change who your father was? Of course, it didn't. So stop thinking you're some kind of monster." Her eyes narrowed. "Or are you suggesting I have such bad taste that I would fall in love with a monster?"

Christian winced as Lilith put him in a position where he couldn't degrade himself. If he did, it would be admitting that Lilith loved a monster, which was close to his previous form of thinking. He'd already decided that it wasn't what a person was, but what they did with their life that mattered. If he didn't apply that same logic to himself, he'd be creating his own double-standard.

"It seems she's got you wrapped around her finger," Azazel said.

"Be quiet," Christian mumbled.

"Your father was the same way with Monica."

"Was he really?"

"Well," Azazel began with a shrug, "who can say for sure? Theirs was a strange relationship."

As the drive continued, Christian could not help but wonder about his parents, who they were, what they did, and whether there were any more massive secrets he hadn't been aware of.

It seemed he hadn't known his parents as well as he thought he did.

Chapter 4

After the battle against Beelzebub, Azazel led the group of RVs to an unused air pad located in the middle of nowhere, so far from civilization that outside of the air pad, there was literally nothing to see for miles.

"There's no way this can be your base of operations," Christian muttered as he, Lilith, and the women of the succubus enclave stood beside Azazel. The vehicles were parked behind them.

The man smirked at him. "Of course not. This is just where we're going to hitch our ride. Can't afford to let the rest of the world see this."

"See this?" asked Lilith, tilting her head. "What is this?"

"This."

Azazel took several steps forward and spun around, spreading his arms wide. In that instant, as if his grand gesture was the signal, something massive suddenly appeared behind him. Long and sleek, the floating fortress—for that's all it could be—looked like something out of a sci-fi film. The gleaming metal hull shone brightly in the sun. Several windows were spaced around selected zones. The front tapered into a rounded end. Four wings jutted from either side. There were some kind of jet engines or repulsors on each one because heat waves were distorting the air around them. Likewise, the end featured a powerful-looking series of rocket-sized engines.

"This is… unbelievable," Christian muttered.

"By the Great Mother," Clarissa also muttered.

"That," Lilith began, "is really big."

Seemingly pleased by the stunned reaction of his audience, Azazel grinned and made another grand gesture.

"Welcome, one and all, to the mobile-fortress… The Watchtower. Now, if you'll all climb aboard, we can get this show on the road."

Lilith gripped Christian's hand fiercely as the two of them, along with the succubus enclave, followed Azazel up a large boarding ramp that suddenly extended from the back. He could understand how she must have felt. Suddenly finding a giant flying fortress that looked like something out of Star Wars was definitely overwhelming, even for him.

When they entered The Watchtower, it was to discover a large docking bay, which Azazel quickly ushered them past before they could fully grasp what they were seeing. He led them into hallway that looked every bit the sci-fi mobile base. Glossy black metal made up the walls. The floor beneath their feet looked like plastic, but the feel when his boots struck it made him realize it wasn't. There were several lights built into either side of the wall, spaced at even intervals. As Azazel led them through it, Christian could feel a sense of dissonance slowly filling him.

I'm in a high-tech sci-fi ship made by a group of fallen angels…

What the heck had happened to his life?

"Since we're in a hurry and I want to get us to your new home as quickly as possible, I won't be able to give you the grand tour," Azazel said. "However, I can at least show you the bridge before directing everyone to their rooms."

"In all my centuries of being alive, I have never seen anything like this outside of fiction. Do you mind if I ask how you built this?" asked Clarissa.

"Not at all." Azazel seemed only too pleased to answer. "You wouldn't know it, but the Grigori have their hands in a lot of businesses that deal with the creation and development of cutting-edge technology. You know NASA, right? Big executive branch of the United States government responsible for aeronautics and space travel? Yeah. The Grigori helped fund that."

Christian couldn't believe what he was hearing, but he was given no time to question the man as they emerged from the hallway and into a massive space that could only be the bridge.

It was three floors. The second floor, which he realized they were on, looked more like an observation deck. There was a section just in front of them that had a table. However, the table wasn't just a table. A holographic map was floating above the surface, revealing more details about the terrain than any map he'd ever seen before. A walkway led to the very front of the bridge, which had numerous displays that, at first glance, could have easily been mistaken for glass. Only a closer inspection revealed that they were actually monitors displaying video feedback of the outside.

"This is the bridge," Azazel informed everyone. "This is basically where all the controls for The Watchtower are located. Piloting, communications, self-defense... basically, all of the vessel's primary functions are here."

Christian wandered with Lilith over to the edge of the walkway and looked down. There he found several fallen angels sitting at a variety of work stations. He didn't know what any of them did. Everything looked so much more high-tech than even he was used to that he couldn't fathom what they might be. Of course, there were a few stations that looked vaguely familiar, like the one with the person speaking into a headset. That must have been communications. There were also several people sitting in seats with joysticks that reminded him of video games. Given the nature of the joystick and the display on the monitors in front of them, he could assume they were responsible for firing whatever weapons this vessel had.

"I wish we'd been able to build something like this," Clarissa said as she looked around. "If we had, maybe we wouldn't have lost so many of our members throughout the years."

The succubi seemed to be in even more shock than Christian. All the girls were gawking at everything as they craned their necks and spun around, as if they simply couldn't figure out where to look and were trying to take in everything at once.

"We only just recently finished construction on this," Azazel admitted. "Until about a month ago, we'd been using regular jets when we need to transport a lot of people. There's also some downsides to using this, like the fueling and maintenance costs, but given what's been happening, I thought having a vessel that could be used in missions that required both stealth and overwhelming firepower would be beneficial to our cause."

"And what is that cause?" asked Christian, turning around to look at Azazel.

"I thought that would be obvious," said the fallen angel governor, smirking at him. "The continued protection of God's creations, of course."

After showing them the bridge, Azazel had a young fallen angel female take everyone to their rooms. This ship apparently had over two dozen unused rooms that had been converted into living quarters. The women from the succubus enclave had to share several rooms amongst themselves since there were so many of them, but Christian and Lilith were given a room of their own.

The bedroom wasn't what Christian would have called first-class. He wouldn't even call it second-class. It didn't have carpet for a floor but used the same material that the rest of the ship's floor was made from, that strange substance that looked like plastic but was metallic. While the room did have a desk, a closet, and a bed, there was literally nothing else.

It wasn't like he'd been expecting something fancy, so Christian didn't actually mind, and having been an Executioner for so long, he could sleep pretty much anywhere. Sometimes during missions, he'd been forced to sleep on the ground outside. That was actually why Executioners had a cloak. It could be used as a blanket to keep warm, or it could be rolled up and placed under the head as a makeshift pillow.

Lilith went straight for the bed and sat down. She paused as her butt sank into the soft mattress.

"Oh. This is pretty comfortable," she murmured. She looked at him and patted the spot beside here. "Come on. Sit down and feel how soft this is."

Doing just that, Christian sat beside Lilith and blinked as he sank partially into the mattress, which conformed to his butt.

"You're right. It is very soft. The mattress is probably one of the newer ones that use memory foam or something." He shifted a bit, feeling the way the mattress adjusted to his position. "I've never slept on one of these before."

"Me neither."

After moving around a bit just to see how the mattress would adjust to them, the two fell back onto the bed. Lying side by side, their feet dangling over the bed, he and Lilith stared at the ceiling as their hands subconsciously sought each other out.

"So much has happened," Lilith murmured. "I can barely keep up with everything that's going on."

"I know how you feel. Even I feel like everything is moving too fast for me to keep my head on straight."

Christian sighed as he thought about everything they'd been through, everything that had happened. When he'd been sent to Seal Beach all those months ago to slay a succubus, he would have never imagined this was what would happen.

"Christian?"

"Hmm?"

"I want to get stronger."

Hearing those words caused Christian to turn on his side. He propped himself up with a hand and stared at Lilith as she looked at the ceiling, her eyes unfocused as if she was thinking about something really hard. Those eyes soon turned to him.

"You're always the one fighting for my sake, but I hate it when you have to go off to fight and leave me alone. I want to become stronger, so I can fight with you."

There were so many things Christian could have said to her, so many things he wanted to say, some of which were even contradictory. Truth be told, he didn't want Lilith fighting alongside him. It was dangerous. He didn't like the idea of her putting herself in danger like that, but he remembered what Lilith had told him before, about how she felt the same way whenever he went off. It wouldn't be fair to her if he tried to forbid her from putting herself in danger when he was already doing just that.

"You will." Christian placed a hand on her stomach, feeling the warm softness hidden beneath the thin fabric of her shirt. "Heather and Clarissa are teaching you, right? I'm sure they can help you master your succubus powers and how to use a weapon, and I'll also do what I can to help you get stronger. I… I don't want what happened during the goblin attack to ever happen again."

Of course, he wasn't just referring to how she'd nearly been killed. He was also referring to how he'd blown his top. After discovering that she had followed him, Christian had grown angry and shouted at her. His anger had been an extension of the worry he felt, but that hardly mattered. What mattered was that he'd said words he shouldn't have. Even though they had made up in the end, he still regretted ever telling Lilith that she was a liability on the battlefield.

"Christian…"

"I will do everything in my power to make sure that you're strong enough to fight by my side," Christian continued as he slipped a hand underneath her shirt, caressing the warm skin directly. Lilith's stomach twitched as his fingers glided over her smooth, taut stomach. "We'll become a team. I promise, once you're strong enough, I'll never fight without you."

"Thank you," Lilith muttered before her breathing hitched. "Christian... I love you so much."

"And I love you."

Christian leaned over and pressed his mouth against hers. Lilith quickly opened her mouth to grant his tongue entrance. The slick wetness of his saliva-coated tongue rubbing against hers caused a haze to settle over his mind. As they exchanged their wet kiss filled with tongue, the accompanying smacking sound of their exchange echoed in Christian's ears.

Lilith's mouth filled with saliva from their activity, but she didn't hesitate to gulp it down and continue kissing him. She tilted her head. This granted him better access to her mouth. At the same time, Christian unclasped her bra and pushed the cups aside, so he could have direct access to her chest.

"Hnn!!"

Oh, yes!!

The voice emerging from Lilith's mouth was a muffled moan, but her inner voice, which Christian was becoming more aware of now that he knew exactly what it was, told him what to do. Not that he needed it anymore. After allowing his fingers to sink into the pliant, elastic flesh of Lilith's breasts, he traced the outline of her areola with his forefinger. He swirled his finger around, then pushed her nipple into her breast, enjoying how it sank beneath her skin. Lilith squirmed beneath him as her nipple soon hardened into a point. Once it did, he rolled it between his thumb and forefinger.

"Mmmm!!!"

H-harder!

He pinched her nipple harder, then tugged on it. Lilith's moans increased in volume.

Wanting more, Christian followed the suggestions of his mate's inner-voice and retracted his mouth from hers, then began kissing, sucking, and licking her neck. He shifted until her was straddling her. Lilith buried her hands in his hair as he left several shiny red love bites on her tender skin. Without his mouth hampering hers, the lovely sound of her voice rang out in the room, as did her heavy pants and hitched breathing whenever he did something she liked.

Reaching down to grab the hem of her shirt, Christian pushed the shirt up until her breasts were exposed. Her skin was already a healthy red as the blood rushed to the forefront. He watched for a moment as her breasts jiggled with every inhale and exhale. His dick twitched several times as it grew hard.

He didn't immediately go in for the kill. Pressing lips in the very center of her chest, he kissed between her breasts, enjoying the way Lilith squirmed and moaned from his actions. Extending his tongue, he licked her skin. The salty taste of sweat hit his tongue.

I can't... can't take anymore!

Her inner-voice was the signal. When she was so bothered she couldn't deal with his teasing, Christian took one of her nipples into his mouth. He bit down on it, not hard enough to hurt, but enough that she could feel it. Lilith released a loud moan that reverberated in her chest. Keeping her nipple in his mouth, he flicked it back and forth with his tongue, then swirled his tongue around the hardened nub before biting again and repeating the process.

Since he could only please one breast at a time if he used just his mouth, Christian cupped her other tit in his hand and began playing with it. He slid his finger underneath her breast. It was heavy. He could only marvel at how much weight this one object had. Grasping it more firmly, he kneaded her breast like a baker making bread.

"Christian! Christian!!"

Don't just focus on my breasts!

Withholding a grin, Christian continued to kiss, suck, and nibble on her breast, but he removed his hand and began trailing down. He crossed her stomach, caressing the soft skin, and then undid the button and zipper on her jeans. It wasn't long before he'd slipped inside and found her sodden entrance. Juices flowed from her depths. Her panties were already so damp her love nectar was soaking through her jeans.

"You're soaking down there," he muttered. It was one of the few times he'd ever spoken out loud during sex.

Lilith flushed. "D-don't say that!"

"Why not?"

"Because it's embarraSSIIIIIING!!! OH!!"

Tease me more!

Christian spreading her glistening lips apart, tracing his finger along the edge of her entrance before slipping a finger inside of her. Even though she was wet, her insides were so tight that moving required some effort on his part. He pushed his finger in, working to loosen her tight passage, and then pushed another finger inside of her.

"OOOH!"

Oh, God! That feels so gooooood!

While he fingered her, Christian used his thumb to work her clit out and begin massaging it. Her hips bucked, and an increased flow of juices flowed around his fingers, drenching her inner thighs and trailing down her butt. The stimulation soon became so intense that Lilith lifted her hips off the bed and began humping his hand. Her elegant toes were clenching the bedsheets as though attempting to stave off the feelings shooting through her. Gasps and moans filled the air before her walls around him tightened. Lilith let out another scream as her entire body seemed to seize up, and then she relaxed back onto the bed, her body adopting a boneless quality.

Christian let go of Lilith's nipple with a loud pop. Removing his drenched fingers from her passage, he sat back up and licked his hand clean, savoring Lilith's taste.

Looking back at Lilith, he smiled when he saw how exhausted she was. Her body was covered in a glistening sheen of sweat. Her breasts jiggled as her chest rose and fell with each deep breath. Likewise, her eyes had a glazed over quality as they stared sightlessly at the ceiling.

As he finished licking his fingers and stared at her, Christian felt his desire spike.

He wanted more.

While Lilith was still recovering, Christian slid her jeans and panties down her hips and legs. He also removed her shoes. Setting her clothing off to the side, he removed his own clothes. He didn't plan on having sex with her just yet, but he might as well remove anything that could impede their fun.

"Christian?" Lilith asked, lifting her head as Christian spread her legs. Lilith was completely clean shaven. Her bald pussy lips were engorged from her arousal. Their beautiful pink coloring made them seem fresh. He wasn't sure that was the word he was looking for, but it was the only one he could think of that fit. "W-what are you doing?"

This looks fun...

"What's it look like I'm doing?" asked Christian as he placed a finger on either side of Lilith's lips and spread them wide, revealing the inner depths of her drenched walls. "I want to see more of you."

Lilith covered her hands with her face. "T-this is so embarrassing!"

I love it!

"You say that, but I can hear your inner thoughts," Christian said as he traced her lips with a finger. "So I know you love this."

He didn't give Lilith time to respond before he leaned down and placed a kiss on her lips. Lilith screamed as a burst of ecstasy shot through their bond. Her hips jerked wildly as she placed her feet on the bed and practically shoved her crotch into his face. Christian didn't mind. In fact, he used her actions to push his tongue deeper inside of her as the walls of her passage closed around him. That said, it was kind of hard to please her when she was squirming around so much, so he hooked his arms around her thighs to keep her from moving.

"Christian! Christian, I—"

Feel like I'm losing my mind!!

Already knowing where her weak points were, Christian went in for the kill, rubbing his tongue against her most sensitive places before pulling out and taking her clit into his mouth. Lilith's toes curled, and her body quaked as she orgasmed again. Juices drenched his face as she squirted into his mouth. Some of it escaped, the rest trickling down her inner thighs and staining the bed.

Her body slumped again. Christian slowly lowered her limp legs back onto the bed. He stood up and looked down. His dick was harder than it had ever been, and it was beginning to ache. Biting his lip, he thought about going in, but then another thought occurred to him as an image he'd seen during their time having sex once flashed through his mind.

Crawling onto the bed, he stroked Lilith's face until the young woman's glazed eyes fluttered and focused on him.

"Hey, Lilith," he said. "There's something I'd like to try. Um, is it okay if we try, er, what was it called? Paizuri?"

"I think... think you mean a boob job." Lilith smiled at him. "I'd love to try. Um... I can't move yet, though."

Christian was a bit embarrassed as he realized he may have gone overboard, though to be fair, he'd just been following the advice Lilith's inner-voice gave to him.

"Don't worry. I'll do most of the work."

"Okay..."

Helping Lilith sit up, Christian pulled her shirt over her head, removed her bra, and then laid her back on the bed. Now bare as the day she'd been born; Lilith flawless figure was completely revealed to him. Her pearlescent skin didn't have a single blemish. Her legs were soft yet firm, and they seemed to go on forever, a paradoxical effect since they ended in a pair of small and incredibly cute feet with delicate toes. As she breathed in and out, her chest expanded and contracted, causing her large breasts to sway and jiggle.

Christian moved until he was straddling her just above below her sternum. He placed his pulsating dick in the center of her chest, and then pushed her breasts together until they had engulfed him. It was quite different than what he was used to feeling. Her tits were soft, like marshmallows or a pair of pillows, but they were also quite warm, and that warmth was engulfing him, causing his already engorged member to feel like it was growing even more. The sweat covering her body gave her skin a slickness that allowed him to slide his dick against her without rubbing himself raw.

"I… I didn't realize it would feel this good," he mumbled.

Lilith smiled underneath him. "I'm glad… I'm glad you feel good."

This is erotic. Why didn't we try this sooner?

"I don't know…" he groaned an answer to Lilith's inner voice.

Christian gritted his teeth as he slid his dick through Lilith's tits. In and out. His stomach muscles contracted as he worked his lower body.

"Hnn. Hk! I don't understand why… I don't get it… but this feels really good for me too! It feels like my breasts have become really sensitive!"

"I'm happy… to hear that…"

Grunting as he felt his balls begin to contract, Christian was about to shout out a warning, but Lilith suddenly lunged forward and engulfed the tip of his cock with her mouth. Her tongue swirled around his head, and then she sucked. Christian was unable to hold back. Her actions were too much. The suction-like sensation caused him to release his load inside of her mouth. Lilith's cheeks bulged obscenely, but none of his cum spilled out. He got a front-row view of Lilith's throat moving as she swallowed every drop of cum he released.

With her task done, Lilith let her head drop back onto the bed. "I don't know why… but you taste delicious. I feel like I could sustain myself on just your cum."

"That's a weird thing to subsist on… but it's not like I don't understand where you're cumming from."

"Ha ha…" Lilith snickered at his bad pun. "Christian?"

"Yes?"

"I want to be on top this time."

"Sure thing."

Lilith sat up as Christian moved onto the bed and laid down. His had already recovered and was standing at attention again. Reaching down, Lilith lovingly stroked his shaft before leaning down and placing a kiss on the tip of his head.

"I love how much stamina you have."

"Me too... I think."

Moving until her dripping entrance was hovering over his dick, Lilith placed her hands on his chest and slowly lowered herself. Christian watched as the tip of his head poked her entrance. Then her lips stretched as she slowly took his dick inside of her. He gritted his teeth and tried not to cum on the spot as her tight walls surrounding and conformed to him. Slowly, inch by inch, Lilith took him in until it couldn't go any further.

"It feels like your hitting my womb..."

I love how full this makes me feel.

"Move whenever you're ready," Christian said as he placed his hands on her hips.

Lilith smiled at him. "I'm ready."

Raising her hips, Lilith retracted until just the tip of his dick was inside of her, and then she moved back down until her ass was touching his thighs. She did it again, faster this time. Then again and again. Each time she moved, Lilith picked up speed. It wasn't long until the slapping sound of her butt striking his thighs mixed with the lewd squelching sounds of their passionate act.

"Ha... ha... oh... this feeling is..."

Hmmm... I might have found my new favorite position.

"You like this?"

"Y-yes!"

"We... should do it more often then."

"Definitely!"

While Christian couldn't do much on bottom, he did what he could to help her, lifting her hips, timing her downward movements with a quick thrust. Lilith became incapable of talking soon. She arched her back and stared at the ceiling, moaning as she continued to ride his dick.

"I... Lilith... I'm about to cum!"

"Me too! Me too!"

"I can't... can't—"

Christian released a loud groan while Lilith screamed, their simultaneous orgasm rocking them both as sensations, jolts of powerful energy and pleasure, raced through their bodies. The feeling left slowly.

When it did, Christian felt drained, like he'd just run across the country without rest, but he also felt satisfied. Lilith, her back still arched, swayed several times before almost falling backward.

"Whoa!"

He reached out and grabbed the girl's arms before she could fall. A quick tug pulled her to him. Lilith fell onto his chest, her breathing heavy as her boobs squished against him. Her chest was so big that a good portion of her breasts spilled over the sides.

As they came down from what Christian could have only considered a small slice of Heaven, Lilith seemed to gain her second wind. She pushed herself up, leaned down, and kissed him again. It was hot, passionate. Her tongue filled his mouth. Christian, still recovering, could do nothing but ride out her erotic kiss.

"Ha... ha... Christian." Lilith was staring at him with a wanton smile that he'd never seen before. It was like she'd become possessed by a lewd spirit. "I want to have more sex. Let's go again."

"Uh..." Christian looked to the side. "I'm not sure I can get it up again just yet. Let me recover some first."

"But I want to have sex now."

"... I can't help you if I can't get it up."

"You say that, but..." Lilith slid backward until her butt came into contact with his flaccid member. Rubbing herself against him, Christian became somewhat horrified when his cock readily responded to her ministrations. It didn't take long before his soldier was standing at attention, nestled firmly between Lilith's pert ass cheeks. "... this little one seems ready to go again."

If Lilith hadn't been in the way, he would have glared at his manhood.

"Traitor," he mumbled with all the hatred he could muster. That is to say, none at all.

***

Samantha did not know if she'd ever felt more awkward than she did now. Leon and Sif were not sitting in the Ford F-150 with her. They were in the trunk. Meanwhile, she was alone with Kokabiel who, thanks to his wings, was forced to sit in the back of the truck. She was sure he could have flown alongside the truck if he wanted, but he had chosen to sit with her. He stated that his reasons was to avoid attracting attention.

She wasn't sure she believed him.

The ride was made mostly in silence. They had to stop several times to refuel and eat, and it took several days to reach their destination. Normally, that would mean spending the night somewhere and continuing in the morning, but Kokabiel had taken the wheel during those times, driving while she slept. She was grateful. However, for whatever reason, his kindness made her even more on edge.

"I am not sure why I sense so much fear in you," Kokabiel suddenly said.

Samantha was startled enough that she almost took her eyes off the road. "W-what? I'm not afraid."

"But you are." Kokabiel's grin was reflected in the rearview mirror. Samantha tried not to shudder. "A fallen angel I may be, but I still have all the abilities granted to me as an angel born in Heaven. One of those abilities allows me to sense the emotional disposition of mortals."

They were almost at the base, which of course meant there was nothing around them for miles. This place was a desert that seemed to stretch on forever. Up ahead, Samantha could just barely make out the abandoned factory that was their makeshift hideout, the last bastion of the Executioners.

"You fear me," Kokabiel murmured. "Of course, you have every right to be afraid of me. With but a single thought, I could eradicate you from existence." He yawned and stretched his arms. "That said, I don't have any desire to exterminate you, and we have become allies. You have no reason to fear me for the moment."

"For the moment. Right," Samantha mumbled.

They soon past an old fence that looked like it had seen better days. Kokabiel glanced out the window, his nose wrinkling as they drove by a large warehouse with peeling paint, a rusted metal roof, and an entrance that looked like it had been torn asunder.

"This is your base?"

"Yes… and do not comment on how bad it looks. I'm aware that this place looks like a decrepit cesspit. I chose it specifically because it is so innocuous."

"It does not look like a decrepit cesspit," Kokabiel muttered, causing Samantha to raise an eyebrow. His next words made her scowl. "That is doing decrepit cesspits everywhere a grave injustice. This place looks like a post-apocalyptic shithole. I've seen porta potties with more class than this."

"Whatever. It is not like I care what you think."

"That is a lie."

Samantha gnashed her teeth together as she recalled this angel could apparently sense her true feelings. If she wasn't frightened of doing so, she would have decked him in the face.

They stopped in front of the smaller warehouse. Turning off the vehicle, Samantha exited, slamming the door shut and stomping over to Leon and Sif, who were climbing out of the back.

"Here's your case, Command—" Sif stopped talking when Samantha snatched the case containing her gun and sword out of the woman's hand. She hesitated for a moment. "Commander, are you okay?"

"I am just fine," Samantha muttered. Meanwhile, Kokabiel was slowly emerging from the back. He closed the door as she turned away and headed for the warehouse.

"She's pissed," Leon grunted.

"She's definitely upset about something," Sif added.

"I'm not upset!" Samantha snapped. "Now come on. Let's hurry this up."

No one said anything as Samantha entered the warehouse, moved between several boxes ranging in size from knee-high to well past her head. Before long, she had reached a large container made of metal. Pressing against her hand against one of the boxes revealed a handprint scanner hidden inside. A part of the floor slid back to reveal a hidden staircase.

"Hmm... a hidden entrance to a secret base inside of a remote abandoned warehouse." Kokabiel's wings flapped. "It's a bit cliched, but I suppose beggars can't be choosers."

"Well, excuse me for being cliched," Samantha muttered bitterly as she walked down the stairs.

The room they emerged from after passing through a hallway at the bottom of the stairs didn't look like much. Leon was so tall his head nearly scraped against the ceiling. As Azazel's eyes wandered around, Samantha walked past several cubicles. Several people stood up to greet her, but the words died on their lips when their eyes landed on Kokabiel. Even if no one knew who he was, the black angel wings on his back let everyone know what he was.

Samantha ignored the murmurs and walked back to her office. She reached her desk, a plain table with literally no decorations, grabbed the intercom, and picked it up.

"How long will it take for someone to pick us up?" asked Samantha.

"Azazel should have already arrived at The Watchtower." Kokabiel crossed his arms. "He is also capable of tracking my location, so he should know where we are. If nothing untoward has happened, I imagine it won't take him more than five or six hours."

Samantha nodded as she placed the intercom to her mouth and said, "I have an important announcement to make, everyone, so listen up. I have just come back from my mission and learned that the Catholic Church has been taken over by the Seven Demon Kings of Hell. Due to this unprecedented situation, we have teamed up with the Grigori in order to defeat them. I know what's happening is unheard of, but I would like to ask for your cooperation as we do our best to liberate the Catholic Church from those demons. We have about five hours before we're changing location. Use that time to gather your supplies and prepare to leave. That is all."

Turning off the intercom, Samantha set the device down and turned to Sif and Leon.

"I'd like you both to help begin directing everyone. Also, keep an eye out for what they say. The Grigori have never been our enemies, but they've never been our allies either. Some people may be distrustful. If anyone dissents with this decision, please pacify them as best you can."

Both straightened their backs at the command. They snapped off a salute, placing one hand over their heart.

"Yes, Commander."

The two quickly left, closing the door behind them. Samantha watched them go, and then brushed some hair out of her face, aware that Kokabiel's eyes were locked onto her.

"Something you want to say?" she asked.

"No." Kokabiel shook his head.

"Good."

Samantha left her office. Kokabiel followed her. She would have told him not to, but she felt keeping him by her side would be for the best anyway, so she said nothing.

This hidden base had two levels. The first level was for the Intelligence Division. The second level was divided into a barracks and science lab. Of course, the lab was not much. It consisted mostly of a large, empty space with several work tables. When she entered, she almost sighed at seeing what the scientists were doing.

"Why can't they ever do something productive?" she groaned.

"What an odd bunch of people. Is that man on fire?" asked Kokabiel.

Kokabiel was, of course, referring to the man running in circles while his head was on fire. She had no idea how his head had become alight with flames like that, but that hardly mattered. As she watched, a man around her age with greasy blond hair, gray eyes, and a lab coat grabbed a fire extinguisher and put it to good use. She twitched several times as the man who'd been on fire flopped on the ground like a fish on dry land.

"What the hell is going on here?" asked Samantha.

"Ah, Samantha." The man who had extinguished the fire turned around.

"Sebastian," Samantha began in a slow, calm voice. "Please tell me you were not performing another dangerous experiment. You know I forbade those in this base. We do not have the resources necessary to repair it, and any damage done to this place could cause it all to collapse around our ears."

Sebastian raised his hands in a defensive, warding gesture. "No, no. We weren't doing any experiments. We were gathering our supplies and putting them away. However, he ended up slipping and one of the fuel cells he was carrying struck him on the head."

Pinching the bridge of her nose, Samantha took a deep breath, held it, and then released it. It was important to remain calm when dealing with the Science Division. They were all brilliant, but perhaps because of their incredible intellect, they enjoyed pushing the boundaries of what most would consider common sense. The number of deaths in the Science Division due to one of their inventions exploding in their face almost matched the number of deaths the Warriors had experienced while on the job.

"I see. Please carry on then but be more careful."

"Yes, ma'am." Sebastian nodded before glancing at the fallen angel standing a little way behind Samantha. "Is that one of our new allies?"

"He is."

"Hmm…" Sebastian walked over to a table, grabbed a small cylindrical device, and stepped in front of Kokabiel. "Would you mind injecting some of your divine energy into this device?"

Kokabiel raised an eyebrow. "And why would I do that?"

"Because I would like a sample of your energy. I've been working on a weapon that can destroy even a high-class demon, but there's nothing on this earth save perhaps nuclear fission that has enough energy to power it. However, if I had the power of a fallen angel, I might be able to power the weapon without needing to create my own atom bomb."

"What have I told you about making crazy experiments?!" demanded Samantha.

"I am intrigued." Kokabiel took the device from Sebastian, and then a bright golden glow covered his hand. The hairs on Samantha's neck prickled as a strange humming filled the air. "I'm curious to see what this weapon can do. Show it to me when you have the chance."

"I will," Sebastian promised.

Samantha pressed a hand against her face as she realized that maybe, just maybe, coming down here to make sure the Science Division wasn't destroying anything had been a bad idea.

Just as this thought occurred to her, a massive rumbling shook the bunker. Samantha looked up as several cracks appeared on the ceiling and some dust rained down on them.

"What was that?" asked Sebastian.

"I sense several demonic presences," Kokabiel said, tilting his head.

"Dammit!"

Hissing, Samantha set her case, which she hadn't let go of, on the ground. She opened it and grabbed her weapon, Zaphkiel. Picking the case up with her free hand, Samantha shouted at the Science Division to hurry up and get their stuff together as she ran up the stairs and into the Intelligence Division's room.

What she found was chaos. Demons were everywhere. Fortunately, they were merely marionettes—demons that had a slightly humanoid appearance. However, these marionettes were all carrying weapons. Some of them had swords for hands. Others had guns for hands. Even as she watched, one of the marionettes fired a hailstorm of bullets into one of her people. As the man's blood splattered against the floor, she felt only a single moment of shock before her anger, irritation, and determination congealed into a single desire.

Destroy the enemy.

With a war cry that she rarely let out, Samantha charged head first into battle.

Chapter 5

Marionettes were low-class demons. Although they were called marionettes, they weren't puppets controlled by another. They merely had a puppet-like appearance. Their bodies appeared as if they had been stitched together. Ball socket joints in the arms, knees, shoulders, and torso allowed them a full range of movement. Even so, the gangly way they walked would make anyone assume they were being controlled by someone else.

Samantha cut down the first marionette to stand in her way without mercy. Zaphkiel was a streak of light as she removed it from its sheathe, swung, and then slid it back into place. The soft *click* that echoed around the room preceded the marionette falling apart.

Not hesitating for even a second, she sought out her next enemy, a group of five that had clustered together and were attempting to harm one of her people. She raced forward. Skidding along the floor as she neared them, Samantha removed Zaphkiel from its sheathe again. There was a flash of light. The glare of her blade. Then she was sheathing it once more, and the marionettes all fell apart.

"I want all the Intelligence Agents to begin evacuation procedures!" Samantha ordered as she sliced another marionette in half.

"We're using the tunnels on the second floor! Hurry through the barracks!"

By this point in time, the other Executioners, members of the Warriors and Assassins caste, must have realized something was going on. They streamed in through the stairway leading to the second basement. It wasn't long before about 25 men and women of varying builds charged into the room and attacked the marionettes alongside Samantha.

Swords were swung. Claws raked across demon flesh. Guns went off with bright flashes, blowing holes in the bodies of marionettes. To her left, a young man slammed a gauntlet-clad fist into a marionette's face, shattering the creature's head. It went down in a tangle of limbs. On her right, a young woman of the Assassin caste leapt to the ceiling. She used the ceiling as a springboard to launch herself at a marionette, which she disposed of by impaling it with a kodachi—a traditional Japanese short sword.

Among the ranks of those fighting, three of them stood out among the group.

Leon, his roaring laughter easily distinguishable from the din of battle, sent three marionettes flying with a single swing of his warhammer. Sandalphon whistled is it was swung through the air. Bodies were broken, heads were crushed, and limbs were removed. The man was so powerful he only needed one hand to swing his weapon. The muscles of his right arm, thick as a tree trunk, bulged as he brought his hammer down, crushing another marionette and cracking the floor.

Another figure darted around Leon. It was Sif. Using her vastly superior speed, dexterity, and acrobatics, the woman leapt at her foes. She used the orichalcum gauntlets covering her hand to pierce the bodies of numerous puppets. She'd kick off one to launch herself at another, and then tear through it like it was made of paper. It wouldn't have been inaccurate to describe this woman as a whirlwind of death and destruction. Numerous demons fell at her hands, though that meant little when six marionettes took the place of their fallen brethren.

Of course, out of all the figures present, none slayed more than Kokabiel. The fallen angel had summoned a pair of light swords. The blades were large. She would have called them claymores, but they seemed more like big broadswords. In either event, the fallen angel calmly wielded his blades with a two-handed style that was both graceful and yet somehow sloppy. He swung his swords in lazy arcs. However, no matter how lethargic his attacks seemed, they never failed to slice apart two, three, or even four marionettes at once.

To top it off, he was fast. His blades were nothing but brilliant streaks of light whenever he swung them. He moved left, swung, and then moved right and swung again. 16 opponents were felled in less than a second. That 16 quickly became 20, 27, 39, with the number increasing after every swing.

Samantha focused on defending the Intelligence Division as they retreated to the barracks.

"Kokabiel! Did the Science Division already leave?"

"They did. All their supplies were packed up. The only one I didn't see leaving down that hidden tunnel of yours was the one called Sebastian."

Samantha clicked her tongue as she avoided a sword swipe from a marionette, leaning back, and then coming back up with a slash of her own. Half the marionette's head slid off. The marionette didn't seem to have realized what happened for a moment, but then it crumbled to the ground.

It did not take more than five minutes for the Intelligence Division to disappear down the stairs. Samantha quickly ordered a retreat. She had Leon and Sif take the lead, while she and Kokabiel defended the rear. Once everyone had filed out, they hurried down the stairs.

"Retreating is a terrible decision. They are just going to follow us," Kokabiel said.

"No." Samantha shook her head as they raced down the tunnel. "They won't."

Kokabiel said nothing, but the frown on his face spoke for him. That was fine. He didn't have to believe Samantha, and of course, considering the marionettes were already rushing to get down the stairs, she understood why he wouldn't believe her.

The barracks were not much. They were like a gloomier version of a hotel hallway. Thick walls of concrete with several doors embedded on either side led to their rooms. There were a few lateral passages, but that was all. At the end of the hallway was a wall that would have been a dead end. However, a large section of the wall had already been removed, revealing the hidden passage that would lead them out of there.

Everyone was already hurrying through it. Samantha pulled out her revolver and took careful aim at the marionettes that had kept pace with them, firing several rounds. She didn't have Christian's incredible aim. Even so, each shot blew a hole through something. Beside her, Kokabiel conjured several dozen light spears that seemed to appear from the ether. He didn't throw them. They just flew forward the moment they were conjured, impaling the demons with impunity and burning them until not even ash remained.

When the last person had entered the passage, Samantha had Kokabiel enter first, and then she typed a few keys into a keypad on the wall. After which, she ducked into the passage and shut it closed. A massive rumbling rocked the tunnel as, from the other side of the now closed off passage, the sound of numerous explosions echoed back to them, the noise barely muffled.

"I see." Kokabiel nodded in approval. "You set up explosives in the event that your hideout was overrun. A good plan."

Samantha shrugged. "I figured if this place was ever attacked, the least we could do was find some way to take down as many demons as possible."

The tunnel was long and had a gentle slope that ascended as they moved. It was also made in a straight line. Samantha had thought about making it long and winding when this backup base had first been built, but she'd ultimately never had the time or money to make the escape tunnel better. She also never suspected she would use it.

Before too long, they had emerged from the passage. It was just a large opening that looked like the mouth to a man-made cave. The sky overhead was a bright blue. That meant those demons hadn't been using a barrier to appear in their world, which meant someone had summoned them. She grimaced but shrugged the thought off and got to work.

"I want everyone to remain calm!" she called out to the group of Executioners. "Before we move off, I'd like to take a quick headcount to make sure everyone is here! Form ranks!"

The Executioners quickly filed in, the Intelligence Division in front, the Executioners in the center, and the Science Division in back. Samantha quickly counted off the number of individuals present. 67. She bit her lip. There had been about 75 when she'd escaped from the Executioners HQ in Los Angeles. Including Leon and Sif, that meant there'd been 77 Executioners. She'd lost ten people… which was ten people more than she could afford to lose.

"It looks like we lost a few people, and I don't see Sebastian anywhere…"

Samantha bit her lip as she thought about what to do. She already knew the answer. They couldn't afford to remain there.

"Let's get a move on," Samantha announced. "I've hidden several vehicles about one mile from here in the event something like this happened. We'll travel there. Let's get going."

The group had no choice but to move off, walking in the direction Samantha led them under the beating hot sun. Several of the intelligence agents grumbled. Unlike the Warriors and Assassins, who underwent rigorous physical training, they only took basic self-defense courses. They lacked the stamina for a long trek through the desert.

Of course, the scientists were even worse off. They didn't do any training.

They were barely halfway to their destination when Kokabiel, walking alongside Samantha at the front, paused.

"What is it?" she asked.

"I'm sensing a massive surge of demonic energy." Kokabiel glanced up as he summoned a pair of light swords to his hands. "It is coming straight for us."

Samantha followed his gaze and gawked when she found a massive shape in the distance. As it grew closer, she recognized that the creature flying toward them was humanoid, but it still looked nothing like a human. It had two arms, two legs, and a head. However, its large body was grotesquely obese. A thick gut swung to and fro alongside a pair of sagging breasts. Of course, this figure was distinctly male. It was just so fat that it's chest looked like breasts. It had no chin or neck, just wobbly folds that jiggled. Red-skinned and naked, the only adornments this thing had were golden necklaces, golden rings, and numerous gold piercings.

"W-what is that?" asked Samantha.

"Mammon," Kokabiel answered with a growing smile. "That is the Demon King of Greed. It seems they have decided to bring out the big guns."

Samantha sucked in a breath. She didn't have much time to let fear rule her, though, for surrounding the Demon King of Greed were numerous other demons. They were nowhere close to Mammon's size, which she judged to be on the scale of a Goliath. These creatures were about the size of a human. As the massive figure drew ever nearer, she was able to make out the other demons' more defining features.

They were not humanoid at all. A round sphere surrounded by a thick membrane and leathery skin, the demons looked like eyes with numerous tentacles surrounding them. Wings flapped behind them, black and leathery, keeping them aloft. Samantha was horrified to admit that she didn't recognize them, which meant they were, at the very least, mid-level demons.

"Eyes of Greed," Kokabiel informed her. "That is what those things are called. They are what you would classify as mid-level demons, but they aren't very strong. Their primary method of attack are those tentacles. If you can avoid the tentacles and hit the eye, they'll go down easily."

"I see."

Samantha attached Zaphkiel's sheathe to her belt and pulled out her revolver. Spinning the cylinder, she made sure the light cartridge was working. This gun didn't rely on bullets. It channeled solar energy to create pseudo-light bullets.

"Intelligence and Science Division members move back! Long-range specialists prepare to fire! Aim for the flying eyes! Close-range specialists get ready to protect the long-range specialists!"

Everyone followed her orders. Those who couldn't fight retreated. Those who could fight stood beside her. Executioners who didn't have a long-range weapon pulled out blades, staves, and gauntlets, while those who did brought their guns to bear. Pistols, sub machine guns... one of them even had a Gatling gun. The 25 strong long-range specialists aimed their weapons as Samantha gave the order.

"FIRE!"

Every gun in the vicinity flashed as the Executioners opened fire. Fortunately, the swarm of demons had grown closer, and there were so many that it was impossible to miss so long as one pointed their weapon in the demons' direction. A few shots glanced off the thick membrane, which seemed stronger than it looked. Many shots, though, struck the things right in the eye, causing them to explode in a spark of gore.

Samantha took careful aim with her revolver and fired several shots, the weapon discharging energy with a sound not unlike the rumbling of thunder. Bright golden bullets shot from the weapon. Each one plowed into an eye. She narrowed her eyes in satisfaction as one, two, three, six, twelve, twenty-four eyes were downed by her in less than a third as many seconds. That said, there were still hundreds of those eyes swarming around the demon.

"Kokabiel, are you not going to hel—"

Samantha turned her head to ask why Kokabiel was not attacking the demons with his light spears, only to be startled when she found him no longer standing beside her. She glanced back up. He was already in the sky. Even as she watched him flap his wings, several dozen spears of light appeared around him and flew with unerring accuracy. All of them pierced in eye. In half the time it took her to kill 24 of the demons, Kokabiel slayed about 60. Samantha felt green with envy.

Even as he launched light spears at the Eyes of Greed, Kokabiel flew toward Mammon like a bolt of lightning. He soon became nothing more than a streak.

A loud sound like crackling thunder echoed around them. The ground rumbled as a shockwave exploded out from where Kokabiel slammed into Mammon, knocking her and the other Executioners to the ground. Samantha looked up to see many of the Eyes of Greed crashing into the ground as well. Some of them exploded from the force, but a few merely bounced and regained their bearings. Knowing that she couldn't afford to get distracted by the battle happening above her, Samantha holstered her revolver and grabbed Zaphkiel again.

"Executioners! To battle!"

The other Executioners picked themselves up and charged toward the flying eyes. Samantha and Sif, the fastest of the group, reached the Eyes of Greed first.

Most of the flying eyeballs seemed disoriented from their impact against the ground. She and Sif slaughtered nearly a dozen before the rest regained their bearings. They soon tried to impale the pair with their tentacles, but the two of them wove around the attacks and cut the tentacles off with their orichalcum weapons. This didn't mean much. The tentacles grew back, but Samantha just took that to mean they needed to destroy the eyes. That was probably their core.

The rest of the Executioners reached the Eyes of Greed and attacked with vigor, slicing the demons to pieces. However, it was not a one-sided fight. The tentacles were incredibly quick. One had to keep a constant eye out for attacks from all sides. A man was impaled by several tentacles. His body was tossed through the air, slamming into a woman who went down under the weight before she was stabbed through the head.

Samantha lost herself to the haze of battle. She used her iaido technique to great effect. Resheathing and unsheathing her blade to increase the speed of her attacks, she spun around in circles, cutting through several Eyes of Greed that surrounded her. The world around her disappeared as she focused only on slaying the monsters before her. Time lost its meaning. Thoughts fled before they could form. She relied only on her instincts to see her through.

She had no idea how long the battle lasted, but it came to an end when something struck the ground with so much force that she nearly lost her balance. A tentacle appeared before her. A jolt raced through her spine. She was off-balance! She wouldn't be able to dodge this!

The tentacle was sliced apart as Sif lunged forward and slashed it with her clawed gauntlet. Samantha used that moment to regain her balance, and then she raced past Sif, cutting another Eye of Greed before it could launch a tentacle at the other woman's exposed back.

"What just happened?! What was that?!" she shouted.

"Over there." Sif pointed at something in the distance. Samantha turned her head.

It was Kokabiel and Mammon. They had brought their battle groundside. Kokabiel, who was so small compared to Mammon he might as well have been a rabbit fighting against a bear, danced across the ground as his demonic foe slammed two massive hands against the earth. Each time the massive demon attacked, the earth shook. Samantha gritted her teeth as she lowered her center of gravity to keep from being knocked to the ground.

The clear majority of those flying eyes appeared to have been defeated, with the remaining few being mopped up by the other Executioners. She looked around. Several of their numbers had fallen, and quite a few were injured. Regret gnawed away at her heart, but she shoved it aside. There was nothing they could do about the loss of life. For now, they had to merely do whatever they could to survive.

"Do you think we should help him?" Leon asked, gesturing toward the battle with his chin.

"How do you propose we do that?" asked Sif. "In case you haven't noticed, that thing is one of the Seven Demon Kings. We wouldn't stand a chance."

"Christian beat one of them."

"Christian is an anomaly. He's always doing impossible things."

Samantha barely paid attention as the two bickered, looking instead at Kokabiel and Mammon as they fought. Kokabiel danced between the giant demon's attacks. Then he would dart forward with incredible speed, slice through the demon's flesh, and then retreat as Mammon raged. It looked like a great hit and run strategy. The problem was that the injuries Mammon suffered didn't seem to affect him.

Shouldn't Kokabiel be more powerful than this? They both should.

The beings fighting before her eyes were creatures far beyond the scope of humanity, with the powers to match. Their battle should have been far more devastating than it was now. Yet as she continued to watch, Samantha slowly realized why the battle hadn't picked up.

Kokabiel was holding back. Because they were there, he couldn't use his more powerful attacks. Of course, he also couldn't let Mammon use his more powerful attacks either. That meant he had to stay in close and pepper the Demon King with smaller attacks that didn't do much damage.

Samantha hesitated. Should she order a retreat?

Before she could make a decision, one of Mammon's fists finally struck Kokabiel, sending the fallen angel rocketing back so fast the earth exploded in his wake. The fallen angel tumbled across the ground. While he somehow managed to right himself and land on his feet, that didn't mean much. He was now several dozen yards from Mammon. What's more, the demon had opened its large mouth and was gathering a massive amount energy, so much that it had become visible.

"Oh, shit," Leon muttered.

"That's—" Sif's eyes widened.

Samantha said nothing as reddish black streamers of energy rushed toward Mammon's mouth, gathering into a tightly compressed ball. It didn't look very powerful. She knew better. According to Christian's report, Abaddon had a similar attack, but that demon hadn't been as powerful as a Demon King. This attack was sure to be several magnitudes more powerful than the one unleashed by The Destroyer.

Mammon closed his mouth around the orb. His stomach suddenly inflated even more. It was like all that energy had caused his insides to expand. Kokabiel grimaced as he stood in front of the Executioners, as if to shield them from the attack to come. The Demon King opened his mouth. Black light emerged from inside—

And then a massive beam of white energy struck the demon's face.

Everyone froze in shock. Samantha, barely able to believe her eyes, could only gawk as Mammon's face was engulfed in a massive explosion that caused a wave of energy to crash over their group. She winced as several people were lifted off the ground and hurled across the airspace. Digging in her heels and impaling her sword into the ground, she covered her eyes, ignoring the burning of her arms as she used them as shields.

When the explosion dissipated, it revealed that the left side of Mammon's head was gone. Flesh hung grotesquely off broken bits of skull. Even his brain, which still pulsed, sagged as several chunks sloughed off. Despite this, Mammon was still very much alive. He opened his mouth and screamed.

"WHO DARES ATTACK MAMMON?! DO YOU THINK I'LL ALLOW YOU TO TAKE AWAY MY PREY?! GREEDY LITTLE—"

Whatever Mammon had been going to say would remain unfinished, for Kokabiel had used that explosion as a distraction to rush forward. Samantha and the others hadn't even realized his intent until he'd become a streak of golden light. At some point, he began rotating his body as he flew low to the ground, twisting around at a pace so fast the light around him looked like a giant drill.

He slammed into Mammon before the Demon King could finish yelling. The creature's stomach caved in grotesquely. Then Kokabiel went straight through the demon's stomach and out his back.

Samantha was used to gore and violence. However, even she felt sick as a massive hole opened in Mammon's stomach. Gore splattered against the ground. The demon's intestines fell out, though he grabbed them to try and keep them inside of his body. However, in that moment, Kokabiel curved around and tore through his upper back, exploding out of Mammon's chest a second later.

As the fallen angel landed on the ground, the golden aura around him disappeared, revealing that he didn't even have a single drop of blood on him. Meanwhile, behind him, the massive Mammon gazed down at the two holes running straight through his body. He teetered back and forth, and then fell backward. He slammed into the ground with a resounding crash.

Samantha and the other Executioners stumbled as they tried to keep their balance. As they righted themselves, she glanced over at where Mammon lay, only to discover black particles like ash wafting into the air as his body dissolved. As more and more of Mammon disappeared, it revealed something inside of him. A person.

Curiosity overcoming her, Samantha walked up to the body, now completely exposed as Mammon disappeared. She vaguely recognized this person. He was a high-ranking member of the bishopric. If she was not mistaken, this aging man who looked about 60, was an archbishop.

"It is impossible to summon a Demon King," Kokabiel said as he walked up behind her. "In order to remain on this plane of existence, the Demon King's tether a small piece of their power to the soul of a human and slowly take over them. Of course, it is best to take over a person who embodies the sin of that specific Demon King." He tilted his head. "I do not know who this man is, but he must have been awfully greedy."

Samantha's throat felt dry as she answered Kokabiel. "There had been accusations against this man claiming he was laundering donation money into his own personal bank account. An investigation was brought against him. However, the lack of evidence caused the charges to be dropped."

"So I see." Kokabiel said nothing more on the subject. "By the way, where did that last attack come from? I should thank whoever launched it."

"Over there." Samantha pointed at the figure several dozen yards away. It was Sebastian. The man was wearing a strange contraption on his back as he held a rifle-shaped object in his hands. It looked almost like a flamethrower. "At least now we know his invention that required your energy works, though I'll have to talk to him about not using a battlefield as a field test."

Samantha looked back at the obviously dead man who'd been possessed by the Demon King of Greed and wondered what she should do about the body. Bury it? Cremate it? Did this man even deserve that?

"The dead have no enemies..."

The words came to her in a whisper. She closed her eyes as she remembered what Christian had told her long ago. Taking a deep breath, she held it in and counted to ten, then released it.

"Leon," she called the large man to her side, "help me gather some wood to start a fire."

While Leon looked incredibly confused, tilting his head to the side, he didn't disobey her order either.

"Sure thing, Commander."

With Leon's help, Samantha created a pyre and cremated the body of the archbishop. As the smoke from the flames surrounding the man's body rose into the air, a massive vessel that looked like something out of a science fiction story closed in from above.

"It looks like our ride has finally arrived," Kokabiel said, turning to face Samantha. "That is The Watchtower—our mobile fortress."

***

Christian and Lilith had not been awake when Samantha and the other Executioners had boarded The Watchtower, but they were made aware of what happened after waking up.

The Watchtower really was a massive vessel. It was about the same size as a cruise liner. There were four floors. Two of the floors were dedicated to living quarters, while the bottom floor was an observation deck, loading bay, and boarding ramp, and the fourth floor contained the bridge, forensics lab, weapons depot, medical wing, and prison block.

Christian and Lilith, upon waking up and learning about what happened, headed for the medical wing.

The medical wing wasn't much. As they entered the modest-sized room, they found several people lying on beds, suffering from various injuries ranging from light to serious. Most of the Executioners present seemed to be suffering from modest injuries, a few cuts, bruises, and fractures. One person was currently having their arm cauterized. It looked like something had nearly ripped it off at the elbow. Now it was just a lump of dangling flesh.

When he and Lilith entered the room, all sense of movement ceased, and everyone turned to stare at them. The Executioners who were less injured muttered as the two of them past.

"That's Christian, isn't it?"

"It is. What is he doing here? I heard he betrayed the Executioners."

"Who is that with him? She's beautiful."

"Think she might be that succubus?"

"Nah. Couldn't be. Everyone knows succubus have that Aura of Allure. I don't feel like I've suddenly become hornier."

While everyone seemed confused by his presence, he knew they'd eventually be informed about what was going on. It didn't really concern him.

He walked past several used tables, studiously keeping his eyes up front. Lilith glanced at the people they past. However, she looked away just as quickly. Their destination was a table in the back, where Samantha was getting a checkup. It didn't look like she was injured except for a few scrapes and bruises, but the dark pants and shirt she wore did have several rips in it, exposing the white flesh underneath. She sat on the medical bed as a very familiar woman in a lab coat was checking over her.

"Christian," Samantha greeted, eyes flickering over to the woman by his side. "Lilith."

"Well, now…" The woman giving Samantha the checkup turned around and grinned at him. "If it isn't my favorite Executioner. Sorry. I guess that's former Executioner."

"Geh!" Christian took a step back as Lilith looked on in surprise. "Doctor Pierce."

Anastasia Pierce was a doctor for the Executioners. She worked primarily with Warriors like himself. Ever since his battle against Abaddon, Doctor Pierce has taken a special interest in him, even going so far as to become his personal physician.

"What's with that response?" asked the doctor, raising a delicate eyebrow. "Are you not even going to tell me it's good to see me again?"

"Er... it's good to see you again."

"How very insincere of you." Doctor Pierce rolled her eyes before she focused on Lilith. "And you must be the succubus he ran off with."

Now put on the spot, Lilith did her best impression of a vampire staring at a cross. She looked left, then right, and then at Doctor Pierce. Squirming just a bit, she stepped forward and bowed to the woman.

"It's very nice to meet you. Um, my name is Lilith."

"I'm perfectly aware of who you are... but it's nice to meet you all the same. You're not what I expected from a succubus." Christian wanted to ask what she had expected, but Doctor Pierce turned back to Samantha and started checking her over again. "Anyway, come see me when you have time, Christian. It's been awhile since I gave you a checkup. I'm keen to see if there's been any changes in your physiology."

"Yeah... okay." Christian didn't really want to get a checkup from her, but he knew denying her would simply result in a home visit. Shaking his head, he turned back to Samantha, his expression slowly hardening. "I heard you guys were attacked."

"We were."

Samantha sighed as Doctor Pierce announced that she had no major injuries and could leave. She clambered off the examination table and walked over to them, and then the three of them walked out of the hospital. According to Samantha, all the people with major injuries had already been treated, but there were still people who'd suffered minor injuries like she had. They couldn't afford to waste space.

"We were attacked by Mammon," Samantha continued as they wandered down a wide passage. It was large enough that five people could have stood shoulder to shoulder without touching each other. "Fortunately, Kokabiel was there. Without him, we would never have made it out alive."

They turned a corner. Several lights illuminated the hallway, revealing a couple of lateral passages. Their destination was the commander center, which Samantha did not know the way to, so Christian took the lead.

"Mammon is... um, who is that?" asked Lilith.

"The Demon King of Greed," Christian answered. "So Kokabiel defeated him?"

"Yes." Samantha nodded. "I have been in a lot of battles, but I've never seen a battle quite like that. It was... frightening, to be honest. Seeing those two fight made me realize how insignificant the Executioners are in all this. It's enough to make me wonder if there's anything we can even do."

The hallway they entered was narrower. A doorway sat at the end. They walked to it.

"The Demon Kings are frightening. I remember my battle with Asmodeus." Christian shuddered. "I don't think I've ever felt so scared in my entire life—not even during my fight with Abaddon."

Upon entering the command chamber, Christian saw that Azazel and Kokabiel were already there. While Kokabiel more or less ignored them, Azazel waved them over.

"I'm glad you two have shown up," he said as they walked up to him. "We're about to pick up Shemhazai and the incubus, and then we can head over to our hideout."

"You know that incubus has a name, right?" asked Christian.

"You're awfully defensive when it comes to him." Azazel raised a curious eyebrow.

Christian straightened his shoulders. "Tristin might be annoying, but... I don't hold that against him. He's helped me out enough times that the least I can do is stick up for him."

Azazel shrugged. "In either event, it will take about ten minutes to reach their location. I just received word that they have Tristin's harem and are at the extraction point. If all goes well, we'll be heading toward our final destination in a few minutes."

"Where is our final destination?" asked Samantha.

"Why? Where else would it be if not the Antarctic?" asked Azazel with a smirk.

***

After picking up Tristin, the group made for their destination, which was apparently located in Antarctica.

There wasn't much to do on the vessel despite its size. None of the places were off-limits to them except for the engine room, but it wasn't like the Watchtower had anything remotely meant for recreation. They didn't even have a room for exercising, which Christian found out was because fallen angels didn't need to exercise. Their physical growth was set the moment they had been created by God. No amount of exercise would ever change how strong they became.

Christian and Lilith spent most of their time inside of their room, though occasionally they'd travel outside to speak with Azazel, Samantha, or Tristin. Speaking of, they saw surprisingly little of Tristin. He only found out later, but it seemed that Tristin harem wasn't letting him go outside very often. The one time Christian had gone to visit him, he'd been introduced to all his friend's women. It had been... quite the surreal experience.

"Take a deep breath for me. Hold it. Good. Now exhale."

Christian followed Doctor Pierce's instructions, ignoring the slight chill of the stethoscope against his bare chest. Today was just a standard checkup. Thanks to how they'd been on the run, Doctor Pierce had not been able to bring any of her normal equipment, and she apparently wasn't well-versed in the equipment inside of this medical wing. That said, she had demanded he see her again once she had all the necessary equipment to do a proper checkup.

"It looks like your breathing is fine," she muttered. "Have there been any changes in your diet?"

"Plenty. I've been on the run for several months. It's not like I've had the time, money, or ability to maintain a healthy balance of food, you know?"

"I suppose being chased would make finding time to eat properly hard." Doctor Pierce took the stethoscope off his chest, which Christian was grateful for because it looked like Lilith, who was watching from beside them, was about ready to begin pouting. "Well, it looks like you're still in excellent physical condition. In fact, I'd say your physical conditioning is even better than when you were an Executioner, which is a bit... odd. I had expected your muscles to have atrophied at least a little."

Christian wasn't sure what to say to that, and so he said nothing. It wasn't in his nature to speak when he had nothing to add.

"In any case, it looks like you're good to go." Doctor Pierce smiled at him, though it turned a tad wry when she eyed Lilith. "I'll give you back to your mate now. It looks like she's dying to hog you all to yourself."

"You're right about that," Lilith muttered as she grabbed Christian's arm after he put his shirt back on and began dragging him out. It seemed she really didn't like other women touching him, not even for medical purposes.

"Next time, I want to examine you, Lilith!" Doctor Pierce gave one last parting shot before they left. "I've never examined a succubus before!"

"Not in this lifetime!"

Lilith could not leave the medical wing fast enough. Christian let her drag him further away from the medical wing at a quick trot, until she eventually slowed down and began walking normally. He quickened his pace to walk alongside her.

"Not a big fan of hers, I'm guessing," he said.

Lilith's scowl was more like a cute pout. "I don't like how she was putting her hands all over you."

"You do realize she's just doing her duties as a doctor, right?"

"She was pawing at you with her grubby mitts."

Christian almost released a sigh, but he decided against it at the last second, knowing that doing so would only invoke Lilith's ire. It seemed the woman had a territorial side. This was his first time seeing it. He wondered if it had been triggered from Doctor Peirce touching him. Probably.

As they wandered the Watchtower with no real destination in mind, the two eventually found themselves on the observation deck. Of course, it was called that, but it wasn't like anything was there. It was a large, open room with no decorations or even a place to sit. The floor beneath their feet was invisible. Christian had thought it was glass at first, but he'd learned that it was a series of monitors projecting real-time video feedback from a series of cameras that were connected to each panel. Currently, it looked like they were sailing over an ocean.

He thought it was a gross waste of money, but what did he know?

"I wonder how long it will take to reach the Antarctic," Christian said.

"I heard that flying from the US to Britain takes about 13 hours, so I imagine this will take even longer," Lilith mumbled. "Well, at least we aren't confined to an aisle."

"True."

"That said, I wonder what's going to happen when we get there."

The two of them walked over to the wall, which was made from the same monitor panels as the floor. Like the floor, it acted as a window to the outside. As Lilith pressed her hands against the monitor, Christian crossed his arms and leaned against the wall, heedless of how it looked like he might fall to the watery depths several hundred thousand feet below.

"I'm not sure." Sighing, Christian ran a hand through his hair. "We joined the fallen angels because they might be the only people who can offer us protection from the Catholic Church... or rather, the demons who've taken over it. However, even if we run to the ends of the Earth, I doubt they'll stop chasing us. It seems like there's a deeper reason for it beyond me abandoning my post."

"Well, considering all that's happened and what we learned, I guess that isn't so surprising." Lilith bit her lower lip as expressive green eyes flickered in thought. She crossed her arms under her chest, the act pushing her bosom together in a way that caused Christian's eyes to stray—not that she seemed to even notice. "Now I'm wondering what they want from us in the first place."

"I'm not sure they want anything from you," a new voice interrupted them. Christian and Lilith turned to find Azazel walking onto the observation deck. "You were merely a convenient excuse to sick the Executioners on Christian. I suspect they forced Christian to accept the contract to kill you because they believed he'd be overcome by your Aura of Allure. Him not being affected and running off with you probably put a huge dent in their plans."

"Their plans?" Christian blinked. "So they're after me?"

"I believe so."

"But why?"

Christian couldn't think of a single reason the Catholic Church—no, the Seven Demon Kings—would be after him. The only thing that might make sense was what Azazel had told him before. He had the Eye of Belial. Did that have something to do with it? He didn't know. However, that was the only clue he had to go on.

Azazel opened his mouth to speak, but just before he could say anything, the entire ship was jostled as a loud explosion echoed from somewhere inside. Lilith screamed as she fell into Caspian, who quickly caught her and steadied himself against the wall. Azazel's wings were flapping like mad as he rushed over to a small comm unit near the observation deck entrance.

"Bridge! This is Azazel! What in Heaven's name just happened?!"

A controlled but slightly panicked voice reached their ears. "Sir, we're under attack! Something just struck the top of the Watchtower! The hull is holding but has sustained heavy damage! There's something on top of it!"

"What?!"

As Azazel shouted into the comm, several of the panels suddenly went blank. Another one winked out. Then another and another. Christian and Lilith looked at one of the panels that hadn't fritzed, and then gasped as something flitted in front of it. They only had a moment to see it, but the creature had been a red-skinned imp with black wings. The screen they were staring at went black seconds later.

"Azazel," Christian called out.

"What is it?" asked a distracted Azazel. "In case you can't tell, I'm a little busy."

"I think we're in trouble."

"Trouble?" Azazel finally looked at them, and then he looked at the black panels. More cameras had been destroyed. When he glanced at one of the panels still working and saw the imp darting by and destroying the camera, his face went pale, and he summed up his thoughts in a single word. "Fuck."

Chapter 6

Azazel, Christian, and Lilith made haste to the bridge, where several other people were already waiting. There was Kokabiel standing next to Shemhazai with his arms crossed. A little way over, Clarissa and Heather were already dressed in their battle gear, looking ready to start a war. Samantha, Sif, and Leon were also present. Tristin was there, too. He was standing in front of the table with the three-dimensional holographic projector, which currently displayed an image of The Watchtower as it flew over the ocean.

There was something big standing on the vessel.

"Beelzebub," Azazel muttered with a grimace. "Damn locust. I should have killed him when I had the chance."

"It looks like he's brought friends," Christian muttered.

"Good. You're here." Shemhazai turned toward Azazel as the three of them walked up to the table, thereby directing everyone else's attention to them. "It looks like Beelzebub managed to track you after you escaped from him previously. While he hasn't broken through the hull yet, it's only a matter of time before our shield fails. As the young man kindly pointed out, he's also brought some friends with him."

"The imps," Azazel said. "I already saw them. Have any managed to get inside?"

"Not yet," Shemhazai began, "but it's only a matter of time before they—" Just then, a loud siren blared through the bridge and red lights flashed in warning. Shemhazai sighed. "It looks like I spoke too soon. They just managed to breach the hull."

Tristin used his hands, which were covered with a pair of gloves, to manipulate the holographic display. The hologram zoomed in until it was showing the inside of The Watchtower. Manipulating his hands some more, he traveled through several hallways until he found the hull breach, which created a surprisingly detailed recreation of what was currently happening. Several imps were rushing in through a hole in the wall.

"It looks like the breach is on the second floor at the south end of section five," Tristin said.

"That's where the living quarters are!" Clarissa gasped. "Heather and I will deal with this! Come!"

"Go with them. Help repel the imps," Samantha ordered Sif and Leon as the two succubi took off at a quick trot. The two Executioners gave her a smart salute before rushing after the pair. The last Christian saw of them was Leon's massive back and the warhammer resting on his shoulder before the door closed.

"Kokabiel and I will take care of Beelzebub," Azazel said. "Shemhazai and Tristin will remain here and provide constant updates on the situation. Direct our forces as needed. Christian—" he turned to the former Executioner "—grab your weapons, and then head over to the weapon depot. You're almost out of ammo, right? I have several ammo clips made specifically for your gun."

"Really? Wait." Christian's face twisted as something occurred to him. "How do you know about Phanuel and Gabriel?"

"What?" Azazel shrugged. "Did you think I wouldn't keep track of Amon's son?"

Christian had so many things he could have said to that, things he wanted to ask, but they would have to wait. They were under attack. Now was not the time to ask questions.

"Lilith, would you mind staying up here for the time being?" Christian looked at the young woman by his side.

Her expressive blue eyes staring into his, Lilith bit her lower lip for several seconds, then sighed and nodded. "I'll stay here. I know that as I am right now, I can't actually help you."

"We'll change that eventually," Christian assured her.

She gave him a wan smile. "I hope so."

Christian smiled back, pecked her on the lips, and then he was running out of the bridge. He flew down a flight of stairs to reach his and Lilith's room. His swords were leaning against the wall. They were already in their sheathes, so he just strapped them to his back and adjusted them for easy access. Then he opened the case sitting on the desk. His two silver and black guns were sitting on top of a velvet cushion. He grabbed the holsters resting in a small compartment of the case first, strapping them around his thighs, and then grabbed the two guns and slid them into their holsters. After a moment of thought, he also took the last few ammo clips he had remaining and attached them to his belt.

While he did not feel like he was ready to fight a war, he did feel less naked. Exiting the room, he traveled back up the stairs, rushed down the hall, took several turns, and stopped in front of the weapons depot. The door slid open and he stepped inside.

As expected of a weapon's depot, it was basically just a big room with a bunker-like feel to it, though that might have had something to do with the numerous racks lining the walls. Each rack had weapons of all kinds. Christian was surprised. Fallen angels did not use weapons. They used divine energy to create weapons: light swords, light spears, etc. Then again, maybe Azazel had known something like this would eventually happen and stockpiled weapons for him and the other non-fallen? He couldn't say for sure.

Among the numerous weapon racks, there was a cabinet with the words "orichalcum bullets" written on it. Christian could only assume that was it. He went over and opened the cabinet, where he discovered several clips of ammunition, all of which would fit perfectly into Phanuel and Gabriel.

It's like he knew I'd be joining him...

The thought made Christian frown, but he took twelve clips, attached them to his belt, and then ran out of the depot. As he did, a loud shaking made him stumble. He steadied himself against the wall as a voice came from overhead.

"Christian! This is Tristin. I'm talking to you through the intercom. I'll be directing you from here on out. Isn't that great?"

"No, it is not great. It's terrible," Christian muttered. He didn't think Tristin could hear his response, but there must have been a microphone or something that allowed people on the bridge to hear him.

"What a horrible thing to say!"

"That was sarcasm."

"In any case, there's been another breech. It's the observation deck this time. A group of fallen are already heading that way, but I would like you to go there too. Show them what for!"

"Right," Christian sighed.

Pepping himself up, Christian ran off again, backtracking as he found the stairs leading down. He went all the way down to the first floor, traveled through the wide hallway, and then burst onto the observation deck, where a battle was already taking place.

Christian paused to take stock of the situation. A large horde of imps, too many to count, were facing off against the fallen.

Imps were tiny creatures that were about half the size of an average adult human, though they looked nothing like a human outside of being bipedal. Their skin was a blistering red. The wings flapping on their back allowed them to dart to and fro, shifting angles and velocity at the drop of a hat. It gave them a wide range of aerial maneuvers. Stubby legs were used to leap from the ground in pouncing actions. Their arms were also stubby, but the ends of their hands were coated in thick claws that could easily slice through steel.

However, while the imps looked disgusting, it was not they who had Christian's attention.

It was the fallen.

Their dark armor looked less like armor and more like a fetishist's S&M costume. The men wore leather straps that covered their chest and wrapped around their shoulders, but it only covered the bits that were important. It left most of their bodies exposed. Their crotch was also only covered by a jock strap. Similarly, the woman wore clothing that looked more like strategically placed leather straps. Three straps went across their bust. A collar attached with a metal ring near their chest was attached to a leather strap that went down the center, between their breasts and over their stomach before disappearing between their legs. Three more straps formed a triangle along their crotch, acting as replacement panties.

Christian spent a full ten seconds wondering if he had walked into a nightmare, but when an imp suddenly spotted and leapt at him, he realized that he had no time for such questions.

The imp who leapt at him was sliced in half when he pulled Rafael from its sheath and swung down. As gore flew from the two halves, he rushed into the battle, quickly falling into his familiar fighting style as instincts took over.

As he delved deeper into that place that was halfway between conscious and unconscious actions, Christian thought something felt different from before. Maybe his mind had expanded. He could feel, or maybe sense, the location of everyone within the room to a startling degree of accuracy.

Someone was in trouble. It was a young man wielding a light spear. He didn't know an imp was coming up behind him. Christian rushed over, ducked beneath a clawed hand, removed said hand before continuing, and then sliced off the head of the imp before it could attack the fallen angel from behind.

What is this?

Another person, a woman this time, was surrounded by multiple imps. She was doing a fine job of defending herself, but she didn't have any time to attack. Christian swerved around several attacks aimed at his vital points. Of course, they were easy to dodge. He'd left those vitals open on purpose. He retaliated by killing each imp that came his way, and then he slid Michael into its sheath, unholstered Phanul, and fired several rounds, catching three imps in the head and dropping them. The fallen angel slaughtered the other three with quick thrusts of her spear.

I feel weird.

Christian blinked several times as sweat fell down his eyelashes. His breathing had grown a bit heavy, but he wasn't tired. In fact, he felt good. Really good.

Darting through the horde of imps, Christian swung Rafael and Michael while simultaneously dodging the numerous attacks launched at him. Duck. Swerve. Swing. Slice. Thrust. Imps fell by his blades in the dozens, until all too soon, there were none left.

I want more... I want to kill more...

The thought startled him. He shook his head, and the strange feeling dispelled. What was all that about?

"Christian," Tristin's voice blared from above as the fallen angels began disposing of the imp bodies by burning them with divine energy. "There is another breach on the second floor. Leon and Sif are currently pinned down trying to protect the succubus. Go help them."

"Got it."

Leaving the fallen angels to their duties, Christian rushed out the way he'd come, traveled back up the flight of stairs, and quickly located Leon and Sif. It wasn't hard. He just needed to follow the sounds of battle.

Leon and Sif were standing on opposite sides of a hallway. Imps rushed at them from both sides, trying to slip by, but they were doing their best to bar the way. Leon was having an easier time of it. He swung his massive warhammer around like it was a feather, smashing imps against the walls, floor, and ceiling. Sif, who was more of a technical fighter, had a more difficult time due to the enclosed space. Several imps were trying to attack her from multiple directions. She already had several cuts from their claws.

Judging that Sif needed more help at the moment, Christian dashed over to her, firing Phanul and Gabriel several times with pinpoint accuracy. The orichalcum bullets were impressive. They blasted right through the imps, leaving gaping holes in their bodies. The imps remaining squawked in surprise. Sif used their distracted states to rend them apart with her claws.

Of course, even though she killed those imps attacking her, that did not mean there weren't anymore. For every one that she killed, four replaced it.

Christian holstered his guns and drew his swords again. He attacked the imps from behind as Sif guarded the hallway. Fighting his way through the swarm, it wasn't long before he and Sif were standing side by side.

"It feels weird battling beside someone smaller than Leon," Sif muttered as she ducked underneath an imp's claw, and then impaled that same imp through the chest. "I'm used to attacking the enemies he fails to strike with that hammer of his." A slight deprecating smile curled at her lips. "I feel almost like you are stealing my job."

Christian would have wondered what she meant, but as he cut apart a dozen imps with precise strokes of his sword, he felt like he understood.

"Sorry for taking your job."

"It is fine. The important thing is protecting this place."

The two of them fought side by side. Christian presented openings in his guard that the imps were drawn to like moths to a flame. They tried to attack the holes he left, but he already knew they would and reacted as if he was omnipotent. One. Two. Four. Eight. Sixteen imps fell in less time than it took to blink. Caspian focused only on defending this position and slaying the enemies before him. Before too long, the number of imps attacking them trickled down, and then Caspian and Sif found no more enemies to fight. Just a pile of corpses.

"It looks like that is all of them," Sif muttered.

"Seems that way," Christian said.

Leon was also finished with his battle. As he turned to face them Christian realized the man was covered in cuts and bruises. He sighed. The big man wasn't really a dodger. His talent lay in using his warhammer to fend off large enemies. Smaller demons like imps were harder for him to fight off because they were so quick, nothing at all like those trolls they had fought back at the inn.

As Christian took several slow breaths to regain his second wind, one of the doors they had been guarding opened and Celeste peeked her head outside.

"Um, is it safe?" she asked.

"Yes," Sif said, nodding. "It is safe for the moment, though I would suggest you remain in your rooms. We don't know when more will come."

"Oh… okay."

The door closed again. However, before it did, Christian noticed Celeste sending a look his way. Sif noticed it too.

"I think that girl likes you."

Christian shrugged. "I'm not sure why you're telling me that. I already have a mate."

"I'm telling you so you can let her down rather than prolong her crush," Sif said. "It is important to know when and how to let a girl down, so she can move on."

"I suppose." He sighed. The woman had a point. On the other hand, Celeste probably already knew nothing could happen between them, given that he and Lilith were mates. "Anyway, where are Heather and Clarissa? I thought you had gone with them."

"We were fighting together, but then the place up here was breached, so we had to split up," Sif said.

"I see. Do you know if they are still fighting?"

"They are," Tristin suddenly said over the intercom. "That is actually your next destination."

Christian blew out a deep breath. "Right." He turned to Sif and Leon. "Can I count on you two to guard this place?"

"Leave it to us," Leon said with a booming laugh.

"We can handle things here," Sif added.

"I'll leave it to you then," Christian said with another sigh as he headed off toward his next battlefield.

It was going to be a long day.

***

Azazel and Kokabiel exited The Watchtower via an emergency hatch. Flapping their wings, the two fallen flew above the Watchtower and looked down.

Beelzebub was there, slamming his clawed hands against the hull, which crackled and sparked. It looked like the shield was holding in this area at least. Sadly, the shield was not meant to withstand the barrage of a Demon King. The shield tech had allocated all the power into protecting the area around Beelzebub, which was what allowed the imps to invade the ship.

As expected of a Demon King, even one whose power was only a tenth of what it should be due to requiring a possessed human to act as an anchor, the creature had already healed from the wounds Azazel dealt it. He sighed. If he'd had the luxury of time, he would have destroyed this demon during the highway chase.

"I'm going to get him off The Watchtower," Azazel said. "I'd like you to wait until I do that, and then blast him with your most powerful attack."

Kokabiel shrugged. "That sounds a bit boring, but it suits me just fine. Beelzebub doesn't seem like he'll provide much of a challenge for me anyway."

"Careful. Your arrogance is showing."

"Tch!"

Chuckling to himself, Azazel descended until he lightly touched upon The Watchtower's hull. Beelzebub hadn't noticed him yet... so Azazel tossed a light spear that struck the brute in the face. The demon stopped bashing its hand against the hull. Lifting its head, the creature pinioned Azazel with a ferocious glare.

"Azazel," Beelzebub said in a buzzing voice. It sounded like a thousand locusts were buzzing around to create something that only vaguely resembled talking. **"I was wondering when you would come out and face me again. That damn child of Belial wounded me last time, putting an end to our fight, but I don't see him anywhere now. That means you are mine. I will make you regret heaping those indignities onto me!"**

Azazel smiled as he spread his arms wide. "I would like to see you try."

Beelzebub let out a terrifying roar that rattled the bones, opening his mouth and launching out a plague of locusts. The swarm of tiny creatures was so thick it looked more like an energy beam than a swarm.

Azazel raised his left hand. A golden barrier shimmered around him. The swarm struck the barrier. Flickers of light surrounded him on all sides as the locusts were burnt to cinders by the millions, unable to withstand the divine energy they were slamming against. Azazel narrowed his eyes. The locust blast slowed down before ceasing altogether.

Dropping his barrier, Azazel created a massive light spear six times the size of a normal spear. It hovered above him. With a gesture of his hand, the spear flew toward Beelzebub—who suddenly disappeared in a swarm of locusts. The spear past through the locusts, and then reformed into Beelzebub.

"That's quite the trick you have there."

"I've spent eons perfecting my techniques for the day our kind would invade the Earth."

"I'm sure you have, though it's not gonna do you much good. I haven't been resting on my laurels either."

Beelzebub slammed his hands together, and a massive wall of bugs suddenly exploded from his body. Azazel raised his hands, palms out, fingers splayed. A brilliant golden wall appeared before him. The locusts slammed into the barrier. It was a lot like watching a tidal wave smash against a wall protecting a coastline. The bugs exploded in bursts of light. However, while he was protecting his front, several bugs snuck up behind him.

"Tch!"

Azazel clicked his tongue as something bit his calf. He flared his powers, which burst from his body in wisps of light. The locusts biting him exploded. Then he spun around and made a slashing gesture with his arm, which emitted a large crescent wave of energy that eradicated the rest of the bugs behind him.

Since he'd been forced to turn his attention to his back, the shield he'd erected at his front dissipated. The bugs that had been slamming against it surged forward. Azazel turned back around, stomped on the hull, and several golden pillars soared into the air. The swirling pillars looked like a tornado on fire, but it was just his divine energy. Azazel directed his attacks with his will. The tornadoes quickly moved, converging on the bugs and destroying them.

"You are just as annoying as before," Beelzebub growled. **"You're like a gnat, always buzzing around and creating problems for me."**

"That's amusing coming from you," Azazel retorted. "Was that pun on purpose?"

Beelzebub roared again, which Azazel took to mean "no." They once more traded long-range attacks. A surge of insects swarmed Azazel, who erected a dome-shaped barrier to protect him on all sides.

It was definitely a good thing that Beelzebub couldn't come to this world in person. The Demon Kings were stronger than a fallen angel like him, on par with the archangels themselves. Had Beelzebub not been forced to possess a human, which limited how much power he could use, this battle would have been decided already.

"I wonder how I can get him off my ship without damaging my ship," Azazel mused as he kept the barrier in place.

Azazel thought for a moment, and then realized he would have to get in close. With a sigh, he compressed the barrier around his body until it encased him like armor. The swarm of bugs slammed into him. They rattled him a bit from the force they struck with, but he didn't receive any damage.

"This is such a pain. I'm not a battle maniac like Kokabiel. I'd much rather find some beautiful woman to bed."

Getting into a starting position like an Olympic athlete about to run the 100-meter dash, Azazel counted down to three, two, one, and then he blasted off like a rocket. Retracting his wings, he raced forward.

Beelzebub seemed to realize what he was doing. The insects gathered into a swarm that slammed against him, as though to prevent him from moving forward. Azazel blinked, tapped his foot against the hull, and then he was suddenly standing right in front of the massive demon.

"What?!"

"You didn't think you were the only one honing his skills, did you?" asked Azazel. The question was rhetorical. He didn't even give Beelzebub a chance to answer.

Slamming both hands against Beelzebub's chest, Azazel let his power surge through and out of his palms. A concussive blast of energy launched the Demon King into the air. Beelzebub was thrown clear off The Watchtower. Soaring through the air, his insect-like wings emitting a fierce buzz, he tried to halt his momentum.

Too late.

At that exact moment, Kokabiel swooped down. He gripped a small spear within his hand. It looked like a normal light spear, but it was nearly ten times brighter than usual. Crackling and pulsating with a barely suppressed energy, the spear emitted tendrils that shot out in violent arcs. Kokabiel drew the spear back, and then he plunged it into Beelzebub's chest.

An agonized scream tore from the Demon King's throat before, without warning, his entire body exploded in a brilliant haze of golden light. Azazel looked away. It was so bright he feared going blind. As the light died down, it revealed there was nothing left of the Demon King. Even the body he had possessed was gone.

"You went overboard again," Azazel muttered as Kokabiel landed by his side.

Kokabiel shrugged. His face remained unchanged. He looked bored. Azazel sighed. As a regular battle maniac, Kokabiel was always seeking out strong foes to fight against, but there was no one on Earth who had the power needed to fight a fallen angel like him. It seemed even the Demon Kings themselves couldn't match him unless they were able to pass through the barrier with their original bodies.

"Better to go overboard and deal a killing blow, then to hold back and need to attack again."

"I suppose… you bring up a good point. Anyway, let's get back inside. The others should be done mopping up the small fry."

Flapping their wings, the two soared back over to the emergency hatch they had exited The Watchtower from. Azazel took one last look at where Beelzebub had been, and then he went back into the flying fortress.

***

It had been a long time since Vertrou had been summoned to the Vatican. In fact, not since the ceremony in which he had been promoted to Bishop had he set foot in this place.

As the largest community for Catholicism and the only entirely Catholic city-state, the Vatican was a sprawling network of buildings built in the Mediterranean style of architecture. Cobblestone roads. Sprawling constructs. All the roofs were made of old tiles, or new tiles made to look old. It gave the Vatican a more rustic, more ancient feel.

He glanced at the numerous people wandering the street as he walked toward his destination in casual clothes. There were so many people. A group of teenagers wandering the area and snapping pictures. A mother was trying to convince her crying son that he couldn't swim in the fountain. Several old people chatting as they sat near that same fountain.

Most of these people weren't Catholic. Since the beginning of the modern age, the Vatican had become more about tourism than worshipping Catholicism, which suited him just fine. He didn't care for religion beyond what it could do to elevate his station in life.

His destination was St. Peter's square, which he could tell he was nearing thanks to the increased volume. It didn't take long before the street he was walking down widened into a circular space surrounded by columns on two sides, forming a sort of two-thirds elliptical enclosure. The place was impossibly crowded with people, so much so that he couldn't even hear the running water of the two fountains over the din of noise. Withholding his grimace, he walked over to the giant obelisk that stood in the center of the square.

A man stood near the obelisk. There was nothing remarkable about him. He leaned against obelisk, a black book in his hand, cobalt eyes absently scanning the pages. The dark cloak he'd thrown over himself lent the already unremarkable man an even more bland appearance, as did his slightly swept back black hair.

Vertrou was not fooled.

"Are you sure it's alright to be out here?"

"Are you sure it's alright for you to express disapproval of what I do?"

Vertrou felt something unpleasant crawl up his spine, but he did his best to remain calm. He slowly walked over to the man.

"My apologies."

"Whatever." The man waved him off, though even that gesture made Vertrou flinch. "It is fine. In any event, you need not be concerned. The, ahem, Pope is currently locked away in his room, praying." The man flashed him a grin that revealed sharp fangs. "I told them I don't want to be disturbed."

Vertrou had no idea what to say to that, so he said nothing, instead choosing to look around at all the people present. The man also looked at the people. However, unlike Vertrou, who was doing so to distract himself, the man seemed to be contemplating something.

"It won't be long before these people become subjects of the new world order. These poor fools don't even realize what is going to happen to them. It's almost sad, really." He paused, then chuckled. "Do you not agree?"

Knowing he needed to tread carefully, Vertrou spoke with honesty. "I'm not really sure I care about what happens to these people. Humans are like sheep. They follow anyone who they believe is even remotely qualified to lead, which normally means they follow the loudest person speaking. I've watched these fools succumb to pretty words, devolve into violence over the most foolish differences in opinions, and hate each other for no other reason than because someone told them to. A new world order might be just what the doctor ordered."

The man grinned some more. "And I suppose the promise of power and untold riches didn't help?"

"I won't lie and say they didn't." Vertrou shrugged.

The grin widened. "That's very honest of you."

Disturbed by the grin on this man's face and the gleam in his eye, Vertrou coughed into his hand and tried to ignore the dread welling up in the pit of his stomach. Just standing near this man—this monster—made his skin crawl.

"I am guessing you summoned me for a specific reason? You normally only require virtual communication."

"Normally, simply talking telepathically is enough." The man nodded. "However, two of my subordinates have been defeated, sent back to Hell, and I have no idea why. I was hoping you could shed some light on that."

Vertrou licked his suddenly dry lips. "Following the orders to locate and retrieve Christian Crux, we managed to discover that he had made contact with Azazel and the few remaining Executioners in the United States. I had been unsure of what to do, so I was going to bring it to your attention. However, Beelzebub and Mammon found out and decided to act on their own. I... had not realized they'd been defeated."

"Hmm..."

Trying his best not to let on how frightened he was, Vertrou kept his eyes on the crowd of tourists as the man studied him. He felt like something powerful was piercing his heart. There was a strange pressure on his chest that left him breathless. The man wasn't even releasing any power. Just the power of his gaze was enough to make people quiver in fear.

"I'm glad you're being honest," the man said at last, causing Vertrou to sigh in relief.

"Lying to you is foolish."

"Indeed." A moment of silence passed between them as the man stroked his chin. "That said, I am going to have to teach those two a lesson when I see them again. Thanks to their foolishness, I am now down three Demon Kings. Accomplishing my goal is going to be that much harder. And Christian has made contact with Azazel. That is troublesome. I still have no idea where the Grigori hideout is located. Now it will take an even longer time to capture him, but we need him in our grasp. The gate cannot be opened without sacrificing someone who contains the blood of the king."

"I know." Vertrou nodded. "I will do everything within my power to locate the Grigori hideout."

"You had better." The man snapped his book shut and pushed off the wall. "And I had better get back to the cathedral. I'm sure by now someone will have ignored my order and entered the check up on me. I would hate to have to replace another servant." The man began walking off, but then he stopped and turned around. "Oh. There is a bit of information that might help you locate the Grigori hideout. Beelzebub was apparently killed in the middle of the South Atlantic Ocean."

Vertrou wondered what Beelzebub had been doing in the Atlantic Ocean, but he realized that Christian must have been located there, though just what that child was doing so far out was beyond him. The Grigori's hideout had to be somewhere outside of the US. Were they on a small island in the South Atlantic? Further out? There were too many possibilities to think about just then.

"Thank you. I will use Lord Beelzebub's last known location as a way point to search for Christian and the Grigori hideout."

"Good. Remember: I'm counting on you."

The man waved at Vertrou from over his shoulder as he headed back toward the Apostolic Palace, the official residence of the Pope. He watched as the man who was not really a man disappeared. Then he turned around and headed back the way he'd come. While it would be a waste to leave after having come all this way, given everything he had learned, Vertrou knew that his workload was going to increase.

He supposed that was the price one paid for power, and Vertrou would do anything to have more power, including selling his soul, and the souls of everyone on this planet, to Satan himself.

Chapter 7

Four days passed. There was very little to do during that time. They could walk around, clean their guns, eat in the cafeteria, or head to either the observation deck or bridge… and that was it. After the third day in the Watchtower, Christian felt like he was going stir crazy.

Lying in bed, Christian gazed at the ceiling as he stroked Lilith's shoulder. Her naked body was nestled against him, breasts pushing into his torso, spilling out due to their voluptuousness. She had wrapped her legs around his as well, further entangling them together. As she shifted against him, getting herself more comfortable even as she continued sleeping, her thigh gently grazed against his manhood. It wasn't erect just then. Given how much sex they'd been having, he'd have been surprised if it could get up right now.

Christian knew they couldn't stay in bed forever. He'd eventually have to wake Lilith, and then they would have to find something to do. Since Lilith wanted to get stronger, strong enough that she could fight beside him, he'd been teaching her about guns, but there was no place to practice so all that knowledge was theoretical.

It was a bit late in the game, but he had discovered that the weapons depot Azazel had on this massive contraption of steel and technology was new. The fallen angel had acquired those weapons and the orichalcum bullets only after deciding to meet with him and the Executioners. That made sense to him. Fallen angels had no need for weapons. Why bother using guns when you can just fire off light spears and create swords with divine energy?

Of course, that left him with the problem of there not being a shooting range. He could teach Lilith all the theory and gun safety tips she would ever need, but it wouldn't do her much good if they couldn't begin practicing.

I wonder what kind of gun I should have her wield...

He pulled Lilith closer, to which she responded by nuzzling her face against his bare chest and thought about that dilemma.

His first thoughts on a long-range weapon had been a self-defense gun like the Glock 43 or the Ruger LC9s. However, he quickly discarded the idea. Those were great for self-defense, but they were terrible for prolonged conflicts. For the average woman whose only need for a gun was muggers and rapists, it would be fine, but for a woman going up against goblins, demons, and all sorts of other nasty creatures, a gun with only 6 or 7 round magazines was asking to be killed.

A weapon for her should be a handgun, or at least the size of one. Something easy to use that doesn't have much recoil. Hmm... maybe something like an MP7?

MP7s were personal defense submachine guns. It had a cycling rate of fire of 950 rounds per minute, and conventionally allowed for 20-, 30-, or 40-round box magazines to be fitted within the pistol grip. Christian had only used them once or twice for missions that required him to mow down a lot of enemies. They were great when fired in short bursts and narrow hallways with very little cover. The MP7 was also compact and light, so a slip of a girl like Lilith could carry it without trouble.

I'll have to see if there's an MP7 in the weapons depot.

As he solidified his thoughts, a knock came at the door.

"Wakey, wakey! Rise and bakey!"

Tristin...

Christian groaned as he briefly considered ignoring the man, but he already knew that would be a bad idea. As if to prove him right, the knocking became louder.

"Come on, Christian! Rise and shine!"

"Christian..." Lilith groaned as she shifted against him. "Tell whoever's at the door to leave us alone."

Snorting in amusement, Christian slipped out of bed, ignored Lilith's moan of complaint for him to come back, and searched for his clothes. They were strewn across the floor. The knocking grew louder as he picked up his boxers and a pair of shorts. Slipping them on, he ran a hand through his hair as he pressed a button that caused the door to slide open.

Tristin was on the other side, looking his usual dapper self. His blond hair hovered over bright blue eyes. Since he was not an Intelligence Agent anymore, he'd changed his outfit. The pants he wore looked a bit tight, and he had a sash-like shirt that had a large gap in the shape of a V going all the way down to his navel. Christian thought the man looked like a pornstar. That demeanor was made more evocative by the women behind him, seven in total.

"You're looking even worse than usual," Tristin announced brightly. "Long night?"

"You could say that." Christian withheld a yawn as he looked at Tristin with flat eyes. "So? What do you want? I hope there's a reason you're bothering me."

"Do I ever need a reason to bother my best friend?"

"I'm closing the door now."

"Wait, wait, wait! I do have a reason! I do!"

Christian had been halfway toward pushing the close button, but he paused at Tristin's word. Letting his hand hover over the button for a moment, he slowly retracted it and stared at the incubus, who had grown suddenly pale.

"Well?" He raised an eyebrow.

Tristin coughed into his hand. "Right. My reason for being here. We've arrived in the Antarctic. We'll be coming up on the Grigori's base soon. I figured you and Lilith would want to see it."

It took a moment for the words to become fully processed by his brain, which had always been slow to start on mornings, but once it did, he realized why Tristin had come to see him.

"I'll wake up Lilith," he said at last.

"We'll be waiting here," Tristin announced.

Christian thought about telling Tristin that he didn't have to and should go on ahead, but he already knew what kind of response he could expect. He nodded instead.

"Give me a minute."

Closing the door, he wandered back over to the bed. Lilith was still asleep. She had turned over on her side after he vacated the bed and was now lying with her legs curled closer to her chest. The covers had partly fallen away, leaving her breasts exposed to the slightly warm air. Golden threads of hair spread across the sheets like streams of sunlight. As he gazed at her, Christian found his eyes drawn to her lips, slightly parted and glossy.

He crawled onto the bed and turned the woman over. Her breasts jiggled. Were he not exhausted from their previous night, he would have already been hard enough to cut orichalcum.

Leaning down, he placed a kiss on Lilith's lips, and when she only stirred a bit, he gave her another one, and then another and another, until a pair of arms wrapped around his neck and Lilith began kissing back.

"Morning," Lilith murmured in a sleepy slur.

"Morning," Christian greeted back. "We'll be arriving at the Grigori stronghold shortly. Let's get dressed."

"M'kay."

Lilith let go of Christian, allowing him to get up and put on his shirt. Meanwhile, she let the sheets pool around her waist and stretched her arms above her head. Christian admired the elegant curvature of her body as she twisted this way and that, along with the way her breasts would bounce and shake with every movement. He sighed. It would have been nice if they could have a quickie before heading off... but nothing they did was ever quick.

"Here."

"Thank you."

Christian grabbed Lilith's clothes and handed them to the woman, so she could get dressed. While he was wearing black pants and a white T-shirt, Lilith wore shorts that showed off her legs and a spaghetti strap shirt.

He briefly considered putting on his armor, but, in all honesty, his armor was currently in ruins. It was dented in some place and cracked in others. He'd need to get it repaired, or maybe he should just have new armor made.

After he put on his boots and Lilith slipped into her sneakers, they wandered outside where Tristin and his harem were waiting for them.

"You two are looking good!" The incubus complimented with a thumbs-up and a wink. Christian and Lilith stared at him, causing Tristin to cough in his hand. "Anyway, are you ready to go?"

"Yup," Christian said as Lilith grabbed his hand. She didn't much care for Tristin. It was an instinctive dislike born from being different species. Succubus and incubus harbored an intense hatred of each other, to the point where that dislike was practically a part of their DNA. It was like a genetic memory passed down through the ages.

Tristin, an anomaly in this regard, ignored her actions as he beamed at them. "Then let's go!"

Together with his harem, Tristin led Christian and Lilith to the bridge. While the young incubus spoke, Christian could not help but study the woman in his harem. There were seven: Jizabell, Marianne, Miyu, Nagendra, Kristine, Listy, and Hannah.

Jizabell was the de facto leader of the harem. A graceful woman with tanned skin and an athletic build, her muscular legs, easily visible in those black spandex pants, flexed every time she walked. She wore a sleeveless shirt, which meant her lean arms were on display. Higher cheekbones and a slightly sharper face gave her a regal appearance. She wouldn't have looked out of place sitting on a throne. The woman didn't talk much, but when she did, everyone in the harem listened.

Glancing and Marianne and Nagendra, who walked side by side, Christian could not help but notice how different the two were. Marianne was a willowy woman with brown hair and fair skin, while Nagendra had dark skin and black hair. Unlike Jizabell, who seemed to prefer workout clothing, they were wearing jeans and a shirt.

Miyu, a pudgy woman of Asian descent, walked behind the two, taking slight glances at Lilith out of her peripheral vision. She seemed to have a thing for kimono-esque clothing. Her shirt vaguely reminded him of a kimono with voluminous sleeves and flower print designs. Likewise, her skirt gave off a similar vibe. He didn't know which country she was from. It wasn't like they had ever spoken.

If Jizabell was the leader, and Marianne, Nagendra, and Miyu were simple harem members, then Kristine, Listy, and Hannah were bodyguards. Kristine looked like a typical California girl with bleached blonde hair and a tan without tan lines, but she also carried a pistol at her hip. Listy seemed a bit more like the bookish type with her glasses and slightly mousy hair. Even so, Christian had immediately spotted the knives she hid in her boots. Hannah, who looked younger than the others by a few years, was a raven-haired beauty who walked with the experienced grace of a martial artist. Being someone well-versed in combat himself, Christian easily noticed the sleight of hand movements that denoted an experienced hand-to-hand fighter.

Neither he nor Lilith had much to do with Tristin's harem. They had been introduced to each other when the group came onboard, but that was about it. The women seemed mostly interested in doing their own things. Running along that same vein, he and Lilith didn't really feel the need to form a close relationship with any of them.

They arrived on the bridge to find Samantha, Sif, Leon, Clarissa, and Heather were already present alongside Azazel, Kokabiel, and Shemhazai. Azazel was standing at the head of the bridge, staring at the large monitor that showed them a panoramic view of the outside. The Watchtower didn't have any windows. Every view outside was a panel connected to a camera.

"It's good that you've come," Azazel said as Christian and Lilith split from Tristin and his harem. "You'll want to see this."

"What are we supposed to be seeing?" Lilith asked the question Christian wanted answered as well. Looking outside revealed nothing but ice.

Antarctica was the coldest, windiest, and driest continent on Earth. It contained 90% of all the ice on Earth in an area just under one and a half times the size of the US. As he stared out the viewport, all her could see was ground slick with ice and massive mountains covered in white. As he and Lilith continued to stare, they saw a glacier several miles below crack and break as it moved across the continent. Cracks hundreds of feet deep spanned the continent, some hidden only by a shallow layer of snow, while others weren't hidden at all.

"Just a minute." Azazel presented them with a mysterious smile. "You'll see it soon."

Christian and Lilith didn't know what they were supposed to be seeing, but just as Christian opened his mouth to say something, it happened. A small section of the air in front of them distorted. Tendrils of electricity or lightning crackled for a brief second, and then a square of space opened before them. The Watchtower flew through.

It was like a rift leading into another world.

The world on the other side of the strange rift looked nothing like he had expected. Large towers jutted into the sky, stopping before they hit a strange dome that Christian realized with a start was an energy field.

There weren't that many towers. One giant one sat in the center, a monolith of perfect symmetry, while several smaller ones were arrayed around it. Most of the landscape looked like an urban development zone. There were houses and buildings, parks and recreational areas. The place didn't have any streets. He found that odd, but as he continued observing the strange city, he saw figures darting through the sky on wings blacker than night.

Fallen angels.

"Welcome to Seventh Heaven," Azazel said with a grand sweep of his hand. "Home of the Grigori, the Watchers of God's children."

"This is…" Lilith began.

"Unbelievable," Christian finished.

While tempted to get right up to the viewport and press his face against it, Christian resisted. As he and Lilith stood there, staring, Samantha wandered up to them, stopping to stand on his other side.

"I've never seen anything like this. What kind of barrier is that? And how can this place be so fertile?"

Azazel grinned. "The barrier is actually something of my own invention. I call it the Divine Oscillation Barrier. It uses the divine energy from us fallen angels to create a field that not only hides it completely from the view of eyes and satellites, but it also protects us from Antarctica's frigid atmosphere. The greenery is actually easier to explain. We just important this stuff from other countries. Even the soil we use to grow crops was imported."

Christian could hardly believe such a place existed outside of the annals of fantasy and science fiction but seeing was believing. In the face of such a sight, he could do nothing but believe, though now he was curious about how long it had taken to make such a place. Also, the technological level of these fallen angels seemed completely disproportionate with the time. Just how far ahead, technologically, were these fallen angels?

The Watchtower slowly descended. As they came closer to the ground, Christian could see more of the city, which really did look like a blend of modern urban zones with technological wonders found only in science fiction. Add in the fallen angels flying through the air, and Christian could not help but feel like all three of these factors were completely dissociated from each other.

They passed by two of the towers, lowered their altitude more, and soon arrived at a massive landing zone. It looked like a flat surface made of black asphalt. It wasn't asphalt, though. The surface had a glossy quality that made him think of polished obsidian, though he wasn't sure it was that either.

"Prepare for landing," the fallen angel piloting the vessel set.

"Extend landing planks."

"Easing thrust."

"Calculating the angle of descent."

The fallen angels manning the Watchtower announced what they were doing as it happened. Christian couldn't help but feel like he had ended up in some really bizarre crossover of Macross and High School DxD.

"All right, everyone," Azazel began. "Prepare to disembark. Get the others, grab your belongings, and meet me at the boarding ramp!"

Everyone hustled out of the bridge in a single group. The living quarters were all located close together anyway. Christian and Lilith headed back into their room and grabbed their meager belongings, which mostly consisted of his weapons and a spare change of underwear, and then met up with the others again.

The groups were already heading down to the bridge, and what a mixed group it was. Christian didn't think he'd ever see the day where so many different people had gathered. Succubus mixed with Executioners, who were all wearing the medallions that kept their sanity from being eroded by the Aura of Allure.

It had taken a long time for the two groups to get used to each other. The Executioners were so used to killing succubus that suddenly living among them was jarring. Several fights had broken out, mostly instigated by the Executioners, but all of them were quickly squashed by either Clarissa, Heather, Samantha, Sif, or Leon.

Of course, there were also the fallen angels. They seemed eager to leave the Watchtower as well. He guessed they had been cooped up in this place longer than anyone else and wanted to stretch their wings.

Streaming through the halls and down the staircases like a river, the massive group of over 100 individuals of mixed races soon gathered by the boarding ramp. Azazel, Kokabiel, and Shemhazai were already there. After fiddling with the controls, Azazel lowered the boarding ramp, allowing a blast of surprisingly warm air to hit their faces.

At the Grigori leader's instructions, everyone descended the boarding ramp. Azazel and his two cohorts were in the lead. After them came Samantha, Sif, Leon, Clarissa, and Heather. Heather's second in command, Kaylee, followed behind her like a faithful puppy. Christian and Lilith followed behind them with Tristin and his harem. Meanwhile, the mixed group of succubi, Executioners, and fallen angels came down last.

A small procession was waiting for them. At the head of this procession was a man with short-cropped blond hair and small eyes. His face was lined with hard angles. Unlike Azazel, Kokabiel, and Shemhazai, who all looked like they were in their 20s, this man appeared more like someone in his late 40s or early 50s. He wore a robe of pure white that descended all the way down to his feet.

Four black angel wings spread out behind him.

"Armaros!" Azazel greeted with a grin.

The one named Armaros smiled. "It is good to see you've returned safely, General-Governor. You were gone much longer this time." He glanced past Azazel to the large group gathered behind the man, specifically the humans and succubus. "It seems you've picked up quite a few people."

"Yup." Azazel shrugged and gave a helpless smile. "We ran into some trouble, and I couldn't very well leave them."

"You have always been a kind person." As Armaros observed them, his eyes suddenly locked onto Christian, who felt his back unconsciously straightening. "Is that the son of Amon?"

Azazel looked at where Armaros was looking, then turned back to the other fallen angel and chuckled. "Yup."

"He looks just like Amon... except he doesn't have sharp teeth and his skin isn't red, of course."

"Of course."

Christian couldn't help but feel like he was being left out of the loop. Everyone seemed to know his father. It felt like so much had been hidden from him, and now he couldn't help but have more questions. Just who was his father? Did the Church know all this when they picked him up? If so, why had they let him live? Surely if he was related to a demon, the Church should have killed him regardless of his age. That was how the Executioners had always operated.

"I know you must be tired, but the members of the Council of Twenty have been made aware of your arrival and gathered in Babel."

"I see." Azazel grimaced as he cracked his back with several deft movements. "I'll head over there right now. In the meantime, could you find some place for these people to stay?"

"Of course, General-Governor."

Armaros bowed low to Azazel, who soon left with Kokabiel and Shemhazai in tow. Christian watched as they lifted into the air and flew toward the massive tower, Babel he presumed, and then directed his attention to the one who greeted them. Armaros. According to the Book of Enoch, this person was the fallen angel known as the "cursed one" or the "accursed one." Not much was known about him, but he was listed among the 20 leaders of the 200 strong Grigori.

"If you will all follow me, I shall show you to your accommodations," he said before turning around and walking. The procession of fallen angels that had stood behind him flapped their wings and took to the sky.

Left with no other choice, the mixed group of Executioners and succubus could do nothing but follow the fallen angel.

"I feel like a fish out of water," Leon said as they walked off the glimmering black landing pad.

"I understand all too well how you feel," Sif muttered. "Everything feels like it's gone to Hell. I would have never imagined we'd be allied with both succubus and the Grigori."

"I'd have never imagined the Catholic Church could play host to Satan and the other Demon Kings, but it's happened and there is nothing we can do about it," Samantha said. "Right now, these people are our only hope for survival."

"We know," Sif and Leon muttered at the same time.

Ignoring the conversation between the three Executioners, Christian glanced at their surroundings.

While Seventh Heaven didn't have any roads that did not mean they couldn't walk between buildings. Christian immediately noticed that while most of the buildings had a very modern shape, they lacked several key features that normal buildings had, such as doors and windows. They were instead just open entrances with nothing barring the way. He would have questioned someone's sanity at such a lack of security, but then realized where he was. Fallen angels probably saw no point in things like doors since no one but other fallen angels lived here.

"Excuse me, Clarissa?" Lilith began as she caught up to the woman.

"Yes, Lilith? What is it?"

"I was wondering if I could restart my training soon?" Lilith asked, worrying her lower lip.

Clarissa nodded. "Yes, I suppose it would be a good idea to renew your training. I heard from one of the Valkyries that you managed to activate your Succubus Form. That is good. It means the next phase of your training should come more smoothly."

"We will also need to pick out a weapon for you," Heather added. "I don't think something like a sword or a spear would be a good fit, but maybe we can find a whip."

"A whip?"

"Like Indiana Jones."

"I know what a whip is. I was just wondering why you would suggest it." Lilith pouted at the woman.

As Lilith listened to Heather explain her reasoning, Christian found he could only partially agree. A whip was a tool which was traditionally designed to strike animals or people to aid guidance or exert control through pain compliance or fear of pain. It wasn't really a weapon. It couldn't kill. Well, he supposed it was possible to flog someone to death, but that would take more effort, and it wasn't a practical way to fight.

The large group was soon led to one of the towers. Looking at it from up close, Christian realized this one was about sixteen stories high. Like everything else, it had no doors or windows, just an open space for them to walk through. It also didn't have any defining features, though from the number of fallen angels flying into the building through the windows, he assumed this place was a housing unit of some kind.

Entering through the door revealed an open space vaguely reminiscent to a hotel lobby, except it didn't have a reception desk. Several tables were arrayed around the room. A number of fallen angels were sitting at them, drinking red wine as they discussed various topics—or they had been. As the group of humans and succubus entered, all conversations ceased.

"Come, everyone," Armaros urged them on. "Do not let yourself be bothered by the crowd. They are merely curious. While we do have some humans living among us, it is not often that such a large number of them appear in one place, never mind succubus."

"I'll bet," Samantha muttered.

"So we're basically like superstars?" asked Tristin. "Heh, I can deal with that."

"More like eccentricities," Armaros said in an odd but amused tone.

Following Armaros, the group was lead to a cylindrical room in the center of the building. It was large enough to fit about half their numbers but appeared innocuous at first, but then the fallen angel passed a hand over a small device, and the floor suddenly shuddered before it began ascending. Christian and Lilith tried their best to keep from being crushed by the group of people. The elevator soon stopped, revealing four doorways that led out.

"All of the rooms on this floor are empty," Armaros said. "You may use any room you wish. There are over one hundred, so there is more than enough space for all of you."

Samantha and Clarissa took the lead. As the head of the Executioners, the raven-haired femme fatale led her ragtag group of former monster hunters through one exit, while Clarissa led her succubus through another, leaving Christian, Lilith, Tristin, and his harem alone with Armaros.

"Well," Tristin began, "I guess we should get settled in. I'll talk to you later, Christian."

"Yeah. Later."

Tristin and his harem left through one of the exits, and then it was just him and Lilith alone with Armaros. The fallen angel tilted his head in quiet curiosity.

"Is there something on your mind, young one?"

Christian swallowed. "Did you know my father?"

"Indeed, I did." Armaros nodded. "I was not as close to him as Azazel was, though. If you're asking because you wish to know more about your father, I would recommend talking to him… though he will probably be busy for some time. Now then, you two had best be off. I have to get the next group up here."

"Okay."

Lilith and Christian exited the elevator, which descended a moment later. They stood in a plain hallway. When it became apparent that Christian wouldn't move, Lilith tugged his hand to get them going.

"Come on. Let's find a room."

Letting Lilith lead him, the two of them found an empty room that suited their tastes well enough. It was just a plain room really. Like the room they had slept in on the Watchtower, it only had a bed, a dresser, a desk, and a closet. This one did feature a window as well. Of course, he only called it a window because he didn't know what else to call the large rectangular hole. The fallen angels apparently used it as a door.

"Are you alright, Christian?" asked Lilith.

"Yeah," he said with a sigh. "I just feel overwhelmed. I keep learning things that I never knew, and it feels like my entire world perspective has been distorted." He paused long enough to shake his head. "No, it feels like my perspective was distorted before and the cloth has suddenly been pulled from my eyes, but now that I have all this new information, I'm confused about how I should feel."

Lilith slowly nodded. "I can see how that would be overwhelming. I've just been sort of going with the flow right now because everything happening seems to be happening despite me, not because of me, but it sounds like you are somehow in the thick of what's going on. It must be a lot to take in."

Gracing the woman with a smile, Christian said, "that might be the biggest understatement I've ever heard."

Shrugging, Lilith pulled Christian over to the king-sized bed. She pushed him down until he was sitting, and then sat on his lap, wiggling her butt to get comfortable before wrapping her arms around him.

"Maybe it is. In either event, right now there's nothing we can do about it. All we can do for the moment is wait to see what's going to happen next."

Christian sighed as he hugged Lilith and buried his face in her hair. The natural scent of her hair and body calmed the raging storm that his mind had become, though it couldn't fully calm his stormy heart. Even so, he relaxed against Lilith and took comfort in her presence.

"I know," he muttered softly. "But I hate waiting when I know something major is going on around us."

"Me too," Lilith murmured as she closed her eyes. "Me too."

***

Azazel entered the meeting room to find 16 of the Council of Twenty already present. They sat at a long table inside of a small office space. The table was made of the same obsidian material that most of the buildings were created from as were the chairs, which featured a high back and comfortable armrest. Four spaces were currently vacant, though Kokabiel and Shemhazai filled two of them, while Azazel filled the third at the head of the table. The last seat was for Armaros.

"I'm so glad you three could find the time to return home," an older-looking gentleman with dark hair, silver sideburns, and wrinkles around his eyes said. His voice was stone cold. Unlike many of the others, who wore white robes, his were a dark black and covered the unique body armor he wore.

"Me too." Azazel ignored the sarcasm in the man's voice, though he couldn't stop the grin from forming on his face. "It was quite the journey, let me tell you. Hm. But, it sounds like you were worried about us, Baraquiel."

"Hmph!" The fabric of Baraquel's robe shifted as he crossed his thick arms over his massive chest. His arms were bare, so the incredible musculature and pulsating veins were easily visible in the bright light of the room. "Given that you have been leaving more and more, is it not the job of those under you to wonder what you are up to? So much is going on in the outside world right now, and most of it isn't what I would call pleasant."

"Wars, famine, racism, politics…" An even older-looking fallen angel with completely white hair and numerous wrinkles listed off topics on his fingers. Of course, all the topics were somehow involved in the growing dissent of humanity. "… there are so many issues on Earth right now that we Grigori can no longer keep up with them. Even before discovering that Satan and the Seven Demon Kings had infiltrated the Catholic Church, there were more problems than we could solve."

Penemue, an old angel who had fallen because he taught mankind the art of writing with ink and paper, was something like their manager of telecommunications. All the spies they had located throughout the world reported to him. Out of all the angels present, he knew the most about what they were dealing with. It was this old angel who had discovered that the Seven Demon Kings were up to something.

"Many of those problems are caused by man," Chazaqiel said with a dismissive wave of his hand. "We cannot solve every problem that humanity creates for themselves. Sometimes it is better to take a step back and observe the situation."

"Yes, but the current situation has nothing to do with Americas war in the Middle East, or the numerous conflicts happening in Africa. The very religion we belong to is under threat. The fragile balance between demons and angels, Satan and God, is on the verge of breaking. As those who promised to watch after God's creations, we cannot afford to do nothing," Penemue said.

"I am not suggesting we do nothing," Chazaqiel said. "I am merely stating that many of those problems you mentioned were brought about by the hands of man and are therefore not our problems. We taught mankind much of what they know, but we are not responsible for their actions. What they do with that knowledge is up to them."

"As interesting as this age-old debate is, that is not the reason we're having this meeting, is it?" Azazel posed his words as a question, even though everyone knew it wasn't. He glanced at each of the fallen sitting at the table in turn. He made sure to make eye contact before starting again. "As of this moment, the Seven Demon Kings have infiltrated the Catholic Church. Sadly, they are so entrenched that right now, we cannot remove them without eliminating more than a third of their bishops and the Pope himself. What we need to decide on now is what we should be doing."

After opening the council for debate, Azazel sat back and listened as several of the twenty Grigori present argued with each other. He let them talk. Numerous ideas were tossed about, some of which sounded good, while others sounded ridiculous. One person even suggested trying to form a new religion with them at the end, but he was immediately shot down.

"This arguing is pointless," Kokabiel muttered. He spoke softly, but it was loud enough that everyone heard him.

"Excuse me?" asked Sariel, a young-looking fallen angel with dark skin and gray eyes.

"If the Demon Kings have infiltrated the Catholic Church, then all we need to do is present them with a reason to head out." Kokabiel looked at everyone with a composed expression. Azazel suddenly felt a chill run down his spine. "And we have one. Amon's son is now among us. We can use him as bait."

At those words, the entire council exploded.

"Amon's son is here?! Now?!"

"Where is he?!"

"What's he like?! Is he strong?!"

"Do you think we can use him in our plans?!"

Azazel held a hand to his face as he listened to the numerous words, mostly questions and ideas on how to use Christian, with a grimace. He didn't know if Kokabiel had realized this would happen. In fact, the man probably hadn't. He was a battle maniac through and through, caring little for political contrivances.

"Enough!" Azazel shouted enough to be heard over the arguments. Everyone went silent. Azazel tossed Kokabiel a mild glare, but then sent his disapproving gaze around the room. "Yes, Amon's son, Christian, is currently among us now. Currently, his power is unremarkable. He has displayed several moments of incredible power, but it is not stable, so we cannot use him in any of our plans. I'm going to have Kokabiel try and coax that power out of him. If we can train him to utilize his full powers, then we might be able to use him as bait to lure the remaining four Demon Kings into a trap. However, before we even think of doing something like that, I need to talk to him and he needs to get stronger."

Given who Christian was and Azazel's relationship with the boy's father, he could ill afford to treat the boy like a tool. First, he had to let Christian know what was going on. Then he had to train Christian to utilize his powers to their fullest, which could take years, depending on Christian himself. Then and only then could they create any plans revolving around the boy.

"Right now, what we should be focusing on is running damage control," Azazel continued. "We need to find a way to impede the Seven Demon Kings from getting any more power. At the very least, we should find some method to prevent more demons from crossing over."

Everyone grumbled a bit, but Azazel sent each person a quick glare of disapproval, quieting them down.

The council proceeded much more smoothly after that. It was agreed upon that they would begin dispatching more of their brethren into the world. The plan was to send them to hotspots of demon activity, which normally meant someone was using a summoning ritual to summon demons directly to Earth, which was different than when demons used a barrier to phase a portion of the world out of alignment. They would be easy enough to disrupt by killing the summoner. The only problem was getting to those places fast enough that they could kill the summoner before the summoning was complete.

"We'll dispatch some of our stronger warriors to places where demon summoning seems likely," Azazel began bringing the meeting to a close. "Penemue, I'll be relying on your intelligence to let us know where we should send our forces."

"Leave it to me," Penemue muttered as he toyed with his long hair.

"Does anyone else have anything to add? No. Then let's bring this meeting to a close."

As the fallen angels filed out of the room in ones and twos, Azazel sat there and stretched his arms, sighing as he realized that it had been a long time since he'd gotten any sleep. While he technically didn't need sleep, it really was a fun past time. It was particularly fun to sleep with a woman in his arms after a night of passionate sex.

Taking a deep breath, Azazel frowned as he saw Kokabiel leave. He stood up and filed out. Quickly catching up with the other fallen angel, he walked down the extravagant but barren of decoration hallway.

"Why did you tell them Christian Crux was with us?" he asked.

Kokabiel tilted his head. "Should I not have? It is not like you told me not to, and you were going to have to bring it up anyway."

"I… I suppose that is true," Azazel admitted with a sigh. He couldn't really be mad at Kokabiel. "Still, I had been hoping to ease them into that knowledge. Now some of the more aggressive ones might try something."

Shrugging as if he didn't care one way or another, Kokabie said, "I'll keep that in mind for the future. Speaking of, when would you like me to begin training him?"

Azazel scratched the back of his head. "As soon as you are able, I suppose. The sooner he can tap into his power at will, the better."

"Understood."

The two of them soon split up. Azazel didn't know where Kokabiel went (probably to a training ground or something), but he decided to head off in search of a nice woman to bed.

Chapter 8

Lilith stood in an open field far from the city proper. Of course, it was not like she had truly left the city. Several buildings surrounded the field on all sides, but they were smaller than the towering skyscrapers closer to the center. The field was covered in a thick layer of grass. She was standing on it bare feet, and the many soft blades tickled her soles.

Standing before her was Clarissa, who was once again trying to teach her how to use illusions, the magic that all succubus possessed.

"I have already given you some basic knowledge of illusions, but I suppose a refresher course might be necessary," Clarissa coughed into her hand, clearing her throat. "Succubus have the ability to cast illusions that affect one or more of the five senses of sight, smell, hearing, taste, and touch. For example, you could cast an illusion that throws your voice several meters away, making people believe you are somewhere else. You could also cast an illusion that makes people feel like they are being bound, affecting their sense of touch. You could even make people see horrible scenes of death and destruction, even their own death, by affecting their sense of sight with an illusion. The possibilities are theoretically limitless."

It was early in the morning. Lilith had abstained from having sex last night and asked Christian to wake her up early, so she could begin training as soon as possible. She wanted to get stronger. She didn't want to be the weak girl Christian had to keep protecting.

On that note, Christian was with her that day. He said he wanted to know more about succubus powers because it would help them work together as a team.

"You said theoretically," Lilith began, "does that imply there are some illusions that are impossible to create?"

"Very good." Clarissa smiled. "Yes, some illusions may be impossible. Illusions are cast by injecting your life essence into another person and disrupting one or more of their senses. There are several key factors when casting an illusion." She held up a finger. "One: The power of the succubus doing the casting." She held up a second finger. "Two: The imagination of the succubus doing the casting." She held up a third finger. "Three: The willpower of the person who the illusion is being cast on."

Lilith bit her lower lip as she nodded. It wasn't easy keeping up with what the woman was saying, but she was using her knowledge from light novels she'd read to fill in some of the blanks. Humans might not have known magic existed in real life. That said, they had a surprisingly realistic view of how magic worked.

Beside her, Christian was nodding along as well, looking the same as she felt.

"Can you figure out what makes these three aspects of crafting illusions so important?" asked Clarissa.

Lilith scrunched up her face a bit as, slowly, she worked out the answers in her head and thought about what she wanted to say.

"For the first point, I imagine it is a simple application of power. Some illusions might be bigger than others. That means casting them will require more power, like, um, for example, an illusion that affects two senses might cost more than one that only affects one sense... maybe?"

Clarissa's smile widened. "Very good. Yes. The bigger the illusion, the more power that illusion will cost to produce. Also, the more senses you try to affect using an illusion, the more it will cost as well. Given your own exceptional powers, I imagine you'll eventually be able to cast multiple illusions that affect all five senses at some point."

Though Lilith tried not to let it show on her face, she was already imagining herself casting vastly powerful illusions and defeating her opponent's magical girl style. It sounded really cool.

"Your otaku is showing," Christian muttered with a smile.

Lilith did her best not to blush. When that failed, she glared at Christian, but her mate had such a kind look on his face that she had to look away for fear of melting. That was too close. If she'd stared at him for longer than a second, she might have jumped him.

Coughing into her hand, Clarissa grabbed their attention again. "What about my second point?"

"I think…" Lilith hesitated for a moment, but then she plowed on. "I think it has to do with how well the succubus can imagine the illusion happening. It sounds like illusions rely on the imagination of the one casting them, so if a succubus can't visualize what her illusion will look like or how it will feel for the person it's being cast on, she won't be able to cast it."

"Excellent." Clarissa clasped her hands together. "Yes, that is it exactly. In order to cast an illusion, you need to be able to imagine what that illusion would be like. Visual illusions are generally the easiest, though they get harder the more complex your illusion is. On the other hand, how does one 'imagine' a sound? Can you hear a sound clearly in your head if you haven't heard it before? Sometimes a succubus can power through this problem by simply shoving more of their life essence into their illusion, but that requires more power than most succubus have."

Thinking about it, that was some fairly standard illusion magic. She remembered reading a light novel about a witch who could cast illusions; her magic had been very similar to this, albeit, slightly different.

Lilith glanced at Christian again, but her mate was staring intently at Clarissa, as if he was trying to burn a hole through the woman's face. He was taking her lesson even more seriously than she was.

"I guess the last point has less to do with the succubus and more to do with the one the succubus is casting the illusion on." Lilith tilted her head, nodded, and then continued. "A person with a strong will can probably resist an illusion. That's basically it, right?"

"More or less." Clarissa shrugged and smiled. "It is a tad more complicated than that, though. The amount of power you put into an illusion will determine that illusion's strength. If the strength of your illusion is stronger than the will of the person it is being cast on, then your illusion will override his or her will. However, if their will is stronger than your illusion, it will be the illusion that ends up getting destroyed."

Lilith nodded several times, as did Christian. While this sort of magic lesson might have made little sense to someone who didn't read fantastical stories about mages, demons, angels, yōkai, and any other number of supernatural creatures, for a pair of nerds like them, it was easier to understand.

"I have a question," Christian said at last, speaking for the first time since the lesson began.

"What is it?" asked Clarissa.

"When we were fighting Asmodeus, something strange happened." He crossed his arms and frowned. "Several vines seemed to emerge from the ground to restrain him. I only saw them thanks to my eye, and I didn't really pay much attention at the time, but it seems to me that Lilith's power is more than merely exceptional. To affect a Demon King, even one who can only use a tenth of his power, means her abilities are on par with some of the strongest creatures out there."

Lilith looked started for a moment, but then she tried to recall what happened during the fight with Asmodeus. She scrunched up her face. However, no matter how hard she tried, only bits and pieces of that time flashed through her mind. Part of it probably had to do with how stressful that moment had been. That said, she thought a good portion of it was because she'd barely been aware of what was happening after the car crash, like she'd only been semi-conscious.

"You are correct." Clarissa chuckled a bit, bringing Lilith's focus back onto her. "You didn't think Lilith was just a name she randomly chose, did you? Every so often, a succubus who inherits the power of one of the original four will come along. Each time this happens, the succubus in question will often adopt the name of the one who's power they inherited. For Eve here, the succubus whose power she inherited was probably Lilith's."

A figure in Jewish mythology, Lilith was often envisioned as a dangerous demon of the night, a creature who was sexually wanton, stole babies, and such. She was generally thought to derive in part from a historically far earlier class of female monster known as Lifitu in the ancient Mesopotamian region. According to Clarissa, Lilith had been a prominent and powerful succubus during the time when Babylon rose to prominence.

"Lilith was often considered the leader of what we now consider the Four Progenitors. It was said that her succubus form was even more enchanting than her human form, and that her powers were so overwhelming that the illusions she cast became real." Clarissa paused for a moment to frown. "Having never seen her powers for myself, I cannot say for certain, but I believe Lilith had the ability to rewrite reality with her illusions."

"And you think I inherited that power?" asked Lilith uncertainly.

"It is not a matter of thinking." Clarissa shook her head as if to dispel any uncertainty. "When you changed your name, why did you choose the name Lilith? There are millions of names out there. Lilith is also a very uncommon name. How did you think it up?"

"Well…"

"It was instinctive," Clarissa said when Lilith trailed off. "That name came to you because your soul is drawn to the name of the woman you inherited your vast powers from. This is what I believe, at any rate."

Without any proof, there really was no way to know whether Clarissa was correct. All she had were theories and conjecture. Ultimately, Lilith wasn't sure where her powers came from mattered. What mattered most, right then, was learning how to use them.

"So… to use these illusions…" Lilith began.

"To use illusions, you must first learn how to use your life essence." Clarissa straightened her shoulders and adopted a more lecture-like pose. "Our life essence is basically the power of life that we consume when we have sex with our mate. We call it life essence because on top of being used to power our magic, it is also what gives us life. Without it, we would die." She gave Lilith a stern look. "This actually brings me to an important point, and that is that you should always be aware of how much life essence you have. If you use too much, you might end up using all your life essence, and then you will die, so please be careful."

Lilith gulped. Beside her, Christian paled.

"Now then, to feel your life essence, you must simply close your eyes and visualize a small sphere inside of your chest. That sphere is your core. It is the core of your power. Once you visualize it, you should be able to feel your life essence."

Taking a shaky breath, Lilith closed her eyes and tried to do what Clarissa told her. Tried. And failed. Sweat beaded along her brow as she struggled to form what constituted as a mental image of her "core," which seemed like such an ethereal and nebulous concept that she couldn't get a decent grasp of it.

"Take a deep breath," Clarissa suggested. "Don't force it. If you remain calm and let your mind go, you should be able to visualize it unconsciously."

"Visualize it unconsciously," Lilith muttered under her breath as she tried to do just that. She took a deep breath. Then she held it. Then she released it. And then she repeated the whole process over again.

As she continued taking deep, even breaths, Lilith felt her body relax. Her shoulders loosened. Her back no longer felt stiff. Her legs slackened. Then something else happened. It felt like she was suddenly floating through a dark void, even though she knew she was still standing on a grassy field. While drifting through this void, a bright light appeared in the distance. She closed in on the light, which grew more luminescent with each passing second, until it turned into a sphere so large and so bright she couldn't look at it without going blind.

Lilith opened her eyes with a gasp.

"You saw it, didn't you?" said Clarissa, smiling.

"I certainly saw something," Lilith muttered as Christian looked on curiously. She noticed that he'd closed his green eye and was looking at her with the red one.

"That was definitely your core. I can feel it becoming more active." Clarissa crossed her arms and nodded. "Now that you've seen your core, you should be able to feel your life essence and draw upon it at will."

While Lilith still wasn't sure she understood what the woman meant, she did feel something flowing through her body. A strange energy moved through her, following what felt like a set of predetermined paths. This flow originated from the center of her chest. If she had to guess, Lilith would have said that her core was located there, and the flow of power was her life essence.

"I believe we've done enough today," Clarissa began. "You have more lessons to attend anyway."

Lilith wanted to learn more, but she knew by this point that Clarissa would not budge on subjects like this. She nodded and released a sigh.

"Do not look so disappointed." Clarissa gave her a look that mixed exasperation with amusement. "We cannot do much until you learn to control your power. Now that you have activated your core, the Aura of Allure, which had been kept under control thanks to you mating with Christian, is leaking a bit. You will want to learn how to reign that power in. Once you can manage that, I will teach you how to craft illusions."

Startled by Clarissa's words, Lilith looked at Christian, who spotted her shocked expression and shrugged. She frowned. So, he didn't feel her Aura of Allure at all. Well, he was her mate, so that mate sense. Lilith could only assume that mating with Christian had caused her Aura of Allure to go dormant since she no longer needed it, but now that she had activated her core, her succubus powers were leaking out of her. Something like that.

"Okay." Lilith agreed with a reluctant nod.

"Good." Clarissa also nodded, though hers was much more decisive. "Now, go seek out Heather. I believe she and the other Valkyries are teaching the younger succubus how to fight right now. Join them."

"Yes, ma'am. Thank you for the lesson."

Clarissa waved them off as she began walking away. Since it looked like they were done there, Christian and Lilith also left the field.

They journeyed into the city proper, which really did look like a normal city if one discounted the fact that over half the people there were had wings and flew to most of their destinations. There were a surprising number of humans, however. Lilith had learned the other day that because the Grigori were small in number (they were 200 strong), they did not have enough people to initiate long-term and large-scale operations. To rectify this, they brought in numerous humans who had special skills. According to Armaros, there were about 500 humans.

That still wasn't a lot.

"That was a pretty informative lesson," Lilith said as they passed by a stall with bread. Everything there was free. The Grigori didn't believe in using human currency for goods. As she and Christian grabbed a small loaf to share, the man standing behind the stall blinked several times before his eyes glazed over.

"There's a lot more to succubus powers than I imagined." Christian agreed as he broke the loaf in half and gave one half to Lilith. "And it seems like you can become pretty powerful if you learn to master your abilities."

"Do you think... I'll be useful to you?" asked Lilith as she nibbled on the half-loaf of bread.

Christian didn't answer at first. He considered her with a casual glance. Lilith wondered what he was thinking, but then he spoke.

"I do not believe you have ever not been useful. You've done more for me than you seem to realize." He paused to lick his lips.

"However, if you're referring to being useful in battle, then I think if you can master your abilities, you might become even more powerful than me."

"So... I'll be useful, right?"

"Yes." Christian finished off his bread and slipped his hand into hers. "You will be very useful."

"Good," Lilith said with a relieved sigh.

As they continued walking toward where Heather was likely training the younger succubus, a figure swooped down from the sky and stood before them. Lilith recognized Kokabiel from his pale skin and dark hair. The fallen angel's wings shook before retracting. He took a step forward, and then he paused, his brow furrowing as he stared at Lilith.

"I believe you might want to turn that Aura of Allure off," he said. "If even I can feel it, then I guarantee you that everyone around us can too."

Lilith blinked several times, then looked at Christian, and then looked at the people around her. It was just as Kokabiel said. Everyone they passed had stopped what they were doing to stare at her. Some were even drooling.

It was just like before she had met Christian. No, this was even worse. While they weren't attacking her, it was clear from the completely vacant expressions every male wore that her very presence had caused them to go brain dead. Even the fallen angels were being affected.

She blushed and turned back to Kokabiel. "I... uh... I just activated my core, so I can't really, um, control it yet."

"I see." He sighed. "I suggest you learn to control it soon. We can't afford to have our people turn into slathering idiots."

"O-of course."

"Did you need something?" asked Christian.

Kokabiel redirected his gaze to Christian. "I need you to come with me. It is time to begin your training."

***

Kokabiel led Christian to a building shaped like a rectangle, with nothing else adorning it aside from a single doorway without a door. It was something he had noticed. The Grigori did not seem to believe in decorating their buildings with anything, so everything lacked any form of individuality. He guessed it was in their nature as angels to be austere.

The inside was like the outside in that it had no decoration. The floor was made of a strangely flexible material that reminded him of a training mat, but it didn't have the same feel or give. It was more like rubber than padding. Likewise, the walls were strangely reflective and shiny, yet for some reason, Christian could not see his reflection in them.

"This is our training room," Kokabiel informed him as he looked around. "Fallen angels do not gain power. Our strength is set the moment we are created. However, that does not mean we cannot improve our abilities. This training hall was created to help us learn how to control our power. It can withstand a lot of punishment, so we can go all out here and not worry about destroying it... supposedly."

"I see," Christian murmured. "You mentioned something about training, but what exactly am I being trained in."

Kokabiel studied him with a slight frown. "I'm sure you've heard from Azazel. You are the son of Amon, a powerful half-demon descended from the Great King Belial. The same blood that ran through your father's veins runs through your veins, as does the power he possessed. Azazel has asked that I train you in drawing that power out."

Christian sucked in a breath, his thoughts being overridden by the sudden impulse to bury his head in the sand. Of course, everyone had been telling him that he had demon blood running through him. Clarissa had been the first. However, Azazel had said more or less the same thing, and he even seemed to know Christian's dad. There was no denying it now, but even so, he still didn't want to face it.

"I... I don't know if I should learn to control that power..."

"Are you a fool?" Kokabiel scowled. Christian felt a shiver run down his spine. "Do you think you can get by if you don't learn to control that power? The world is teetering on the brink of darkness. The balance has been lost. The Seven Demon Kings have infiltrated the Catholic Church and stand on the cusp of sending the world over the edge. As you are now, you lack the power to do anything. You were lucky when you killed Asmodeus, but you won't be so lucky next time."

Christian twitched, struggling to contain his emotions. What Kokabiel said made sense. It did. At the same time... at the same time...

"If you cannot learn to master that power, then you will put your mate in danger." That got Christian's attention. He looked back at Kokabiel, whose penetrating stare made him want to look away. "And it won't come from the demons trying to overrun the world. It will come from you."

"What do you... mean?" Christian felt like he'd swallowed a rock.

"I mean that power you possess comes at a price." Calming down, Kokabiel began pacing back and forth. "I'm sure you must have heard it by now, the voice of your inner demon."

Christian shuddered as he suddenly recalled all the times a voice had spoken inside of his head. He'd always done his best to ignore it. When he couldn't ignore it, he tried to pretend it wasn't there. However, he'd heard it plenty of times by now. He knew what Kokabiel was talking about.

"You are a human. However, you have the blood of Belial flowing through your veins. It is a powerful bloodline that cannot be extinguished by your humanity. I imagine the blood inside of you has created a separate persona made up of all the aspects the Great King himself was admired among demonkind for. Power. Greed. Malice. Hatred. The dark emotions of your persona are currently separate from you, but they will grow stronger in time. They are already growing stronger, evidenced by how your abilities are becoming more active. It won't be long before the other you tries to claim your life for his own. If that happens, you will cease to exist. No doubt your mate will suffer at the hands of the other Christian should that happen."

Closing his eyes, Christian tried not to imagine what would happen to Lilith if this other self of his ever consumed him, but he knew. He'd already met his other self before. That version of him had no sympathy for others, no love. If he took Christian's place, Lilith would become a toy for that beast.

I can't let that happen.

"What should I do?" asked Christian.

"There is only one thing you can do," Kokabiel said. "You will have to confront your other self in mortal combat and emerge victorious. However, when you do this, you will not have any of the powers that he does. You will be human, which means you will be at a disadvantage." At this, Kokabiel's lips pulled back into a grin that revealed his sharp fangs. "Unless you become strong enough to steal that power and make it your own. That is what I'm going to help you with."

Christian wasn't sure how Kokabiel planned to help him, but if everything the fallen said was true, then he could ill-afford to stand around doing nothing. He needed to become stronger. If this man could make him stronger, then Christian was willing to accept his offer.

"How do you plan to train me?" asked Christian.

"Is that not obvious?" Kokabiel undid his robes, revealing a lithe body that was covered in muscles and scars. He shucked the robes away, then slid his feet apart, bent his knees, and adopted a guard stance. "There is only way surefire method of growing stronger. That is to beat it into you. Try not to die."

Christian barely had time to register those words before Kokabiel attacked.

The world around him exploded as white-hot lances of agony shot through him.

*　*　*

Lilith didn't think she'd ever felt sorer than she did now. After meeting up with Heather, Lilith had been forced to exercise alongside the other succubus. For a woman who never really exercised, the drills she had been put through were like torture—no, not like. They were torture. Her body ached. Her shoulders hurt. Her back was sore. Her legs felt like jello. Even her arms, neck, and butt hurt like no tomorrow.

She was in bad shape.

After the exercises, which had lasted for well over two hours, Heather had Lilith hold several different weapons. She said they wouldn't choose one for her right now. According to Heather, Lilith didn't have enough strength, stamina, or dexterity to properly utilize any of the weapons they had. However, she said it would be good to find out if any weapons they did have on hand felt comfortable.

Lilith hadn't felt particularly comfortable with any of the weapons. That said, of the weapons she had been shown, the one that felt the least uncomfortable to hold had been the whip. Heather had nodded as if she expected that. She said that Lilith's primary weapon would be her illusions, and that using a whip to keep people away would be more beneficial than using a sword or spear to slay people. Aside from that, she would also have Christian fighting alongside her.

Heather told Lilith that her main role in combat would likely be support magic and long-range attacks. Once she got the hang of casting illusions, she could support Christian by confounding their enemies, keeping them distracted so he could finish them off. The whip would serve as self-defense, but her ultimate purpose would be rear support.

Of course, that was only in her human form. Her succubus form gave her a significant boost to all her physical attributes. While in that form, she could easily act as a frontline fighter alongside Christian and decimate the enemy. That was what Heather said, at least.

She trudged into the room that belonged to her and Christian, closed the door behind her, and then turned back around and walked further in.

She stopped.

Then she squawked.

"C-Christian?!"

She rushed over to Christian, who was lying on the bed, looking like a piece of beef that had been shoved through a meat grinder. His bare torso was covered in lacerations and contusions. Most of his skin had turned black, though some of it was blue. Several large bruises covered his face. One of his eyes was even swollen shut.

"Christian?! Are you okay?! Answer me!"

A groan emerged from Christian's chapped lips. He seemed to come to, though it was hard to tell because his face looked so swollen.

"Christian? Can you hear me?"

"Lilith..." he mumbled, his voice low and raspy, as if he'd spent so much time screaming that he had lost it. "W-where am I?"

"You're in our room," Lilith answered.

"Our room? How... did I get here?"

"You don't remember?"

Christian began to shake his head, but then he seemed to think better of it. Lilith imagined even the simple act of a head shake caused undue pain.

"I remember... yes, I was with Kokabiel. He said he was gonna train me. I was supposed to fight him... and then... I don't know. Everything is blank after that."

Lilith quickly put two and two together from his words and arrived at what she believed was the correct conclusion. More than likely, Kokabiel had decided on a more Spartan method of training than what Heather did. Basically, he tried to beat up Christian, who tried to avoid getting beaten up. It seemed her mate hadn't succeeded.

An intense surge of red hot anger suddenly shot through her. Lilith wanted nothing more than to find Kokabiel and make him suffer for what he'd done. She wanted to tear him apart. However, the intense surge of anger she felt dissipated as quickly as it had come. Her mate was more important than getting revenge.

There has to be something I can do...

Lilith thought hard, trying to recall everything she'd ever learned about succubus. Clarissa had taught her some things back at the enclave, before they had been forced to flee, and she recalled a very brief lecture on how a succubus could heal their mates and be healed by their mates in return. She believed the key lay there.

There was something... something about, um, er... what was it? Healing by sharing my powers through sex?

She quickly recalled all the things she remembered and finally recalled what it was Clarissa had said.

The act of a succubus having sex with her mate generated a powerful amount of life essence that the succubus drew upon to increase her energy and therefore her life. While generally, a succubus drew all that life essence into herself, she could share it with her mate. It acted as a stimulus to promote healing.

Right. We need to have sex, and then I have to share the life essence with Christian... but, um, how do I do that?

While she would gladly share the life essence with Christian, she had no idea how one went about doing that. Was it something she did unconsciously? Did she have to, like, will the life essence into him? All she knew about this particular power was what Clarissa had told her, and unfortunately, the woman had left out just how, exactly, one went about using this power.

I suppose... I will just have to wing it.

Lilith decided that the first thing she should do was clean him off. It was a good thing they had their own shower. Given how unusual this place was, she wouldn't have been surprised to discover there was no shower.

Grabbing a towel from the bathroom and soaking it in warm water, she came back, sat on the bed, and began rubbing the dirt and sweat off his face and chest. Christian hissed in pain at her actions. However, she spoke to him with gentle reassurances, kinda like a pet owner might talk to their pet when they were scared. The thought was kind of amusing.

"Okay," Lilith mumbled once she finished cleaning him. "Now what?"

Since Christian's face was basically a mess, she wasn't sure kissing it would make things better. It would probably make things worse. His chest was in similar shape. She really had to wonder what kind of idiot Kokabiel was to just dump her mate on the bed without even healing him.

Figuring she had nothing to lose, Lilith undid his pants, grabbed them by the ends, and pulled them off his body. It was a lot harder than it looked since the pants were stuck to his skin, which was covered in a layer of sweat. Still, she managed to get them off.

The moment she did, a strong scent filled the air. The masculine scent of Christian's sweat. It wasn't quite as pleasant as usual, but she imagined the irony smell of blood mixed with it was the cause.

Crawling back onto the bed, Lilith reached down and grabbed his flaccid dick, which, most fortunately, did not have any injuries. That at least meant Kokabiel hadn't hit below the belt. She supposed that was good. Frowning slightly, she slowly stroked him, alternating between rubbing his shaft and playing with his head. It took longer than normal, but Christian's manhood eventually stood fully erect.

As Christian's scent became even stronger, a haze clouded over Lilith's mind. She leaned down and placed the tip of his head against her mouth. Taking in just his head, she swirled her tongue around it, then sucked as though she was trying to draw something out. Christian groaned as he bucked his hips into her, causing Lilith to nearly gag in surprise.

Christian was already harder than the swords he wielded. She knew she could have begun the healing process at any time, but part of Lilith wanted to savor this moment. It must have been her succubus desire acting up. She tried to fight it for a while, but really, fighting against her own nature was, well, it went against her nature.

Sticking out her tongue, Lilith licked Christian like he was a popsicle, traveling from his ball sack all the way to the tip. He groaned again as she coated him in her saliva. Then she took his head in again. While she sucked on the mushroom-shaped top and flicked his tip with her tongue, she wrapped her fingers around his shaft and stroked him.

This was a very different experience than she was used to. Lilith normally let Christian take the lead. She thought that was odd for a succubus, but Clarissa had once told her that different succubus were into different fetishes, which she guessed meant she just preferred being the submissive one. However, now she was taking charge—sort of taking charge. Did this count as taking charge if he was barely conscious?

Deciding to ponder such thoughts later, Lilith fondled Christian's balls until she felt the buildup signaling his impending orgasm. As his hot seed shot from his dick, painting her throat white, Lilith slurped up everything, until not even a drop remained.

I want more, but...

Resisting the rest of her impulses, Lilith lowered her head to take as much of Christian into her mouth as she good, slurping and licking his shaft to get him back to full hardness. She removed his dick from her mouth. Then, climbing on top of him, Lilith placed her hands on either side of his body, which forced her to lean over more than normal. As her breasts swayed from side to side, she frowned.

When she was normally on top, she placed her hands on his chest. She had avoided that because she was afraid of hurting him. This position wasn't quite as comfortable. Oh, well.

Raising her hips, Lilith did her best to line Christian up with her already dripping lips, and then, ever so slowly, she lowered herself onto him.

Lilith groaned as her lips were stretched by Christian's girth. She sucked in a deep breath. Focus, Lilith. Focus. She couldn't afford to lose track of what she was doing. Once she had bottomed out, Lilith waited for a moment to see if Christian would stir. He didn't.

"Okay," she whispered. "Here I go."

Slowly raising her hips again, she lowered them back down just as slowly. The glacial pace was agonizing, sending jolts of pleasure racing along her love canal. This new position made it feel like Christian's manhood was hitting a whole bunch of new places they'd never explored before.

Before she could get herself lost in the haze of pleasure, a pair of hands suddenly landed on her bottom with a loud slap. She shrieked. Then she moaned when the hands massaged her butt cheeks like a master sculptor creating art.

"C-Christian!" Lilith clenched her teeth as one of his fingers slipped into her puckered hole. It felt so good! Why did it feel so good?

"You couldn't... wait until I recovered?" asked a now conscious Christian. He still seemed a tad daze, but maybe that was because his left eye was swollen shut.

"I-I'm trying to heal yoooOOOUUUU!! OH!" Lilith cried out in pleasure when a second finger was inserted into her butthole.

"Heal me? I thought that only worked on succubus?"

"C-Clarissa said I can share the life essence p-produced by—ah! Ah!—produced by sex with you!"

"Hmm... I see... Well, I guess I can't complain either way... Do what you need to."

"Mm!!"

Lilith struggled to retain her sanity as Christian toyed with her butt, while she continued riding his dick like it was a Gundam's joystick. What did she have to do again? She had to heal him. Right. How did she do that?

No matter how hard she thought, she kept coming up blank. Granted, it was hard to think when her mate was pushing buttons she hadn't even known existed, but she should have been able to remember something.

"You can do this…"

A voice whispered to her.

"You've got this. Just trust your instincts."

M-my instincts?

What did that mean? Was the voice telling her to just let go and give into her instincts? But if she did that, wouldn't she instinctively take in all the life energy being produced.

The voice didn't answer her, so she was left with no other choice but to make her own choice. Perhaps it was in her nature. Lilith didn't know, but she ended up giving into her instincts.

She picked up the pace of her actions, raising her hips and slamming them back onto Christian's shaft. The lewd sound of their skin slapping each other echoed around them. As she increased her pace, she let herself fall onto Christian's chest and began kissing, licking, and sucking at his wounds.

"Hmmm… Lilith… that feels really good…"

Christian's words spurred her to continue. She left no wound untouched, which meant Christian's chest was basically lathered in her saliva, though he didn't seem to mind. The slickness of her spit combined with the sweat their bodies produced to create a thick, wet lubricant. Lilith cried out as her stiff nipples glided along her mate's skin. Electricity raced through her body, causing her back to arc.

"Christian! Christian! Christian!"

Because of the bond they shared, she was aware of what he was feeling as they connected. She could sense the pain in his body fading. She could feel it being replaced by pleasure. Her body moved faster of its own accord. Faster. Harder. She slammed her hips against his crotch over and over in off-rhythm attacks that became more frenetic as she felt her end coming closer. Lilith wanted this moment to last longer, forever, but at the same time, she knew it wouldn't.

Her end came all too soon. Her walls clenched around Christian's dick, practically squeezing the cum out of him. At the same time, her body felt like it had seized up. An unfathomable white light blinded her before, with a soft sigh, the pleasure faded, and her body grew slack. She slumped forward against Christian and closed her eyes.

For some reason, she felt tired. That was odd since she normally felt energized after having sex. It felt like all her energy had been spent Why… why was… that…?

Chapter 9

Christian woke up feeling more refreshed than he'd ever felt in his entire life. Light filtered in through the window and hit his closed eyelids. It was warm and gentle, like a lover's kiss. Sighing as he took a moment to bask in the warmth, Christian slowly opened his eyes.

The room looked the same as always, but the bed seemed a tad messier than usual, and then there was also Lilith, who lay resting against his side. She seemed a bit tired to him. There were bags under her eyes. He couldn't put his finger on it, but it was like her sleep had been restless or something.

Shifting, Christian slowly rolled Lilith onto her back. Her right arm flopped against the bed and her breasts shook, jiggling in an enticing way that he couldn't help but notice. He shook his head. Now was not the time.

As had become a custom, Christian kissed Lilith awake. Their last kiss lasted several seconds longer than the others.

"Morning," Lilith murmured in a heavy voice.

"Morning. You okay?"

"I'm exhausted," she admitted. "What about you? You were very injured the other day…" she paused to look at him, blinking her weary eyes several times. "It looks like you're okay now, though."

"I am okay." He smiled. "I'm pretty sure I have you to thank for that. Thank you."

He couldn't really figure out what had happened, but he did remember bits and pieces. He'd sparred with Kokabiel, who'd so thoroughly wiped the floor with him that he blacked out and woke up to Lilith's worried voice. His consciousness had faded in and out after that, but he distinctly remembered Lilith riding him, and then feeling better, and then—he'd woken up. The conclusion he had reached was that Lilith somehow healed him.

Lilith smiled back, but then…

"I'm hungry."

Christian knew she wasn't talking about food.

"Let's take a shower," he suggested.

Their showers tended to last on the long side, but that was mostly because their showers weren't just showers. They got dirty before they got clean. Of course, shower sex was a problematic activity that came with much slipping and sliding, so they avoided actually having sex in the shower and did it outside before getting in the shower to wash each other off.

Once they were clean, the two got dressed.

Christian's clothing from the day before was ruined. His shirt was gone, his pants had become shorts, and his boots had been so thoroughly trashed they looked more like strips of hide. He ended up having to use one of the robes that were located in the dresser. It was a pure white robe that went down to his feet. He didn't think it fit him, but he wasn't one to complain.

Lilith donned what she'd worn the day before. Her jeans still seemed fine and the shirt wasn't too dirty. He did worry about how they didn't have many clothes. That was something he would need to speak with Azazel or someone else about.

"What are your plans for the day?" asked Christian.

"I want to meet back up with Clarissa and begin practicing how to cast illusions," Lilith said.

"Then let's go find her. I'm sure she's probably still in this building."

Clarissa's room wasn't too far from theirs, so they made it there in record time. However, when they arrived, the pair was surprised to discover that the woman they had come to see was nowhere to be found.

The rooms here did not have doors. It was another eccentricity of this place. He assumed it had something to do with how Jerusalem's architecture didn't have doors back in the day... but maybe he only thought that way because he wasn't an angelic being.

In either event, when they arrived at the room and entered through the entrance, it was to find that Clarissa was missing. They quickly left the room. It was rude to step inside someone's abode without their permission. However, now they had a problem.

"She isn't here. Do you think she's already at the training field?" asked Christian.

"Maybe..." Lilith mumbled.

"Are you two looking for Clarissa?" asked a voice. The two turned their heads to find Kaylee looking at them with a frown.

"We are," Lilith said. "Have you seen her?"

Kaylee nodded. "She and Heather got special permission to leave Seventh Heaven. They took some of the Valkyries and are traveling back to the US to pick up our mates."

Selected from a group of women who volunteered, the Valkyries were succubi trained extensively in combat. They were on par with all but the strongest Executioners, the XIII. Christian had been impressed with their battle prowess several times. Their talent lay in ambushes and hit and run tactics, but they were adept at numerous types of martial discipline.

They were also older than the other succubus. While the other women who belonged to the enclave were young, between 12 and 16, the Valkyries were all at least 100 years old. Each of them had already had their first mate and had moved onto a second one.

Being supernatural creatures, succubus lived far longer than humans. The natural lifespan of a human male was 76, though medical technology and other advances in bioscience had extended that. Most humans could live to their 90s and some even beyond that. However, succubus, if they wanted to, could live for as long as they were willing to mate.

In general, a succubus would have one mate. When her mate died, she would never mate again and wither away. Christian supposed there was some romantic aspect in that, something like, "he was the only man I'll ever love!" or that kind of thing. It was proof of their monogamy.

The Valkyries were those who disregarded their solely monogamous lifestyle in order to extend their life. When their first mate died, they found another human male who was genetically compatible with them. Extending their life in this way, they were able to gain more worldly knowledge and experience, as well as become expert warriors, and they taught what they knew to the younger succubus, who would then be released into the world to find their own mates once they gained control over their Aura of Allure.

On a side note, Clarissa was the oldest succubus. He didn't know how old. However, she was already on her sixth mate, which meant she must have at least been between 500 and 600 years old.

"I see." Lilith bit her lip.

"Since Heather and Clarissa aren't here, why don't I help you find a gun that suits you?" Christian suggested as his mate stood there in indecision. She looked at him. "I already promised you we'd find one that you can use, right?"

"Yeah. Yeah, you did." Lilith nodded, and then smiled at him. It was like rays of light shining through parted clouds. "Thank you, Christian."

"You're welcome."

Kaylee scoffed at the pair, but they didn't pay attention to her anymore. Leaving the building they were staying at—Christian didn't know if he could call it an inn—they asked a passing fallen angel where the armory was. The fallen, a woman who looked uncomfortable being so close to Lilith, answered them in a hurry, pointing off to the north before scurrying away.

"That woman didn't seem to like you."

"I haven't regained control over my Aura of Allure yet. She probably felt threatened."

"Hmm... I couldn't tell."

As someone who's genetics were compatible with Lilith, Christian could not feel her Aura of Allure at all. That said, as they walked through the streets, he saw the effect it had on those around them. One man walked into a building. A pair of fallen angels stopped flapping their wings and crashed into the ground. A group of women stopped chatting and stared at Lilith like she was the most disgusting thing they'd ever seen. No matter where they walked, her very presence caused some kind of commotion.

"It's been awhile since this has happened." Christian frowned at the people they walked past.

"It's been so nice not having people stare at me like this that I'd nearly forgotten what this was like," Lilith admitted with a resigned sigh.

They spoke about her Aura of Allure as they walked toward the weapons depot. Lilith wanted to regain control over it soon, but she didn't really know how she was supposed to do that, and with Clarissa gone, she didn't have anyone to turn to. Christian suggested asking one of the other succubus, but Lilith wasn't as well-acquainted with them. She was reluctant to ask for their help.

"But you need to reign in your Aura of Allure, right?" Christian pointed out. "There's no shame in asking for help."

"Says the man who tries to do everything himself."

"That was a low-blow."

Joking aside, they soon reached the weapons depot, a large building shaped like a rectangle. It didn't look any different from the others outside of being longer than it was wide. The building was even made from the same obsidian material as everything else. However, the inside was completely different.

"I'll never get over how mixed up this community is," Christian muttered as he looked at the completely brand-new, high-tech shooting range and racks upon racks of guns. The floor was made of that obsidian material. It had a glossy finish and creaked as they walked into the building.

"Most of these guns look really big." Lilith worried her lower lip.

Christian nodded. "It seems they've stockpiled mostly automatic weapons. There's Adaptive Combat Rifles, ADS Amphibious Rifles, AEK-971s, AMP-69s... they even have rocket launchers and grenade launchers. I wonder what they were planning to do with all these?"

Fallen angels did not use weapons themselves since they had their divine powers. That being the case, Christian could not help but wonder if they planned on recruiting human soldiers to their cause, or maybe they had stockpiled these weapons because they knew the Executioners would be joining them. He wasn't sure.

"It looks like they have some basic weapons." Christian tugged on Lilith's hand. "This way. We'll start you off with something small and work our way up from there."

"Okay..."

They had already worked with some 9mm pistols back at the enclave, so Christian decided to begin with one of those. Fortunately, the Grigori had numerous handguns. Christian chose a Glock 17 for her to use. It was a full-sized handgun. Good for starting out.

"You remember how to hold it, right?"

"Um, yes. I think so."

Lilith assumed the position she vaguely recalled Christian showing her, spreading her feet a bit as she placed one leg behind her and bent her dominant leg for stability. She held the gun in both hands. Her right hand was up top, bottom hand below for support. Just like he had taught her, her trigger finger was not on the trigger but resting against it.

"Yes. That's it. Let's begin practicing."

The weapons depot had a shooting range set up on one side. Like most shooting ranges, this one featured a sloped earthen berm with reinforced baffles situated along the roof and side walls. The partitioned shooting range even had earplugs hanging from the walls. Unlike most modern shooting ranges, this one did not have an air-locked corridor for sound-proofing, but he guessed the fallen angels, who weren't very gun savvy, hadn't thought to add one.

Christian attached a paper target that looked like a man onto a board that was attached to a crane. He pressed a button on the side of the wall, which caused the crane to slide along a set of gears located on the metal beam it was attached to. He narrowed his eyes and judged the distance. 5. 10. 15. 20. 25. He stopped the target at 25 feet.

"Okay." Nodding to himself, he turned to Lilith. "Show me how to insert a magazine into your gun."

"Um, okay. Like… this?"

Lilith slowly inserted the magazine into her pistol, glancing at Christian every so often to make sure she was doing it right. He watched her while keeping his expression carefully blank. He didn't want her relying on him.

She eventually finished loading her gun. After which, he nodded several times and let her know she'd done it right.

"Now take your stance and aim at the target."

Keeping her breathing even and steady, she assumed the firing stance he'd taught her. Once she did, Christian put a pair of earphones on her head. She looked at him, but he just smiled and pointed at his ear, which got her to nod. The earphones were to protect her from the sound.

Coming up behind her, Christian carefully adjusted her stance a bit, making sure that she was using the most stable and easy to fire stance as possible. Then he looked down the sight of her gun and adjusted her aim. Nodding to himself, he stepped back and gestured for her to begin firing.

She did.

The loud thunderclap of a gun going off echoed all around them, muffled through their headphones. Lilith's hand jerked slightly, but she kept a firm grip on her gun, just like Christian had taught her. Sadly, even though she did everything right, her bullet still veered off to the side and struck the berm without going through the target. She frowned. Adjusting her aim, she fired again.

Christian smiled as the target shook from getting hit. Her aim was still off. She hit the paper, but not the human-shaped target printed on it. Even so, Lilith didn't give up. She adjusted her aim again and fired once, twice, thrice, and then again. With each shot fired, she came steadily closer to her goal, until she eventually began hitting the target every time, though her aim still tended to be veer off course, with her hitting the chest, shoulder, stomach, and head at random.

When the gun clicked empty, Lilith released a sigh and relaxed her stance. Her arms were shaking.

"Nice job," he congratulated as Lilith pulled the earphones off her head. "You did pretty good. We'll have you practice some more after you rest up a bit. Firing a gun for the first time can be exhausting."

"It is exhausting." Lilith set the gun on a table and raised her arms to stretch. "I don't know how you manage to fire those two big guns of yours like they're nothing."

"Lots of practice." Christian shrugged.

They spoke for several minutes before Lilith felt recovered enough to begin practicing again. After that, they practiced for another hour before her arms began to feel like lead weights. Christian decided it was enough for now. It wasn't good to overwork oneself, and Lilith had done a pretty decent job.

"We'll continue practicing while Clarissa and Heather are away," Christian said as they began walking back toward their current residence.

Lilith nodded. "It'll be good to have a skill under my belt, and it's not like I can practice using my succubus powers without Clarissa around."

"Hmm…"

As they neared the tower they lived in, the two of them stopped when Kokabiel emerged from the entrance. He paused upon seeing the pair. Blinking, he looked at Christian in something resembling surprise.

"I had not expected you to be up so soon." He tilted his head as if staring at a puzzle from a different angle before he switched his gaze from Christian to Lilith. He nodded once. "I see. You helped heal him."

While Lilith glared at Kokabiel, Christian asked, "was there something you needed? Have you come to train me again?"

Kokabiel shook his head. "Actually, I did not expect you to even be awake. I came because I had intended to heal your wounds. I couldn't do so the other day because I can't use my powers to heal you. As someone with devil blood, the divine healing abilities of us fallen angels is poisonous to your kind."

"I see."

Christian did not like being reminded that part of him wasn't human, that he had the blood of Belial inside of him, but he was trying his best not to let it bother him. Denying the truth, running from it, would not help him.

"Since you are awake, though, I suppose we can pick up where we left off."

Christian nodded. "I'm all for it."

"Well, I'm not," Lilith suddenly interrupted. She was still glaring at Kokabiel. "Christian got so injured sparring with you the other day that it looked like someone had shoved his body into a wood chipper. I'm not going to let something like that happen to him again."

Kokabiel gazed at her with his indifferent stare and, much to Christian's surprise, Lilith did not back down at all. He remembered a time when the very gaze of a man would cause her to panic. Now she was glaring at a fallen angel, of all beings, with anger clear in her eyes.

"You do realize that while my methods may be brutal, they are the fastest way to help Christian unlock the power he has at his disposal, yes? The longer he goes without being able to use his power, the more danger he places himself and you in."

"Even so…"

"It's alright, Lilith."

"Christian?"

He cupped her face, rubbing his thumb against her cheek in gentle strokes. Lilith leaned into him. As she rubbed her face against his hand, she reminded him of a cat, and the amusing thought that she might start purring entered his mind before he could stop it.

"I know you don't want me to get hurt, but just like you, I really do need to get stronger. Please let me do this."

Even as he continued tenderly stroking her cheek with his thumb, a conflicted look crossed Lilith's face, letting him know that she really didn't want to let him do this. Christian knew, however, that she knew he had to. The world was on the brink of chaos. The Demon Kings had infiltrated the Church and were coming after them. If they wanted to have any hope of survival, he would need to master his power.

"F-fine…" Lilith turned her head, though she did not remove his hand. "You can train, but I want to be there, to make sure nothing bad happens."

Christian debated for only a second. He didn't want Lilith to see this. He was sure she'd be horrified, but he wanted her to worry about him even less. If coming with him while he trained would alleviate her worry, then the choice was obvious.

"Are you okay with that?" Christian turned to Kokabiel.

The fallen angel shrugged. "I care not what you do. However, if she gets injured during our training, she'll only have herself to blame."

***

The training hall looked the same as last time. The difference was that Lilith was also present. She stood far away from Christian and Kokabiel, who were less than a dozen feet apart, eying each other.

"I hope you are ready," Kokabiel said. "I will not be holding back."

Christian shifted into his preferred fighting stance, though it felt a little awkward without his swords. The goal of this spar was not to get better at sword fighting. It was to help him gain access to his power, which Kokabiel said was buried deep inside of him and could only be drawn out by combat.

"That's fine by me."

"Then… here I come!"

Kokabiel shot off like a rocket. Christian barely had time to ponder this man's insane speed before the fallen angel was upon him. The air shook as he just barely dodged his sparring partner's punch, and even then, the force of his punch was so strong that the displaced air pushed Christian back.

Instead of trying to regain his balance, which would have given Kokabiel the opportunity to attack, Christian fell backward, rolling across the floor and springing to his feet. Sadly, Kokabiel was already there when he stood up. The fallen angel swung his left leg in a powerful kick at Christian's midsection.

Bending his legs, Christian lowered himself until his back was touching the floor. He placed his hands behind his head, biceps and triceps straining, and then he launched a powerful mule kick at Kokabiel. It was stopped. Kokabiel reached out and caught both feet with the palms of his hands.

"You're still not even trying to access your power."

The man didn't give Christian time to respond. He spun around, lifting Christian into the air. Round and around they went, spinning faster and faster, until the howling in Christian's ear was only matched by the nauseating feel of his stomach leaping into his throat from the centrifugal force acting on his body. He would have tried to kick his way out, but Kokabiel had both of his feet.

It seemed like forever, but the man soon let go, and Christian soared across the room in an uncontrolled spin. Everything passed by him in a blur. He wanted to throw up. Then he crashed into the hard ground with bone-jarring impact. He couldn't even scream as he tumbled across the floor. It was like he'd swallowed his tongue.

Christian eventually stopped. However, as he tried to get up, he found that his arms weren't working properly. They wobbled and shook. Every time he placed his hand on the ground and tried to push up, they would slip all over the place like they had minds of their own.

"How long are you going to lie there?!"

The voice caused Christian to look up. He was just in time to receive a kick to the face. It was such a powerful kick that Christian's head was snapped back as blood welled up in his now broken nose. He flew through the air, struck the ground again, bounced, and then tumbled across the floor.

Rolling over onto his stomach, he tried to get back up.

"How long are you going to let your fear control you?!"

A kick to his side made Christian gasp in pain. The world spun around him again. When he landed on his back once more, the air left his lungs in a loud whoosh. Before he even had a chance to recover, something powerful slammed into his chest, making him gasp as agony overrode his ability to think.

"Do you think I don't know what you are doing?!" The object on his chest, which he realized was a heel, ground into him. "The last time you and I did this, no matter how badly I beat you, no matter how many bones you broke or bruises you got, you refused to use the power inside of you! Do you think I don't realize that you're running away?!"

Christian would have liked to say that he wasn't running from anything, that the entire reason he had agreed to fight this man was because he wanted to learn how to control his powers. He wanted to say that, but he didn't. Kokabiel was right. As much as Christian said he would try to control his power, control the power of the demon blood flowing in his veins, he was too afraid to seek it out. He didn't want to become a monster.

"Hurry up and use your power!" Stomp. Crack. Christian barely held back a scream. "Use your power now, or I'm going to kill you!"

Christian groaned each time Kokabiel slammed a heel into his chest. He could feel his ribs slowly giving in, could feel the fractures spreading across his bones like spiderwebs. The agony was quite unlike anything else. It wasn't the sharp pain of getting stabbed or the slow burn of poison. It was like his body was being crushed at a pace so agonizingly slow that he could acutely feel every injury as it formed.

"What are you doing?!" a shriek made Christian blink. "Stop it! You're killing him!"

"That's the point!"

Through his blurry vision, Christian could just barely make out the blonde hair and green eyes of Lilith. What was she doing?

"H-hey! Ouch! Let go of me!!"

"I've got another idea. Hey, child of Belial. If you do not use that power of yours, I'll kill your mate."

Christian felt a chill seep into his bones. This man would kill his mate? He was going to kill her? The words echoed in his mind, sounding out like a gong signaling an end to his world. As the cold chill spread through his body, entering his bloodstream and finding its way into his heart, a strange heat emitted from the center of his chest.

"Well, now. Hehe. Looks like you're in trouble again."

It was the voice. Christian groaned and tried to tell it off, but the heel digging into his chest, breaking his ribs, didn't allow him to talk, not even in his mind.

"I see that you are in no position to do anything, so I'll lend you my help again. The only thing it will cost is this body of ours. Don't worry. I'll take good care of it."

Christian tried to tell the voice to shut up, that he wouldn't give his body to it, but darkness was seeping at the edges of his vision. He couldn't see anything beyond slight blurs of color now. Pain was overriding everything.

He tried to hold on for a little longer, tried to regain control over the situation, but then there was a flash of light and everything went dark.

***

Lilith could only remember a few times she'd ever felt this terrified. The first time was when Damien, the No Life King who had kidnapped her when she lived in Seal Beach, revealed his true colors by killing her adoptive mother. The second time was when Christian almost died after they jumped out of a train. The third time was on another train when Asmodeus, possessing the body of Nicholas Cruer, had tried to torture and rape her. The fourth time was during hers and Christian's fight with Asmodeus. And now... for the fifth time in her life, she felt true fear.

The moment Kokabiel began crushing Christian underneath his heel, she had tried to do something. She wouldn't let her fear control her. She banged on his back, shouted at him, and even bit him on the arm. It didn't even phase him. Worse still, Kokabiel grabbed her, pressed a light sword to her throat, and said he would kill her if Christian didn't use his powers.

It was just as she started struggling again that something happened.

A chill ran down her spine as something like electricity raced through her body. No. It wasn't coming from her. The sensations she felt was coming from outside of her body.

She looked down at Christian.

The chill froze over.

It was strange. He didn't look any different than before. His skin hadn't changed color, horns hadn't grown on his head, and his nails hadn't become claws. Christian looked the same as always. It was just...

Those eyes.

Something about his gaze frightened her.

Before she had time to really figure out what was happening, a loud crunching noise, like twigs being snapped, echoed around the room. It wasn't a twig, however. It was Kokabiel's leg. Christian had grabbed onto the calf holding him down and crushed it.

"Wha—"

Kokabiel's words were halted when a beam of light shot from Christian's red eye, striking the light sword resting against Lilith's neck and dissolving it. Once the sword was gone, an incredible forced shoved Lilith out of the way. She landed on her butt. As she rubbed her backside, a loud crashing sound that caused the ground to quake made her look up.

Christian was standing in front of her. She couldn't see Kokabiel anywhere, but there was a massive hole in the wall several dozen yards away. Christian's hand was outstretched, showing that he'd probably punched Kokabiel. A grin stretched across his face. It was a grin that sent a shiver down her spine.

"Heh heh..." A throaty chuckle belonging to a voice that sounded like Christian but was not Christian emerged from his throat. *"Hahahaha! This is great! So this is what it feels like to be on the outside world! I like it!"*

"C-Christian?" Lilith asked, even though she could tell the person before her was not her Christian.

"Oh, Lilith." Christian turned to her, and Lilith froze in place. Something about his eyes just made her entire body lock in place like it had been turned into ice. *"Wait right there. I'll be back in just a bit."*

Lilith could do nothing as Christian suddenly vanished. She blinked. Then she turned her head to try and find him, except he wasn't there anymore. No one was. It was just her.

Before she could try and figure out what happened, another massive quake rocked the building. Lilith rushed toward the hole in the wall and looked outside. Her breath left her as she found Christian fighting against Kokabiel.

The young man she had come to love was laughing as he slammed his fist into Kokabiel's face. A shockwave exploded from where Christian punched Kokabiel, causing the ground around them to be destroyed when the incredible force impacted against it. Lilith screamed as the massive wave of wind and energy slammed into her.

Kokabiel went flying, but he proved to be far more resilient than a human, whose face would have been pulped by that. He flapped his wings and righted himself. Grinning widely, he summoned a massive spear that was easily ten times larger than the sword he had held against her neck.

"This is excellent! Yes! Show me more of your power!!"

He threw the spear at Christian, who didn't even bat an eye as he pulled his fist back and threw it forward. His fist slammed into the spear, which pushed against him, sending his feet sliding along the ground, digging a trench through the dirt. A grin still on his face, Christian's muscles bulged as he shouted.

A flash of brilliant light forced Lilith to close her eyes. Even though she could see nothing, the sound of an explosion warned her of danger. She screamed and crouched against the wall, listening to the loud banging of debris pelting the building she was hiding behind.

The storm eventually died down. Lilith waited for several seconds. The sound of distant thunder, of impacting fists, echoed back to her. Remaining wary, Lilith opened her eyes and peeked back out from behind her cover.

Christian and Kokabiel were still battling. In fact, the battle had become even more intense.

A grinning Christian held his hand aloft, a small sphere of crackling energy appeared within it, which he then lobbed at Kokabiel. The fallen angel created a shield that blocked the attack, but the resulting explosion sent plumes of blackish red energy everywhere.

A crack appeared on the shield. It spread quickly.

Laughing like a madman, Christian slammed his fist into the shield, shattering it. His fist, which Lilith realized was covered in reddish black energy, then crashed into Kokabiel's face. An explosion of energy emitted outward. Kokabiel went flying. He struck the ground, causing the earth to explode in a violent spray of dirt. Then he rolled along the ground for several yards before skipping back to his feet.

Christian was already there.

Blood flew from Christian's body was swords of light sliced into his flesh. Bruises appeared on Kokabiel as Christian's fists impacted against his torso and face. Loud thuds and bangs like rolling thunder resounded across the land as the two traded strikes.

Lilith wanted to do something, to stop the battle happening in front of her, but her body was frozen, mind overcome with fear. She could scarcely understand what was happening. Everything had happened so quick that her mind was having trouble keeping up.

By this point in time, their battle had drawn the attention of everyone else. Floating above the battlefield were numerous fallen angels. Meanwhile, standing on the ground were the succubus and Executioners. She recognized many of the succubus, but among the executioners, she only knew Samantha, Sif, and Leon. Tristin was surrounded by his harem as usual.

Lilith didn't know what else to do, so she rushed over to the group of Executioners.

"What is going on?" asked Samantha, her voice shocked.

"That's Christian, isn't it?" Leon looked as befuddled as the rest. "That is Christian, right? Why is he leaking demonic energy?!"

"Commander," Sif began.

"I know what you are going to say, and no, I don't know anything about this," said Samantha with a shake of her head.

"E-everyone!" Lilith yelled at the group, causing them to turn around and stare at her. "P-please! You have to stop this! Stop them from fighting!"

Even as she spoke, Kokabiel impaled Christian with a light spear. Blood gushed from the wound and steam hissed as the divine energy ate into his flesh, but Christian just laughed as he snapped the spear in half. The wound vanished. Then he punched Kokabiel so hard that the fallen angel's chest dented inward. He skidded backward along the ground for several yards, but then stopped himself and created nearly a dozen light spears that he sent at Christian, who punched each one into oblivion.

"I'm not sure we can stop that." Samantha eyed the battle with the wary gaze of an experienced warrior. "This battle is far beyond anything we've ever fought." She looked up. "The only ones who probably have the power to stop these two is them, but it looks like they're content to watch."

Lilith bit her lip as she tried to think of something, anything she could do. Yet all she did was draw a blank. She couldn't do anything.

"Everything will be okay..."

Just as she was ready to give into despair, a voice spoke to her. It sounded a lot like her voice, but there was a confidence in it that she lacked.

"Believe in yourself. You can stop them."

But... what can I do.

"You have the power to stop them. Trust in yourself and do what you feel is right."

But how am I supposed to do that?

The voice did not answer her again, having disappeared from wherever it had come. Lilith bit her lip. What could she do? She wanted to stop them from fighting, but she had... no... power...?

What about my illusions?

Would her illusions work on these two? They seemed so powerful, so strong, that she wasn't sure her illusions would be enough to overpower their will. At the same time, she couldn't afford to do nothing. If no one else was going to help them, then she would.

Lilith hesitated for a moment before resolving herself. She took a deep breath and recalled her feelings for Christian, her love for him, which was so powerful it overwhelmed her at times. She wanted to be with him. She wanted to protect him. She wanted to be protected by him. All her feelings swirled around her like a storm.

And then Lilith changed.

She wasn't fully conscious of the change, but she could feel that something was different about herself. The people around her were staring at her in shock. Lilith glanced at them, and then looked down at her hands, which were now pink with long claws. Something wagged behind her. She turned her head to see two wings flapping on her back, and then she tilted her head down to observe the tail that she could just barely see but felt sticking out of her pants. Along with her transformation, Lilith felt an incredible amount of power flowing through her.

She took a deep breath and closed her eyes.

I need to stop them.

Her eyes snapped open and she locked onto the still fighting Christian and Kokabiel, both of whom looked like a mess of blood and bruises. She raised her hand and commanded them.

"Stop."

The two froze. Of course, it was not like they were truly frozen. It was an illusion that made them think their bodies had become locked in place. Either one of them could have broken free, and in fact, it looked like they would overcome her illusion at any second.

She needed to hurry.

Activating another illusion, Lilith imagined herself standing in front of Christian, and then, suddenly, as if her illusion had become real, she was there, between the two of them. She locked eyes with Christian. His face was covered in blood and cuts. He stared at her with an inquisitive frown.

"Get out of the way, Lilith. I told you I'd come back once I deal with him."

"No." Lilith shook her head. "I won't. I refuse. Christian, come back to me."

Christian's lips curled into a smirk. *"What do you mean? I haven't gone anywhere. I'm right here."*

"You are not the Christian I fell in love with." She narrowed her eyes. "The man I fell in love with would never battle against someone with the intent to kill without good reason. You aren't him."

"Tch! What's wrong with fighting against someone who tried to kill me?! He threatened to kill you! You think I can just let something like that go?!"

"Yes." Lilith's simple response stunned Christian. She didn't give him any time to react either. Closing the distance between them, she reached out and stroked his cheek. "This isn't you. You aren't someone who mindlessly fights for the sake of fighting. You are kind and loving. You are a protector. Please. Come back to me. I need you here."

"Che." Christian's face morphed into a grimace. *"That fool really is loved, isn't he? Just another reason for me to hate him."* Lilith didn't know exactly what he was saying, but the person wearing Christian's face looked at her. *"Tell Christian this when he wakes up.*

I'll be coming back soon, and when I do, this body, and you, will both be mine."

Lilith couldn't say anything as Christian's eyes rolled up into the back of his head and he pitched forward. She caught him in her arms. His weight normally would have held her down, but Christian seemed lighter than normal, even though he was dead weight right then.

As she pulled him close and lowered herself to the ground, Azazel floated down and confronted Kokabiel.

"It looks like you went overboard," Azazel said.

"I couldn't think of another way to force his powers to activate." Kokabiel didn't appear concerned. "A demon's power is activated through negative emotions. Anger, hatred, fear. This was the only way to trigger his power."

"Fair enough." Azazel sighed, then looked at Lilith. He eyed her for a moment. She felt a sudden sense of revulsion at the appreciative look on his face. "Why don't you follow me to the hospital? We made one recently just in case something like this happened."

"I'll do as you ask, but please wipe that look off your face."

Azazel chuckled as Lilith stood up and lifted Christian into her arms. "Fair enough. Now, let's go. I'd like for us to be away from all these prying eyes."

As Lilith followed Azazel, she glanced at the people around them, the angels in the sky and the mixture of humans and succubus on the ground. Staring into their faces, she came to understand something.

None of these people would look at Christian, or her, the same way ever again.

Chapter 10

Lilith, having reverted to her human form again, sat on the bed inside of a place that screamed medical wing. The white hospital floor and white walls were a dead enough giveaway to understand what this place was used for, but the examination table, bed with its plane white sheets, IV hookup, and monitoring equipment made it even more obvious. The thick scent of antiseptics further emphasized this room's use.

Christian was lying on the bed. His eyes were closed, body unmoving. All his injuries, suffered at the hands of Kokabiel, seemed to have healed, but he wasn't waking up. She wasn't sure what to do here.

She had cleaned up his body as best she could, but really, all she'd done was use a hot washcloth to wipe the sweat and grime coating him.

As she ran her fingers through his hair, the door to the hospital room opened. Lilith looked up as several people stepped inside. Azazel was in the front, but she also spotted Clarissa, Samantha, and Tristin. She wondered where Sif and Leon were. They were almost always with Samantha, but she dispelled the thought.

"Can I help you?" she asked.

Azazel stopped before the bed. "We were wondering how Christian was doing. Is he okay?"

Lilith shrugged. "I don't know. He seems fine, but he hasn't woken up."

"Hmm…" Azazel glanced at Christian with a frown, eyes flickering as if he was reading something from a script. Lilith thought she noticed his eyes glowing. However, it could have just been a trick of the light. "I believe he's currently lost inside of his mind. When Kokabiel forced him to use his power, it appears something inside of him took over and forced his psyche deep into his unconsciousness."

Having been a light novel fan her whole life, she understood what he was getting at. There were plenty of light novel series that dealt with characters who have to travel into their own subconscious, or the subconscious of another, to fix a problem they were dealing with. That said…

"Is there any way to bring him out?"

"I'm afraid not." Azazel shook his head. "He'll find his way out eventually. We just need to be patient. Although…" Running a hand through his hair, he frowned at her. "I guess you kind of need him to regain consciousness soon, huh?"

Lilith didn't say anything, but she didn't need to. A succubus could not survive without a steady stream of sex. The life energy created from the act was what sustained them. That said, Lilith, as a succubus who'd only recently found her mate, required more physical contact than someone like Clarissa, who had numerous mates and didn't require as much sex to sustain herself.

"If the worst comes to pass, I might be able to forcibly wake him, but I'd rather we not do something so drastic," Clarissa said. "It could prove damaging."

"While I'm glad everyone here is so concerned about Christian's well-being, could someone please explain what is going on to me?" Samantha crossed her arms, not looking the least bit happy to be left out of the loop. "What happened to Christian? Why was he releasing all that demonic energy?"

"I'd actually like to know that, too." Tristin raised his hand.

Lilith looked back and forth between the two, and then she looked at Azazel and Clarissa for help. She didn't want to be the one who explained this to them.

Clarissa sighed and rubbed her face as though she was exhausted. However, it was Azazel who spoke up.

"I'll explain everything to you, though I'm sure some part of you has already guessed."

Lilith left the explanation to Azazel, who carefully went on to tell Samantha and Tristin about Christian's origins, explaining how the blood of Belial flowed through his veins, how his father had been a powerful half-demon, and how they were trying to get Christian to master that power. Tristin took it fairly well. He whistled in surprise but seemed to accept it. Samantha, on the other hand, was shaking as she struggled with this knowledge.

"You are telling me that... that all this time, the man I trusted the most was... was a demon?" she asked in a whisper.

"That's about the gist of it, though does it really matter if Christian is part demon?" asked Azazel.

"Of course it matters!" Samantha snapped. "Succubus, werewolves, incubus... those are one thing. I can at least accept they aren't all evil, but demons? They were born evil! Now you're telling me that the man I lo—that the man I placed all my trust in is one of those evil beings! How can it not matter?!"

The woman's entire body seemed to shake. An intense aura unlike anything Lilith had ever felt was leaking out of her, though she understood that it was all in her head. Samantha was human. She didn't have any special powers. This intense aura was nothing more than a figment of her imagination. That said, the woman still intimidated her.

"Could you tell us a bit more about his father?" asked Clarissa. "I had always suspected Christian to have the blood of Belial in him since we met, but I don't really know anything about his family."

"I suppose it couldn't hurt." Azazel cupped a hand to his chin and stroked his face. "Amon was a powerful half-demon. We're not really sure how, but somehow or other, Belial was able to inseminate a woman with his seed and she gave birth to Amon. I do not know much about his early life, but I know he went on to become a powerful mercenary. He would accept any job regardless of what it was so long as the person hiring him was willing to pay his price."

"Did you know him back then?" asked Tristin.

"I knew of him, but I didn't associate with him until later." Azazel half-grinned as if he was remembering something funny. "Actually, my first meeting with Amon was during a mission I had. Some demons had managed to slip through the barrier, and I was going to take care of them, but Belial beat me to it. At the time, he had been consumed by bloodlust and attacked me without provocation. I fought him, of course, but he was so strong that our battle ended in a stalemate and both of us etreated. I met him a few more times after that. Sometimes he was an enemy and sometimes he was an ally. It really depended on who contracted him."

While Azazel told the story of her mate's dad, Lilith reached out for Christian's hand. It was still warm. She took his hand in both of hers and ran her thumbs over his knuckles. He didn't stir.

"What about his mom?" asked Lilith.

"His mom didn't come until much later," Azazel admitted. "I couldn't tell you when she was born, but I can tell you that Monica Calmonte was a famous member of the Executioners and—"

"Did you say Monica Calmonte?!" Samantha's head suddenly whipped toward Azazel so forcefully Lilith worried the woman would snap her own neck.

"I did." Azazel paused. "I'm guessing you know of her? I'm not surprised."

"How could I not know of her?" Samantha looked like someone had just shot her between the eyes. "Monica Calmonte is infamous for being one of the most powerful Executioners to have ever existed. It was said that she was so capable she could defeat a horde of A-class monsters on her own. However, at some point, she disappeared, and no one ever heard from her again."

Lilith looked at Samantha, and then back down at Christian. She wished he was awake. The information they were being given was about him, and she was sure he would have wanted to know more about his parents.

"Her last mission had actually been to defeat a powerful demon." Samantha appeared to be struggling with something. "But she... never returned. Everyone assumed she was killed and wrote her off as KIA."

"Well, I can tell you right now that she wasn't killed." Azazel crossed his arms as he shifted from one foot to the other. "Her last mission was to kill Amon, but she failed. I couldn't tell you what happened. I only know that instead of killing him, the two of them fell in love and had Christian."

Samantha didn't speak, but the look on her face was enough. Shock, confusion, betrayal, anguish... there were so many emotions plastered over her face that anyone could have figured out she was not feeling good.

"What happened after they fell in love?" asked a curious Tristin. "I'm really curious now! Come on! Tell me more!"

"After they fell in love, the two of them got married, had Christian, and eventually founded a small village in the US." Azazel stroked his beard. "I visited on occasion, but I tried not to stick around too much. The village itself was sort of a safe haven for supernatural folks and their families. You might find this hard to believe, but there are a lot of beings out there who are married to humans. Fae, mermaids, werewolves, vampires, succubus… I even knew an ork who once married a human woman."

Lilith blinked at that. Orks were, according to every story she'd ever read, these large, hulking brutes with more muscle than brains. They were often portrayed as being exceedingly violent and killing whoever stood in their way. She tried to imagine someone marrying a creature like that, but she couldn't.

"In any case," Azazel continued. "The village was a community for people like that. However, sometime later the Catholic Church caught wind of it and sent an entire army of Executioners to the village. Everyone was slaughtered except for Christian, who miraculously survived and was sent to live in a Catholic Church funded orphanage."

"That… doesn't make any sense." Samantha furrowed her brow. "Why would they spare Christian? If he was the son of a half-demon, protocol would demand that he be slaughtered with the rest of them."

Azazel blew out a deep breath, seemed to debate with himself for a moment, and then glanced at the people around him. His eyes flickered briefly to Christian. Then he sighed.

"While I have no evidence to support this, I believe the Catholic Church may have already been infiltrated by the Seven Demon Kings back then." Samantha sucked in a deep breath. "I have reason to believe they were searching for the son of Belial. More than likely, it was Satan who gave the order to destroy the village. He likely told them to bring Amon back alive, but a man like him would have never let himself be captured."

"But… but there had been a different Pope back then, and—"

"And that doesn't mean Satan couldn't have possessed the previous Pope either," Azazel interrupted. "Do you not remember how the last Pope died?" Samantha said nothing, prompting the fallen angel to continue. "According to reports, his heart simply stopped working. He wasn't that old, in perfect physical health, and should have lasted another decade or two. There's a good chance Satan possessed him. Once someone has been possessed by a Demon King, their body becomes reliant on his power. Should the Demon King ever leave…" Azazel trailed off, shrugged, and moved along. "Well, I still have no proof. This is just a theory."

No one said anything for the longest time. Samantha looked like someone had just pulled a rug out from underneath her. After a moment, she took a slow breath, though it still appeared unsteady to Lilith.

"If you'll excuse me," she murmured, spinning on her heel and walking out of the room. Azazel, Clarissa, Lilith, and Tristin watched her go.

"Do you think she'll be okay?" asked Clarissa.

"I'm sure the boss lady will be fine," Tristin said. "She's a pretty resilient gal."

"I wasn't asking you."

"Why are you so mean to me?!"

"Azazel," Lilith said softly.

"Hm?" Azazel turned to gaze at her.

"The way you told that story, you made it sound like the Seven Demon Kings were after Christian's father."

Azazel nodded. "Yes, I imagine they were."

"Why?" she couldn't help but ask.

"That's a pretty loaded question." Azazel rubbed the back of his neck as he presented them with a mirthless smile. "It's because the only way to get past the barrier that separates Earth and Hell is by sacrificing someone who has the blood of Belial, the former King of Hell."

***

An emergency meeting of the Council of Twenty was called. Azazel had, of course, called it immediately after leaving the hospital. Given what happened, he judged there would be a lot of people whose excitement he needed to quell before it could get out of hand. There were also other matters the disturbance had caused that would need to be taken care of.

"Did you see the power that boy displayed?"

"To go up against Kokabiel like that is incredible."

"The power of Belial is indeed a frightening thing."

Azazel let the comments from his fellow fallen angels continue for a while, but he eventually called everyone to order.

"I'm sure all of you want to know what will happen from here on out, but before we get to Christian and what should be done about him, there are some other things we need to take care of." Azazel glanced at Shemhazai. "How long do you think it will take to repair the damage done by Christian's and Kokabiel's little spat?"

"I have a rough estimate of how much damage was done," Shemhazai began. "The damage was fairly extensive. Our training hall was destroyed, and the surrounding area was completely demolished. It's a good thing we decided not to build anything else there. All told, it will probably take around four months to completely repair, and of course, we're going to have to import supplies, which will extend that time. I'd say six months, give or take a few days."

"Cost of repairs?"

"About fifty thousand."

The Grigori did not use currency in their home. Everything people had there was free. However, the world outside of their hideout required money, and all the materials they used to build this place came from outside.

Fortunately, the Grigori had spent years amassing their fortune, and now they had businesses in just about every venture. They made enough that they wouldn't need to worry about costs. $50,000 was negligible.

"Sounds good to me. Now then…" Azazel cleared his throat. "About the matter of what we should do with Christian. I have decided to take him under my wing."

The words caused the other members of the council to mutter and whisper to each other. Azazel watched them with a frown, and then raised his hand toward them, asking for silence.

"It seems there are more problems with Christian's power than we first suspected. There's never been a case of a human with a quarter of demon's blood in them. That was a miscalculation on my part. It will require a bit more research, but I believe that with my advice, we can turn Christian into a capable asset."

A lot of heads nodded at his words. However, there were a few people who did no such thing. Kokabiel looked somewhat cross. His arms were crossed, and he was glaring at the table, not saying a word. It wasn't unusual for him to be quiet. However, he looked like a child who'd had his favorite toy taken away. Likewise, Shemhazai and Baraqiel were not saying anything.

"Are you sure this is a wise idea?" someone suddenly asked. It was a woman. Her long hair was black but had silver streaks, remnants of her time from when she had been an angel of Heaven. Her eyes were a vibrant green. Skin so pale and smooth it appeared as silk gave her face a soft appearance.

"What do you mean, Ezekiel?" asked Azazel.

"I mean training that boy," Ezekiel stated. "We all saw what that child was capable of. His powers are unbelievable. Are we really certain we should train him at all? It might be better if we just used him as bait."

Azazel frowned when several of the fallen angels nodded, but he had no intention of letting them agree with this woman. He had to get them all on his side with this.

"What you are suggesting his dangerous." Azazel placed his hand against the table and tapped on it several times. "Say we don't train him at all, and then use him as bait. First, the possibility of him being captured increases exponentially since he cannot use his powers to defend himself. Should that happen, we can basically kiss this world goodbye. However, what if what happened when Kokabiel was training him happens again? Can you imagine the destructive power he could unleash if we let him go without teaching him to control his powers?"

Ezekiel paled, as did several of the people who had agreed with her. No doubt they were imagining what would happen if Christian lost control like he'd done training with Kokabiel. He had fought their strongest warrior to a standstill. Had it been any other fallen angel save maybe himself or Baraqiel, they undoubtedly would have died.

"Having someone with that much power inside of them but unable to control it is dangerous," Azazel continued. "That is why I am going to train him."

"I retract my previous statement," Ezekiel said softly, withdrawing into her chair.

The meeting didn't last for much longer. They spoke a bit more about what they would be doing, Azazel received a few reports on the outside world, but the main purpose of this meeting was over.

"There is still the matter of the succubus," Arakiel said. "Lilith, was it? The power she displayed was also exceptional. She managed to freeze Kokabiel's movements completely, if only for a brief instant."

"Her powers are indeed admirable," Azazel agreed. "However, I do not think we need to do anything about her. Christian is her mate. Where he goes, she'll follow."

The meeting came to an end soon after, and the other fallen angels stood up from their chairs and left. Azazel remained seated. He had one more matter to attend to.

"Kokabiel, stay here a moment," Azazel said, still sitting.

Kokabiel looked at him, and then lowered himself back into his chair. The other fallen angels looked at them. However, none of them said anything as they filed out. Azazel believed most of them assumed he was going to scold the other fallen angel for his reckless stunt. They couldn't have been further from the truth.

"I need you to do something for me," Azazel said.

"I assumed as much." Kokabiel sighed. "What am I being asked to do this time?"

"I would like you to find out more about the situation in the Church. We're not getting enough information from our contacts, and I fear that what information is coming out might be misinformation designed to lead us astray."

"You do not trust our informants?"

Azazel winced and shrugged at the helplessness of his feelings. "It is not that I do not trust them. It is that I cannot afford to underestimate Satan and his ilk. There's a chance that many of our informants have been corrupted or caught. If they've been corrupted, then they'll no doubt give us information that is false. If they have been caught, the Demon Kings can give them incorrect information that will ultimately result in the same situation as the first problem. Right now, I need someone strong who can get the information I need. You're the only one I can trust with this."

"And you're sure it's not because you want to get me out of Seventh Heaven due to what happened?" asked Kokabiel, his eyes glowing as he stared at Azazel.

"No." He shook his head. "I have no reason to do that. I merely need someone who can get the information I need, and since I've decided to train Christian myself, you don't have anything to do. If you stay here, you'll be bored to tears."

"That is true." Kokabiel nodded several times as he crossed his arms. "Very well. I'll leave for the outside world today."

"Thank you."

As the fallen angel's most powerful member left, Azazel looked down at the table and furrowed his brow. The easy part was done. Now it was time for the hard part.

"How the hell am I going to train someone to use their demonic power?" he asked of no one in particular.

***

Floating in an endless abyss, Christian could see nothing but darkness in all directions. He couldn't tell if this place had any beginning or end. Blackness encompassed him. It was like his senses were all blocked off. He could see nothing, smell nothing, touch nothing, and hear nothing. Where was he? How had he gotten here?

"It looks like I failed yet again," suddenly, his hearing returned, and a voice spoke up.

"Who is there?" asked Christian.

"Aww. What's with that ignorance? Are you telling me you can't even recognize your own voice?"

A figure suddenly materialized in front of him, a man who stood with his back straight and wore an arrogant smirk. Messy dark hair. Heterochromatic eyes. A muscular physique. Christian frowned. It was like he was staring into a mirror, except he couldn't remember a time he'd had such an arrogant look on his face before. This man wore it like a mantle.

"Who are you?" asked Christian.

The figure smirked. *"That should be obvious. I am you. I am the you that you keep locked away in the deepest recesses of your soul, fueled by the demonic blood flowing through our veins."*

Christian twitched at the mention of his demonic side, something he still didn't like admitting to even though he was trying to control it. Now that this being had mentioned it, he remembered what happened. His glare hardened.

"You used my body. You possessed me."

"Possessed is such a strong word. This is my body too, you know. I prefer to think of it as me simply taking my rightful place as the lead actor in this little play."

"What do you want?" asked Christian through narrowed eyes.

"What do I want?" The arrogant reflection of Christian parroted, his head tilting from side to side as he cackled. *"I thought that would be obvious. I want out of here. I don't want to be cooped up in this place any longer. It's dark, damp, and cold. I don't like it. Is it so wrong of me to wish I could walk in the light for a change?"*

Christian narrowed his eyes further. "I'm not going to let such a dangerous person out. I don't know who you are exactly, but you are staying here. There's obviously a reason I imprisoned you."

His arrogant reflection snarled and looked ready to rush him, though he didn't move from his spot. Christian assumed this meant he couldn't move.

"You imprisoned me because you can't accept the side of you that isn't human! And so long as you continue, you will never gain the power you seek! You'll never gain the strength to protect Lilith! I'm the only one who has that power! Just wait! Soon, you'll see how helpless you are!! You'll see how much you need me!"

The arrogant-looking Christian, which he decided to call Nox began fading away. His body slowly became more translucent, until it eventually disappeared entirely. Now alone, Christian wondered what this confrontation meant. He closed his eyes.

And then he woke up.

Taking a deep breath, Christian almost winced as the scent of antiseptics stung his nose. He immediately realized he was in a hospital. He wondered if this was going to become a habit. Actually, now that he thought about it, passing out and waking up in different locations might already be a habit. He passed out after fighting the werewolf in Seal Beach, then again after fighting Damien, the time where he jumped off the train with Lilith, and then when he fought Asmodeus. It really did seem like he had picked up a bad habit.

As he lay there, trying to regain his bearings and not feel depressed about his bad fainting habit, two loud voices reached his ears. He cracked his eyes open and sought out the voices. He easily recognized Lilith, but it took him a moment to recognize the woman she was arguing with. A white lab coat, black skirt, and a dark shirt covered her body. She was a middle-aged woman. He blinked several more times as he realized it was Anastasia Pierce, his physician back when he had been an Executioner.

What are they arguing about?

Curious, Christian pretended he was still asleep and listened in.

"I'm not letting you go near him when he can't even defend himself!"

"You make it sound like I'm going to cut him open or something. I assure you that I have no such intentions. I just want to check up on him."

"Then why are you carrying a scalpel with you?"

"A scalpel is a standard medical tool. I also have a stethoscope and several other supplies with me."

"A likely story."

Christian frowned as he inferred what was happening from their conversation, and now that he understood the gist of it, he wondered what he should do. Keep pretending to be asleep, or wake up? He supposed letting things play out by pretending to be asleep wouldn't be a very good idea.

Waking up it is.

Opening his eyes, Christian groaned as he sat up in bed. His actions caused Lilith and Dr. Pierce to stop arguing. Their heads snapped over to him as he made a show of stretching his arms above his head.

"Christian!" Lilith was at his side immediately. "Are you okay? How are you feeling?"

"I'm feeling fine," Christian muttered, then winced. "A little stiff though."

Lilith's smile was relieved. "Considering what happened, being a little stiff is probably natural."

Christian rubbed the side of his neck for a moment. "I don't really know what happened after Kokabiel pinned me down. Would you mind telling me?"

"Sure."

Lilith did her best to inform Christian of what happened, explaining that he'd suddenly exploded with intense demonic energy, and then proceeded to fight Kokabiel on even grounds. Having been at ground zero, she had the most extensive knowledge of the battle. She provided him with a lot of details, including how he and Kokabiel had almost killed each other.

"To be honest, your incredible show of power reminded me a bit of… of Asmodeus," Lilith said reluctantly as she looked at her hands, which rested on her lap. "It was kind of frightening."

Christian flinched. "I'm sorry. I didn't mean to frighten you."

Long blonde locks swaying as she shook her head, Lilith placed her hands over his. She made eye contact. Her gaze pinned him in place. It was warm and made him feel safe and comfortable. He felt like she was trying to reassure him with eye contact alone.

"I didn't mean that you were scary," Lilith said. "You could never frighten me. It's just… when you used that power, it was like you weren't yourself. You acted like someone else entirely. The thought that the Christian I love might be gone is what frightened me."

Her words made Christian recall the dream he'd just had, where he was confronted by someone who looked like him. He knew he'd been possessed. That one he decided to call Nox had said they were the same, but he wasn't sure he could believe that.

As the two of them were talking, Dr. Pierce set a case on a counter and opened it up. There were several devices inside. She pulled out one of them, which looked like a far more streamlined version of the scanners people found being used at a cash register.

"I don't mind if you two keep talking," she said, coming up to them. "But, Caspian, do you mind if I begin scanning your body for any abnormalities?"

While Lilith opened her mouth, the expression on her face making it obvious she was going to tell this woman off, Christian nodded.

"Sure. Go ahead."

"Christian!"

"What?" Christian shrugged. "I trust her. Besides, it looks like she got a new scanner finally. I haven't had a thorough check up in a long time, so it would be good to know if there's anything wrong with my body."

Lilith pouted a bit, but she eventually conceded with a reluctant pout. "Well… I guess, but I'm going to watch her and make sure she doesn't do anything strange to you."

"Your jealousy is showing."

"Can you blame me?"

"I guess not."

"You two really are adorable," Dr. Pierce said as she sat on the other side of the bed and brought the scanner to Christian's chest.

Lilith sent the woman her most vicious pout, though to Christian, it reminded him of a cute poodle trying to growl at a rottweiler. Dr. Pierce didn't even seem to be paying attention. She pressed the scanner against his chest, stared intently into the screen, and frowned as she read whatever information appeared.

"What's the diagnoses?" asked Christian.

Dr. Pierce sighed as she removed the scanner. "Well, you definitely aren't fully human. There's some strange changes going on inside of your body right now. These changes actually started after your battle against Abaddon. We assumed it was because Abaddon's blood mixed with yours. The changes stopped with your eye, so we didn't think much of it at the time, but now your body is changing even more. I can even see what looks like white and red blood cells actively regenerating your body like the nanomachines we gave you back in Seal Beach."

For just a moment, Christian found himself too stunned for words. However, Dr. Peirce's comment reminded him of something he'd read back at the succubus enclave.

Belial is known to possess a trident of incredible power, one capable of piercing anything by distorting reality. Some believe this trident to be Gae Bolg, a spear wielded by Cu Chulainn, the famed Hound of Ireland. Others think Gae Bolg is merely a part of the trident wielded by Belial. Regardless of what mythos are to be believed, it is well-known that the trident wielded by Belial is one with incredible destructive capabilities.

Like many demons of his class, Belial is known for possessing incredible amounts of raw power. It is said that with nothing but a wave of his hand, he can create hellfire powerful enough to wipe out several dozen acres of land.

He is also known for his ability to steal the powers of others. It is said that drinking even a single drop of blood is enough for him to gain all the powers someone has, be they demon or something else. This, above all else, is what makes him such a terrifying enemy.

The words from book he'd read came back as if to haunt him. Now that he knew, without a doubt, that he had demon blood in him, Christian realized that the reason he healed so well was because his Belial bloodline had copied the nanomachines' ability.

Furthermore, the changes he experienced after defeating Abaddon was likely this same copying power. Christian had noticed a marked increase in his physical abilities after that battle. To top it off, his eye had gained the ability to see in 360 degrees, infrared, and could be used to zoom in to a certain extent.

"Christian, is everything okay?" Lilith placed a hand on his shoulder, which helped calm his thoughts and emotions. "You look pale."

"I'm fine." He gave her a wan smile. "Just shocked is all."

"Shock or not, you're in great shape." Dr. Pierce walked over to the counter, placed her scanner back in the case, and picked it up. She turned around. "It's amazing after you were in such a hard battle, but you are in even better shape now than you were before fighting against Kokabiel."

"I see..."

Dr. Pierce must have realized her words were having an adverse effect. She sent him a brittle smile, bid them both goodbye, and exited the hospital room. Now alone with Lilith, Christian couldn't stop himself from feeling the weight of his affliction.

"What am I supposed to do about this?" he asked. He didn't exactly expect to receive an answer.

"Can't you just beat it?" Lilith answered his question with one of her own.

He looked up. Her bright eyes like a pair of vast oceans the color of topazes, shone with a determined glint.

"Beat... it?"

"Yeah." Lilith nodded. "This power is yours, right? It seems like there's this second version of you, like an... an alter-ego, and he's the one who currently controls that power. If you beat him, maybe you can learn how to control that power."

"How very light novel of you." Christian smiled when Lilith pouted, but then he leaned over and placed a kiss on her lips. "But you might have a point. Maybe I just need to confront Nox and defeat him inside of my mind... or whatever."

It wasn't like he had a better idea, and Lilith's suggestion did sound like it had merit. He'd read the same light novels as her. This was a very common theme. Of course, he'd never expected it to happen to him, but maybe he could draw upon the knowledge gleaned from what he'd read in fiction. It felt a little silly, but without any other options, what else could he do?

"I'm not sure fighting against yourself is the best idea right now."

At the sound of the voice, Christian and Lilith turned to find Azazel strolling into the room. He looked at the two with a smile. Yet even though he was smiling, it looked strained, like he had something serious he wanted to talk about.

"Sorry. I couldn't help but overhear your conversation." Azazel pulled up a chair and sat down at the end of the bed. "It is true that you will probably have to confront your... your... well, why don't we just call it your dark half for now."

"I decided to call it Nox," Christian said.

"Nox it is then." Azazel didn't seem to care and continued. "Anyway, while I think you will have to confront Nox, I don't think doing so right now is a good idea. Don't forget that he currently has the ability to use Belial's power, and you do not."

Christian and Lilith glanced at each other.

"What do you suggest we do then?" asked Christian.

"Kokabiel's form of training was too Spartan," Azazel said. "He has a very trial by fire method, but I don't think that's going to work here. Therefore..." he placed a thumb against his chest and grinned. "I'm going to train you in how to draw upon Belial's power. This is going to be something of a trial by error method. We'll try different things to see what works. I'm sure we'll eventually stumble upon a method that does."

"Stumble upon?" asked Lilith with a raised eyebrow.

"That doesn't inspire much confidence," Christian added.

Azazel gave them both a shrug. "We're in uncharted territory here, so everything we're doing is basically an untested trial. So..."

Azazel held out his hand to Christian. "What do you say? Do you want to see if we can't find some way to help you control that power of yours?"

If Christian was being honest, he really didn't want to use his power at all. He hated this power. He hated being part demon. The very thought made him sick. At the same time, the enemies he was facing were getting stronger, and if he didn't get stronger with them, he wouldn't be able to protect Lilith.

"Sure." Reluctantly reaching out, Christian gripped Azazel's hand in a firm shake. "Why not? It's not like I've got any other ideas."

Chapter 11

The days wore on, and the Executioners, the succubus, Tristin and his harem, and Christian and Lilith had all settled in.

The Executioners had become a part of Seventh Heaven's armed forces. Their job was primarily to defend the community should it ever come under attack, but they were also occasionally sent out on missions alongside some of the fallen angels. Most of their missions involved intelligence gathering or demon extermination.

Their uniforms had also changed from the traditional black clothing with matte armor into something a little more unusual. Unitards with orichalcum armor. They might have looked a little odd, but there was no denying they were far sturdier than what they'd had before.

The succubus were not part of the armed forces, but the Valkyries did occasionally work alongside the Grigori as repayment for being allowed to live there. In exchange for their services, whenever a succubus mastered her Aura of Allure, the Grigori helped send her out into the world so she could find her mate.

Christian didn't know what happened to the succubus who went out. However, everyone who left had a direct line to Seventh Heaven, so he guessed they would know if there was any trouble.

It didn't come as much of a shock, but Tristin soon proved his worth at gathering and disseminating information. Once the Grigori realized his worth, they sent him to work with Penemue, who oversaw their spy network. Tristin had bragged once over drinks about how he had cut the rate at which their forces were led into traps by over 60%, an impressive number to be sure, provided it was true. Of course, Tristin wasn't really one to lie, so Christian assumed he was being honest.

He didn't know what Tristin's harem was up to these days. That was fine. Christian had never really spent much time with them to begin with, and if he was being honest, he didn't approve of polyamory. Being around them was awkward.

He and Lilith continued their training.

They would train together in the mornings, going to the shooting range and practicing their shooting. Lilith was a quick study. She had already gotten down the basics of gun use, and she could even shoot a target from over 75 feet away with a good degree of accuracy. Her gun of choice was the Glock 19. She told Christian she liked it because of its versatility. It was a compact pistol with a 4.01-inch barrel and a total length of 7.63 inches. When combine with the polymer frame that reduced the weight to 30.18 ounces when loaded it made for an easy to use gun. Reliable and simple.

Lilith was not ambidextrous. She could only fire one gun at any given time. She had once been about to try shooting two, but Christian had stopped her.

"I can fire two guns because I was born ambidextrous and trained myself extensively to be equally strong in both arms. You're right-handed. I know you want to be able to fight, but please trust me when I say that trying to dual-wield is not a good idea for most people."

Lilith had pouted at his words, but she'd decided to stick with a single gun in the end.

After their training at the shooting range ended, the two of them split off to train separately. Lilith trained alongside the Valkyries. He never saw her training, but they always exchanged notes and talked about what they had done after training finished in the evening.

While Lilith went to the Valkyries, Christian trained with Azazel.

Of course, he wasn't sure it could be called training.

"I believe the reason why you always lose control whenever you call upon that power is because your emotions are always running hot."

They were inside of what Christian could only think of as a lecture hall. There were no seats or anything of the sort, but there were several low-rise tables where people sat on the floor. The tables were lined up in six rows of two. At the front of the room, Azazel paced back and forth as he lectured Christian.

"Emotions like anger, hatred, lust, and envy are the keys to activating a demon's ability. The emotion used as the trigger is normally dependent on which Demon King a demon is aligned to. However, your case is different. You have the blood of Belial running through you."

Azazel paused as though to make sure Christian was listening, which he was, though he still felt reluctant. Even so, he kept his eyes on the fallen angel leader and listened to every word the man said.

"A lot of people confuse Satan as the King of Hell, but the truth is that Satan is just another angel who fell from God's grace. In fact, he was the first angel who fell. That's another misunderstanding as Lucifer is often considered the first angel to rebel against God. For future reference, Satan is the serpent who tempted Adam and Eve into eating the apple from the Tree of Eden. After his fall to Hell, he became a member of Belial's servants. You with me so far?"

"I think so," Christian said as Azazel once more paused to make sure he was following along. "I do have a question, though. How did the Seven Demon Kings come about? It sounds like Belial was defeated."

"He was." Azazel nodded. "Six more angels rebelled against God and fell from grace: Lucifer, Mammon, Asmodeus, Leviathan, Beelzebub, and Belphegor. Satan was the strongest of these seven. He formed an alliance with them and together they overthrew Belial. In either event, my point in this lecture is that you are not affiliated with any of the Seven Demon Kings, and so the method in which you activate your powers are also different. I believe there is a way to do so without relying on negative emotions and near-death experiences."

"And what method is that?"

"Accepting yourself."

Christian froze. The words made his entire body grow cold.

"What do you mean by that?"

"Come on, Christian." Azazel gave him an admonishing look. "You are not dumb. I know you understand what I mean."

Christian looked away. "You make it sound so simple."

"I suppose it wouldn't be easy for someone who was raised as a devout Catholic, but I believe that is the only way to use those powers you have."

Even though he knew Azazel was right, Christian wasn't sure he could accept this part of himself—no, maybe it wasn't so much that he couldn't as he didn't want to.

He sighed. "I'll try. I can't promise anything more than that."

Azazel nodded, though the look on his face said he wasn't satisfied. "I suppose that is acceptable for now."

Despite his words about trying, Christian really didn't know what to do. How did one go about accepting themselves? Was it as simple a matter as telling himself that he accepted himself? If it were that easy, he probably wouldn't be having this problem.

They tried many different methods. Azazel had Christian meditate, try to speak with his inner self, induced hypnosis to force Christian into accepting him, and many other methods that didn't work. It was a frustrating experience for Christian, but Azazel seemed interested in going through these numerous experiments. He didn't appreciate how the fallen angel appeared to be having fun over his plight.

That day, as all days, ended in what Christian believed was more or less a failure. While Azazel didn't seem to mind, it bothered him that he couldn't access that power, made him feel like he was wasting his time. At the same time, he also felt relieved.

As he walked through Seventh Heaven, Christian did his best to ignore the gazes, whispers, and fingers pointing his way.

It had been like this ever since his training gone wrong with Kokabiel. His battle against the strongest warrior among the Grigori had sent ripples through the residents. While a few of the fallen angels looked at him like he was a curiosity, most of the residents gazed at him in fear. According to Azazel, he had leaked a massive amount of demonic energy and bloodlust, enough that everyone had been able to feel it. That was why he didn't blame them for fearing him. Even so, he couldn't deny that it hurt.

Seventh Heaven was an odd place to him, even now. It wasn't like any city he'd ever visited. The architecture appeared old for the most part. Aside from the skyscrapers, everything else reminded him of the buildings that could be found in Jerusalem. Of course, this was only on the outside. The inside blended modern aesthetics with ancient traditions.

The place where he was traveling to was a small cafe, and again, while the outside looked like an ancient building that had been transported through time, the inside almost resembled a Starbucks.

Christian walked between low-rise tables where several people, a mix of fallen angels and humans, sat around and sipped their coffee or munched on a sandwich. These people were probably on break or something. Several of them looked his way, but they quickly averted their gaze once they realized who he was.

A young human manned the counter. His light brown hair was flecked with blond. He had green eyes and unblemished skin. Christian had realized something about all the humans who lived here. They were all very beautiful. He wondered if the Grigori had selected humans to live with them based on their appearance.

"Christian," the young man said without a hint of the fear most people displayed. "You'd like the usual, I take it?"

"Yes, please."

"And for Lilith?"

Christian paused as he thought about what Lilith would want to have. Christian preferred sticking with what he knew he liked, but his mate enjoyed trying new things.

"Let's go with…" Christian glanced at their menu, which changed on a weekly basis depending on what sort of food got shipped in. Seventh Heaven was not a self-sufficient place. "We'll do the fig and prosciutto sandwich and a chai latte."

"Sounds good," the young man said. "I'll have your order right up."

"Thanks."

Because Seventh Heaven didn't use currency, there was no register to pay for food. Christian left the counter and found a seat near a corner of the room. It was an empty table surrounded by several cushions, which were more comfortable than their plain appearance would suggest. The cushions were made of memory foam. They basically conformed to the shape of someone's butt when they sat on them.

Lilith arrived before the food did. As she entered through the entrance (he still didn't consider them doors because they were nothing but holes in the wall with no covering), she glanced around, spotted him, and made a beeline for his table. The way her face lit up caused Christian to smile as well, though his smile did crack a bit when he saw how she was limping.

"Everything alright? Did something happen during training?"

"Just a little bruise."

After taking a seat, Lilith gingerly stretched out her legs, and then leaned over and placed a soft kiss on Christian's lips. She was wearing jeans that day. They covered her legs so he couldn't see the injury but knowing that she didn't like to make him worry, he worried that her "little bruise" might not be as little as she suggested. That said, he would see it tonight anyway when he helped heal her.

"Mind telling me what happened?" asked Christian.

"Heather said I was in good enough physical shape to begin sparring with the younger succubus," Lilith said as she reached down and rubbed her thigh. "I think I did pretty well, but of course, my opponent had more experience than I do, so I lost. She used a staff. Struck me on the thigh and then disarmed me."

Christian decided to let her explanation for her injury go at that. How she got injured ultimately wasn't important.

"Speaking of, what kind of weapon are you using?"

"A whip. Heather had me try one out and she says I have a knack for it. She told me that since my greatest assets were my illusions anyway, having something that would let me keep my opponents back would be better than a weapon to use at close-range."

Christian agreed with Heather's assessment of Lilith's fighting prowess and abilities. Given Lilith's overwhelming power, the illusions she could cast would eventually reach a point where she could probably turn all her illusions into reality. It would be better in the long run to focus on what would become her primary method of attack.

"That reminds me: How are your illusions coming along?" asked Christian as their meals arrived. He thanked the young man who delivered them, then focused on Lilith as she grabbed her chai latte and took a sip.

"They're going better than I expected, actually." Lilith set her cup down and tilted her head, brow furrowing in thought. "Once I got the basics of casting illusions down, I learned how to expand them and affect more than one sense at a time. Right now, I can affect two of the five senses, but I'm working my way up to three. I think I can get the third sense down with a bit more practice."

"It sounds like you're doing better than me." Christian scratched the side of his head and sighed. "I'm honestly a bit jealous at how well your training is going."

Of course, he was also quite proud of how well Lilith's training was coming along. She might have been a succubus, but she was still a civilian with no combat experience. However, in the span of a few weeks, she'd learned how to accurately shoot a gun, how to fight with a whip, and how to cast illusions. The speed at which she learned was honestly impressive.

"I'm sure you'll get there eventually." Lilith leaned into him briefly and kissed his cheek. "You're not the kind of person who gives up. You'll keep going until you've mastered your power. I have faith in you."

"Thank you," Christian said as Lilith took a bite of her fig and prosciutto sandwich. She gasped. "What is it?"

"This is really good! You should try some!"

Lilith held her sandwich out to Christian, who leaned in and took a bite. It was good. Not really something he'd eat normally, but still good. However, as he thought this, a thought occurred to him, a question, a doubt.

How long was this peaceful life going to last?

***

I wonder how long it's been since I last saw this sight... centuries at least.

Tasked with gathering information, Kokabiel had come to the Vatican to meet with one of the Grigori's informants.

He sat at a quaint cafe and sipped some black coffee. Fallen angels like himself did not require sustenance. Most of them ate or drank simply because they liked eating and drinking, but Kokabiel generally did not indulge in such base pleasures. He was drinking for appearances... and because the cafe owner had told him he couldn't loiter around.

Watching the humans walk past the cafe, Kokabiel couldn't stop the feeling of mild disgust welling up inside of him. He didn't hate humans. That said, he didn't like them either. Humans were weak, inferior, and incapable of providing him with even a modicum of entertainment. Even those Executioners like Samantha and Leon were pathetic in his eyes. They might have been strong by human standards, but they were weak by his.

I want a challenge.

In the days of old, when the angels of Heaven fought against the forces of Hell on a near constant basis, Kokabiel had been at the front lines almost every day. He had fought and bled and fought and bled some more, and it had been glorious. However, then God had come back from wherever he'd disappeared to. He pushed the forces of Hell back like they were nothing, then created a powerful barrier that kept demons from traveling to Earth.

Kokabiel had been resentful of God. He hadn't rebelled like Satan and his ilk had. He just left. He went down to Earth against God's will and began seeking out strong opponents, and thus he became a fallen.

That didn't bother him like it did some of his brethren. All he wanted was to find and battle against powerful foes. He sought out No Life Kings, Ancestors, Lycaons, and even the Dragon Kings. He fought them all. Sometimes he won. Sometimes he lost and had to retreat. But no matter whether he won or lost, Kokabiel always felt his best when he was fighting against a strong opponent.

He hadn't battled like that in a long while—not since Azazel had recruited him.

Kokabiel wasn't sure what possessed him to accept Azazel's offer. Maybe he'd been bored, or perhaps he'd seen some benefit in joining the Grigori. It had been so long ago that he no longer knew why he'd decided to join their ranks. The last several centuries had been dull.

Until just recently.

Looking at his hand, Kokabiel clenched it into a fist as he recalled his battle against Christian. Battling against that child had reminded Kokabiel of the thrill he used to feel during combat. He wanted to feel that again. He wanted to experience that sensation again.

Maybe he will lose it if I kill his woman...

Azazel had forbidden him from touching Lilith, but it might be worth if he could bring out Christian's full power.

"Now here's a face I haven't seen in a while," a voice said in his ear.

Kokabiel turned around to find a man standing behind him, grinning down at him. There was nothing particularly remarkable about this man's appearance. He wore dark clothing. His eyes were cobalt. His features were plain. This man had the kind of face that could easily blend into the crowd.

But that was only on the surface.

Kokabiel narrowed his eyes. "I did not expect to see you in such a young body, Satan. Our intelligence reported that you were possessing the Pope."

"Hehe." Satan glared at Kokabiel with barely restrained anger, his lips splitting into a massive grin. "I am, of course, possessing the Pope. However, everyone would recognize the Pope, so I change his appearance and make him younger whenever I go out."

"So I see."

Changing the appearance and age of the person you were possessing was dangerous and ultimately killed the host, but he guessed Satan didn't care about that.

"If you are here, then I assume our agent was discovered."

Kokabiel kept calm. Satan was confronting him, not fighting him, which means this demon wanted something.

"Oh, we discovered him a long time ago." Satan waved off the accusatory glare Kokabiel cast at him as he sat down. "We just didn't do anything because we thought we could use him for our own purposes." His cobalt eyes flared crimson as he grinned. "However, when I found out that none other than Kokabiel was coming to meet him, I knew I just had to meet you myself. I believe you and I have a lot we can offer each other."

"I'm not interested in whatever you have to offer." Kokabiel made to stand up and leave.

Satan wouldn't let him. "What if I could give you the challenge you've been craving since the war came to an end all those centuries ago?"

Halfway out of his seat, Kokabiel paused as a debate raged inside of him. However, the debate did not last long. He sat back down and gestured for Satan to continue.

"Go on. I'm listening."

Satan's malicious, wrath-filled smile stretched across his face as he informed Kokabiel of his plans.

***

As the days turned into weeks, Christian felt like he was slowly getting used to his new life. At the same time, he also felt like he was losing his edge. With no powerful enemies to fight, no threats to confront, he had nothing and no one who could give him a challenge. The Executioners wouldn't fight him anymore. They basically ignored him with the exceptions of Samantha, and even she acted wary around him. He had asked Azazel to be his sparring partner, but the man had said he wouldn't spar against him until he learned how to use his powers.

He did spar occasionally with Heather and Clarissa. Both of them were good, but Christian often defeated them within fifteen minutes. Ever since his battle against Kokabiel, his body had become stronger, faster, and altogether more powerful than before. Azazel theorized that it was because his demonic blood was growing more powerful.

The thought terrified him.

His training with Azazel wasn't yielding any results either, and even the Grigori leader was at a complete loss. The man had been so sure he could help. He couldn't figure out why Christian couldn't access his power.

Christian didn't say anything. He knew the reason he couldn't access his power was not Azazel's fault; it was his own fault. No matter how many times he was told to accept the demonic side of him, no matter how often he told that to himself, he still couldn't accept it. He didn't want to.

Since his training with Azazel wasn't doing anything for him, that day he had decided to spend his time sparring against Heather and Clarissa. He was fighting them at the same time.

The two charged at him from either side. It was a classic pincer maneuver, but in a battle where a person could move more than just right or left, it was ultimately useless.

Christian ran forward to avoid the pincer attack, spun around on the balls of his feet, slammed his left foot into the ground behind him, and used the kinetic energy built into his leg to blast forward. He was on the two within seconds. Wielding Michael and Raphael, he swung his blades at them, a loud clang, the sound of clashing metal, echoing around them as Heather blocked his swords with her tonfas.

While Heather locked blades with him, Clarissa slipped behind him and thrust her spear into his side, but Christian had already known it would happen. He left that opening on purpose. Before she could complete her attack, he pulled away from Heather, who'd been placing all her weight into her weapons. Now that the resistance he offered was gone, she stumbled forward—right into Clarissa's thrust.

"Shit!"

Clarissa managed to avoid having her naginata impale Heather. She yanked her weapon to the side. However, now both of them were knocked off balance.

Christian capitalized on their openings, swinging his swords at them. His first attack, a horizontal swing of Rafael, was avoided by Heather when she shoulder-rolled across the ground. Spinning around, Christian turned and slashed at Clarissa with Michael. She raised her naginata in time to block. However, the force of his swing knocked her aside, causing her to stumble forward.

Continuing to keep the pressure on, Christian attacked Clarissa and Heather, keeping them from being able to attack by using his dual-wielding style to great effect. Clarissa had a bit of an advantage over him. Her naginata gave her a longer attack range. Even so, he could avoid that by forcing his way into her guard.

The two of them soon split up. They must have realized that attacking together was working. Christian held his blades loosely at his sides and waited for them to make a move.

That move came when a stake made of mud shot from the ground and tried to impale him through the side. Christian instinctively slashed at it, but he realized a second too late that it had been nothing more than an illusion. His blade passed through it.

Heather closed the distance, swinging her tonfa around as she danced across the battlefield. Christian narrowed his eyes. A tonfa tried to jab the opening in his side, but he knocked it wide with Rafael. Heather swung her arm down from overhead. The attack would have cracked his skull, but he twirled to the side and aimed a thrust at her neck.

The attack was stopped by a naginata.

He followed the naginata's pole to the hand holding it, then up the hand to the face of Clarissa. Her arms were shaking as she struggled against the strength of his thrust.

Christian pulled Michael back, spun around, and struck the naginata with Rafael. The polearm weapon went wide. Clarissa stumbled.

He would have used that moment to attack before she could recover, but Heather was already there, protecting Clarissa with a series of powerful swings. His hair was ruffled as she jabbed her tonfa at his temple. It missed when he tilted his head. Bringing up Rafael, he knocked her attack away, and then swung Michael into her other tonfa. He hooked his blades against her weapons, rotated his wrists, and forced to the tonfas into the ground. Then he took a single step forward and slapped her hands with the flat end of his blades.

"Ack!"

Heather was forced to drop her tonfas. Christian used her pain as a distraction to close the distance. He took one step, lifted his right leg, and then rotated his body and kicked her in the sternum. There was a loud "OOF!" as her lungs were deprived of oxygen and she was sent to the ground.

By that time, Clarissa had recovered and was coming to attack him, but Christian placed Rafael against Heather's throat.

"I think this is my win," he said.

Clarissa bit her lip for a moment, but then she lowered her naginata, setting the butt end on the ground.

"We surrender."

Taking a deep breath and holding it, Christian let the tension ease from his muscles as he removed his sword from Heather's neck. The woman looked pretty put out. However, she clambered to her feet as he sheathed his swords and shook her head in amazement.

"You've improved a lot since the last time we sparred."

Christian shook his head. "It's not that I've improved. This is how I've always fought."

"Is that so? Well, I guess you were having an off-moment back then."

Back then. Heather was referring to when he and Lilith had been avoiding each other. Christian had been so out of sorts that he made numerous rookie mistakes, and his fighting style had been nothing like the one he'd spent years of blood, sweat, and tears perfecting.

A loud round of applause alerted Christian to their audience. The other succubus from the enclave had stopped their own training at some point to watch their spar, including Lilith, who was also clapping.

"That style of yours really impresses me," Clarissa said. "Where did you learn it?"

"It's not learned." Christian ran a hand through his hair, slick with sweat. "I created that style myself years ago."

"Even more impressive. Can it be taught?"

"Maybe…" Christian tilted his head. "However, it won't work if you already have your own style. To learn this, it's best to start out as a blank slate. Also…"

"Also?" Clarissa prodded.

He took a deep breath and looked her square in the eye. "It requires you to completely cast away your life to use. The style I created is considered suicidal because you have to flirt with death every time you fight. You're inviting your enemy to attack your vital points, and if your timing is even a little off, if you show a fear of death, you'll give yourself away and the style won't work."

While Heather paled a little, Clarissa rubbed her chin and nodded. "I see. It is as you say. That style is not something just anyone can learn. That is unfortunate."

He shrugged. "I think it's better this way."

As their conversation finished, Lilith came up to them and gave Christian a towel.

"Here. It might be a bit sweaty because I already used it, but…"

"I don't mind being covered in your sweat," Christian said with a chuckle as he used the towel to wipe his face and neck. Lilith beamed at him, but Heather and Clarissa rolled their eyes.

The training session ended soon after. Christian and Lilith joined the succubus in their walk back to their residence. There were less of them than before. There used to be a little over 50 succubi, but now there were only about 29, not including the Valkyries and Clarissa. Many of the succubi who'd survived the battle in the underground enclave had finally mastered their Aura of Allure. The ones who were at least 18 years old had been sent into the world. All the succubus that remained were below 18, with the youngest being 8.

Just as they reached the tower they were staying at, a loud crackling sound like a burst of static filled the air, followed by a powerful rumble that shook the bones.

"What was that?" asked a young succubus.

"I'm not sure," said another.

Christian also looked around to see if he could determine the source of the noise. It happened again. He couldn't see anything, which meant...

"An attack from outside?" Christian wondered out loud.

Just then, Armaros descended to the ground in front of them. He looked a bit harried. His wings were ruffled and there was a sense of panic about him.

"I'm glad I found you all," he said without preamble. "Christian, Clarissa, Heather, and Lilith, Azazel is requesting your presence."

The fact that their presence was being requested caused them to worry enough, but as the strange rumbling and crackling noise emanated around them, faint as though it was coming from a distance, the four of them couldn't help but feel a thrill run down their spines.

"I'm guessing there's some trouble?" Heather said as she set a hand on her tonfas as if using their presence to reassure herself.

"It's a little worse than 'just some trouble.'"

Armaros wore an expression far graver than Christian had seen from him before. It was so serious and filled with such worry that the fallen angel appeared to have aged a couple of decades.

Christian soon found out why when Armaros muttered his next words.

"There's a massive army of demons just outside our barrier."

Chapter 12

Despite having been given a tour of Seventh Heaven, there were some places Christian and the others who recently arrived had not seen. The mission briefing room was one of those places.

They sat in normal chairs made of metal and plastic. The chairs were in rows of 15 and there were 10 rows in total. Christian sat with Lilith at the front of the big room, which was large enough that at least a dozen tanks could fit inside of it and have room to spare. Surrounding him were the succubus warriors, the Valkyries. They were currently the only group who would still talk to him.

Well, Tristin did too, but that man was usually busy with his intelligence work or spending time with his harem.

Azazel stood on top of a podium at the front. It didn't look like much, just a slightly elevated platform with a desk, but then he flipped a switch on the desk and a holographic projection suddenly appeared.

It took Christian a second to realize that he was staring at a map. It took him even longer to realize it was a map of Antarctica. The topographic map was built in three-dimensions as opposed to two, revealing far more details than a normal map could. A large dome sat within the center. That must have been Seventh Heaven. Surrounding the dome were red splotches, which Christian was going to assume were enemy forces until someone told him otherwise. There were also red dots flitting around the dome.

"As you all know, we are currently under attack," Azazel began. "I'm not exactly sure how they found us, but there is currently a large army of demons just outside of the barrier. That sound you all heard was them trying to break through."

"Should we be worried about them breaking through?" asked a fallen angel decked in armor that looked more like S&M cosplay.

"I wouldn't worry about that." Azazel shook his head as he pointed at the dome-shaped object in the middle of the map. "Our barrier is one that's powered by using the thermal nuclear energy of the earth. The amount of power behind this barrier is enough that it could easily withstand four or five atom bombs without trouble. Even one of the Seven Demon Kings won't be able to break it down so easily."

That was another place Christian hadn't seen, the powerplant that generated the barrier. It was off-limits to everyone except a few people.

"However, just because they can't get in, that doesn't mean we can let them stay," Azazel continued. "Seventh Heaven is not a self-sufficient community. We rely on importing numerous supplies to survive. We'll have to expel them."

"How large are their forces?" asked Samantha. Christian whipped his head around to seek out the woman who'd once been his commanding officer. She was closer to the back, surrounded by her comrades. He frowned. They hadn't spoken since his powers had run amok.

"Estimates gathered from our satellites put their forces at about ten thousand strong," Azazel stated.

Whispers broke out amongst everyone present. Christian could hear the worry in everyone's tone as they muttered to each other. He and Lilith didn't say anything as they held hands, but the Valkyries were saying plenty.

"Forgive me for saying so, but our forces don't even number a thousand," Heather brought up the concern everyone else had. "How do you expect us to defeat an army that large?"

It was easy to see that everyone was thinking the same thing. They couldn't really be blamed. Counting the 150 fallen angels capable of combat, there were the 50 Executioners, the 20 Valkyries, him, and Lilith. Combined, their total forces weren't even a tenth of the demon army's.

"Who said anything about defeating them?" asked Azazel, grinning at the group of now befuddled people. He coughed into his hand. "The barrier keeping Earth and Hell separated is still operating. That means these demons did not travel here on their own. They were summoned."

Everyone nodded. That was common knowledge.

"Do you know how summoning works?" asked Azazel.

There was a slight pause before everyone shook their heads.

"Summoning works by creating a magic circle and using a sacrifice to summon a demon. Normally, a simple blood sacrifice would suffice. However, to summon this many means they probably sacrificed several dozen humans."

A cold chill swept through the room. No one could say they were pleased to hear that several people had been sacrificed for this, but they all knew there was nothing they could do about the deceased. It was a bitter pill to swallow.

"Furthermore, for a ritual of this size to work, they also need someone who is willing to act as the medium for all of these demons. If the medium dies, then the summoning will be dispelled, and the demons will go back to where they came from." Azazel grinned as the people sitting before him gained expressions of comprehension. "Someone out there is currently standing in a large magic circle, unable to move or defend themselves. All we need to do is find this person and take them out."

"Do we know where this person is?" asked Leon, his booming voice echoing loudly in the room.

"I'm going to have Penemue answer that. He knows more than me."

At those words, an old fallen angel who looked like he might break if hit with a strong breeze stood up. Decrepit didn't even begin to describe him, but despite looking ancient, he walked with his back straight and head held high. He climbed the podium and turned to face the group.

"We currently do not know where the medium is," Penemue said. "The demons have gone to great lengths to hide the medium's location, though we do know that he or she is on this island. There are several potential locations where the medium could be hidden away."

Azazel fiddled with something on the desk. No one could figure out what he was doing, but then several blue circles appeared around specific locations on the map.

"There are several bases located on Antarctica that are being operated by scientists and survey teams," Penemue began, though he paused soon after. Christian and Lilith shifted as though something unsettling had wormed into their gut. Penemue then continued, his voice grave. "Given the nature of what is happening, it is unknown whether anyone from the survey teams are still alive. They were likely the ones used as a sacrifice to summon such a large army."

A grim silence settled over the group. Of course, it was obvious that someone had to have been sacrificed, and they all knew that, but hearing it put so bluntly was tough on everyone. Christian looked around at the grave faces. He was sure the expression on his face matched theirs.

"Our plan is to create several teams," Azazel picked up where Penemue left off. "Each team will head to one of the bases marked on the map. Of course, given how many demons are out there, we can't just let you all loose. Myself and the other Council of Twenty members will fight against the army head on and provide you with a distraction."

Christian's spine stiffened as he thought about the implications of those words. The Council of Twenty were the leaders of the Grigori. Each one was said to have powers surpassing regular angels. Their power was represented in the number of wings they had. Most fallen angels only had two, but some like Azazel, Baraqiel, and Shemhazai had twelve. Kokabiel was something of an anomaly. He had ten wings, but he was more powerful than the other Council of Twenty members.

"There are currently fifteen bases," Azazel said. "We'll split you up into fifteen teams of fourteen. The teams will be Alpha, Beta, Gamma, Delta, Epsilon, Zeta, Eta, Theta, Iota, Kappa, Lambda, Omicron, Sigma, Upsilon, and Omega. The team leaders will be Samantha, Leon, Sif, Clarissa, Heather, Oberon, Nigndara, Malthos, Talia, Rebecca, Bennet, Nicholas, Lilac, Uther, and Christian."

The moment Christian heard his name being called, he nearly leapt from his seat as though something had shocked his butt.

"H-hold on," he said.

"What is it?" asked Azazel.

"You can't possibly mean you want me to lead a team," Christian began, his voice shaking. "I mean, I've never led a team before in my entire life. I've only been on teams or done solo missions. I don't know the first thing about leading a group of people into battle."

"I'm sure you'll be fine." When Christian opened his mouth to refute Azazel, the man continued before he could even begin. "You're one of our strongest fighters right now. While that might not necessarily equate to a strong leader, no one is going to follow a weakling. Besides, you might not have experience with leading a unit but you have more experience with missions than many of my fallen angels."

"Yes, but—"

"That's an order, Christian."

Christian froze as he tried to figure out how he should respond. His natural inclination was to snap off a salute and tell Azazel that he'd do his best, but this wasn't something he could just agree to. What if he led these people on a mission and all of them died because of his incompetence? He was already carrying the burden of being the only survivor of his village, of being the only person to come back alive from the battle against Abaddon. He didn't know if he could deal with having another burden placed on him.

Just as he was about to tell that to Azazel, someone grabbed his hand, sending a jolt through his body. It traveled up his arm, across his shoulder, and straight into his brain, an electric sensation that made him pause.

He looked down. Lilith was staring up at him, her hand firmly gripping his.

"It'll be okay," she said. "You can do this."

Christian stared at her for several seconds, took a deep breath, and then released it along with all the boiling emotions threatening to overwhelm him. He looked back Azazel. The fallen angel leader was eying him with a raised eyebrow.

"I… I understand. I'll do my best."

"That's the spirit!" Azazel clapped his hands together. "Now then, let's organize our forces and get ready! Your missions will begin once myself and the other Council of Twenty engages the enemy in combat, which will be in about… one hour."

The three races were quickly divided and mixed into groups of fourteen. Aside from Lilith, Christian ended up having three succubus, five fallen angels, and four members of the Executioners in his squad. The succubus were women recognized by face but not by name. Of course, he didn't even know the fallen angels or the Executioner members.

With their groups all assigned, they headed toward the weapons depot, where the Executioners and Valkyries equipped themselves with whatever weapons they felt they would need.

"Are you sure you know how to use that?" asked a blonde succubus named Valerie.

The woman she was a talking to, a female with dark skin and dark eyes, held Browning M2 .50 caliber machine gun. She didn't seem to have any trouble lifting it. Christian wasn't sure he believed his eyes.

"Yeah... I've used one of these before," the dark-skinned succubus, Taryn, said as she hefted the weapon up with both hands.

"You've always loved big guns," the last succubus, Natashia, muttered. She was a slip of a girl. Her red hair traveled all the way down to her butt, though it was currently tied into a ponytail. She had green eyes and soft features. If Christian hadn't been aware that she had lived long enough to be on her second mate, he would have assumed she was a child.

Taryn grinned at Natashia. "You know me."

The Valkyries were wearing their standard skin-tight unitards, but Taryn and Valerie also wore orichalcum chestplates over their standard outfits. Natashia's chestplate was more compact and unlike the other two, whose plates were black, hers was a light silver, but the main feature to her outfit was the two falchions strapped to her back and the submachine gun resting in a holster on her thigh.

While the succubus were getting ready, the four Executioners did not appear as enthused as they checked their weapons.

"I can't believe we're stuck on that monster's team," muttered a woman named Hannah Green. She was a member of the Assassins, meaning she specialized in stealth. She wore a black unitard and orichalcum armor. Her head was wrapped in cloth, covering everything but her brown eyes. Several throwing knives were strapped to her thighs and an extendable spear was attached to her lower back.

One of the men nodded. "I know what you mean. I used to respect him, but now that I know what he really is... well, now I'm just wondering why we haven't killed him yet."

The one who spoke was a big man—not quite Leon's height, but definitely bigger than Christian himself. The muscles in his arms and legs bulged beneath his clothing. He had two uzis at his hip, ammo clipped to a bandolier, and his primary weapon, a massive claymore that was easily as tall as Christian was. His shock blond hair and blue eyes gave him a typical American appearance.

Two other Executioner members, both men, said nothing, though it was clear from the dissatisfaction practically oozing from them that they were also not happy.

The one on the left, his body covered in sturdy armor, carried several long-range weapons. He had two 9mm pistols in holsters at his hips, a submachine strapped across his back, grenades stuck to a belt, and ammo poking from several pockets. It didn't look like he had a close-range weapon at first, but that was only until Christian looked down and saw the massive machete strapped to his left boot.

Standing next to him was the last man, a tall, lean male who didn't look very strong with his clothes on. He wasn't carrying any guns. However, he did have a crossbow strapped to his back along with a quiver of arrows. Christian didn't know if that was his primary weapon, or if the rapier strapped to his waist was the one he used more.

As the two Executioners continued talking, Lilith, who had been silently checking and cleaning her Glock, finally exploded.

"You people are disgusting," she snapped at them.

The Executioners paused. As one, they turned to her, eyes glaring with malice. Lilith didn't back down. Showing just how much she'd grown from the woman who feared men, she glared at the group.

"What was that?" Hannah asked with a hiss.

"You heard me," Lilith snapped. "Christian used to be one of the most devoted members of your group. He fought and bled for you people without a second thought, but the moment you learned he's different from you, all of his accomplishments and hard work mean nothing. You are the most disgusting people I've ever met."

The guy who looked like a walking armory growled at her. "Listen here, you cunt. That person you're defending so much isn't even a human. He's a thing. A monster. Why should we respect something like that?"

"The only monsters I see here are you people." Lilith raised her head to glare at the man, who stood almost two heads taller than she did.

Those words caused the group of four to send her fierce glares that could have melted through steel. The man with all the weapons— Alex, Christian thought his name was—was practically spitting with rage. His eyes were almost bloodshot. He looked apoplectic.

"You little bitch!"

The man raised his hand to strike Lilith, who looked like she was ready to throw down as well, but Christian quickly moved in between the two. He redirected Alex's attack to the side. Then, grabbing the man by his wrist, he twisted Alex around and locked his arm behind his back. A scream echoed from his mouth. He tried to struggle free. Christian let him go, kicking him in the back and sending him sprawling forward.

"You fucking monster! What was that for?" asked the man carrying the crossbow. Christian believed his name was Gregory.

"Do not touch my mate," Christian said.

His voice was quiet, but the four Executioners stiffened as he spoke. A chill seemed to run down their spines as he stared at them with his red and green eyes. Everyone had always found his heterochromia intimidating.

"Let me make one thing clear," Christian began. "I do not care what your feelings are toward me. Hate me if you want. However, I was put in charge of this mission, and if you want to live to see tomorrow, then you will do as I say. Do you four understand?" They didn't say anything. Christian growled. "Do you understand?"

"Yes… sir," they mumbled reluctantly.

"Good." Christian nodded and went back to attaching clips of orichalcum ammunition to his thighs. However, he had one last thing to say, so he turned around and stared at the four humans. "Also, I shouldn't need to mention this, but if you ever raise a hand to my mate, mission or not, I will break your arm."

Maybe it was his words, the quiet confidence he spoke with, or perhaps it was his glare, but the four humans shuddered before turning back to getting ready. Christian tried his best to ignore the group as he and Lilith finished preparing. Meanwhile, the three members of the Valkyries stood alongside the five fallen angels. They had all been watching the scene play out without interfering.

"Something tells me that if this mission goes FUBAR, it's not going to be because of the demons," Natasha muttered.

The two other succubus and five fallen angels nodded.

***

The Council of Twenty was mostly assembled. Azazel gazed at the group of fallen angels. Armaros with his calm demeanor; the inscrutable Araqiel who always acted like a sour puss; Baraqiel whose arms were crossed and whose expression remained stern; Chazaqiel and his mild grin as if he found everything amusing; Ezekiel, the beautiful woman who seemed a touch nervous about the coming battle; Gadreel floated alongside Ezekiel, doing her best to calm her fellow fallen angel; Kasdaye, one of the first who had fallen and one of the oldest alongside Penemue; the former high-ranking angel Raziel who was always looking morose; Penemue and his deceptively ancient appearance; the young-looking Shamsiel who had once been a guardian of Eden; the one who taught men of the moon, Sariel, remained in the back.

A few of their members were missing, out on assignment in the world at large. Including himself, there were currently 13 members from the Council of Twenty assembled before him.

That was more than enough.

They were floating just before the dome's entrance. Azazel had yet to open it, but once he did, they would all fly out and begin the battle against an army of 10,000 strong.

"Is everybody ready?" asked Azazel.

None of the council members cheered or gave a wary cry like a human might. Instead, all of them created the weapons of their choice. Spears of light crackled brightly as they were gripped in powerful hands. Swords of varying shapes and sizes suddenly flared into brilliant incandescence. A number of the Grigori like Shemhazai and Baraqiel created bows. Each member belonging to the Council of Twenty was ready.

Azazel nodded, satisfied. "Since it seems all of you are prepared, let's get this show on the road." Pressing a hand to his ear, he activated the communication device inside and said, "open the barrier in sector E75."

"Understood. Deactivating a portion of the barrier now."

As the words came over the comm unit, crisp and clear, a small square hole appeared on the barrier. It wasn't very large. However, it was enough for several angels to fit through at the same time.

"Let's go!" Azazel commanded.

Leading the charge, Azazel flew straight out of the hole. A demon, red-skinned and flying on leathery black wings, had stopped in front of the now open barrier. It looked shocked. That expression of surprise remained on its face even after Azazel sliced its head clean off. The creature fell, striking the barrier and evaporating.

The other fallen angels followed him out. However, they didn't remain with him. The idea was to spread out and begin attacking as many demons as possible. They split off into groups of two, seeking out demons wherever they were and attacking with swift strikes of their light spears, swords, and bows.

Shemhazai stuck with Azazel, throwing several spears at the demonic entities threatening them with pinpoint accuracy. Some spears pierced chest, others pierced shoulders, and one poor demon even got stuck in the eye. It honestly didn't matter where they were struck, though. Demons could not stand the divine powers of an angel. Those who received even a graze from a light attack were burnt to ash.

Azazel flew toward the largest horde of demons. They were all low-class. Red skin covered their gelatinous bodies, while wings of leather flapped to keep them aloft. Their faces were sort of human. They had noses, eyes, ears, and mouths. However, their nose was pinched and small. It looked more like a flat nose with two slits on either side acting as nostrils.

Their bodies were not hard, which was apparent in the way their distended guts wobbled as they flew. Fat sagged off their arms. Even their legs looked like gelatin.

These are... Belphegor's demons.

Belphegor was the Demon King of Sloth. Demons under his reign were humans who bore the sin of sloth. Their sin was so great they became these monsters in death.

As he flew toward the group, several massive spears of light easily larger than he was tall appeared around him, twelve in total. Azazel didn't hesitate to send the spears straight into the horde. Unlike with Shemhazai and his pinpoint precision, these spears did not impale. They incinerated. Bodies were burned to ashes, disappearing as the spears engulfed them, causing the putrid scent of burning flesh to mix with ozone.

Most of the demons he attacked were destroyed during his initial assault, but a few survived. Shemhazai shot those down with more thrown spears. Azazel didn't even bother watching him finish off the survivors as he flew higher, higher, and higher still, until he reached a point where he could see almost all of Antarctica.

Looking at the progression of the battle, Azazel saw that things were well in hand.

Baraqiel, a bow of light in his hands, fired off numerous golden arrows that crackled with power. He shot so many that his hands were a blur. Arrows flew from his bow like machine gun fire, striking dozens of demons at a time, causing the foul beasts to burst into holy flames that burned their insides and ignited their fat.

Alongside him was Araqiel. The man flew through the hailstorm of arrows with a sword and buckler in hand. He sliced off heads, arms, legs, and anything his sword touched was instantly burned. Demons squealed in pain as he slew them like a man possessed. However, those squeals were quickly cut off when he killed them.

Several yards from where Baraqiel and Araqiel were fighting, Ezekiel and Gadreel battled back to back against a horde of demons. He could barely see them through the wall of red flesh closing around them. Had they been lesser angels, it would have looked like they needed help, but then, just as the demons fully closed ranks, several lines of light appeared from within. They were small incisions that ran along the demons' bodies. Not even a split second after the light appeared, the demons were felled, their bodies falling apart at the seams before they disappeared into ashes.

"It looks like we've already taken care of most of the flying demons," Shemhazai said as he, too, observed the battle.

"Yeah, but there weren't that many of them. Belphegor doesn't have a lot of flyers in his army." Azazel looked toward ground, where a demonic army like something out of a biblical reference amassed. "The real battle begins now."

Spreading his arms wide, Azazel created two dozen spears of light even more massive than the previous ones, and then, in the span of a single breath, he sent them toward the ground and began decimating the demonic ranks.

***

After everyone was equipped, the nearly 200 strong force, divided into 14 groups of 15 individuals, stood ready near the underground entrance to Seventh Heaven. It was a lot like a parking garage. The space was open and large, easily capable of fitting upwards of a thousand cars inside. There even were a few vehicles, though none of them would serve any purpose here. They were snow vehicles, slow, lumbering, and big. Driving in them would make them an easy target.

Everyone had been given a set of communicators. According to the fallen angel who handed them out, these would allow them to keep in contact with the Grigori's intelligence network, who would be providing them constant, up-to-date information.

Christian and Lilith stood with their group near the gates. Hannah leaned against the wall, her arms crossed. She looked almost calm. Only the minute tapping of her left foot let people know otherwise. Alex, Gregory, and Laine stood next to her. None of them were talking. He could tell from the way they stood, with their limbs akimbo and awkward, that they were all nervous.

They must be rookies.

Rookies always had certain habits they did when they were nervous; tapping their feet or fingers, looking around, appearing anxious to get started, smack talking. It was easy to tell who had never been in battle before by how they acted while waiting for the mission to start.

Lilith was a great example. She shifted from one foot to another, trying to casually observe the others while she fingered her pistol. That reaction was nothing like the Valkyries and fallen angels, who remained calm as they quietly spoke to each other.

"Waiting is always the worst part of missions like this," Christian.

"E-excuse me?" Lilith looked at him.

He smiled and gestured toward the door. "You've been in dangerous situations a lot of times, but most of those times, you and I were too busy running to feel any kind of tension. Everything happened to fast. Missions like this, which involve waiting until it's time to start our mission, are some of the worst. When you're left with nothing but your thoughts, you begin to think about all the things that could go wrong. Then when the time finally comes for the mission to begin, you hesitate, which could cost you your life."

Christian had been in a number of situations like this. In fact, his greatest example was the battle with Abaddon. On the trip there, the Executioners had all been left to their own thoughts, sitting in the back seat of a giant military vehicle, just waiting to arrive so they could begin the battle. He still remembered how some people had talked up how they would give Abaddon an "asskicking," while others had cleaned their guns for the umpteenth time. Christian had used that time to pray.

He still recalled how nervous he'd been, how his heart had pounded in his chest, how he'd worried about whether or not he'd perform well. Worries had filled his mind and doubt entered his heart. Perhaps if he'd not let his anxiety get so bad back then, he would have been able to save his comrades.

Cupping Lilith's cheeks, he caressed her smooth face. "It's okay to worry, but try not to let that worry consume you, all right? Letting your anxiety overwhelm you is like admitting defeat before the battle even begins."

Christian had spoken loud enough for everyone else to hear him as well, not just Lilith, though his words had been primarily meant for her. He couldn't see how the others responded to his words. He only had eyes for the woman in front of him. She looked at him with her big, blue eyes that reminded him of gemstones scintillating as light reflected off their glittering surfaces. Then she smiled.

"Mm. You're right, Christian. I'm worried, but you're here with me. I'm sure things will work out."

"Right. There's nothing we can't do together."

"Yes!"

Christian and Lilith slowly leaned down, their eyes slowly fluttering closed. They were mere inches away from a kiss.

"You two really are an adorable couple," a voice interrupted them.

They jerked their heads apart like their faces had a polarizing effect. Blushes spread across their cheeks as they realized that, in their desire for an intimate physical connection, they had completely forgotten where they were.

The person who had spoken was one of the two male fallen angels in the group of five. Silvery blond hair reflected the light from lamps overhead, making it look like he was surrounded by a halo. They contrasted with his two black wings. He wore the same bondage-like armor as every other fallen angel, which Christian still didn't really understand. What kind of protection was that going to offer them?

"Don't tease them, Kel," one of the woman said. She had hair the same color as her wings, so black they reminded him of raven feathers. Like most fallen angels, she had a body that could invoke sin, not in the least bit hidden by her S&M cosplay. He wondered if these fallen angels even had a sense of shame.

"I'm not teasing them." Kel shrugged. "I'm just being honest."

"He does have a point." This girl looked young. With a shorter frame and thinner figure, he would have put her at around 14 years old, though he knew better than to judge a fallen angel by her appearance. "Forgive my saying so, but you two do look awfully cute. It's adorable how you completely forget where you are the moment you start staring into each other's eyes."

The other male fallen angel was a quiet man named Paledius. He didn't talk much. In fact, he hadn't said more than two or three sentences since they were introduced.

His hair wasn't long like Kel's, being just of a few inches short of a buzz cut. He had olive-colored skin and more middle-eastern features than the others. His appearance seemed out of place among the mostly porcelain-skinned angels. That being said, Christian didn't really think angels were of any particular nationality. They were angels, not humans.

The last two remaining angels were twins. They wore the same S&M type armor as the others, but because their figures were a bit... better proportioned than the other female angel, their bodies were barely constrained by the outfit. Their breasts, which were even larger than Lilith's, practically spilled from between the straps keeping them in place, and their thighs, which held a misleading softness, were squished into their thigh-high heeled boots.

"I know, right?" Natashia said with a grin as she gestured to the other succubi. "We all think so too."

The two of them looked at each other. Christian imagined his face was the same color red that Lilith's was, though he was unwilling to admit it. He coughed into his hand, prepared to tell everyone that now wasn't the time for jokes, but just before he could say something, the massive steel doors blocking the exit creaked and slowly started to open.

"It looks like it's time." Mastering his features into a blank mask, Christian looked at the people in his squadron. "Are all of you ready?"

He received verbal confirmation from the succubi, the fallen angels all produced light spears to display their readiness, and the Executioners, after some hesitation, nodded.

"I'm ready as well," Lilith said, patting both her gun and the whip at her side.

"Good." Christian took a deep breath before giving his order. "Then let's move out."

Chapter 13

The snowy winds hit Christian's face as they emerged from the underground exit. A chill immediately seeped into his bones despite the unitard he wore having a thermal layer that regulated his body temperature underneath. He was able to shake it off, though it was far colder than anywhere he'd ever been to before. Beside him, Lilith and the others were shivering.

"Come on," Christian said, directing his group to head off toward their destination.

Off in the distance, explosions echoed like thunder, and when he turned to look, he saw large spears of light plow into the ground and detonate with concussive force. The Grigori leaders had begun their battle against the demon army. It was happening barely a few dozen yards from where they were standing. More explosions struck the ground in the opposite direction. A glance skyward revealed Baraqiel and another angel firing exploding light arrows into a horde of demons.

"This looks dangerous!" Natashia had to shout to be overheard. "If we don't get out of here soon, we're gonna get caught up in that!"

"Let's move!" Christian commanded.

"My squad!" Samantha shouted. "Follow me!"

As he looked around, Christian saw the other squadrons all moving off in separate directions. Each one had been assigned a different base to travel to. Samantha's squad headed north. He spotted her racing across the white terrain, avoiding the explosions from stray attacks that struck the ground too close for comfort. Leon, Sif, Clarissa, Heather, and the other group leaders were also leading their squadrons off in different directions.

Christian stopped paying attention to what the others were doing. He took off in the direction of the base his group had been assigned to scout, the others following close behind him.

Given the freezing atmosphere, it was not surprising that the members of his squadron were breathing heavily as they ran. Natashia, Taryn, and Valerie were running alongside him and Lilith, their breathing coming out in heavy puffs. He could hear the footsteps of the Executioners behind him. The sound of feet crunching against the snow was mixed with their ragged gasps.

This would be a good place to train.

The terrain of Antarctica was rugged. Snow coated the ground in a thick sheet that caused their feet to sink, making it harder to run. Several times one or more of them tripped. Furthermore, the ground was unstable, and several sections of the snow was deeper than others. If they weren't careful, they'd fall flat on their faces.

Numerous mountains surrounded them, covered in snow, with only a bit of the black rock underneath peeking out. It kept them from being able to see too far in any one direction. As they came up on one of those mountains, the group was forced to change their course and travel around it.

"Hey, hey, hey!" a voice suddenly blasted in his ear. *"Can you hear me, Christian and company? It is I, your favorite intelligence agent! The great, the magnanimous, the—"*

"Who the heck put you in charge of communications!" Christian snapped at Tristin, a voice he could easily recognize.

"That's mean! Obviously, they put me in charge because I'm your best friend!"

"You're friends with this guy?" asked Natashia with a disgusted look on her face.

"It's complicated," Christian muttered.

"Was there something you needed to speak to us about?" asked Lilith.

"Yes! There is! I've been assigned to provide you constant intelligence on the location of the demon army's forces. Speaking of, there is a large squad of demons in the direction you're heading."

If their bones hadn't already been chilled by the cold, that would have frozen them solid.

"Is there another direction we can go?" asked Christian.

"Well, there is, but there are even more demons in those directions. I think your best option is to plow straight through them. If you can defeat this group quickly, you should be able to slip past their primary army. There are only a smattering of demons further out."

"I see. Thanks for the info. Keep us posted."

"Will do. Good luck~!"

Christian scowled as Tristin sang that last bit out, but he put the man out of his mind, called for everyone to stop, and turned to the group of fallen angels. He hadn't seen any of them in combat. However, fallen angels were said to have all the powers and abilities of regular angels. They might have fallen from grace because of their decision to remain on Earth, but they were still God's creations.

"How good are your long-range offensive capabilities?"

The five fallen angels glanced at each other, uncertainty clear on their faces. They turned back to him.

"Kel is the only one who is any good at long-range offense," the young-looking girl, whose name was Phoebe, said.

Christian nodded and began giving his orders. "In that case, I want you and Taryn to team up and lay down suppressive fire against the demons the moment we round the mountain. Keep them pinned while the rest of us close the distance, and then join us quickly."

"Got it," Kel said with a nod.

"Heh. I wonder if a fallen angel's power can match up to my baby here." Taryn grinned as she lovingly stroked the Browning M2.

"Lilith." He turned to his mate. "If you can, please try to cast an area wide illusion that makes us invisible to the enemy. If that's too much, then cast an illusion on one or two of the demons to make them look like us."

"I can do the first one easily," Lilith said with a smile.

Christian nodded. "Natashia and Valerie, you two will be protecting Lilith while she's casting illusions. I'd normally be the one providing protection, but I'll be leading the charge with these four." He gestured toward the Executioners, who looked a bit put out at knowing they'd be with him, and then the other four fallen angels.

"Sure thing," Valerie said with a nod.

Natashia thumped her chest. "Leave this to us."

"Right." Christian took a deep breath and centered himself. "Let's do this!"

On the count of three, Christian, Alex, Gregory, Hannah, and Laine rushed out from around the mountain. Following close behind them, their wings flapping, were the four fallen angels. He couldn't see them. However, Christian could hear them over the howling winds.

The demons were up ahead.

They were not your regular, run of the mill demons. Their bodies were covered in a thick layer of bristling black fur tinged with red. Four strong legs crashed against the snow-covered ground, kicking up a layer of powder, while their four arms carried an assortment of weapons—bows, swords, spears. Faces reminiscent of a goat's sat on a thick neck with a long mane traveling down their backs. Their upper bodies looked almost human if one discounted their four arms. Meanwhile, their lower bodies were like a bull's.

Christian had never seen anything like these monsters, which he judged were mid-level demons. His Eye of Belial showed their powers as a dense bluish-black energy. It was far more potent than many of the demons he had faced during his time as an Executioner.

A quick count revealed there were about two dozen. This was going to be cutting it close.

They hadn't noticed his group yet, showing him that Lilith had already woven her illusion over the group of demons. She must have gone a step further, too, because several of the beasts screeched at each other and began fighting amongst themselves. They clashed with sword and shield and mace and spear and bows. Two of their own kind were quickly felled before their group even reached the demons.

Lilith must have cast both illusions I asked for... she's really going above and beyond.

He'd have to do something for her when they got home.

At that moment, the roar of a machine gun opened up and several hundred bullets struck the remaining demons. Some of the bullets glanced off their fur. However, the rest tore through their bodies, blood splattering against the snowy ground.

As if not to be outdone, arrows of light began pouring in from above. One demon went down when its head was pierced. Another died from an arrow through the heart. Several arrows stabbed through arms, shoulders, legs, or the bull-like body, causing the demons to thrash around as the holy energy invaded them from the inside. Nine demons were killed from the long-range bombardment.

There were only twelve left. Much better odds.

Christian and his group crashed into the demons. A whirlwind of blood sprang from a large gash in one of the demon's sides as Christian swung Rafael into it. He felt some resistance, but he muscled through, tearing the beasts hide wide open and causing its entrails to spill onto the ground. The creature screeched in pain as it went down and thrashed about. It would die soon, so Christian moved on.

He sensed movement behind him. Turning around, he found one of the demons barreling toward him. It was holding four scimitars with its massive hands.

Christian shifted into a loose stance, waited for the beast to close the distance, and then acted.

He danced around the thrust aimed at his chest. Bringing up Michael, he knocked the weapon aside, and then he swung Rafael up, intercepting another scimitar. His arm shook as his orichalcum blade squealed against the black weapon, sparks igniting along the two sharp edges. Christian ignored the slight pain as he rotated his wrist, flicking the scimitar over his head.

The demon was knocked off balance by his actions, but despite this, it continued moving forward as if to mow him down. Christian slid between the creature's legs and swung both blades out to his sides. The first pair of legs were removed quickly and easily, his swords slicing through them like butter. The second pair weren't so easy. He didn't have enough time to get a good swing in.

His swords got stuck in the demon's bones. That didn't bother him. He swung his body as the beast, unable to remain upright with its front legs missing, fell to the ground. As he flew through the air, his swords pulling free, he flicked the blood off, sheathed them, and unsheathed Gabriel and Phanul. Still in the air, he swung his arms to rotate his body, aiming for two demons who had cornered Laine and Gregory. He took quick aim, then fired.

His first four bullets penetrated the demons in the eyes. His next four bullets knocked their weapons out of their hands. Laine and Gregory used that opportunity to down their opponents. Laine pierced one through the chest with his spear, while Gregory opened the other demon's underbelly. As the snow was dyed an even deeper shade of crimson, the two glanced at him in shock, but Christian had already landed on the ground and was attacking his next foe.

All around him, his group was fighting against the demons, who had been confused at first thanks to Lilith's illusions, but were now regaining their bearings.

Out of the corner of his eyes, he spotted Natashia and Valerie attacking one of the demons. They weren't strong enough to just slice through the demon. However, they utilized teamwork to inflict hundreds of small wounds that quickly added up. It wasn't long before the beast was covered in hundreds of tiny cuts that slowed down its reactions. Once it began moving about more sluggishly, Valerie hopped onto its bull-like body and stabbed it through the back. The beast let out a gurgle as it plummeted to the ground.

For a moment, Christian wondered where Lilith was, but then he realized she was right behind the two, keeping a pair of demons busy. It looked like they were fighting against invisible opponents. Lilith used their distracted state to wrap her whip around one of the demon's legs, and then she yanked.

In most circumstances, Lilith would not have enough physical strength to yank this creature's legs out from under it. That said, the snow covering the ground had far more yield and was much more slippery than grass or dirt. The demon's leg was pulled to the side, and the demon went down with a loud crash.

Christian rushed over to the fallen demon. He leapt into the air, spinning around like a top, and sliced the monster's head clean off. As the head slid off its neck and hit the ground, he landed on his feet and raced toward the one still fighting an invisible enemy. It didn't even notice when he slid underneath it and sliced the beast's underbelly open from left to right. The demon shrieked as its stomach opened and stained the snow in blood and innards

Coming back up, Christian ignored the dying demon and rushed toward Lilith.

"Are you okay?" he asked, checking her for wounds.

Lilith was breathing heavily, but she gave him a smile. "I'm fine…"

He nodded after not finding any injuries, and then looked at the others.

The battle was mostly concluded. Even as he watched, the four fallen angels, Phoebe, Pelagius, Graf, and Ignatius were slaying the last two demons with their light swords and spears. He turned his head. Natashia and Valerie were also finished with their battles, as were Laine, Gregory, Alex, and Hannah. Kel and Taryn were also running toward them.

No one seems to have suffered any serious injuries. I'm pretty surprised.

Granted, they had surprise on their side, but he had honestly expected some of them to at least have been injured during that assault. He supposed it just meant he had underestimated the strength of his comrades, or maybe he had overestimated the strength of his enemies. It probably didn't matter.

"Is everyone okay?" he called out. "Is there anyone here who doesn't think they can keep going?"

No one in the group seemed ready to quit, so the group quickly moved off. Tristin's voice came again. He helped them avoid more demons by informing them of any groups located nearby whilst simultaneously telling them what routes they could take to avoid them.

The battle between the demon army and the Grigori leaders appeared to have picked up. Even now, Christian could see members of the Council of Twenty flitting through the air, attacking the demons on the ground with large spears of light that destroyed huge chunks of ice and land. Entire hordes were wiped out in an instant. It just went to show him how much more powerful the fallen angel leaders were compared to the others.

It's no wonder they were able to defeat three of the Demon Kings.

Of course, the reason they could fight the Demon Kings was because their enemies could barely bring a tenth of their power to bear. If they managed to destroy the barrier separating Earth from Hell... well, Christian didn't think even Kokabiel would survive an encounter with one of the Demon Kings at their full power.

The group continued on, and they eventually found the base they were supposed to investigate. A series of buildings spread across a large hill that was surprisingly free of snow, revealing brown gravel. Most of the buildings held a general rectangular shape. They were about two-stories tall, and they were being elevated above the ground by support beams. Christian counted three buildings. One that was a combination of grayish-green and red, a brown structure with blue roofing, and a warehouse that was all silver. There was also a spherical object a little way off. It looked like an observatory.

Naturally, the base was not empty. There were even more demons. Most of them were walking about as though patrolling the perimeter. A good few of them were those bull-like creatures, but there were also strange eyeballs walking around on tentacles that jutted from their bodies like legs. He guessed they were like snipers. Knowing what he did about demons, he wouldn't be surprised if they shot beams or something from their eyes.

Aside from the bull demons and the eyeballs, there were also a number of flying demons. Black pinions spread from their back, leathery like those of a dragon's, and their shoulders, knees, and elbows had spikes jutting from them. Ashen gray skin covered every part of their muscular bodies. They reminded him of gargoyles, but their shape was more human. Looking at them through his Eye of Belial showed him that the amount of power they possessed was weaker than the bull demons but stronger than the eyeballs.

Since they were completely outnumbered and couldn't afford to be seen, the group hid behind a large boulder emerging from the ground.

"What's the plan?" asked Gregory as they crouched low to avoid being seen.

Laine looked at him with a frown. "Don't tell me you're willing to follow this thing's orders now just because he saved you?"

"Don't look at me like that." Gregory scowled. "We're in the middle of a mission. I may not like it, but if we don't work together, I doubt we'll survive."

Laine scowled as if Gregory had said something stupid, but the other two Executioners, Alex and Hannah, appeared to be more in line with his way of thinking. Laine was outnumbered.

"It looks like this place is heavily fortified," Natashia muttered as she peeked out from around the boulder. She quickly ducked her head back down, placed a hand against her chest, and sighed. "I'm not sure how we're gonna be able to get close without being spotted. Maybe we should just rush in?"

"That's a bad idea," Phoebe said.

"Why is that?" asked Taryn.

"Those eyeball demons are long-range attackers," Kel answered for her. "They shoot condensed beams of demonic energy from their eyes."

"How powerful are their attacks?" asked Christian.

Kel tilted his head. "I don't know. I've never seen one in action. I just know about them because the fallen angel's study up on demonology in case events like this happen. That said, I've been told that they could easily slice through a boulder like this one with no problem."

"So, if they find out we're here, we're as good as dead," Valerie sighed. "That's just great."

"Should I use one of my illusions?" asked Lilith, looking at Christian for confirmation, but it wasn't Christian who answered her.

"No," Graf said. "Those eyes have the ability to see through and dispel illusions as well."

"Oh…"

Lilith's shoulders slumped as her plan was summarily rejected. Christian said nothing as he thought about what they should do. A frontal assault was obviously out of the question, which meant they would have to be sneaky.

He drew a map of the base on the snow, making sure to include the differences in elevation. Cupping his chin, he studied the map, and then placed small dots in specific areas to mark where the demons had last been.

"It looks like most of the demons are on our side," Christian muttered. "There aren't that many on the other. I guess they're expecting us to come from this direction because Seventh Heaven is inland."

"Should we move around to the opposite side and attack from behind?" asked Valerie.

"Not all of us." Christian looked up from the map to eye his current squadron. "I want Taryn, Kel, Valerie, and Alex to head around the base and get behind them. Once you're in place, the rest of us will attack from the front as a distraction. While they're distracted, I want you, Kel, to destroy those eyes as quickly as you can. Taryn, your job will be to dispatch as many of those flying demons as possible. Valerie and Alex will protect you both in the event some demons decide to split off and attack you."

"Got it," Taryn said as she thumped her chest. "Just leave this to us!"

"I'll do my best not to disappoint you." Kel nodded at Christian.

"Lilith, you, Paledius, and Phoebe will hang back until the eyes have been destroyed. Once that happens, I want you to begin casting illusions. I don't care what they are, just so long as they distract the enemy."

"I can do that." Lilith nodded. "I won't let you down."

Christian smiled. "I know you won't."

Natashia coughed into her hand. "Why don't you two stop making googly-eyes at each other, so we can get this party started, yeah?"

Glad the air was so cold no one could tell whether his face was red from the frigid atmosphere or his embarrassment, Christian tried his best to master his emotions.

"You're right. Let's hurry up and get this plan started. The sooner we can find the medium used to summon all these demons, the better."

Taryn, Kel, Valerie, and Alex split off from the main group. They would have to backtrack and take the long way around to avoid being seen by those eyes. There was a hill just beyond the first building, which meant they would have to stop at the hill, and then climb up it after Christian and his group had distracted the demons.

"Sounds like you guys have your plans all set," Tristin chimed in.

Christian sighed. "Was there something you wanted?"

"I wanted to let you know that most of the other groups have also reached their assigned bases."

"Most of? I'm assuming some didn't?"

"We lost two squadrons."

Lost, meaning they were dead. Christian closed his eyes.

"Which squadrons?"

"The groups led by Ningdaria and Clarissa."

Lilith gasped. He glanced at his mate to see her already pale cheeks become nearly translucent. She wasn't the only one. Natashia's eyes were shaking, pupils dilated, as she stared at him.

Biting his lip, he wondered if he should say anything to reassure them, or maybe tell them they would check on Clarissa and her squad after this, but he didn't. He couldn't. There was no telling what would happen right now, so making her an empty promise wouldn't do any good.

"We're in position," Kel's subdued voice came in through their comm units.

"Good." Christian stood up. "Then we'll begin our assault."

There was no time for him to worry about another squadron when he and his companions were about to fight an uphill battle. Hesitation led to death on the battlefield. They couldn't afford to let their fear make them hesitate at such a critical juncture.

"Is everyone ready?" He looked back at his squadron. They were all standing, weapons at the ready. No one spoke, but they did nod to signal their readiness. "Then let's go in three, two, one."

The moment the word "one" left his lips, Christian spun around and darted out from around the boulder. Pounding feet let him know the others were following.

The eyeballs were the first ones to spot them. They swiveled around and took aim. The area around their pupils became distorted like the kind of heat wave distortions someone might see in desert states like Arizona, but then dark crimson energy crackled around the pupils and formed a small sphere.

"Everyone dodge!" Christian shouted his warning.

The eyeballs, all six of them, released beams of bright energy at the incoming group. Christian didn't stop moving forward as he ducked into a slide. The beam passed overhead, its heat almost overwhelming. He only saw a quick glance of what it could do, but a glance was all he needed. It continued on, slicing into a boulder—not the one Lilith was behind—and cleaved straight through it.

Better not get hit by that.

A scream alerted him to the fact that not everyone had escaped unscathed. Laine's horrified and agonizing screams echoed all around them as a beam sheared straight through his arm, causing the arm to drop to the ground with a dull thud. Stumbling forward, Laine landed on his face, which ultimately saved his life as another beam tore through the spot he'd been standing.

Fortunately for Laine, Phoebe was able to fly in from the air, lift him by the waist, and fly off to safety. Unfortunately, one of the eyeballs targeted her. The beam that was fired sliced straight through her left wing, cutting the pinion off. She fell to the ground and disappeared behind a large boulder.

Laine wasn't the only one who suffered. Hannah was pierced straight through the head. She stumbled forward, rag-dolled across the ground, and stopped. There would be no getting up from that.

Christian didn't allow himself to let what happened distract him. He charged straight into the enemy lines and darted around to present a hard to hit target. His primary focus was on making himself the biggest, most noticeable target possible. If all the demons focused their attention on him, it would give the others a chance to strike.

Beams came in from multiple directions, but Christian had grown quite apt at dodging attacks like this. It helped that the beams were very slow, and it was easy to see when they were being fired. There was an incredible buildup of energy before an eyeball could fire one. That made it easy for him to figure out when he was going to be attacked.

The Eye of Belial also helped. To his chagrin, it remained active while he was fighting, providing him with a 360-degree view of the battlefield. It was a little disorienting. His vision felt like he was looking at everything in a panoramic view, which made it a bit difficult to determine which direction he was looking at. Despite this, Christian used the Eye of Belial to the best of his ability, avoiding attacks from behind and in front equally.

By this point in time, the other members of his group were also engaged in combat. He could see them doing their best to fight against the bull demons. Graf was darting through the sky overhead, throwing spears of light down at their opponents, but he also had the gargoyle-like demons to tangle with. He dodged them to the best of his ability. Even so, it was clear that if Kel and Taryn didn't come through soon, the fallen angel was gonna get ripped to shreds.

Fortunately, the other two fallen angels used the demons' distracted states to tear into them from behind. One had created a sword and buckler shield from her light energy, while the other was using a chakram, of all weapons. The swordswoman sliced through the back of the gargoyle-like demons' necks, while the one using the light chakram tossed her weapon into the back of one, then created another chakram and threw that too.

Gregory was also fighting alone. With Laine gone, half of his fighting strength had been depleted. He could no longer rely on the other Executioner for backup. Despite this, he fought as fiercely as he could, screaming out a battle cry that echoed around the base. However, as he tried to fend off two of the bull demons, one managed to grab his spear and snap it in half. Now weaponless, Gregory could do nothing as the other bull demon grabbed his arm.

Thinking fast, Christian pulled Phanul from his holster, took aim, and fired. His bullet pierced the demon's eye. The bull demon released Gregory, pressing a hand to the blood now gushing out of its destroyed eye. Christian fired two more shots. The first bullet struck the Achilles heel of the other bull demon's left hind leg. The creature squealed as it went down. His second shot struck the back of the creature's head, going straight through. The bull demon swayed for a moment before collapsing on the ground.

Christian couldn't help Gregory anymore. The eyeballs were all targeting him, and he was doing everything possible to avoid their attacks. Several beams were far too close for comfort. He could feel the heat singing his skin. They missed by only a foot or two, but even that could prove dangerous. It seemed the closer one got, the hotter the attacks became. He could get damaged from heat alone.

Just as the situation was beginning to look hopeless, one of the eyeballs suddenly exploded. A loud roar split the air. More eyeballs burst like overripe fruit, their innards spraying across the ground. One. Two. Three. All six eyeball demons were destroyed by the boisterous gunfire of Taryn and her Browning M2.

Like how Christian was saved by Taryn, Graf was also saved when Kel fired off numerous light arrows. His aim was impeccable. Each arrow struck a demon somewhere—the back, the head, the wings. The gargoyle-like monsters went down with screeches of rage and pain.

As they fell, Graf used their agonized states to finish them off with swift thrusts to the chest and neck.

Very soon, only the bull demons were left. However, there were about 12 to fight against, and Christian and his group had lost some of their manpower.

That was when six of the 12 the bull demons began thrashing around. Christian didn't understand what was happening at first, but then Paledius and Lilith raced out from behind the boulder. After another second, Phoebe, now with only one wing, also ran into view. He didn't see Laine, but he hoped the man wasn't dead.

Leaving the six thrashing bull demons to the others, Christian raced toward the nearest one that hadn't been affected by whatever illusion Lilith had cast. It gripped two massive claymores, which it swung the moment he came into view, though Christian danced around the attacks.

These demons were powerful. The claymore split the ground when it struck. Even more impressive, it swung them at him just as quickly from with an upward attack that would have bisected him had he not ducked.

Firing Gabriel and Phanul, Christian unloaded several bullets into the monster's hands. His guns clicked empty. The beast roared as it dropped the claymores. Holstering his guns, he unsheathed Michael and Rafael, spinning around as he cut the demon's two front legs off. As it fell forward, Christian danced left, swinging Michael in a wide arc that relieved the demon of its head.

He looked around. The six bull demons that Lilith trapped in an illusion were dead, impaled through the chest, burnt from light attacks, or decapitated. Valerie and Natashia were working together to deal with one of the other bull demons, Graf and a one-winged Phoebe were in the process of killing a third, and Alex and Gregory had taken out a fourth. There were only two left, but even as he took that in, one of them died so suddenly he had to blink.

What the—

He couldn't rightly figure out what happened. The bull demon had been charging at Lilith, but then several holes had suddenly opened in its chest. There had been no discharge from a gun, and he didn't think anyone on his squadron had a gun that powerful anyway. The demon quickly tripped over its own legs, struck the ground, and tumbled before rolling to a stop. At the same time, the last demon was felled by the combine fire of Kel and Taryn.

The battle was over.

Everyone quickly gathered around him, and Christian took a quick observation. Laine wasn't there, but Alex and Gregory were. Natashia, Taryn, and Valerie had also survived, though Natashia was bleeding from a large gash on her forehead and Valerie's left arm was dangling limply by her side. It looked broken. None of the fallen angels had died, and only Graf and Phoebe seemed injured.

"Laine?" asked Christian. Phoebe shook her head. "I see. Let's keep going."

Alex and Gregory looked like they wanted to say something, but they held it back. They were undoubtedly not happy with Laine's and Hannah's deaths. However, they were Executioners. They knew as well as he that nothing could be done for the dead, and right now they were on a mission.

They split up into three groups. Christian, Lilith, Valerie, and Phoebe made up one group. They went into the largest building present. If the summoning circle and its medium were at this base, they assumed it would be in this building.

When they entered, a massive stench hit them hard, causing Lilith, Valerie, and Phoebe to nearly lose their lunch. Christian didn't, but that was only because he'd grown used to the decaying scent of dead bodies.

Corpses littered much of the interior. Bodies were strewn across tables, and some of those bodies weren't in what he would have called the best of shape. Many of them looked like they had been torn apart. As their feet thudded against the floor, he glanced at the headless corpse of a woman dressed in snow gear, a thick jacket, and pants, which were drenched with blood.

"This is terrible," Valerie muttered with a hand clasped to her mouth.

"I have never seen anything like this in all my centuries." Phoebe wasn't looking much better.

Christian glanced at Lilith. While her face was stoic, her eyes betrayed how affected she was by this. He reached out and grabbed her hand. She didn't say anything, and she didn't smile, but she did squeeze back.

This base had six rooms, four on bottom and two on top. Most of them looked like they were designed to hold experiments. Many of them featured advanced computer systems and various pieces of equipment that Christian knew nothing about. From the data scrolling across some of the computers, it looked like they were digging into the ice. That said, it wasn't like he could read it well. Christian wasn't well-versed in Chinese.

After checking both floors and finding nothing, the group went back outside, where the others were waiting.

"Did you find anything?" Christian asked.

Kel shook his head. "No. Outside of the bodies of several scientists, we found nothing."

"We didn't either," said Gregory.

"Damn it." Christian bit his lip. "It looks like this wasn't the one with the summoning circle."

"I feel like Laine and Hannah's deaths were in vain," Alex muttered.

"What should we do?" asked Valerie.

Christian placed a hand against his ear. "Tristin, has there been any word on one of the other squads finding the summoning circle?"

"Negative. All of the squads that made it to their bases have confirmed that the summoning circle isn't at their location."

"Which means it's probably at either the base Clarissa was going to, or the one that Ningdaria was going to."

"That's my guess."

"Which one is closer to us?"

"Clarissa's."

Christian shut off his communicator and turned to face the others. "You heard the man. It looks like the summoning circle is at one of those two bases. We could head back to Seventh Heaven, but given that the summoning circle has not dispelled, there are bound to still be a lot of demons attacking. Lilith and I are going to be heading to Clarissa's last known location. You can choose to come with us or head back."

"Of course we're going," Natashia said for not only herself, but also Taryn and Valerie, who nodded. "Clarissa is our leader. We can't just head back to safety knowing she might be in trouble. Besides, it's like you said: We're more likely to get killed on the way to Seventh Heaven than we are heading to this base."

"I don't know how much use I'll be with only one wing," Phoebe began, looking forlornly at her only remaining wing. She sighed and shook her head. "But I'm going to travel with you two."

"As will I," Kel added. Paledius nodded, while Graf and the two female twin fallen angels gave their own verbal agreement to follow him.

"Going back by ourselves will make us seem weak," Gregory muttered. "We'll go as well. We can't let Laine and Hannah's deaths be in vain."

"Okay then." Christian glanced at his companions. Beside him, Lilith squeezed his hand in support. "Let's go save Clarissa's squad and locate that other base."

***

Clarissa's squad was made up of two other succubus, six fallen angels, and six members of the Executioners.

The two succubus, Samantha and Delia, were an inseparable pair who couldn't have been more different if they tried. Samantha's golden hair and blue eyes contrasted with Delia's black hair and brown eyes. They also acted vastly different, with Samantha's less outgoing and shy personality creating a juxtaposition to Delia's party-girl attitude.

While their appearance and personality differed in many ways, the beauty inherent in all succubus was the same. Both were charming women who were possessors of an unnatural beauty that caused heads to turn. Their womanly figures were revealed in all their splendor as the clothing they wore fit snugly across their bodies, revealing their feminine curves and body lines.

Three of the Executioners were men. While the six fallen angels were also men, they were able to resist whatever temptations might lay in their hearts, but the human men were a different story. Even though they were suppressing their Aura of Allure, she, Samantha, and Delia had been subjected to their stares before the mission had even started.

"Look at how the men stare at them. Disgusting."

"Hmph. It's only possible to have a body like that because they aren't human."

"Scarlet women. Every last one of them."

The three female Executioners were not pleased by the men's inability not to look, but instead of putting the blame where it belonged, they blamed it on Clarissa, Samantha, and Delia for being too beautiful. This was also natural. Women who felt threatened by other women would often blame the woman they were threatened by. *"If only you weren't so beautiful, then my husband would have never left me!"* they would say, never placing the blame where it belonged—on the men who couldn't remain faithful.

It disgusted Clarissa.

"If you ladies have a complaint, then you can say it to me in person," she told the women, her voice cold and her eyes colder still.

She had been alive for many centuries now, and she'd perfected the bone-chilling stare that caused hearts to freeze. "If you do not have a complaint, then keep your mouths shut. The lives of everyone here is in our hands. We do not have time for petty squabbles."

That shut the three women up.

Clarissa didn't think it was a good idea to have their teams mixed like this. None of these people had any experience working together. It would have been better if they'd been put into teams where everyone was already familiar with everyone else.

However, she also knew that was impractical. Putting a group of humans together and telling them to fight an army of demons was insane—no, it was suicidal. Humans were ill-equipped to deal with a force this large. Likewise, succubus were not much better off. Even if they could increase their strength while in their succubus form, it only lasted for a few minutes. Among the races currently present, only the fallen angels had the power to truly deal massive amounts of damage. Mixing their forces was the only viable method right now.

The six fallen angels were all men, and each one of them was actually quite pretty. There was the black-haired Liem who looked kind of like a goth, the blond Haciel with his longer than normal locks, Oliphus and his large muscles, Mazkiel, who had a tall and willowy figure, Prekeil, whose slicked back hair made him look like an exceedingly handsome entrepreneur, and Joseph, a shorter than average angel who looked like a little boy. Of course, Clarissa would never underestimate someone just because they had a childlike appearance. She was, after all, a succubus who had lived for many centuries.

Once the mission began, she and her group raced across the white plains with as much haste as they could muster. Thanks to the intelligence agent talking through their communication devices, they were able to avoid the worst of the fighting, though that did not mean they avoided battle entirely.

"Don't let yourselves fight alone! Fight together as a group!"

The chaotic throng of battle filled the air as Clarissa tried her best to work alongside Samantha, Mazkiel, Prekeil, and Justina (one of the female Executioners) to bring down one of the large demons that were attacking them. There were three of them. Massive frames towered over the group like Goliath over David. Each giant had black skin that was cracked and blistering, covered in boils and seeping lava-like blood. Their legs were thicker than the trees found in Yellowstone National Park. Each step they took caused the ground to quake. And their faces…

So frightening.

Clarissa had never seen anything like it. Their faces looked like a mashup of thousands of human faces all screaming in torment. Somehow, the human faces were congealed together to form a larger face. It was the most hideous thing she had ever seen.

Mazkiel was their heavy hitter, throwing light spears into the demon's torso. The spears were made of a divine angel's power, so they pierced the creature with ease, causing blood to gush out and stain the ground. However, the blood that struck the white snow hissed and sizzled, not just melting the snow but eating through it like acid.

Clarissa avoided the blood, dancing around the creature as she sliced into its Achilles tendon. However, this beast's hide was something else. Her naginata's blade barely scratched it. Furthermore, the creature turned around and tried to swat at her, though she deftly avoided its attacks by leaping into a series of back handsprings.

While she provided this distraction, Justina raced in and stabbed the monster in the foot, and perhaps because her sword was made of orichalcum, it sliced through the demon's big toe. As the beast roared, Justina tried to leap back. She wasn't fast enough. The beast swat at her before she could move away, and it was only thanks to Prekeil swooping down and slicing the demon's hand off that she avoided a terrible fate.

"Are you alright?" asked the fallen angel as he landed on the ground. The hand he'd sliced off hit the ground next to him with a heavy, wet thud, and then it began hissing.

"Y-yes." Justina placed a hand against her chest and took several panting breaths. "T-thank you."

Prekeil nodded and launched himself back into the air. Clarissa and Samantha had been harassing the creature from down below, keeping it occupied by slowly widening the cuts they made as they darted around its legs like a pair of gnats. This angered the demon, who roared in frustration and continued trying to swat at them with its only remaining hand. As they distracted it, Prekeil and Mazkiel created a pair of light swords and descended upon the creature. They swung their blades in unison, cutting through its thick neck. Had it just been one of them, there was no way they'd have been able to cut through it on their own. They couldn't create a big enough weapon. However, together, their combine swords sliced through the neck and severed the demon's head.

Clarissa and Samantha leapt out of the way as the head slid off the demon's body, which wobbled to and fro as if not sure which direction it should fall in. Then the body fell forward, tumbling to the ground with a cataclysmic rumble. The two succubus and Justina almost lost their balance themselves.

As the demon was defeated, Clarissa took a quick breather and surveyed the battle. It looked like the others were finishing off their demons as well.

The groups had split up with two fallen angels on each team. It made sense. The fallen angels were the ones who did the most damage.

As the other demons were felled, the groups quickly joined with Clarissa, who frowned when she noticed something off.

"Delia and Markus?" she asked. Markus was one of the male Executioners. She didn't see either him or Delia. A cold chill pierced her heart.

One of the females, whose name Clarissa believed was Francesca, bit her lip and looked away. "Delia is... she pushed me out of the way when that thing tried to squash me and..."

"No..." Samantha whispered in horror. "NO!"

She tried to rush over to where Delia had been battling, but Clarissa grabbed her hand.

"Let go of me! Let go of me!"

"Pull yourself together!" Clarissa snapped. "The ground around the battlefield is covered in demon blood! If you set foot over there, you're going to have your feet melted off!"

"I don't care! Delia! I have to find Delia!"

Clarissa was struggling against her own tears, her own sorrow. She'd known both Delia and Samantha since they were children. They had been personally taught how to control their Aura of Allure by her, so in many ways, they were like her children.

She had lost many children in her lifetime.

Clarissa shocked Samantha into silence by slapping her across the face. Her hand stung, but that was nothing compared to what she felt in her heart.

"Do you think you're the only one who is hurt?! What do you think would happen if you went over there now?! We have to... to keep going... otherwise what happened to Delia will just keep happening!"

Samantha clutched a hand to her cheek as tears welled up in her eyes. "But I... I..."

"I'll try to find Delia," Liem said softly.

He flapped his wings and took to the skies. Clarissa watched him go with a frown. The giant demon Delia had fought was about twelve yards away. Liem hovered above the battlefield and looked around for a moment, then came back over. His face was grave when he set down. He gave Samantha an apologetic look.

"I couldn't find her," he said. "I think she was crushed."

"No…" Samantha lost all strength in her legs and would have gone down had Clarissa not picked her back up.

"Come on," Clarissa muttered. "We must keep going."

She hated doing this, but she urged the group on, half-carrying the somewhat listless Samantha.

They continued on. The intelligence agent guiding them reported when they would run into demons, allowing them to avoid confrontations. As they marched, Samantha regained her strength and resolve enough to walk on her own, though she didn't say anything. The tears streaming down her face froze over in the frigid air. Francesca looked at the woman in pity, and perhaps out of guilt.

Their journey took them through mountainous terrain that made walking hard. Sometimes they would go uphill and other times down. Sections of the ground were not covered in snow, presenting a stark contrast to the otherwise white plains.

It was fortunate that the area they were traveling to was mercifully clear of demons, though this was in part due to the mountains they passed blocking the view. According to their guide, several demons were located on the other side of many of these mountains, and she was merely choosing the path that had none. Of course, the paths with no demons were harder to travel, the terrain being far rockier and more treacherous.

The base they were asked to search was the British Antarctic Survey. It was a highly unusual building, not only in shape but also in formation. Clarissa thought it looked more like several buildings linked together similar to sausage links. Each building was shaped like an elongated octagon on stilts. Most of them were blue, but the one in the very center was red. Located in a wide, flat expanse of land, Clarissa and the others were forced to hunker down several dozen yards away to avoid detection.

Numerous demons roamed the area around it.

"I count at least twelve snipers, six gargoyles, and another twelve bulls," Joseph muttered softly.

They had created names for the demons. Snipers were the eyeball demons that moved around on tentacle-like feelers, gargoyles were the ones with wings that stood on top of the structures like sentinels, and bulls were the strange demons with four arms and bull-like lower bodies.

"We need to take out the snipers first," Clarissa said.

"I'm surprised they haven't already seen us," Melvis, one of the male Executioners, admitted.

"It's because we are covered in snow," Joseph told him. "Those things locate people through body heat."

"I want each person who is skilled at long-range attacks to target one of the snipers," Clarissa ordered as she set her naginata on the ground and removed a rifle from her back. It wasn't a sniper rifle, but it did have a scope that would allow her to aim accurately at this distance.

The fallen angels were all moderately skilled at attacking from range. This was because they could create and throw spears, or fire of bows and arrows. Among the humans, Justina, Derick, Melvis, and Kristen had talent at sniping from a distance, though they were still better at close range combat. Samantha didn't have any shooting skills.

Clarissa and the humans readied their respective weapons and picked out their targets.

"I've got the one on the far left."

"I'll take the right then."

"That one on the second building on the left is mine."

"I can take out the one behind the stilts."

As each one called out which sniper they would hit, Clarissa chose the one on the opposite side of the buildings. She was confident in her ability to hit it.

"Okay. On the count of three, we fire." Clarissa took a deep breath as she stared down the scope of her barrel. The sniper she was targeting came into clear focus. She adjusted her rifle. "Three. Two. One."

All at once, five gunshots rang out. Her own target was blasted backwards as she shot it through the eye. The other four also went down, though one of the attacks was only a glancing blow.

The fallen angels all created either spears or arrows that attacked their targets. Mazkiel unloaded a torrent of arrows that appeared above his head, perforating his target. Joseph launched a spear that went straight through a sniper. Liem threw two swords that spun around and sliced into his enemy. The beam fired from Oliphus' finger penetrated the sniper's eye and caused it to disintegrate. Haciel and Prekeil both targeted two snipers, hitting them with a powerful barrage of spheres that appeared from out of nowhere.

While all of the snipers were downed, their surprise attack alerted the gargoyles and bulls of their presence. The gargoyles screeched and shot into the air with a flap of their wings. Roaring their own battle cry, the bulls stamped their feet and charged at the group hidden in the snow.

"To arms!" Clarissa called.

Everyone stood to their feet and grabbed their melee weapons. Clarissa held her naginata at the ready as she stood beside Samantha, who was holding her sword in a two-handed grip, face set in a mask of rage. She likely wanted to kill these demons as revenge for Delia's death. Clarissa understood, but she also didn't want this woman flying into a mad frenzy. That would only result in her death.

"Stay by my side, Samantha. Let us slaughter these demons together."

"Right."

Two of the bulls were felled before they reached the group by the fallen angels, who had taken to the skies. They were going to engage the gargoyles. Since there were six gargoyles, it meant they were forced to fight one on one.

The bulls crashed into the group of humans and succubi. There were ten now, which meant their group was outnumbered.

Clarissa and Samantha attacked their first bull together, charging forward in separate directions to force it to choose between them. The bull hesitated. It didn't know which was the greater threat. That hesitation cost it when Clarissa used her naginata to pierce the demon's chest. It roared and tried to attack her, but she removed her weapon and leapt back. As the monster made to follow, Samantha swung her blade into its left front leg, cleaving through it. The bull roared and went down. Clarissa then ran up and thrust her blade into its neck. Gurgling as blood welled up inside of its lungs, the bull could do nothing as she twisted her blade, removed it, and then swung it again, this time splitting its throat wide open. The creature died quickly as it bled out on the snow.

While she and Samantha managed to make their first kill, Justina and Melvis were not so lucky. They tried to attack it together. However, Justina got too careless and moved in close, not realizing that the creature's eyes had locked onto her.

It grabbed her with one of its four hands. Justina screamed as she was lifted into the air, but that scream soon became a squeal of pain as her bones were crushed in the bull's iron grip.

"Let her go!" Melvis shouted as he charged at the beast, but he was swatted away by the demon, who used Justina herself as a bludgeon. The attack must have snapped the woman's neck, because she dangled limply in the demon's grip as Melvis was sent flying.

Not wanting to lose anymore of people, Clarissa threw her naginata at the bull that was coming up to crush Melvis. Her weapon pierced the beast's chest. It stopped moving, and she and Samantha used that time to close the distance. Samantha swung her sword opening a large gash along its left flank, while Clarissa grabbed her weapon and pulled it free. With its lifeblood spilling out of the massive wound on its side, the bull died quickly.

Clarissa and Samantha then turned their attention on the one holding the now very dead Justina.

"Melvis, can you still fight?"

"Don't worry about me." Melvis grunted as he stood up. "Just help me kill this thing."

"Let's attack it together."

Samantha rushed in from the left, Melvis from the right, and Clarissa charged in from the front. The bull focused on her. It swung Justina's body in a wide arc, but she deftly ducked underneath the attack, came back up, and cut into its chest. The beast roared in anguish, but that roar became a whimper as Melvis and Samantha came in from the sides and chopped off its legs.

It crashed to the ground, releasing Justina, who tumbled limply from its grasp. Melvis then leapt onto the bull's back and thrust his sword into its neck from behind. The orichalcum blade sliced clean through it. Giving out one last gurgle as blood poured from its mouth, the bull shuddered and died.

As the three rushed to help the remaining members of their team defeat the bulls, high overhead, the fallen angels were fighting against the gargoyles. Spears of light flew through the air. None of them hit. The gargoyles moved far faster than their appearance suggested they could, darting in and out of view, forcing the fallen angels to get in close.

Of course, even while fighting close, they had the advantage. Mezkiel jabbed a spear into his foe, killing it near instantly. Joseph flew around his gargoyle at high speed, slowly whittling away at it by creating numerous cuts with his blade. Each cut burned something fierce. The gargoyle screamed in pain as its body was slowly burned by the holy energy. However, not everyone was so lucky.

Ophilus tried to attack his gargoyle with a pair of knucklers made from his holy energy, but this gargoyle seemed particularly fast. It flew down, avoiding the attack, and then came up and raked its claws across his chest. Ophilus released a pained cry, but even that was silenced when the gargoyle leapt forward and clawed out his throat. As Ophilus fell, landing on the ground with a heavy thud, the gargoyle released a cry of victory before a spear impaled it through the back.

Clarissa was breathing heavily as she finished off the last bull. Ignoring the blood that spurted from the wound in the bull's side, she removed her naginata and wiped the nearly black ichor on its hide.

Looking around, she saw that among those who fought with her, only Ophilus and Justina had died, while everyone else had suffered injuries of varying severity. Some had cuts. Prekeil's left leg was twisted at an awkward angle. Samantha had blood running down her face. Clarissa herself was favoring her left side. She'd taken a nasty hit to the torso, and while she couldn't see through her clothing, she imagined there was gonna be a large bruise when she got home.

"That was… that was the last of them, right?" asked Melvis as he took several lungfuls of air.

"I believe so," Clarissa said as the others congregated around them.

"We lost… Justina," Kristen mumbled, now the last of the female Executioners. There were only three of them left, her, Melvis, and David.

David was an awfully big man with compact muscles covering every inch of his body. His brown hair was spiky, and there was a scar running down the left side of his face. He had browned skin, covered almost entirely by his unitard and chestplate. Unlike Melvis and Kristen, who used broadswords, he was hefting a large battle ax over his shoulder.

"Given what we are up against, the fact that so many of us are still alive can be considered a miracle," he said.

Kristen glared at him. "I know that, but still…"

"Now is not the time to mourn." Joseph glanced at Ophilus' body and gnashed his teeth together. He took a deep breath, sighed, and then glanced at them. "We can mourn after we complete our task."

Clarissa agreed and opened her mouth to speak.

"Oh, I'm afraid you won't be completing your task at all," a voice said before she could.

The next moment, before Clarissa or anyone else could even react, three of the six fallen angels—Joseph, Prekeil, and Haciel—were killed. Clarissa stared in horror as something speared straight through the back of their necks and out their throats. Their eyes widened for a moment in shock. Then they shuddered before going limp.

Their bodies were lifted into the air. They dangled for a moment, but then the they were tossed aside, revealing that what had pierced them were black tendrils that looked almost like hair. As the tendrils retracted, Clarissa followed them to its source.

A man stood before them, his pale skin and white robes blending perfectly into the snowy backdrop. He was old. Clarissa couldn't judge his age, but his face was lined with wrinkles around his eyes, mouth, and large nose. His robes were the kind worn by the bisophoric. He also wore a hat on his head, the kind expected of a bishop.

Presenting a complete contrast to his humble appearance, which resembled a kind old man, three black tendrils writhed behind him. His eyes were currently squinted. However, he opened them further to reveal crimson irises that were anything but human.

"Hello, children," the man said. "My name is Belphegor. I hope you don't mind, but I'd like to kill you all quickly, so I can go back to sleep."

As the man named himself, shock and fear raced through the group. However, as the three tendrils shot forward again, everyone recovered enough to leap out of the way, avoiding certain death.

"Oh, no. That won't do at all."

Without pause, the tendrils chased after Melvis, who screamed in shock and slashed at them. While his weapon did cut the tendrils apart, that didn't stop them. Before long, they had wrapped around his legs and left arm. His screams of anger soon became pain as the tendrils pulled on him. There was a moment where his screams reached a crescendo, but then, barely a second later, that scream died as the Executioner was ripped apart.

"Hmm…" Belphegor mumbled as he flung the body parts away. "I'm not really a fan of all this fighting. I'd prefer to nap. You people are fortunate. I'll be killing you quickly and painlessly."

"Everyone! Let's split up and attack him in different directions!" Clarissa ordered. The fallen angels took to the sky, David and Kristen raced around to attack from behind, and Clarissa looked at Samantha. "Let's change forms!"

Transforming from their human form to their succubus form was something they did sparingly, mostly because their succubus formed drained them of their life energy more quickly in exchange for increased power. However, in this situation, they didn't have a choice.

The two of them transformed.

Clarissa had transformed many times in her life. As she did, the familiar feeling of her bones popping and growing cascaded over her, as did the increase in power, the rush of energy that flowed through her body. While she couldn't see it, she knew that her body was growing aller, that her breasts and hips were getting bigger, and that her skin was going from olive-colored to a dark red. Nails became claws. Horns grew from her head. When her transformation was finished, she glanced at Samantha, who was now taller, had a pair of wings on her back, and blue skin instead of red.

"Oh ho." Belphegor's eyes opened a little wider. He seemed completely unconcerned with the light spears and arrows that were about to rain down on him from above. "That is quite the transformation. I'm most impressed. It's very interesting."

Just as he finished those words, almost a hundred spears and arrows slammed into him from above. Powdered snow flew everywhere, blocking their view of the Demon King. David and Kristen stopped moving, wondering if perhaps the demon had been finished.

That was a mistake.

Two tendrils shot from the cloud of powdered snow. The first one pierced Kristen through the heart, while the second one impaled David in the neck. They died instantly, and their bodies were quickly tossed away.

"That was a good effort." The powdered snow cleared and revealed an unharmed Belphegor surrounded by a red barrier. "A good effort indeed. However, you little fallen angels do not have the power to harm me."

While the remaining fallen angels quaked, Samantha and Clarissa rushed forward on swift feet. Belphegor turned his attention to them. Tendrils shot from behind his back and tried to skewer them, but instead of blood soaring through the air, the tendrils phased through them like they weren't even there. Belphegor blinked. Then Clarissa dropped the illusion around herself, which made her look further away than she really was and swung at the barrier with her claws.

Even Belphegor looked shocked when her claws sheared straight through his barrier. However, doing so caused her to cry out in pain as her claws melted from the contact with such potent demonic energy. Even so, she pushed through the pain.

"Now Samantha!"

At that exact moment, Samantha appeared behind Belphegor, shouting out as she sliced apart the tendrils with her sword and then plunged it into the man's back. The blade emerged from his chest, coated in blood. Belphegor looked flabbergasted for a second as ichor ran down his mouth, and his expression twisted into one of intense pain.

Then it cleared.

Belphegor began laughing.

"Very good. Very good. You two make quite the pair. I suppose should get rid of you to make things easier for me."

Before they could react, the bishop's back bulged, the skin stretching before a large hand tore through the flesh. Samantha could do nothing as the hand grabbed her.

"SAMANTHA!"

Clarissa's cry was lost to the wind as fist closed around Samantha While they could no longer see her, a loud crunching sound, like the snapping of a thousand bones, echoed across the landscape. Blood dribbled from between Belphegor's finger, which slowly opened. The figure that hit the ground with a wet thud didn't even resemble Samantha anymore. It was twisted and mangled.

The body of the bishop tore completely while the fallen angels and Clarissa stared in shock at the sudden death of Samantha. Emerging from within the body was a massive figure. It stood on two legs, but its toes looked more like tendrils than actual toes. With the body of a man, the gray-skinned creature reached a height that put him almost level with the still flying fallen angels. A long tail sprouted from his hind end. His face didn't look human. His ears, long and pointy and his nose, far larger than a human's, made him resemble a classic goblin. However, the horns on his head and the thick beard covering his chin made the resemblance end there.

"It feels interesting to stretch out my true form like this," Belphegor muttered. **"Though I feel quite weak. Damn mediums. If only I could use my full power. Then I could finish this battle quickly and get back to napping."**

At the sight of such a massive, demonic figure, Clarissa found herself unable to move. She didn't know what to do. Should she attack? Would it even matter?

While she hesitated, Liem and Mezkiel attacked, creating spears of light that rained down on Belphegor. Light was the weakness to all demons. It would not have been an exaggeration to say that their attacks had done more damage to the demons they had fought than the succubi and Executioners combined. However, perhaps due to Belphegor's overwhelming demonic power, all the light spears did to him was leave small scratches.

"Hey now. That tickles."

The tail behind his back shot forward, split into two, and then attacked Liem and Mezkiel. Clarissa's eyes widened as she snapped out of her stupor. She cast an illusion just in time. The tails quickly swerved away from Liem and Mezkiel, missing them entirely. Belphegor paused for a moment, then looked down.

"I had not realized succubus could affect me even while I was in this form. I should remove you first."

Before Belphegor could attack her, Mezkiel darted forward. A sword appeared on his hand. He quickly flew behind Belphegor and sliced into the Demon King's tail. Clarissa could not see what was happening, but then the huge entity in front of her screamed in pain and his tail fell to the ground, wriggling around like a headless snake before going still.

"Damn gnat! Do you know how long it takes to regrow those?!"

Rather than try to swat Mezkiel out of the air, Belphegor slammed his hands against the ground, which somehow caused several stakes to suddenly pierce the sky. Clarissa gritted her teeth as she summoned her reserves of life energy, pushing them into casting another illusion on the two fallen angels. However, she didn't have enough. Shock coursed through her as her body reverted back into her human form to conserve energy.

One of those stakes also pierced Mezkiel could he could fly away. The man gasped in pain as the stake went through his chest, shuddered once, and then went limp. Liem was able to avoid a similar fate by flying up, but he didn't see the tail coming in from behind him. Clarissa shouted a warning.

It was too late.

"There." Belphegor flicked the dead Liem off his tail and turned to her. **"I guess that just leaves you."**

As she stared at the monstrous form before her, Clarissa could do little but accept her fate.

She was going to die here.

Chapter 14

After getting the location for the British base, Christian, Lilith, and the rest of their group headed for their destination as quickly as they were able. Valerie's arm had been healed by Kel. It seemed the fallen angels were talented healers. Of course, divine energy from angels and even the fallen had miraculous healing properties, so it only made sense.

They relied largely on Tristin's constant feedback to avoid battles. Christian had no intention of getting into an unnecessary fight when there was so much at stake. While he didn't say anything, a chill had been running down his spine nearly nonstop.

Christian didn't know what to expect when they reached the British Base. Would they find Clarissa and her group pinned down? Would they be dead? The reason he had decided to head to this base was two-fold. First, he wanted to find out what happened to Clarissa and her group, for Lilith's sake if not his own. Second, on the off chance this base was the one with the demon summoning circle, someone would have to close it. They could not leave it open or the horde of demons would remain on Earth.

The first thing they saw upon running around a large hill was a massive, truly gigantic, monster towering over everything. It had the body of a man, but it's face reminded him of a goblin. A long beard hung down its chin. There was a tail swaying behind it. This thing, which could have only been one of the Seven Demon Kings, was battling against several people.

"That's Clarissa!" Lilith shouted as she pointed at the lone figure standing in front of the monster.

As they watched, the two figures darting through the air, a pair of fallen angels, were swiftly felled, one by a spear that shot from the ground and impaled him, and the other by a tendril that stabbed him from behind.

"Liem and Mezkiel," Paledius mumbled softly as he and the other fallen stared at their two now dead kin.

"There." Belphegor's voice rumbled across the vast, snowy landscape as he flicked the dead Liem off his tail and turned to Clarissa. **"I guess that just leaves you."**

"Natashia! Valerie! Taryn! Enter your succubus forms if you can and charge in to attack with me! Lilith, I need you to save Clarissa with an illusion! Phoebe, Graf, Paledius, Kel! You four are with us! Let's go!"

Time was of the essence, and Christian knew that, which was why he snapped off his orders in rapid succession before charging straight toward the Demon King.

The Demon King, who Christian recognized from the scriptures as Belphegor, the Demon King of Sloth, raised his hand high into the air. He was seemingly prepared to squash Clarissa. However, the moment he tried to bring his hand down, something stopped it. Christian closed his green eye and stared at the arm with his red eye. There was something wrapped around it, a chain that seemed to be coming from a black portal that reminded him of a vortex.

One of Lilith's illusions, no doubt.

"What is this?! Why can't I move my arm?!"

By this point, Christian had already raced by Clarissa. He only had enough time to see the woman look at him in shock before he was charging at Belphegor's legs. Using the Eye of Belial, he saw that most of his skin was covered in a bluish black energy, but there were several lines of white where the energy didn't cover.

He aimed for those.

"GRRRRRRAAAAAAAAA!!!"

Christian swung Michael and Rafael, slicing through those lines, his blades digging in deep and causing blood to spurt out of the gashes like overflowing waterfalls. He danced to the side as the blood struck the snow. Steam hissed from the spots as the blood melted through the white powder. Like most of his demonic legions, Belphegor's blood was corrosive.

"Avoid getting any blood on you!" Christian called out as he ran around behind Belphegor and attacked more of the giant demon's weakness points.

"You damn pest!!"

While he was keeping the demon distracted, Valerie charged in. Her skin was now a pale pink. Swirling patterns ran along her face, which had somehow become even more refined, more beautiful. Her long hair had transformed into vibrant red locks. They descended along her back like waves rolling in from the ocean. She had no wings, horns, or tail. However, her ears had grown long and pointed.

Valerie wielded her two falchions with expert precision. She spun around Belphegor's legs, attacking the massive limbs with numerous attacks. The blades were made of orichalcum, so they did damage. The strength granted to her by her succubus form also allowed her to dig the weapons more deeply into their enemy's flesh. Christian actually saw her slicing through the bluish black energy field surrounding Belphegor.

Her swords are coated with energy...

Christian didn't have time to analyze what Valerie was doing beyond that, as the succubus' attacks meant she was now the target of Belphegor's rage.

He darted back in, targeting more of the cracks, his blades cutting into the flesh of the demon's legs. Belphegor's enraged cries were bone-chilling. Out of anger, the mighty demon stamped on the ground. Christian only had a brief flash of warning before several stakes shot from the floor beneath him and Valerie.

They quickly took several leaps backward to avoid being skewered. More stakes were launched from the ground. Christian winced as several cut into his flesh. A cry made him turn to look at Valerie, who'd been unfortunate enough not to avoid one of them. The stake was piercing her left shoulder. She had dropped her falchions and was trying to remove it.

He darted forward, dancing left and right to avoid more stakes, and sliced the one holding Valerie in place with Rafael. Spinning

around, he swung the blades with calculated recklessness. Each swing
cut through a stake that tried to impale him.

While he protected Valerie, high above their heads, Graf,
Paledius, Taryn, and Natashia were attacking.

Like Valerie, Taryn and Natashia had changed. Natashia's skin
had become completely white, so white it was nearly translucent, and
her hair had turned platinum. Horns the same white as her skin jutted
from her head. Similarly, her wings and spaded tail were the same
color. Taryn's skin was darker, more of a burnt red, but she also had
wings and a tail, and her hair had become a surprisingly deep shade of
blue.

The two of them held out their hands, and quite unexpectedly,
Belphegor seized up. Through his Eye of Belial, he could see the
illusory chains binding the Demon King of Sloth. Belphegor tried to
break out of them. He seemed unable to recognize that it was an
illusion—at first. During that moment of shock, Graf and Paledius
swooped down, light spears appearing in their hands. The impaled
Belphegor through the neck.

"Ggkk! Nnnn! Damn... you...!"

This distraction was all Alex and Gregory needed to attack
Belphegor. They charged in, attacking with their respective weapons.
However, while their blades were also made of orichalcum and
therefore strong enough to cut through Belphegor's flesh, the two
Executioners only had the strength of a normal human. All their attacks
did was leave small scratches.

By this point, Phoebe and Lilith had reached Clarissa. His mate
was fretting over the woman while Phoebe healed her. Clarissa didn't
seem too injured. Christian was more concerned by the look on her
face, which suggested she was in shock. Given that she was alone, and
he could see several corpses strewn across the ground, she had watched
her entire squad die.

"Do not think you can hold me with these petty illusions!!!"

At that moment, Belphegor roared and unleashed a demonic wave
of energy that crashed into all of them. Alex, Gregory, Taryn, Natashia,
Graf, and Paledius screamed as they were tossed away like flies in a
storm. Christian had to bend his knees and struggle against the
ferocious wave. However, his feet slid across the snow. What's more,
the skin on his face felt like it was blistering as the demon's powerful
energy burnt him.

"Ah!!"

Unlike Christian, who fought to remain in place, Valerie was too weakened by her injury and flew backward, crashing into the snowy bank.

Crossing his blades, Christian used them as a makeshift shield to protect his eyes. He waited until the outburst of energy died down before lowering them.

Belphegor's unleashing of energy had done more than just launch everyone away from him. The snow beneath his feet had melted completely. There was a circle with something like a 56-yard circumference surrounding Belphegor now. The Demon King of Sloth stood in the center of this circle. With bluish black energy now visibly wafting off his skin, healing his wounds as he glared at them with eyes glowering in rage, he looked like something out of a nightmare.

"You pests keep showing up one after another. Annoying bugs. I'll put all of you down now!"

Christian looked around for Lilith, finding her in the same spot she'd been standing in, along with Clarissa, Phoebe, and now Kel. There was a perfect circle surrounding their spot. One of them, Kel he guessed, must have been able to create some kind of barrier that protected them from the attack.

Belphegor placed his hands on the ground. Nothing happened for a moment, but then an uncountable amount of black tendrils broke through the ground and came for them.

Christian strained his muscles to move quickly, dodging several of the tendrils while cutting through what he couldn't dodge. Kel had erected another barrier. The golden shield sprang to life, a dome that gleamed against the backdrop of snow. However, the shield wasn't enough. The tendrils stabbed into the shield, and while they didn't tear it apart, the more tendrils that impaled it, the more cracks that appeared on its surface.

Rushing forward, Christian winced as several tendrils scraped against his face, arms, and legs. He ignored the blood leaking down his new cuts. Swinging Michael and Rafael in a flurry of quick attacks, he cut through the tendrils threatening to break through the barrier, which flickered and died seconds later.

I made it just in time.

Christian breathed a sigh of relief as he looked at the group. The light from his red eye faded. He'd used it so much that maintaining it was becoming hard.

His eyes quickly sought Lilith. They looked at each other, locking gaze, but then Lilith's eyes went wide, and her mouth opened in a scream of warning.

Pain erupted from Christian's back, then his stomach. The world seemed to stand still as he looked down. Wiggling around as it emerged from his stomach was a black tendril. He barely had time to contemplate the offending thing protruding from his belly when his feet suddenly left the ground. Everything spun around him in a dizzying blur of colors. Then his face struck something hard, though he could not feel it. White and blue filled his vision as he tumbled along, eventually coming to a stop face first on the snow.

I feel numb.

He couldn't feel the snow on his face.

I let my guard down.

It had only been for a second, but a second could mean the difference between life and death.

That was stupid of me.

He closed his eyes and sighed. Why was he suddenly so tired?

***

Lilith's first inclination was to run over to Christian, who's still form lay several yards from where she sat, but her body was frozen in shock. Denial warred with anger and anguish. Part of her couldn't believe what she was seeing. The rest was forced to believe.

A loud roar filled her ears. Belial was battling against Graf, Paledius, Valerie, Taryn, and Kel. The five were hitting Belphegor with hit and run tactics. They darted in, attacked, and then darted back out as the demon raged. Graf and Paledius were attacking with light spears, punching holes through the demon's flesh. Valerie and Taryn must have been using illusions to trip the demon up. All of Belphegor's attacks missed his intended targets by a wide margin. Kel fought from the ground, flying between their enemy's legs and flaying off large chunks of flesh.

Lilith barely paid attention to the battle. Her eyes were still focused on Christian.

How did this happen?

She didn't understand. One moment Christian was looking at her, and the next he was being stabbed from behind and flung away.

There's no way. I mean, Christian fights like he has eyes in the back of his head.

She knew that, logically, it was impossible for Christian to be aware of everything happening around him all the time. He'd been distracted for one second. That single second had been enough for Belphegor to take advantage of and launch a sneak attack. It still didn't seem real.

Christian...

She wanted to go to Christian. She wanted to kneel down and begin healing him. However, part of her was afraid of what she might find. What if he was already dead? Lilith didn't think she could bear that thought.

"Lilith! Lilith!" Clarissa shook her by the shoulder. "Lilith, you need to snap out of it! Get ahold of yourself!"

"Clarissa…"

"Christian isn't dead yet, but he will be if we don't do something soon!" Clarissa said as Lilith focused on her.

"Something…" The words snapped Lilith back into reality. "What should… I do…?"

"We can't heal him while that thing is still around." Clarissa pointed at Belphegor. "If nothing else, we'll need to distract this monster, so we can get away. If we can at least escape from Belphegor, we can find a place where you can heal Christian."

"Belphegor…"

He was the one who had hurt Christian. He hurt her mate.

Lilith did not consider herself a vengeful person, nor did she think she got angry very often, but in that moment, something boiled inside of her. Christian was hurt. Belphegor had hurt him. Something had to be done about this. Belphegor had to pay.

Standing up, Lilith clenched her hands into fists as the energy locked away inside of her flowed out. She was vaguely aware of the changes her body was undergoing. Her body felt like it was growing. Blood swelled beneath her skin, which had turned a soft pink. Two objects grew out of her head, curving around until the points met in front of her forehead like a crown. Her ears felt like they were stretching. Something was growing from her just above her bottom, crawling along the inside of her pants, and the straps of her chestplate ripped as two pinions jutted from her shoulder blades and spread out wide to reveal large pink and white wings.

"This is a complete transformation!" Clarissa muttered in awe.

Lilith didn't know what Clarissa meant by that, but she looked down at the woman. "Grab Christian and get out of here please. I will hold Belphegor back until you are a safe distance away."

She didn't give Clarissa time to say anything. With a flap of her wings, Lilith soared high into the air.

The others must have noticed her presence, for Belphegor, the three succubus, and the four fallen angels all looked in her direction. Lilith ignored their gaze. She glared at Belphegor and raised a hand eye above her head. She imagined a massive drill spinning at supersonic speeds as it barreled down toward her enemy, and as if her imagination was enough to conjure it, a drill appeared.

Perhaps sensing something unusual about this drill, or maybe just plain frightened, the fallen angels and succubus darted away. The drill spun faster and faster and faster as it shot toward Belphegor. The Demon King of Sloth had no time to escape, so he raised his hands to try and catch the attack. Lilith thought it was a stupid thing to do. Even though he caught the drill, his hands were shredded apart, causing him to cry out in agony. The drill continued. It hit him in the chest and began drilling a hole straight through him.

Gritting his teeth, Belphegor released a mighty roar and his powers skyrocketed. The bluish black energy struck the drill and dissolved it, then the wound on his chest, the gaping hole, sealed shut as if it had never happened. His hands also healed quickly.

Lilith spread her arms wide. She imagined a dozen drills each the size of that first one appearing and drilling holes through Belphegor's body, and just like before, the drills appeared. This time, there were too many for Belphegor to block with his hands, but he unleashed his energy to destroy them.

Frowning, Lilith decided to be subtler. She created a massive tornado that appeared in front of Belphegor and struck him in the face. The demon growled in danger, his energy flaring again to dispel her attack, and while he was distracted with that, she imagined a massive spear appearing behind him and impaling him through the lower back. Belphegor's pained roar as something stabbed through his back and protruded out his stomach made Lilith offer an uncharacteristic smile.

"Damn... you... What is this? Succubus can't create something out of nothing! What are... you...?"

Lilith didn't answer him. This monster had hurt Christian, and so, like a vengeful angel, she would make sure he suffered terribly.

No one hurt her mate.

***

Christian came to when something tugged on his arm. He jerked awake, blinking several times. His neck felt stiff, bent forward as it was. Staring at the ground, he wondered why his feet looked so small, but then he realized they were not his feet, which he now realized were dragging against the snow. Furthermore, his arm had been slung around someone's shoulder.

"Are you awake?" asked a familiar voice. He lifted his head and found Clarissa's face mere inches from his own.

"Clarissa... what happened?"

"You were impaled by Belphegor," Clarissa answered succinctly. "It was pretty brutal. I'm honestly surprised you're still alive, never mind awake."

"Lilith. Where is she?"

"She's battling against Belphegor alongside the others."

The words brought everything into stark focus. Lifting his head and craning his neck, Christian spotted four fallen angels and four succubi battling against Belphegor. All of the succubi had transformed. However, one of them stood out more than the others.

Her skin was a soft pink, wings spread along her back, and two horns curled around her head like a crown. He had only seen it once. Even so, he recognized Lilith even if she had more appendages than last time.

Out of all the people present, she was the one doing the most damage.

Lilith waved her hand and a torrent of icicles suddenly speared into Belphegor.

Blood gushed from the wounds in copious amounts, but the Demon King of Sloth quickly healed from them and tried to attack her.

He was blocked. Kel and Mezkiel intercepted the tendrils by combining their power to create a bright shield of golden energy.

While this happened, Valerie, Taryn, and Natashia raised their hands and, quite suddenly Belphegor screamed in agony as he gripped his head.

Lilith raised her hands above her head. Gathering above her head was a massive drill-shaped flame. It spun like a spiral as she launched it at Belphegor, striking him dead in the chest and blowing a hole clean through his body. The gaping hole was massive too. It easily spanned most of his chest, allowing everyone to see through it. His flesh had been cauterized. However, barely a second had passed before it healed completely.

"That won't be enough to defeat me!" Belphegor roared as he slammed his hands on the ground and created several rock spears that tried to impale the group. He must have been under an illusion because his attacks didn't hit anyone. Christian noticed Valerie struggling against an invisible force as she stood behind the Demon King.

"Impressive, isn't she?" Clarissa asked, forcing him to look her way. "Lilith's powers exceed even what I had imagined. She has the ability to turn her illusions into reality, and they are powerful enough that even a Demon King is affected by them."

Even as she said that, Lilith landed on the ground and tapped her boot against the snow. A massive hand even bigger than Belphegor suddenly appeared. It opened its palms wide and then swooped down, slamming into the demon, who raised his hands to keep from being squashed. A roar echoed from Belphegor's lips. His tail split into hundreds of tendrils, which pierced the hand and destroyed it.

The others were harassing him. Kel threw light spears, Phoebe attacked with a sword alongside Valerie and her falchions, Taryn and Natashia had taken charge of casting illusions to disorient Belphegor, and Mezkiel and Paledius swooped down to cut open the demon's neck and chest. All of them were basically harassing the creature to provide Lilith time to conjure her illusions.

Despite how well the group seemed to be doing, Christian could tell they were tiring. What's more, their attacks didn't seem to leave any lasting damage. Belphegor healed from his injuries almost as fast as he received them. The only one who dealt real damage was Lilith, and even the damage from her attacks were dealt with quickly.

"They're going to lose..."

The voice of his dark half, of Nox, came to him as if it was a whisper on the wind. Everything around him became monochrome as time seemingly stood still. Belphegor no longer moved, Lilith was locked into place, and the fallen angels and succubus were not doing anything either. Even Clarissa now appeared frozen.

"You..."

A figure appeared before him. He looked just like Christian. His skin was pale and covered in several scars, but his shoulders were broad and well-defined, even hidden as they were beneath his armor. Rafael and Michael were strapped to his back. Gabriel and Phanul rested in holsters against his thighs. The dark hair covering his head had the same messy appearance as his own, and the eyes that gazed at him were green and red just like his.

"Nox..."

"Is that what you've taken to calling me?" Nox grinned. It looked nothing like his own grin. This one was cruel and twisted. If there was

one difference between them, this would be it. *"Look at you. You're in a sorry state."*

This would normally be the part where Christian clicked his tongue and told his dark half off, but that was not what he did. He stared at his other half and thought.

Nox was, according to Azazel, the negative emotions inside of him given form from the power of his demonic blood. At the same time, Nox was also him. He and Nox were one and the same. Christian didn't want to admit it, hated the idea down to his very core, but here and now, with everything that was happening around them, he had no choice.

"You… love Lilith, right?"

Nox blinked. *"What kind of stupid question is that? Of course, I love Lilith."*

Christian nodded. "Yeah, that's what I thought. I've been thinking about this for a long time now, but you and I are the same person, and if we're the same person, it means your feelings are the same as mine."

"Did you just now come to realize that?" Nox rolled his eyes.

Shaking his head, Christian stared at Nox. "No… I think I've always known that. I just didn't want to admit it. I didn't want to accept that you were also a part of me."

"That's why I've never liked you," Nox grumbled. *"Whenever you felt sadness or regret, you always shoved those feelings onto me. When you felt anger or hatred, I was the one who had to bear the burden of carrying them. Of course, with each negative thought or feeling you sent my way, I grew more powerful, but you know something? Power isn't everything. I hate being locked in that dark cage you call a mind."*

This might have been the first civilized conversation the two of them had ever had. As they spoke, Christian thought he could feel Nox's own emotions pouring into him. Anger, depression, desire, hatred, greed… and something else, a scar that had been inside of him for so long he'd almost forgotten about it.

Christian closed his eyes as a wave of regret washed over him, as the guilt from being the only survivor of his village slammed against him like crashing tidal waves.

Long ago, Christian had shoved the guilt he felt deep into his subconscious. He'd had no choice at the time. At the tender age of six years-old, there was no way he could have dealt with survivor's guilt. Thanks to what he'd done, Christian had been able to function as a regular human being. However, in pushing that emotion away, he had created Nox, who'd lived with his feelings of guilt and regret.

"You're right." He sighed. "I'm sorry."

"Sorry?" Nox sneered. *"If all it took to make things better was 'sorry,' this world wouldn't be so fucked up. Why the hell do you think I've been pushing you so hard? I don't want your apologies and platitudes. I want you to take responsibility."*

"How do I do that?"

Nox narrowed his eyes. *"By accepting me. In accepting me, you will bear all of the emotions you foisted onto me."*

Christian didn't need long to think about what he should do. He nodded.

"You're right. I've run from myself long enough."

"You've been running for far too long." Nox strode up to Christian, who noticed that when his other half walked, the snow was unmoved. Then a hand was placed on his head and Nox grinned down at him. *"It's time you wake up and come to terms with what you've done. I should warn you, this is going to hurt."*

Christian didn't have time to ask Nox what he meant, for the man disappeared a moment later, and then he was hit with an unbearable pain. This pain wasn't physical, however. It didn't feel like his bones were being ground into a fine power. His muscles didn't feel like they were tearing. There was no sensation of his body being burnt, impaled, or crushed. This pain, which rushed through his body and left him breathless, was emotional.

The guilt from having been the only survivor of his village.

The guilt of surviving against Abaddon when everyone else died.

The regret he felt at taking the lives of others, even monsters.

The self-loathing that threatened to crush him when he realized that he and the Executioners had been wrong this whole time.

The self-deprecating hatred he felt at learning he was not human.

Every negative emotion he'd had ever felt pressed down on his mind. They threatened to erode his sanity. This was what Nox had been dealing with this whole time. That just added to his guilt and self-loathing. However, Christian didn't want to run anymore. This time, he would bear the burdens that he'd refused to acknowledge.

As he gasped and panted for breath, the world around him returned to color and everything started moving. His dead weight caused Clarissa to lean over.

"Christian? Are you okay?"

"I'm fine…" Christian gasped as he pressed his hands against the snow. The coldness contrasted against his burning hands. "I'm just fine…"

"We need to get you out of here."

Clarissa attempted to pick him back up, but Christian pushed her hand, forcefully but gently, away and picked himself up.

"No. I can't run while everyone else is fighting."

Staring at him with narrowed eyes, Clarissa gave him a disapproving glance. "What can you do when you're in that state—"

Clarissa was forced to stop speaking, eyes widening, when Christian tore off his chestplate and the upper half of his unitard, showing off his bare torso. Goosebumps broke out on his skin, but the heat searing his body kept him from getting cold. Energy was flowing through him, dark, negative. The emotions he felt coursed through his body and granted him power. However, whereas before that power overwhelmed him, this time, he was the one controlling the power.

He directed the energy toward his wound, which hissed and steamed as it closed up, just like what Belphegor did when injured. That done, he picked up his sheaths and strapped them to his bare back.

Christian looked at the battle against Belphegor. It was currently locked in a stalemate, but that would change soon.

"I'm going," Christian said to Clarissa before he took off, running in the direction of the battle, running to where Lilith was.

***

Lilith was getting tired. She wouldn't admit it, but her reserves of life energy were already dwindling. Exhaustion was seeping into her bones.

How many illusions had she cast? 10? 20? 100? She had lost track. What's more, all of her illusions were more than just illusions. Everything she created became real, which expended more life energy than if they had been just illusory images.

Belphegor's tail punched through the ground, which somehow caused hundreds of tendrils to shoot from the earth and attack them. Lilith raised her hands and conjured a shield for everyone. She imagined shields, ones strong enough to defend against even a Demon King, appearing. The shields looked like gleaming bright kite shields. The tails slammed into them but couldn't break through.

Lilith gasped. Her breathing had become ragged. Her lungs were burning.

Belphegor glared at her, and then opened his mouth wide, revealing a gaping maw surrounded by a row of razor sharp teeth. Something pink and fleshy suddenly shot out of it, a tongue.

Gritting her teeth, she imagined fire appearing in front of her. A great conflagration suddenly burst out from the ether. It tore through the space between her and Belphegor, striking the tongue and burning it to cinder. Belphegor roared in anguish as he stumbled backward.

Mezkiel, Paledius, Graf, and Kel surrounded Belphegor as he stumbled across the ground, launching spears and firing arrows at him. They peppered him with attacks. While they attacked from above, Natashia, Phoebe, Valerie, and Taryn struck from down below. Their attacks didn't seem to cause much damage. However, the more they attacked, the more Belphegor stumbled. If they could just make him fall, they might be able to deal a finishing blow.

But it was not to be.

Power suddenly burst from Belphegor's body, launching everyone away. The three succubus crashed into the ground, tumbling backwards, their transformations disappearing as they struck their heads. Phoebe tried to maintain her balance, but she only had one wing. She was able to remain upright as she was thrown backward by the force. She crashed into a boulder covered in snow.

High above, Mezkiel, Paledius, Graf, and Kel were launched high into the air. Lilith gritted her teeth as she hunkered behind the shield she'd conjured from her illusions. However, the shield was flickering. Her breath came out in white hot puffs of smoke as she struggled to keep the shield up, but she knew it was only a matter of time before it dissolved.

She was just about out of energy.

With one last gasp, Lilith was forced to relinquish her hold on the shield. The energy that had been crashing into her shield was now barreling right for her. It was like a bluish black tidal of malevolence.

Just before it could reach her, a dark red wave of energy cut straight through the demonic force heading her way. Lilith blinked. Then she looked down, toward where the energy had come from.

That's—

It was Christian. The last she'd seen of him, he'd been impaled and was lying on the ground, but now he looked healthier than ever. Even though he was covered in blood, he stood straight. His posture was erect as he gripped Rafael and Michael, his two swords, in a loose stance at his side. He was looking directly at her.

"That energy!!" Belphegor stared at Christian as well, his eyes bulging in shock. They looked like a pair of dish pans. Then his eyes narrowed. **"So I see. You are the spawn of Belial. Heh... we knew you were holed up inside of the Grigori's hideout, but I had no idea you would show yourself to me like this so brazenly."**

"So you're after me? Is that why you've come here?" asked Christian.

"That's only part of the reason." Belphegor grinned. **"Of course, I'm not going to tell you the other reasons we are here."**

"Of course. Wouldn't want to become too cliched now."

"I don't know what that means, but now that you are here, I'm going to be taking you back to the Vatican with me."

"It sounds so weird that a demon is telling me he's going to take me to the Vatican."

Belphegor roared as he lunged forward, but then, just after he finished taking a single step, his body froze.

"W-what... is going... on...?!"

Lilith wanted to know what was going on as well. She looked around, seeking an answer, and then found Clarissa standing several yards away. She was in her succubus form again. Her teeth were grit as she held out her hands, no doubt casting an illusion on Belphegor to keep him in place somehow.

"Hurry up, you two! I don't have much energy left!" Clarissa grunted.

"Lilith!"

Landing next to Christian, she turned to face her mate, who looked at her with a serious expression.

"Do you think you can conjure a sword?" he asked.

"A sword?"

"Something stronger than even my orichalcum swords. A big sword that can slice through a Demon King with ease."

"I-I'll try, but I'm almost out of energy."

She couldn't create such a large sword if she didn't have any energy. However, even as she said that, Christian wrapped an arm around her waist pulled her close.

"Don't worry. I've got all the energy you need right here."

So saying that, Christian hampered her mouth with his own. Lilith's eyes widened. However, as her body filled with energy, more energy than she would have expected, she found herself closing her eyes and leaning into the kiss. She wanted more. Her mouth opened, and her tongue probed his, but Christian pulled back.

"The sword," he reminded her.

"Oh. Right."

Lilith hid her embarrassment by holding a hand above her head. She imagined a sword, one that was so large it towered over even Belphegor, a blade that was so strong it could cut through this demon with the greatest ease. Large. Sharp. A gleaming blade that nothing in his world could stand against.

A hilt appeared first, clad in red fabric, and then came the guard, a pronged guard made of gleaming gold with an emerald gem in the center on one side and a crimson gem on the other. After the guard came the sword. While the hilt was massive, easily the same height as Lilith herself, the blade was even bigger. It stood above even Belphegor, reaching a height that must have been at least four stories.

Perhaps sensing the danger he was in, Belphegor struggled against whatever invisible bonds were restraining him. Clarissa fell onto a knee. She placed one hand on her knee, while the other remained pointed at Belphegor, though it looked like her hand was seconds away from falling limp.

Christian placed a hand over Lilith's. She felt a flood of energy flowing through her illusion, not only strengthening it, but also causing ethereal red flames to surround the blade. The negative emotions fueling the energy washed over her, but she surprisingly didn't get goosebumps from them. Anger. Hate. Regret. These emotions fueled the energy, but it was acceptance, compassion, and love that guided the energy.

"You ready?" Christian asked.

Lilith looked into his eyes and nodded. "I am."

"I… I can't hold him any longer!"

At that moment, Clarissa's succubus form disappeared as the illusion she'd used to bind Belphegor in place shattered. With nothing holding him back, he rushed toward them, his hands outstretched, fingers extending beyond what was normal, stretching like rubber out to grasp them.

With a loud shout, Christian and Lilith brought the sword down, slicing straight through Belphegor, who didn't even have time to scream before his soul was sent back to Hell.

***

Christian and Lilith took deep, rasping gulps of air as they stared at the spot where Belphegor had been. There was nothing left now. A large chasm traveled through the ground, wide enough that a person could have fallen into it, though it didn't seem very deep. The area around the chasm was scorched. Steam rose from the ground like it had been superheated and was now being rapidly cooled by the freezing temperatures of Antarctica.

The sword they were grasping began breaking apart. Like particles drifting into the air, small pieces of it flecked off, flew upwards, and slowly vanished. As the sword disappeared entirely, Christian and Lilith, still holding onto each other, glanced at the person in their arms.

"We… we did…" Christian said.

"We did." Lilith nodded.

"We defeated another Demon King."

"I'm kinda surprised. We didn't hit its weak point, did we?"

"Well…" Christian tilted his head. "I don't think it really matter in this case. I mean, we kind of obliterated him, so it's likely we did end up destroying the Mark of Possession when we split him in half."

The Mark of Possession was the symbol located somewhere on the Demon King's body. A representation of the deadly sin that particular Demon King represented, the Mark of Possession acted as an anchor that kept the Demon King's soul sealed away inside of a human body.

"Yeah… that makes sense," Lilith said after giving it a moment's thought.

"You two…" Before they could get any further with their conversation, Clarissa came up to them, her eyes wide in shock. "That… what did you… that sword…"

"Are you okay, Clarissa?" asked a concerned Lilith. "You're not making much sense."

As the other members of Christian's squad began gathering around them, Clarissa took several deep breaths. It was like she was trying to center herself. While Lilith merely tilted her head in confusion, Christian realized what had spooked their friend so much.

"That attack you two just did… what was that?" Clarissa finally managed to ask the question burning on her mind—and not just hers. Valerie, Taryn, and Natashia, Kel, Graf, Phoebe, and Paledius, all of them were also looking at the two with expectation in their eyes.

"That was…" Lilith trailed off as she tried to find the words to explain what they'd just done, but it wasn't like they had a clear idea either.

"I suppose you could say we just combined our powers?" Christian offered, but he really wasn't sure.

Clarissa looked at them, then at the massive chasm they had created with their attack, and then back at them. Her expression was surprisingly flat.

"I've never seen a collaboration attack like that."

Christian shrugged. "You've probably also never met a succubus who could make her illusions real, or a human with demonic powers—never mind both at the same time."

"That... that is true," Clarissa sighed. "You two are an unprecedented phenomenon. That you both got together is probably a one in one billion chance."

"While I am curious about that attack they just used as well," Kel began, "I think we should check to see if that summoning circle is here."

Everyone agreed with Kel, especially Christian and Lilith. Of course, their reason for agreeing had more to do with not wanting to be the center of attention any longer.

The group didn't bother splitting up this time. They entered the British base though one of the stairs that led up to a small door, which was locked. Christian put several bullets into the lock, kicked it open, and stepped inside.

Halley VI was a series of eight modules that could be detached and individually toed. The struts each structure stood on were actually skis to help it move across Antarctica. As they stepped inside that first module and looked around, nothing seemed out of the ordinary. Christian had been expecting dead bodies to litter the floor, but there were no traces of the team that had been deployed there.

"This is eerie," Valerie mumbled.

"You said it," Taryn agreed.

Christian raised his hand for silence, turning his head left and right as he tried to get a sense of whether or not anyone was there.

The module they had entered was the second module in the series of four on the left side. To that end, they checked the last module on this end first. It looked like an observation deck. There was plenty of research equipment, but there wasn't anything noteworthy, so they moved on. The third module also had nothing. It was a medical lab. There was all the standard medical equipment present, a bit more outdated than what was at Seventh Heaven, but still leagues above anything in normal hospitals. Since this module also didn't have anything, they moved on to the fourth module, the big red one.

It was there where they found something.

The room had been cleared of any sort of furniture. Given that it was a two-story module with a staircase leading to the upper floor, Christian would have expected this to be a living quarter. However, on top of having all furniture removed, seven obelisks surrounded a circle painted in blood. While he'd never seen one before, the strange lines, eerie symbols, and unusual glow emanating from the circle made it obvious that this was what they had been searching for.

As they moved closer, Christian realized that the obelisks had people inside of them. It vaguely reminded him of that time Han Solo had been frozen in carbonite. The people were inside of the obelisks, their faces sticking out, frozen in horror. With the Eye of Belial, he could see the power flowing from each obelisk and into the circle.

A man was in the center of this circle.

He was a nondescript man whose age was difficult to determine, though his gray hair, the wrinkles around his eyes and mouth, and the way his shoulders sagged did suggest he was old. The bulbous nose protruding from the center of his face shadowed his large lips. White robes with purple trimming adorned him, looking pristine—the stately robes of a Bishop. Christian recognized him.

"Bishop Vertrou," he said.

The Bishop's eyes snapped open.

"C-Christian Crux," he stuttered, taking a step back. He'd been standing in the center of the circle. "W-what are you—wait! I can explain this!"

"You can explain your misdeeds in Hell," Christian stated as he raised his gun and put a bullet through the man's head. Bishop Vertrou was launched clean off his feet as the bullet tore through his skull. Ragged chunks of brain matter splattered against the ground, followed by the hollow thump as the man himself hit the floor.

With the Bishop dead, the summoning ritual was disrupted. The demons could not remain in this world without a medium. The glow emitting from the summoning circle died down before vanishing altogether.

"After everything that just happened, that ending felt very anticlimactic," Phoebe admitted with a frown.

"Christian?" Lilith looked at her mate, who had closed his eyes and seemed to be thinking.

"Bishop Vertrou was the man who ordered me to kill you back when I was still with the Executioners." He looked at the now cooling corpse of the man who had betrayed the trust of his colleagues for power. "On the one hand, I would have never met you if not for him.

On the other... well, I can't say I'm too pleased about everything this man has done."

Lilith nodded. "I understand."

"We should search the base some more," Clarissa suggested. "I doubt there will be any survivors, but..."

"We should at least figure out what happened to them," Christian agreed.

Even though Bishop Vertrou was already dead, the group stuck around for nearly an hour longer. Most of them went off to check the other modules. Christian began the process of getting rid of the summoning circle. While there was no longer any danger presented by it, he didn't like leaving things to chance, so he found out where the buckets and cleaning supplies were, and then used a powerful cleaning agent to remove the circle.

During that time, Christian also let Tristin know about what happened. It was important that the Grigori be informed of what they had faced.

Christian also didn't want to leave the people who'd been used as a sacrifice inside of those obelisks. However, the strange substance that formed them seemed to have hardened and made it impossible to get those people out. Since they couldn't remove the people from the obelisk, he and Graf began the laborious process of taking the obelisks outside and giving them a makeshift burial.

As they finished burying the last obelisk, Christian clapped his hands together, ridding them of the powdered snow.

"You have an awful strong sense of justice, huh?" said Graf.

"Excuse me?" asked Christian.

Graf shook his head. "It is nothing. I was just noticing how unusually strong your sense of righteousness is."

"I can't tell whether that's a compliment or an insult."

"Does it have to be one or the other?"

"I suppose not."

The others were coming outside now, trickling onto the snowy fields in twos and threes. Valerie, Taryn, and Natashia had formed a group, while Kel, Phoebe, and Paledius were also in a group. Lilith and Clarissa were the last to emerge from the Halley VI Research Facility. As the two began walking down the stairs, Christian smiled as he looked at his mate. Even covered in blood and thick clothing, she was so beautiful.

"Christian! Look out!"

"What?"

At the sound of the shout, Christian turned toward Graf, but before he could figure out what was wrong, a powerful force slammed into him. For about one second, the world around him passed by in a blur. For one second, a sense of vertigo overcame him, causing him to feel nauseous. Then the second was over. Christian slammed into something hard, the breath leaving his lungs. His vision faded as he felt something grab him by the arm.

"CHRISTIAN!!"

The last thing he heard was Lilith's scream.

***

The battle was over. Azazel couldn't help but wipe the sweat from his forehead as the demonic army, which they had been battling for far longer than he would have liked, disappeared. It was a bit strange to see. Azazel had been engaged in a ferocious battle against over a dozen demons, and then, so suddenly it was startling, the demons surrounding him had vanished like ghosts, leaving behind nothing but their footprints and blood in the snow.

"Governor General," Baraqiel said as he flew down, landing beside Azazel as the Grigori leader observed the battlefield now bereft of any battles.

"Did we lose anyone?" asked Azazel.

"We did not," Baraqiel said. "Although several of us were injured. Penanume and Chazakiel both suffered severe injuries and were sent back to Seventh Heaven to recover. Everyone else only suffered minor wounds."

"Good. It would be embarrassing if all of us received grave injuries against mid-level demons like this."

Mid-level demons were no threat to the Grigori, who were composed of powerful seraphim that had fallen because of their desire to remain on Earth. Everyone in the Council of Twenty had powers that could only be outmatched by an archangel. Only a high-level demon like Abaddon or Mephisto would prove to be a challenge for them. Saying that, there had been a lot of demons in this army, so some injuries were expected.

"Let's head back inside," Azazel ordered. "I would like to hear a report on everything that happened. I also want to know about the status of the groups we sent out to disrupt the summoning ritual."

"Of course." Baraqiel placed his hand on his chest and bowed slightly at the waist.

The Council of Twenty members all gathered and headed back inside Seventh Heaven the way they'd exited, through the opening in the roof, and then made for the Tower of New Babel, named after the ancient structure God had sent his angels to destroy. Of course, New Babel was not a monument attempting to reach God's domain. It was a watchtower symbolizing the fallen angels will to protect God's creations.

While a pair of lower-ranked fallen angels guarded the entrance, the Council of Twenty sat in their seats around the long table as someone from their Intelligence Division gave a report.

"Reports are still coming in, but it seems we lost about fifty-two of the one hundred and seventy-two people we sent out to disrupt the summoning ritual," the fallen angel said. "Two of our squads were completely annihilated. It seems Clarissa's squadron, which had been tasked with searching the Halley VI Research Facility had run into Belphegor."

Murmurs erupted among the council members. Azazel remained silent for a moment, allowing the whispers to continue, but then he raised his hand. The council chamber fell silent.

"I had sensed Belphegor's presence at some point during the battle," Azazel said with a frown. "I'm a bit surprised Satan sent one of the four remaining Demon Kings. I figured they would send a high-ranking demon, but I was expecting someone like Mephisto or Astaroth."

"Perhaps we should have expected a Demon King to appear," Shemhazai admitted. "It is obvious they realized this is where the Grigori Hideout is. That being the case, they must have known that Christian is here too. Since they need him for their plans, it only makes sense that they would send in one of their strongest to protect the summoning site and ensure the plan's success"

"That is true." Azazel turned back to the Intelligence Division member. "I'm assuming Clarissa did not defeat Belphegor?"

The fallen angel shook his head. "No, sir. While the reports don't tell us how Belphegor died, it seems the ones who finished him off were Christian and Lilith."

While some of the council members once more erupted into murmurs, Azazel nodded. It made sense that those two would be the ones who defeated the Demon King. Christian had already defeated Asmodeus. If there was anyone who could face off against a being like that and win, it would have to be those two.

"What about injuries?" asked Baraqiel.

"There are numerous members who were injured," the fallen angel giving the report said. "At last count, there were about seventy injuries ranging from minor to severe. However, none of the injuries are life-threatening."

Azazel felt a slight sense of relief, an easing of the tension in his shoulders. It looked like they had survived another crisis.

Just then, shouting echoed from the hallway, where the guards were stationed.

"Hold on! You can't go in there!"

"Get out of my way!"

The doors suddenly burst open as Tristin rushed into the room, his face haggard and pale, his expression far from the jovial and teasing one that Azazel remembered seeing the few times they met.

"What is the meaning of this?" asked Baraqiel.

Tristin huffed as he placed his hands on his knees, shoulders and back heaving as he struggled to regain his breath.

"It's... it's Christian..." Getting his second win, the pretty boy who even Azazel felt a bit threatened by looked at everyone with wide eyes. "I just received word that someone has taken Christian."

A string of shocked murmurs spread through the table. Azazel stood to his feet.

"Who?" he asked as a cold chill swept through his body. He didn't know why, but part of him feared the answer Tristin would give.

"It was Kokabiel," Tristin said, setting off a shouting match that erupted around the table. While this was going on, Azazel did nothing to stop the fallen angels from screaming, some spouting denials while others shouted about how they knew Kokabiel was no good.

The Grigori leader slowly sat back down. He leaned over and placed his hands on his face.

We have been betrayed.

Chapter 15

Satan was sitting behind his—technically the Pope's—desk when he felt the powerful presence of a fallen angel soaring toward his location. With a chuckle, he waved his hand. The window several yards to his left opened just as a black figure swooped in.

Kokabiel landed on the floor and straightened. He turned toward Satan, an object dangling limply in his arms. The object was actually a person. While Satan had never seen this young man face to face before, he had seen plenty of pictures, so he knew very well who it was.

"Welcome back. I see you've completed your task," he said.

"It was easy." Kokabiel dropped the body he was carrying onto the floor with little care. "He was exhausted from fighting against Belphegor. He didn't even sense my presence when I attacked him." The fallen angel shook his head. "I'm honestly a little disappointed."

"Hmm… I thought I had sensed Belphegor being sent back to Hell." Satan hummed in thought. "I suppose I will have to punish him for letting himself be defeated so easily, though that can wait until later."

"I've done my part. Now I expect you to do yours."

Satan smiled at Kokabiel's words. "Do not worry. I want to open a Hell Gate as much as you do."

"Hmph."

"Are you going to stick around?" asked Satan.

"No." Kokabiel walked over to the window again. "I have no intention of remaining in your presence for even a second longer. I'll wait until you've opened the Hell Gate, and then I'll come back. Be prepared. I expect you to give me the fight I've been looking for."

"Ever the battle maniac, I see."

Kokabiel didn't respond to Satan's words as he flapped his wings and took off through the open window. Watching as the fallen angel warrior disappeared into the night sky, Satan released a sigh as he waved his hand and closed the window again.

"That fool hasn't changed at all."

Of course, it wasn't like he had much room to talk, but even he was changing at least some things. Several hundred years ago, Satan would have never considered infiltrating the Catholic Church itself. Then again, the protection God offered to those who were faithful had never been this weak before, so this plan wouldn't have worked several centuries ago anyway.

Standing up, Satan moved over to where Christian lay face down on the floor. He looked down at the boy and grinned.

"I suppose I should be grateful that Kokabiel hasn't changed since the war. It makes him a lot easier to manipulate," he mused as he nudged Christian with his shoes. "Wouldn't you agree?"

Of course, the boy lying on the floor did not respond.

***

Azazel sat behind his desk in an office located in the same tower where the Council of Twenty held their meetings. He'd designed the office to look like the ones he had seen in human dramas and TV shows. The wide space gave it an open feel, but he had a lot of amenities that kept it from feeling empty. There was the coffee table and couches sitting in the center of the room, the bookshelves filled with a combination of books and DVDs, and of course, the high-definition 102 inch flat screen against the wall on his left.

The desk he sat behind was wide and shaped like a crescent. It had two computers, one that was for personal use like checking his Twooter and Friendbook, and another that he used solely for work. The other third of his desk had a stack of reports. The reports were currently closed because he had already read through them, but he kept them on hand in case he wanted to look something up again for verification purposes.

Most of the reports were damage reports, though not for Seventh Heaven, which had received no damage to its infrastructure. They were about the damage received by the groups he'd sent out to locate and dispose of the summoning circle and medium.

So many people dead. So many injured.

On top of all the people they had lost, and the ones who were out of commission until they recovered, the loss of Christian was the worst. It meant they had lost. The entire reason they had brought Christian with them was because of his Belial blood, because the demons needed him to pass through God's barrier.

What are we going to do about this?

Of course they had to rescue Christian. The problem was they didn't know where he was. He knew where the ritual would take place; there was only one place where the ritual could happen. The problem was it wouldn't happen for a while yet. If at all possible, Azazel would like to rescue Christian before the ritual rather than wait until the day of. It would mitigate the possibility of them being too late.

As these thoughts went through his head, shouts echoed from the other side of his office door.

"You can't go in there—urk!"

"What are you do—ugh!!"

"Back off!" a voice shouted seconds before the door slammed open.

Azazel did not know Lilith all that well. They had only spoken a few times since meeting. Even so, the look etched on her face, the fire blazing in her eyes, and the brisk stride as she walked over to his desk did not fit the quiet and slightly shy woman he was used to seeing.

"Azazel, when are we going to mount a rescue operation for Caspian?"

"Er…" Azazel leaned over to look past Lilith. He couldn't see all of his two guards, but both of them were lying on the floor, their unmoving bodies partially visible. He leaned back again and looked up at her. "Once we figure out where Christian is being held, I plan on getting together a team."

"I want to be on it."

Azazel paused. "Um, are you sure that's a good idea?" When Lilith narrowed her eyes, he leaned back just a bit. "What I mean is you don't have much energy left right now, right? I heard you used a lot of energy fighting against Belphegor. Shouldn't you conserve what energy you have?"

"You're telling me to sit back and wait for my mate to be rescued by everyone else instead of going myself?"

Azazel didn't want to admit it, but he actually felt a cold sweat break out on the back of his neck. He didn't really understand. Even if she had the powers of the original Lilith, this woman's strength was currently weakened by her lack of life energy. Without her mate, she had to be careful with how much power she used, but even so, something about her suddenly overpowering and aggressive demeanor put him on edge.

Is this how a succubus acts when her mate is in jeopardy?

"W-well... I don't see why not, but there's a lot more that we need to do," Azazel said. "First, we need to find out where Christian is —"

"I can find him."

"Excuse me?"

"I can find him," Lilith repeated. "Christian is my mate. I can find him wherever he is."

"You can?"

Azazel didn't want to admit to being dubious, but, well, he was dubious. He did know that succubus had the ability to locate the men they bonded with. However, everything he'd heard suggested they could only locate their mates from a certain distance.

Then again, this woman's power is pretty out of this world. Maybe she can find him.

"We also need to put together a team..."

"I'll find people to go on this mission with me."

"O-okay." Azazel was beginning to actually get a little freaked out now. Lilith had placed her hands on the desk and was leaning over. The look in her eyes really did not suit her at all. "T-then... um... if you can get a team together, I'll see about getting the Watchtower prepped for launch in... uh... two weeks?"

"Tomorrow."

"You know I can't do that. It takes a long time to prep that thing, and also—"

"Tomorrow."

It was hard to believe the normally polite and quiet woman was being so forward and invasive. Did she even realize she was getting into his personal space?

"How about... three days from now? That's the fastest I can get the Watchtower ready."

Lilith frowned, her face scrunching up. Azazel spine suddenly stiffened as an erotic aroma unlike anything he'd ever smelled suddenly invaded his nose. He blinked once. Then shook his head to clear it However, that didn't do the best job. It was beginning to feel foggy.

Has she... always looked this alluring?

Maybe it was because he was staring at her from so close, but her eyes seemed much bigger and more innocent than usual. Her lips were also fuller. Even her small, pert nose seemed unusually alluring. Granted, he'd always known this young woman was stunning, but that was only natural because she was a succubus. They were basically a race of ticking sex bombs. He'd never met a succubus who wasn't drop dead gorgeous.

Finally, after nearly thirty full seconds of staring, Lilith leaned back.

"Fine. Three days. I think I can last that long."

Azazel waited until Lilith had strode out of the room before collapsing onto his seat. He took several deep breaths. For whatever reason, his heart was hammering in his chest and his libido was going full-throttle. He'd never been this hard before in his life! And he had lived a long, long, long time.

It wasn't until he'd sufficiently calmed down that Azazel realized something shocking.

Lilith's allure had been so powerful it affected even him.

Truly, she was a dangerous woman.

***

Christian jerked awake as though jolted by an electric current. He stifled the groan that threatened to escape his mouth as his body, achy and stiff as though he'd been sleeping in the wrong position, told him that he was not in the best of shape. He took a deep breath. Then he held it for three, two, one seconds. Releasing his breath slowly, he forced himself to remain calm and opened his eyes.

The room was dark, but thanks to the Eye of Belial, he could see just fine, almost as if it was daytime and the sun was shining without a cloud in the sky.

Immediately in front of him was a door. There wasn't anything spectacular about it. It was just a plain, average door. It was gray, had a basic handle, and didn't offer any sort of identifying marks that would let him know where he was.

He turned his head.

There was nothing in this room. It was just a room with four gray walls, a gray floor, and a gray ceiling. However, when he looked up, Christian did discover the potential culprit to explain why he felt so stiff. His wrists were bound in chains the kept his hands pinned above his head. He shook his wrists a bit, but nothing happened.

I can probably break free if I enhance my strength...

Now that he and Nox were one, Christian knew how to enhance his strength using demonic energy. Closing his eyes, he slowly thought about all the people who had died by his hands, the regret he felt killing people who had probably just been trying to live their lives. He thought about Asmodeus and what that demon had tried to do to Lilith. He thought about how the people of his hometown had been killed, how the Executioners had chased him, how the Church had been infiltrated by the Seven Demon Kings of Hell.

Hatred. Regret. Rage. A deluge of negative emotions flooded through him, threatening to overwhelm his mind.

He took a deep breath and shifted gears. Instead of thinking about things that made him angry, he thought about what made him happy. He pictured Lilith's face, her smile when she was happy, the look of satisfaction she wore after they'd had sex, the times when they would read together, and the way she had changed his life. He took those feelings, love, happiness, and the desire to protect, and he used them to protect his mind from the negative emotions flooding through his body.

I can do this.

Christian prepared to break the chains.

"I wouldn't do that if I were you."

He froze. There was a man in the room. Christian hadn't even heard the door open or close.

He didn't look like much, just an unremarkable man with a nondescript appearance that would easily blend into any crowd. It was hard to tell his nationality for precisely this reason as well. He had lightly tanned skin, a bland face, and swept back black hair. Of course, his nondescript ness presented a stark dichotomy to what he was wearing.

The all white robes he wore appeared quite austere, but there was a sense of majesty to them as well. They were adorned with a shoulder cape and a tassel around his waist. A cap sat on his head, also white.

How did this man get in here? And why is he wearing the robes of the Pope?

"Who are you?" Christian asked in a raspy voice that surprised even him. How long had he been unconscious?

"One day," the man answered, hands in his pocket and a smile on his face. "You have only been unconscious for one day, but I imagine you're feeling quite parched after what happened. I'd get you some water, but, well, I doubt you'd drink it."

Christian wondered if this man could read his mind, but he decided not to ask it, even in his head, for fear that the man would hear him.

"Who are you?"

"Hmm? You mean you don't know who I am? Well, I suppose you wouldn't recognize me in this form. Hold on for a moment."

Wondering what the man was talking about, Christian soon went from curious to shocked when the man's body changed. His black hair grew short and turned white. His skin went from soft and youthful to haggard, covered as it was in sunspots and wrinkles. His shoulders became stooped. Suddenly, standing before Christian was a man whom he'd seen on TV numerous times.

"Pope Judecous… no." Christian shook his head before glaring at the man. "I suppose calling you Satan would be more appropriate, wouldn't it?"

Satan chuckled. "I'm guessing you heard that from Azazel. His intelligence network never ceases to amaze me. You know I tried getting him on my side? He refused. I'm going to kill him for that, but it'll have to wait until I can actually come to Earth in my real body."

"So you kidnapped me," Christian stated. "And now you want to use me in that ritual to break the boundary between Earth and Hell, right? That is your goal, if I'm not mistaken."

"Correct… well, mostly correct." Satan crossed his arms and adopted a very human-like posture. "The barrier can't be broken by anyone but God. Let's face it, God is far more powerful than all of us demons combine. There is a reason we lost and were sent down to Hell. However, by using someone with the blood of Belial as a power source, we can open a gate that goes through the barrier. With it, myself and the other demons will be able to finally return to Earth once again."

"Right," Christian muttered. "That's how this sort of scenario usually goes."

"It does indeed." Satan grinned. "Now, I actually didn't come here to gloat. I thought I would warn you not to use your power to try and escape."

"And why is that?"

Satan possessing the Pope's body grinned at him, eyes glowing a malevolent red. "Because if you do, that little doohickey on your hand will explode and release a torrent of demonic energy that will burn you to a crisp." The Demon King pointed to something strapped to Christian's hands. It looked like C4 plastic explosives. "You'd survive, of course. I can't have you dying on me, but you'll never be the same again. Even that powerful regeneration of yours will not be able to heal you once you've been poisoned with my demonic energy."

"You could be bluffing."

"I could. Are you willing to take that risk?"

Christian stared at Satan with a hard look for several seconds, but he looked away in the end. Part of the reason Satan was able to seduce so many was because he never actually lied. Rather, he distorted the truth to suit his own purposes. That was how he had turned so many angels to his cause. If he was telling this to Christian, then he was probably being honest.

"Smart man." Satan chuckled. "Someone will come by to give you some food. I suggest you sit tight. The ritual will begin once we've finished our preparations."

As Satan disappeared in the same manner he had arrived, vanishing without warning, Christian leaned his back against the wall and closed his eyes. He would bide his time, collect his strength, and come up with a way to get out of this situation. He couldn't afford to remain there.

After all, Lilith would undoubtedly be coming to rescue him, and he'd rather she not use up anymore life energy when she was likely running low.

***

The first thing Lilith did was go to Clarissa. Out of all the people she could ask, the one she was most sure would help her was the leader of the succubus.

"Of course I'll help."

They were standing outside in a park, though she felt that calling it a park was being kind. There were no playsets or sandlots. It was just a grassy field surrounded by trees.

She and Clarissa weren't the only ones' present. Clarissa's mate, a man who looked to be in the prime of his life, with brown hair, brown eyes, and a fairly average build, was wrestling with a kid who couldn't have been older than four or five. The child, a girl whose unnatural beauty immediately identified her as a succubus, laughed up a storm as she climbed all over her father like a monkey.

"Thank you."

"You and Christian have done a lot for me," Clarissa continued with a shake of her head, as if stating without words that she had no need for thanks. "Besides, it is dangerous to go for too long without your mate. I... couldn't save your mother. The least I can do is save you."

As they stood there, the little girl, whose dress was completely ruined and covered in grass stains, ran over to them and hugged Clarissa's legs.

"Mommy, mommy! Come wrassle with us."

Clarissa smiled down at her child and patted her head. "I would, but I don't think your father likes it when I join in."

"That's because you two team up on me every time!" her husband shouted.

Lilith smiled at the small family before deciding to leave them so they could spend that time together. She glanced at them one last time to see that, indeed, Clarissa and her daughter were teaming up on her husband—not that he seemed to mind.

Her next stop was Samantha. It took a while to find her, but she soon discovered the woman training at the shooting range with the other Executioners.

The moment she entered the shooting range, almost everyone stopped and turned to look at her. Stares of curiosity, confusion, disgust, lust, and everything in between followed her every step as she walked toward Samantha, the only one not paying attention to her. She ignored the looks.

"Samantha?"

The woman was firing a gun, a pair of earphones over her head. The sound of thunder splitting the air made Lilith wince. Samantha probably couldn't hear her. Standing a few feet behind the woman, she patiently waited until the ex-commander was finished firing before tapping the woman on the shoulder.

"Lilith?" Samantha frowned at her as she pulled the earphones off her head. "What are you doing here?"

"I want you to help me rescue Christian."

It was probably not the most eloquent way to ask for a request, and Lilith understood that she likely sounded pushy. Truth be told, she had been intending to speak with more tact, but perhaps because of how worried she was, her ability to speak politely seemed to have flown out the window.

"I'm afraid I can't help you."

"What?"

"I can't help."

Lilith froze on the spot. She opened and closed her mouth several times, trying without success to speak for almost a full minute. Finally,

"May I ask why?"

"Do you even need to ask that?" Samantha said in return. "You should know why. The Executioners exist to slay demons. Christian is part-demon."

"You're going to not rescue the man who remained loyal to you for years... because you found out he's part-demon?"

Samantha looked away. "... Yes."

There were so many things Lilith could have done just then. She could have argued with Samantha, tried to make her see reason, tried to make her understand that it wasn't Christian's fault he'd been born with Belial's blood in him, that it was just a twist of fate and didn't change that her mate was a good person. The temptation to do just that was so strong it nearly overpowered her.

But she didn't.

She took a deep breath.

"Fine," she said, releasing her breath. "I figured you would be able to look past someone for their lineage after everything they had done for you, but I guess twelve years of loyal service means nothing to the Executioners."

Samantha narrowed her eyes. "That's not being fair."

"No, you're not being fair. I thought you of all people would be able to understand Christian's true nature, but I was wrong." Lilith's hair swayed as she shook her head in disgust. "I'm disappointed in you."

Not looking back at Samantha, Lilith turned around and stormed out of the shooting range, disappointment filling her soul. Given how much Samantha liked Christian, she'd been sure the woman would aid her. It was sad to know she couldn't rely on such a strong ally for help.

Since she'd asked all the people she knew would help—or thought would help—Lilith decided to try and find the fallen angels who had been with her and Christian during the demon army's attack. The problem was she didn't know where to look. However, while she was looking, another familiar figure sprang up to greet her.

"Hey, Lilith! You are looking lovely today!"

"Tristin…" Lilith did not have the strange love/hate relationship with Tristin that her mate did, but she felt wary around him. It was because he was an incubus and she was a succubus. That said, she didn't harbor the hatred her kind had for his kind. Just an instinctual disgust. "I'm sorry, but I'm a bit busy, so I can't talk to you right now."

Lilith quickly tried to walk past Tristin, but he moved in front of her before she could go anywhere. She narrowed her eyes and tried to move around him again. He moved with her. Frowning further, she turned around and tried to march back the way she'd come; he slipped around and blocked her path.

"I hear you're going to rescue Christian," he said. "I'd like to help."

"Uh…" How should she respond to that? "No offense, but won't you be kind of useless in a situation like this?"

"H-how mean! Did Christian tell you that?! He did, didn't he?!" Tristin placed a hand on his chest as if he'd been shot. "I'll have you know that I can help plenty! You're going to need someone who can hack into the Church's database and provide constant, up to date information! I can also coordinate your efforts, so you'll have a better chance of finding Christian and escaping there alive."

"Well… that is true."

"Let me help. I won't be on the ground like you and whoever goes with you. I'll be like your eye in the sky!"

Lilith thought about it and, well, she couldn't see anything wrong with the idea. It was sound. If she had him providing her with information like the layout of wherever Christian was being held, she'd be able to find her mate that much faster.

"I… okay. I'll be counting on you."

"You can count on me!"

As Tristin thumped his chest, Lilith wondered who else she could bring along. It was time to ask more people for help.

Chapter 16

The Watchtower had been prepped and ready to go in three days' time, just like Azazel had said it would.

Because of the nature of this mission, the Watchtower was given a skeleton crew, which meant outside of the people who would rescue Christian—and Tristin who would be providing online support—there were only fifteen crew members. Of course, Azazel was going too.

Lilith heard that Azazel had gotten a lot of flak for deciding to go with her. They were nothing more than rumors, but according to what Kel said, the Council of Twenty was not happy that their leader was going to go gallivanting off again. It was apparently something he did quite often.

Two more days had passed since the journey to rescue Christian had begun, and in that time, Lilith had been responsible for guiding them to her mate's whereabouts.

She did this by "feeling" his presence. As her mate, Lilith could always sense where Christian was. The concept itself was a bit hard for her to explain, but it was like something inside of her gut was tugging her in a specific direction. When she concentrated on that tug, she could feel Caspian, murky and indistinct but clearly him, and sometimes she could even get a sense as to what he was feeling.

At that moment, he seemed to mostly feel frustrated.

Standing on the Watchtower's bridge, Lilith looked at the newly repaired panel monitors that displayed the outside world. At her side was none other than the Governor-General.

"Are you sure we're heading in the right direction?" asked Azazel.

"Yes. It is definitely in this direction."

Lilith pointed at a specific direction. Azazel sighed as he turned around and walked further back onto the bridge. She followed the sound of his footsteps before they stopped, then she also turned around.

Azazel stood beside a large, holographic map of the world, a sphere that hovered several inches above the table, which acted as a projector that created the images. She walked up to the table. However, halfway through her walking, she stumbled as a slight wave of dizziness washed over her.

"Are you okay?"

"I'm fine. Just a bit dizzy."

Azazel didn't look convinced, but Lilith merely shook her head and repeated that she was fine. He probably knew she was running low on life energy.

Sighing, the fallen angel indicated a spot on the map.

"It sounds to me like Christian is right here."

The place he pointed to was located in the Middle East, just off the coast of the Mediterranean Sea. Lilith wasn't very good with her geography, so she looked at Azazel for an explanation.

"This is Jerusalem, one of the most important cities in the Hebrew, Arabic, and Christian religions." Azazel ran a hand through his hair. "Thanks to this city's strong religious background, it has a lot of power for Catholicism. I suspect the ritual they plan on holding to break the barrier between Earth and Hell will be there."

"When do they plan on having it take place?"

"If I had to guess, I'd say the night of the lunar eclipse."

According to Azazel, the lunar eclipse was a time when demonic rituals were at their strongest. It was not because of the reasons most people thought, though. There was no real significance to a blood moon in Catholicism. What gave the lunar eclipse its power was the belief that it had power.

"Belief is a form of power in and of itself," Azazel told her. "Religions get their powers from their followers. The more followers a religion has, the more powerful that religion and the deities involved are. Right now, Christianity and Catholicism are the largest internationally recognized religions, so the power we possess is at an all-time high. Because of that, even if only a few people believed in the power of a Blood Moon, it would be enough to invoke great power."

"I see," was all Lilith said.

Having read a lot of light novels and been inundated with popular nerd culture, she kind of did understand what he meant. She'd even read stories where similar faith-based powers were used.

The trip to Jerusalem only took one day. The Watchtower, Azazel proudly boasted, could easily cross the entire world in less than three days. Lilith was inclined to believe him.

Because of how conspicuous a floating fortress would be—even one with a powerful stealth mode—Azazel set the Watchtower down on the outskirts far from the city. The plan was for Lilith and her group to slip into Jerusalem, find Christian, and get him out. Once Christian was secured, the Watchtower would head into the city and pick them up. Until then, it was best to play it safe.

"These cards should get you into Jerusalem unimpeded."

Azazel handed each of them a small booklet that reminded Lilith of a passport. She flipped it open and saw her photo, a falsified name, and some equally false details about herself.

"I wish I had a cool fake passport," Tristin said with a huff. He crossed his arms and pouted like a petulant child as he watched everyone else. "It's not fair."

"You're not going on this mission." Lilith stared at the man. "Why would you even need one?"

"Because it's cool!"

After nearly a full minute of staring, Lilith turned back to look at Azazel.

"Good luck," the fallen angel said, taking a step back. "I wish I could go with you, but Satan and his cohorts would surely sense my presence if I got too close."

"You two are ignoring me, aren't you?!"

"Don't worry." Lilith gave him a determined look. "We'll get Christian out of there."

Azazel shook his head but grinned. "I know you will."

As Tristin fell onto his hands and knees in despair, Lilith hopped into the large red van alongside the others. Kel and Graf, who had agreed to join them, sat in the front, with Kel in the driver's seat and

Graf in the passenger's seat. Their wings were hidden currently. Also with her was Clarissa, Heather, and Kaylee.

"Are you ladies buckled up?" asked Kel.

"We are," Clarissa answered for everyone.

"Good. We're heading out now then."

As Kel drove the bus down the Watchtower's exit ramp, Lilith looked through the window and thought about the person she was going to save.

***

Tristin stood with Azazel and watched as the bus disappeared. He wished Lilith and her group luck in rescuing Christian. It really would be a shame if he didn't get to tease his best friend anymore.

"Do you think they'll be okay?" he asked Azazel.

The old fallen angel scratched his head. "Well... Lilith isn't doing too good. She may try to hide it, but it's been almost a week since she was able to sleep with her mate. Combine that with her fight against Belphegor and she's probably nearly out of energy. However, with some luck, they'll be able to find Caspian quickly and escape."

"So it's down to luck?"

"More or less."

"Hmm..." Tristin rubbed his chin. There was a bit of stumble on it. He would have to shave soon. "Their odds of victory might go up if they had some help. Wouldn't you agree, Samantha?"

No sound emerged from the loading bay for a moment; it was so silent one might have assumed there was nobody present except him and Azazel. A noise soon echoed throughout the bay. It let them know they were not alone. The odd pair turned to look at a large stack of crates filled with supplies. Walking out from around those crates was a young woman with dark hair and ice blue eyes.

"How did you know I was here?" she asked.

"Uh, incubus here." Tristin rolled his eyes. "I can sense a hot chick from a mile away. There's no escaping this keen sense."

Samantha wrinkled her nose. "You sound like a dog."

"Bark! Bark!"

While Samantha twitched as Tristin playfully barked at her, Azazel gazed at the woman with a bit more calmness.

"Are you not going to join them? I figured that's why you snuck on board."

Samantha turned her head. "I'm... not sure I have the right to join them after the things I said to Lilith."

Tristin had known Samantha long enough to guess what had happened. He wondered if he should say something. Teasing this woman was almost as fun as teasing Christian. He thought better of it for a second, and then decided what the heck?

"Let me guess... Lilith asked you for help, but you turned her down because Christian has demon blood in him, right? Then I'm guessing Lilith must have said something that hit you right in the guilty bone, which prompted you to sneak aboard this vessel without her knowledge and hide away here. Am I close?"

Samantha winced at Tristin, letting him know that he was probably more than just close. He'd definitely hit the nail on the head.

"Well, it's too late for you to join them now," Azazel muttered with a sigh. "However, if you want, you can always act as backup. They might get into a tricky situation that requires someone to rescue them."

Samantha bit her lip for a moment. Her eyes flickered around the loading bay, looking at all the crates and vehicles lined up in there. It was an awfully big place. The Watchtower was a state of the art mobile fortress, and as such, the loading bay was more like a garage than a simple place to load and unload supplies.

After several seconds of looking around, she turned back to Azazel.

There was a fire burning in her eyes.

"Do you have a motorcycle or some other two-wheeled vehicle that I can use?" she finally asked.

***

Getting into Jerusalem was easier than Lilith would have expected, but then, it wasn't like she had known what to expect either.

After arriving in Jerusalem, they were stopped by a small security detail and asked to show identification. They showed the booklets Azazel had given them. The guards had glanced at the booklets, then waved them inside.

Jerusalem was unlike anything she'd ever seen before. The buildings were an unusual blend of old and new. Some of the buildings looked quite modern, and there were even quite a few skyscrapers, though none were as tall as the kind she expected to find in Los Angeles and other US cities. Situated alongside these modern buildings were structures that looked old and weathered. As she pressed her face against the window of the van, Lilith could see one building that appeared to be made from grayish brown stone and was crumbling apart, while another building made her think of an Egyptian palace because it had a golden domed roof.

Christian is somewhere in this city.

"Our first priority should be to find lodgings," Clarissa said as Lilith narrowed her eyes. "After that, Lilith, we'll be counting on you to locate Christian."

Lilith didn't look away from the city. "Just leave it to me."

Thanks to Kel, who seemed familiar with this place, the group were able to find lodgings at a hotel called the Leonardo Plaza. They parked their van and stepped outside. The architecture looked different from what she was used to. A one-story extension was built beside a large building that seemed several stories tall. At about the third way point, a series of balconies protruded from it.

They walked through the entrance, which was made mostly of glass, and walked up to the reception desk. Lilith glanced around at the mostly empty space. She could admit this place was very chic. Even the desk looked like a piece of modern furniture with its strangely asymmetrical appearance.

Kel began speaking to one of the two female receptionists in a language she didn't understand. Hebrew maybe. Lilith didn't know, but she wasn't about to begin questioning it. She waited and watched as they spoke. Money was exchanged, and then Kel was given three sets of keys.

"Come on," he said. "We have our rooms."

He handed Clarissa one set of keys, Lilith another, and kept the last set himself.

Their rooms were all located across from each other. Lilith entered her room. Black carpet with brown triangle patterns covered the floor, the bed was large and took up most of the space, off-white walls covered three of the four walls while the one behind the bed was made of wood paneling, and the ceiling had a strange cutout in it. There were also two nightstands, a long table pressed against the wall opposite the bed, a balcony, and a flat screen TV.

Lilith stepped further into the room, then stumbled forward and collapsed onto the bed. She blinked as she laid half on the bed and half off. Her mind went numb, then snapped into sharp focus. She shook her head and stood back up. Her legs wobbled, but she willed them to stop and went into the hallway, where Valerie, Clarissa, Heather, Kel, and Graf were waiting for her.

"This room has a restaurant attached to it," Kel said with a gesture. "Let's grab a bite to eat, and then Lilith can use her ability to locate Christian."

"You certainly know a lot about this place," Heather said as the group moved off.

"This is Jerusalem," Graf said before Kel could. "Any angel worth his salt knows the historical significance of this city... though Kel knows a lot more about tourist attractions than the religious side of it."

Kel shrugged. "I've come here several times before."

The restaurant was open invitation. Anyone could go in. They were met by a man in a black and white suit, who led them to a table near a paneled window that gave a view of the pool outside. Being early in the evening, there were quite a few people in the pool, and there were even more people sitting at tables. Their group garnered some attention. It was impossible for them not to, but thanks to all of the succubus being able to control their Aura of Allure, it wasn't as bad as it could have been.

As they sat at the table, everyone looked at Lilith, who was frowning in concentration.

"Are you trying to find Christian?" asked Kaylee.

"Don't bother with that yet," Clarissa added. "Conserve your strength for when we need it."

"F-fine," Lilith sighed and slumped in her chair.

Dinner was nice, but Lilith barely tasted any of it. Her thoughts were centered solely on Christian. Was he okay? Was he safe? What if he was hurt? She didn't like the fact that she was sitting there, having dinner, while he was locked away somewhere.

After dinner, the group gathered inside of Kel's and Graf's room, which was bigger than Lilith's. Kel spread a map across the floor and looked at her.

"I want you to find Christian. If you can, try to point out where he is on the map."

"Okay."

Lilith swallowed nervously as the group watched her. She tried to feel that spot inside of her that belonged to Christian, the place inside of her where he lived. It was easy to find. She knew the general direction now as the tug on her gut indicated where he was, but it was difficult to put where that was on the map. However, as she leaned over and drew her finger along the smooth surface, her hand suddenly stopped moving.

"Here. Christian is right here," she said with certainty.

Kel grimaced as he looked at where Lilith was pointing.

"What is it?" asked Kaylee. "Is something wrong?"

"Not necessarily, but..." he sighed. "That is where the Tomb of the Virgin is. It's believed to be the burial site of the Virgin Mary."

"Is that bad?" asked Heather.

"No, but it could prove problematic," Graf answered. "Sites of historical significance always have a security detail patrolling the perimeter."

"When should we begin the operation?" asked Clarissa.

"Can we not begin right now?" asked Lilith, squirming. She was anxious to find Christian.

"We can at least scout the place out," Kel said. "We'll head inside and look around, but we won't be able to begin really searching until tonight. Jerusalem has a strict curfew, so night is when everyone goes to sleep. That will be the best time to slip in unnoticed, though it will also be the time when the guards are patrolling the streets."

They ended up leaving the hotel and heading toward the Tomb of the Virgin, which appeared incredibly ancient from just a glance. It was made from the same faded brick as most old structures in the city. The door leading inside was marked by an arched entrance.

They walked inside and traveled down a long flight of stairs. Chandeliers hung from the ceiling and there were tapestries on the wall. The ceiling wasn't flat. It was also arched, and the bricks were so worn down it looked like they had sunspots.

When the stairs ended, the space opened to reveal a room that would have made Lilith astonished in other circumstances. All kinds of decorations were strung from the ceiling. The numerous people walking through the room were looking at the paintings and artifacts that literally covered every wall and corner. Lilith wished she could say she knew who the paintings depicted, but the only ones she really recognized were the ones of Jesus Christ, who was an easily recognizable figure.

The room wasn't necessarily a room and more like a series of wide hallways. Lilith walked along with her group, who were pretending to act like tourists. As they did, she concentrated on trying to feel out where Christian was.

As they walked down one hall in particular, Lilith felt something tug at her navel again. She stopped. Glancing in the direction of the tugging, she found a small section carved into the wall. The wall was painted. She recognized the depiction showing baby Jesus standing on

Mary's lap, while Joseph and the three wise men and three kings stared at the newborn in awe. Immediately below the depiction was writing. She couldn't read it. However, something about this small section of the wall tugged at her.

"Lilith?" Clarissa tugged at her arm.

"I think Christian is somewhere past this wall," Lilith mumbled as she let Clarissa pull her away.

"Really?"

"Yes."

"Let's tell the others."

"Okay."

Informing the others about what Lilith felt, the group decided it was time to head back to their hotel.

***

The sun had gone down. Lilith stood inside of her bedroom, pulling the matte black unitard up her legs, hips, and torso. The fabric stretched across her body. Even though it basically clung to her skin, it didn't feel uncomfortable. After zipping up the unitard, she strapped the holster for her Glock 17 across her right thigh, attached her whip to a loop on her left thigh, put on her boots, and then donned a Kevlar vest. She threw a cloak over her ensemble to hide the firearms.

The weapons had been hidden inside of a compartment in the van. Kel and Graf had gone to the car and grabbed them for everyone.

Now that she was dressed, Lilith exited the room and headed for Kel's and Graf's room. Everyone was already waiting for her. Clarissa, Kaylee, and Heather were dressed in the same outfit as her. Meanwhile, Kel and Graf were wearing that strange bondage suit again. She wanted to make a comment about how their junk was practically visible, but she was too self-conscious.

"Now that everyone is here, let's quickly go over the plan," Kel said.

Lilith picked up where he left off. "We're going to fly to the Tomb of the Virgin by having you two carry us. Heather and Kaylee will cast an illusion to make sure no one sees us. When we get there, I'll lead you to where I felt the strongest reaction and we'll search for a hidden passage."

"That is about the gist of it." Kel nodded. "We'll want to be wary of traps. Here. Put these earbuds in your ear."

Kel handed everyone a small bud, which they turned on and put inside of their ear. It was a snug fit.

"Testing. Testing. One. Two. Three. Can everyone hear me?" came a voice.

"We can hear you, Tristin," Lilith said.

"Oh, good! Now then, as you know, I will be providing you with whatever information I can. Thanks to the system on the Watchtower, I was already able to hack into the Catholic Church's database. There isn't any information on a secret base located underneath the Tomb of the Virgin, but it might be something that the Demon Kings either purposefully erased or it was never recorded. In either event, I can at least provide you with information on guard patrols and the like. It should help you avoid getting into trouble with the local authorities."

"Is everyone ready?" Kel asked.

Everyone was ready, and so Kel and Graf led them onto the balcony, spreading their wings in preparation to take flight. Lilith and Clarissa each took one of Kel's hands. Kaylee and Heather took one of Graf's.

This was the first time Lilith had ever willingly touched a man who was not Christian. She felt a mild amount of disgust, but despite that, it was not as frightening as she thought it would be. That said, she didn't plan on making this a habit either.

With a flap of their wings, the two fallen angels took to the sky. Lilith almost screamed as her feet left the ground. Dangling from someone else's grasp as they flew across the sky was a frightening experience. The ground was so far down. All it would take was for their grip to slacken, and she would fall to the ground below and become a splat on the street.

They passed over numerous buildings. Just like Kel had said, there were quite a few guards out patrolling that night. Despite this, a few places still looked fairly lively. She could see lights and hear laughter and music coming from several buildings, which she guessed were bars and clubs or something.

Lilith had never been more grateful to be on solid ground upon reaching the Tomb of the Virgin. Her legs felt even more like jelly than she was used to. She wanted to kiss the ground, but that would have been disgusting.

Two guards were standing by the entrance, though they couldn't see her and the others thanks to the illusion cast over them. Clarissa raised a hand in their direction. The two guards blinked, then wobbled, and then leaned back against the wall before slowly sliding down. Loud snores echoing from them told Lilith they'd been put to sleep.

"Let's go, everyone," Clarissa said with a gesture of her hand.

The group moved up to the tomb's entrance. It was locked, but she picked it and the group slipped inside.

Making their way back to the depiction of Mary, Jesus, Joseph and the three kings and three wise men, Lilith and her group began looking around for something that looked like it would open a secret entrance.

"Hey, you guys and gals! I just found something interesting." Tristin's voice came over the earbud. *"While there are no maps showing something beyond this point, by overlapping the signals of every electronic device in the city and using them as a sonar, I was able to discover that there is, in fact, something beyond this door. It's a bit sketchy, but it looks like there's a tunnel of some kind down there. The image gets grainy about twelve feet in."*

"That means we are on the right track," Lilith murmured.

As the group continued searching, they were forced to pause when voices reached their ears and a light shone from another hallway. Two people emerged seconds later, wearing the uniforms of security guards. Once more, Clarissa raised her hand and cast an illusion on them. The two guards swayed and fell back, but Kaylee and Heather caught the pair before they could hit the ground and gently lowered them to the floor.

"Have either of you found something that looks like it might open a secret passage?" asked Lilith.

"No," said Kel.

"Nothing here," Graf added.

Lilith frowned as she stared at the painting. She leaned over and pressed a hand against the wall, letting her fingers glide across the words written below the painting. It looked like Hebrew. Well, she thought it looked like Hebrew. Nothing happened when she touched it. However, as she leaned forward, Lilith placed her hand on the small pedestal in front of it. When she did, her fingers curled over the edge and pushed against something. A soft click echoed through the hall. Then the small section carved into the wall rotated just enough to reveal a passage.

"I found it!" Lilith said excitedly.

"So you have," Clarissa said. "Let's go."

The group traveled through the passage. It was a tight squeeze, so Kel and Graf had to retract their wings again. Past the entrance was a dark tunnel that looked... surprisingly modern. The floor was made of smooth tiles polished to a shine instead of old bricks and the walls and ceiling were a single, uniform white. This was definitely suspicious.

"Are we heading in the right direction?" Clarissa asked Lilith.

Scrunching up her face, Lilith frowned as she followed the tug. "It feels like Christian is somewhere beneath us... but it's hard to tell. It feels like there's a thin wall separating us somehow."

"We should look for a staircase or something," Heather said.

There was indeed a staircase further into the hallway, and so the group walked down it, traveling ever deeper beneath the tomb. When they emerged from the stairs, it was to discover another hallway with more lateral passages than they knew what to do with. Lilith frowned as she tried to get a sense of where Christian was.

"This way."

Lilith turned down a passage. The others followed her.

She found it eerie that there was no one around to guard this place. Of course, there were those guards up top, but they were security guards for the tomb. Lilith had been expecting demons or something to be guarding this passage. However, so far, they had not run into a single soul.

Following the tug on her gut, Lilith found herself standing before a nondescript door. This was where the feeling was leading her. Without hesitating to see if it was trapped, Lilith opened the door and rushed inside.

"Christian! I'm here to save you—" She stopped talking.

The room was empty.

As the other members of her group filed into the room, Lilith spun around as though searching for Christian.

"I thought you said Christian was here." Kel frowned.

"H-he was. This is where the feeling led me. He should be here!"

Lilith didn't know what was going on, but she could tell that something wasn't right. The tug she felt telling her where Christian was indicated that he should have been in this room. Yet he wasn't. All this room had were a set of chains dangling against one side of the wall.

At that moment, the door slammed shut and locked with a click. Everyone spun around and became shocked to find a man standing in front of the door. His white robes were embroidered with gold. A large hat with the same gold embroidery running up the middle sat on his head. He held a shepherd's staff in his left hand.

There was a smile on his face.

Lilith felt a chill run down her spine.

"I thought I sensed the presence of some fallen angels, but I never would have expected to find a group of succubi with them." The man bowed before them. "Hello, my name is Lucifer, and you six will not be getting out of here alive."

Before anyone could respond, their shadows stretched and twisted. The group looked down. Screams of surprise escaped from them as the shadows suddenly reached out and latched onto their feet and ankles, and then began pulling them into the floor. They struggled to break free of the shadows. Kel and Graf even unleashed their divine energy in an attempt to beat it back. However, no matter how much they struggled, no matter how much they fought, nothing happened.

"Sayonara, ladies and gentlemen," Lucifer said, raising his hand as if waving goodbye to them.

That was the last thing Lilith saw before her entire world went black.

***

Azazel stood on the bridge of the Watchtower, wondering what he should do to pass the time. It had not even been half a day since Lilith and her group had left for Jerusalem. He knew they couldn't be expected to find Christian right away. Even so, he was getting impatient. This waiting was easily one of the most horrid feelings he'd ever dealt with.

It's probably because of the nature of this mission.

If Lilith and the others failed to rescue Christian, it would mean the end of the world as they knew it. Demons would invade Earth. This place would become overrun, and with God currently away, Heaven would be unable to stop them.

"Hey... Azazel, I think something bad just happened," Tristin called out from the command station.

Azazel walked over to Tristin's station. The man was sitting in the central control chair, his fingers flying across two keyboards as he stared at the pair of monitors in front of him.

Being someone who didn't know much about technology, Azazel had no idea what the characters scrolling across the screen meant. Everything here had been built by other fallen angels.

"What is the problem?"

"I just lost contact with Lilith and the others," Tristin admitted in a grim voice.

"What?"

Just then, a powerful sensation unlike anything he'd felt in a very long time washed over him. The hairs on his arm prickled. Turning his head, he, Tristin, and the other fallen angels looked out of the viewport and saw something that caused his blood to run cold.

"That is not good," he murmured.

Visible even from several miles away, the city of Jerusalem was covered in a dark, crimson glow.

Chapter 17

When Christian woke up, it was to discover that his surroundings had changed. He was no longer in that room with the gray walls, manacles binding his hands over his head, and was instead in a large room shaped like a cylinder. The ground was made of a dark obsidian. Marking the ground, breaking the blackness up with color, crimson lines like blood ran over the floor, forming a circle covered in symbols he could only think were demonic.

There were thirteen pillars surrounding him. He could only see seven, but the way they were spaced let him know there were seven more behind him. A person was attached to each pillar. Christian recognized them, if not for their white robes, then because he had met quite a few of these people. They were clergy members. Each one was a high-ranking Bishop.

While he could tell they were still alive, the Bishops moaned in agony as they writhed against the pillars they were chained to. They couldn't say anything. Their mouths had been hampered by the chains, which also dug into their flesh. All of them were covered in lacerations. Whoever bound them to these pillars must have beaten them as well.

"I see you are finally awake," a voice said.

Christian turned his head and glared balefully at the man standing before him—no, this person could not even be called a man.

"Satan."

"Good morning, sleeping beauty." Satan grinned. "I hope you're ready to begin the ritual."

"Ritual?"

"Oh, yes." Nodding, Satan walked among the pillars. The Bishops all flinched away from him, but they could do nothing except release a muffled scream as he dragged his nails along their flesh. "It is time to begin the ritual to open the Gate to Hell. I was originally going to wait until the lunar eclipse, but then I realized that would take too long and give those pesky Grigori a chance to rescue you, so we'll be using you as a medium and these flesh bags as fuel to initiate it in place of the eclipse."

The Bishops began crying, but Christian ignored them in favor of glaring at Satan. "What makes you think I'll go along with this?"

"You don't have to go along with it." Satan shrugged. "It will be happening whether you decide to help or not."

Saying this, Satan walked over to a pedestal outside of the circle. The demon disguised as a man pressed his hands against the pedestal. Dark energy flared from his hands. Its malignance was so overpowering that Christian flinched. The pedestal glowed with an ominous luminescence, then a single line of power lit up beneath the pedestal and spread to the circle, causing it to glow as well.

Almost as one, the Bishops screamed in agony as the pillars they were on became wreathed in dark flames. Christian could only watch in horror as their bodies started decomposing right before his very eyes. Their flesh became saggy and wrinkled. Then their skin started sloughing off, splattering to the ground. It only took around ten seconds for the bodies to wither away, but those ten seconds felt horrendously long to Christian.

With no bodies left to bind, the chains clattered to the ground. Meanwhile, the pillars had begun glowing even brighter than before. Christian realized that whatever was going to happen would not be good for him, so he started to struggle, but his hands had been staked to the cross Satan had bound him on, and his body was further bound in chains. He tried to channel his power. However, for whatever reason, his demonic power wouldn't flow through him the way he wanted.

"Oh, I forgot to tell you: those chains you're being bound with are called Hell Chains," Satan said almost as an afterthought. "They block a demon's ability to use their power. I imagine they work even better on someone who's barely a third demon."

Christian snarled at Satan, but he couldn't do anything else because the energy from the pillars had traveled along the circle and engulfed the cross he'd been bound to.

A scream escaped him as he opened his mouth wide. Christian thrashed and struggled as agony tore through his body. It felt like his insides were being boiled with lightning. Tendrils of arcane energy danced across his body, black lightning that covered him and flowed through him, wreaking havoc. His internal organs were on fire! He was being burned alive!

Darkness engulfed him as the last thought to flicker through his mind was how he hoped Lilith was safe.

***

Lilith jerked awake when her body shook as though someone, or something were incessantly shaking it. She blinked. Her eyesight was blurry, so all she could see were indistinct shapes and colors, but it soon became sharp enough that she could see the curve of a shoulder and strands of dark hair.

As she became more aware of her situation, Lilith felt the way her legs were swinging back and forth, the hands underneath her thighs, how her arms were slung over someone's shoulder, and the scent of sweat mixed with perfume. She realized that someone was carrying her. From the familiar scent and olive-colored skin, that someone could only be...

"C-Clarissa?"

"Are you finally awake?" Clarissa asked, though she did not stop running.

Lilith nodded even though she knew Clarisse couldn't see it. "W-what happened?"

"I'm not surprised you don't remember. You passed out soon after we were pulled into this strange place."

"This place?"

Lilith shifted and placed her hands on Clarissa's shoulders as the woman kept running. She glanced at the dark walls. Covered in a thick layer of grime, the walls were not only disgusting, but she could make out strange patterns on them that made her think the walls were made of bone. Likewise, the floor and ground had similar bone-like patterns. There weren't many lamps either, and what lamps hung from the walls emitted a dark light that almost seemed evil.

"Where are we?" she asked.

"I do not know," Clarissa said. "Lucifer brought us here. You passed out, but the rest of us tried to battle against Lucifer. We were no match for him, however."

"No match..." Lilith parroted, still quite out of it. "The others? Where is everyone else?"

"Probably dead," Clarissa admitted softly. "They told me to take you and run while they held off Lucifer."

"N-no..."

Lilith felt tears stinging her eyes as Clarissa kept running, taking random turns with seemingly no rhyme or reason. She couldn't believe everyone who'd gone with her was dead. She just... she couldn't. If they were dead, then it was all her fault. She was the one who'd asked them to come with her, to help her.

"If you have time to feel sorry for yourself, then you have time to focus on our mission," Clarissa suddenly interrupted Lilith's moment of self-loathing.

"Excuse me?"

"We're still here to rescue Christian," Clarissa reminded her. "Can you sense him?"

Shoving her anguish into the back of her mind, Lilith remembered their purpose for coming all this way. They had come to rescue her mate. She hated that people had died for her, died because she asked them to help her, but if nothing else, she should at least find Christian. If she could do that... if she could just locate and rescue him, then at least the deaths of her companions wouldn't be in vain.

Lilith closed her eyes and concentrated. She felt weak. Her bones seemed brittle, the flow of blood through her veins was slow, and her breathing was becoming stagnant. It seemed not being able to recover her life energy in several days was affecting her. Even so, she reached out and tried to find Christian.

"He's this way!" She pointed in the direction she felt him. "We need to hurry, though! He's in pain!"

"Gotcha!"

Clarissa kept running. Lilith could do nothing but lament her own uselessness as she let the other succubus carry her. The woman went through several more lateral passages, down a staircase, and soon burst into a large room.

Not being a good judge of size, Lilith could only tell that the room was large and shaped like a cylinder. A circle filled with strange symbols was in the center of this room, and inside the circle were 13 pillars with chains laying on the floor around them. A man stood on the opposite side of the room as them, concentrating on something, sweat beading down his face. And in the center of the room, inside of the circle was…

"Christian!"

Lilith struggled to get out of Clarissa's grip. Even though she felt weak, she pushed herself off the other succubus and stumbled toward Christian, but she couldn't reach him. The moment she reached the magic circle, a red dome of energy sprang up. Lilith screamed as she ran into the barrier, which shocked her. She stumbled back, landing on her backside, her face and torso smoking as though burned.

"Ho? It seems we have visitors," the man said, glancing in their direction. "If I'm not mistaken, you are this one's 'mate,' are you not? How precious. You came all this way just to save him. I guess Lucifer didn't do his job properly." The man's smile frightened Lilith, sending shivers down her spine. "I'll have to punish him later. As for you two, just stand there and watch. The ritual is almost complete."

Christian was screaming in agony as a dark energy engulfed his body. His screams, more than anything else, tore at Lilith's heart. Blood welled up in Christian's eyes, leaking down his face. His hands, staked to a cross, were covered in blood as the man thrashed against his restraints.

"This is it! Look at this! It's magnificent!" The man standing behind the pedestal crowed.

"I don't know what's going on," Clarissa muttered, "but we should try to stop him from completing this ritual."

Clarissa moved around the circle and raced toward the man, but with barely a flick of his wrist, the person fired off a spear of crackling dark energy at her. It struck her straight in the stomach. The woman staggered as the spear pierced her flesh and then disappeared. With blood gushing from the wound, Clarissa fell onto her knees, and then onto her stomach, a pool of crimson spreading out beneath her.

"Clarissa!"

Lilith scrambled over to the woman and placed a hand on her shoulder, turning her over. She gasped when she saw the wound. The ends were ragged as though something had torn her skin apart. The gaping hole had blood surging from it, leaking down her sides.

"W-we have to stop the bleeding!"

"I… I don't think you can stop this by applying pressure," Clarissa muttered as Lilith tore off her Kevlar vest and pressed it to the wound.

"But I... I have to try!"

Clarissa opened her mouth to say something in response, but then she coughed up blood. Lilith shushed her.

The ritual continued unabated. However, Christian's screams had disappeared. The man now hung limply from the cross, blood streaming from his eyes, mouth, ears, nose, and hands. Over by the pedestal, the man's grin widened as the ritual circle dimmed, flickered, and then stopped glowing.

"And now the ritual is complete," he said, turning to face them. "You two are quite lucky. No mortal has ever gotten to see a ritual like this before." He tilted his head. "Then again, maybe you aren't lucky, since I have no intention of letting you leave here alive."

Lilith could do nothing as the man flicked his wrist at them, sending two more dark spears in their direction, his aim obvious. Her life flashed before her eyes. She had so many regrets. Even so, she didn't look away as the spears traveled toward her and Clarissa in what appeared to be slow motion.

The ground rumbled as the wall on her left exploded. A bright beam of condensed golden energy washed over the spears. Lilith had to close her eyes, but when the light died down and she opened them again, it was to find several people racing into the room.

"Azazel? Samantha!"

Azazel and Samantha were there, along with Heather and Kel, though Kel only had one arm now. The other was a stump that gushed blood.

Heather and Kel rushed over to her and Clarissa.

"This doesn't look good," Heater muttered. "Damn... Clarissa is in bad shape."

"You two... you're alive," Lilith muttered as tears gathered in her eyes.

"Thanks to those two." Heather pointed at Azazel, who stood protectively in front of them, and then Samantha, who had made an immediate rush for Christian. The barrier was gone now that the ritual was complete. She stepped into the circle without pause. "They swooped in just as we were about to be killed. Anyway, let's get you out of here."

Heather helped Lilith sling her arm over the now one-armed Kel, and then she lifted Clarissa into her arms, heedless of the blood gushing from the wound in her leader's stomach. Lilith struggled to remain upright as Kel began dragging her toward the exit they had made. Heather, carrying the limply swaying Clarissa in her arms, was already running in that direction. Meanwhile, Samantha had removed the stakes and chains from around Christian and was now carrying him in a fireman's carry over her shoulder.

"Oh ho! Azazel, who would have guessed that you'd have the audacity to confront me," the man said, eyes glowing with malice.

"I'm not really here to confront you." Azazel shrugged. "I'm actually just here for the kids, though I guess it would be impossible to escape without a fight breaking out."

"I'm assuming you sent Lucifer back to Hell?"

"I did."

"Hmph. Consider yourself lucky that I no longer have any time to play with you." Black steam erupted from the body of the Pope, which began aging before their very eyes. "Now that the Hell Gate is open, I have more important things to do. But don't worry. It won't be long before I arrive on Earth in person, and then I'll show you what it means to incur my wrath."

With those last words, the Pope's body erupted into black flames and quickly dissolved. All that remained was the white robes.

Azazel stared at the robes for a second, then turned to them.

"Let's get out of here. All of you need medical attention."

Lilith struggled to keep her eyes open as the group began moving, yet the harder she worked to stay awake, the more tired she became. Unable to keep her eyes open, she descended into darkness.

***

Christian opened his eyes when he felt something poking and prodding him. He glanced around, recognizing the room he was in as a medical wing. White walls. White ceiling. IV drip. Someone prodding him. The person poking him with the strange device that resembled a wand was none other than Dr. Anastasia Pierce.

"Finally awake?" she asked.

"Doctor Pierce," Christian mumbled as he felt a wave of exhaustion sweep over him. His limbs were sore and stiff, and it felt like his insides had been turned into jelly. "What… happened? How did I get here? The last thing I remember was being crucified and feeling excruciating agony…"

"Lilith and the others rescued you," Dr. Pierce announced, causing Christian to jolt. "They traveled all the way to Jerusalem to save you."

"Lilith… where is she now?"

Dr. Pierce sighed. "You never change, do you? Still thinking of others more than yourself. Well, I won't tell you where she is right now. You still aren't fully recovered, so even if I did tell you, it's not like you can do anything."

If he didn't know any better, Christian would have said it felt like Dr. Pierce was purposefully avoiding the subject of Lilith. That made him nervous.

"You have become quite weak," Dr. Pierce said as she continued prodding him with that stick. "It is as if all the energy was drained from your body. Azazel told me about what happened. You were used in some kind of ritual to open a Hell Gate. Currently, your body is trying to recover the energy you lost, but it's going to be a slow process."

"How slow are we talking?"

"Slow enough that you'll probably be here for quite a while."

"Well... that sucks."

"I hope you're not saying that it sucks to be with me."

Dr. Pierce smiled at him, and Christian looked away as he broke out into a cold sweat.

"O-of course not."

"Good."

When Dr. Pierce had said that Christian was weak and had very little energy, she really did mean it. Talking even for five minutes left him exhausted. Christian ended up falling asleep almost immediately after his conversation with Dr. Pierce. He didn't know how long he'd slept, but when he woke up, the doctor was gone, and Samantha was sitting next to the bed.

He wondered what she was doing there. After learning that Christian was part demon, Samantha had all but avoided him.

"You're awake," Samantha said at last. She seemed to have realized that he was staring at her because she looked away. "How are you feeling?"

"Tired," Christian answered immediately, "but a bit better than before."

"That's good."

An awkward silence fell between them. Christian wasn't sure what he should say to this woman, who used to be his commanding officer and someone he trusted with his life. It felt like they were now standing on opposite ends of a chasm. He could no longer say he knew this woman the way he used to.

"Listen..." Samantha began, "I wanted to apologize."

"For what?"

"For avoiding you." Samantha's eyes flickered over to him, but then she looked away just as quickly. She placed her hands in her lap. "After I found out that you weren't fully human, I... well, I didn't know what to think. I felt betrayed, so I decided to treat you like you didn't exist. I know it was dumb. You didn't ask to be born this way, but I still couldn't accept that the person I lo—that the person I knew for so long wasn't human."

Saying this must have taken a lot of courage. Samantha was a lot like him. She'd been raised in the Church for years, indoctrinated in the ways of the Executioner, and never once questioned their cause. Humans needed to be protected. They were good. Demons and other monsters were bad and needed to be exterminated for the sake of humanity. Admitting that she was wrong, that he wasn't bad just for being born with demon blood in him, would take a lot for someone who'd been taught to believe otherwise for so long.

"It's fine." He sighed. "I understand where you are coming from. I don't blame you."

Samantha's lips twitched into a small smile. "I assumed you would say that. It's just like you."

"I guess."

Samantha didn't stay long, and he fell asleep soon after. Another day passed with Christian still bedridden, but after getting another good night's sleep, he felt a lot better—good enough that he climbed out of bed and tried to stretch his limbs. He still felt stiff. His muscles were sore from disuse.

While he went through some basic stretches, the door to his hospital room opened and Azazel walked in. The man looked a bit different since the last time he'd seen him. The Grigori leader normally wore such a nonchalant and even lazy expression, but now his face appeared haggard. He looked worn down.

"I'm glad to see you're in good health," Azazel said.

"I wouldn't say I'm in good health, but I do feel better." Christian stopped stretching to look at Azazel. He felt a bit uncomfortable since he was only in a hospital smock, but he couldn't let that bother him. "If you're here, then I'm guessing there's a reason for it."

"A lot has happened since we rescued you. Given the nature of what's going on, I felt it was best to inform you of everything that's happened."

Pausing, the fallen angel seemed to be thinking really hard about something. Christian remained silent as the man's brow furrowed. Finally, he sighed and scratched his head.

"There's no way I can put this delicately, so I'm just going to come out and say it. We currently have a crisis on our hands. A Hell Gate has opened up in Jerusalem and is spewing demons out of it. We've currently managed to seal the city off with a barrier, but that's only a temporary solution. The Council of Twenty is currently working on a plan to close the close the gate. We'll have to do something soon."

"What happened to the people inside the city?" asked Christian.

Azazel shook his head. "We don't know if any of them are alive anymore. The moment we put up the barrier, all contact with the city was cut off. There's a good chance everyone is dead."

Christian closed his eyes as he realized what that meant. To keep the demons from spreading, Azazel and the others erected the barrier around the city. While doing so prevented the demons from traveling to other cities, it also meant that everyone inside of Jerusalem couldn't leave either, and considering the cruel nature of demons… well, Christian couldn't see anyone who lived there surviving.

"There's one other matter I need to talk to you about," Azazel said. "It's about Lilith."

Christian froze. "What about Lilith? Is she okay?"

"She's alive, but that's about all I can say." Azazel turned around. "It would be best if I showed you."

Christian was left with no choice but to follow Azazel as the man left the medical room. He was given a pair of black pants and a white shirt, then exited the room and traveled through the hospital wing toward another room. When the door slid open to admit them, Christian froze.

"Lilith…"

His mate was currently inside some sort of pod. The sleek design was made of a white material with silver lining the opening. The shape reminded him of a flower bud. A section of the pod was made of glass, which revealed Lilith, her skin so pale it was nearly translucent, lying inside.

"She's been comatose ever since we rescued you," Azazel said as Christian walked over to the pod and placed a hand against it. "According to Heather, Lilith is almost out of life energy. Her body is currently in the process of breaking down. We managed to preserve her life by getting her into this cryo capsule. It's currently put her in a state of suspended animation, keeping her body and what little life energy she has left preserved."

Touching the glass, Christian ran his fingers over it as if to stroke Lilith's sleeping face. Her skin was so pale she looked like a corpse. It also appeared much gaunter than he remembered.

"This is all my fault," he muttered, frowning just a bit as his fingers moved over a circular section on the window that was not glass. It looked like this part was connected to the outside. A strange tube connected to a breathing apparatus covered Lilith's mouth. "Because I got captured, Lilith wasn't able to replenish her energy, and she used a lot during our battle against Belphegor."

"I wouldn't say it's your fault." Azazel wandered up to the pod and looked inside. "It was just bad luck. If anything, the fault lies with me for trusting Kokabiel."

"He was the one who betrayed us?" Christian had been knocked unconscious before figuring out who'd kidnapped him, so he knew nothing about this.

Azazel sighed and nodded. "I had always known that Kokabiel was dissatisfied with our current way of life. He craves combat. While the rest of us fallen angels chose to remain on Earth because we loved humanity more than we should, all Kokabiel has ever wanted was to fight against strong opponents. Thinking on it, I should have known he would betray us if someone offered him a chance to fight against the Seven Demon Kings."

Christian didn't know what to say to that, so he said nothing. Gazing into the capsule that was keeping his mate alive, he let his thoughts, his guilt, and his regret about not being able to do anything run wild.

"Fortunately," Azazel perked up, "we can heal Lilith now that you're awake. The problem we have is that we can't open the pod and let her out. The moment we do that, she will most likely die immediately. However, while you were recuperating, we devised a method that can help replenish enough of her energy that she'll survive until you and she can get to practicing procreation."

Christian didn't know if he approved of the way this man said, "practicing procreation," but he ignored his annoyance and focused on the rest of what Azazel told him. He could heal Lilith.

"What do I do?"

Azazel wandered over to a series of cabinets, opened them, and rummaged around. He mumbled to himself, though Christian couldn't tell what he was saying. After a moment of awkwardly looking at the fallen angel's back, he looked back at Lilith.

"Ah! Here it is!"

Finally returning to the bed, Azazel held a strange device in his hands. A long tube made of plastic composed most of it. On one side there was a cylinder that looked sort of like a cup or maybe even a really long beaker. It was about three inches in diameter, and the tube was connected to the beaker through the bottom. On the other side of the tube was a dome-shaped device that had a screen and several buttons located on it.

"What is that?" Christian couldn't help but ask.

"This is how you're going to save Lilith," Azazel announced as he held up the device. "I call this the Masturbator. What you're going to do is stick your penis in here. Then you stick this part on here." He tapped the dome-shaped part on the capsule that Christian initially assumed was to provide oxygen. "After that, you just turn it on, and the device will suck out your sperm and feed it to Lilith, which will give her the life energy she needs to remain alive."

Christian stared at the device now with something akin to horror, like it was an abomination the likes of which he'd never seen. He looked from the device to Azazel. The man looked so proud of himself. He was even puffing out his chest in pride.

"That is the most disgusting idea I've ever heard," he said at last.

"It is also the only idea we were able to come up with," Azazel countered. "Sebastian created it after learning about succubus physiology."

Damn that stupid scientist!

"Besides, it isn't like Lilith hasn't drunken your sperm before, right?"

Christian blushed at the implications, and then felt his cheeks grow even hotter when he recalled all the times Lilith had woken him up with a blowjob. She'd once told him that drinking his sperm was like her breakfast. She even jokingly referred to it as a protein shake.

A lecherous grin spread across Azazel's face as he held the device out for Christian. The former-Executioner glared at the device like it was the evilest thing he'd ever seen, but then, with great reluctance, he took it from the man's hand.

"This is the most humiliating thing I've ever had to do," he muttered.

"Just think of it as using your body to save your beloved mate," Azazel suggested.

"I would gladly use my body to save Lilith but using my body and having a weird device suck sperm from my junk are two very different things," Christian snapped as he removed his pants. He left his boxers on for now.

While he was attaching the dome-shaped device, which he realized acted as the machine-part that would suck out his sperm, onto the small round section of the capsule, Christian could not help but wonder if Sebastian had grown even more deranged since their last meeting. What sane man would come up with this?

He was about to pull down his pants, but then he paused as he realized something.

"Do you mind?" he asked Azazel, who was still in the room with him.

"Not at all." Azazel waved a hand as though gesturing for him to continue. "Please proceed."

"Not with you here. Get out."

"Now Christian," Azazel began. "I know this can be embarrassing, but I need to make sure everything proceeds smoothly."

Christian glared at Azazel as he pointed toward the door. "Out."

Azazel sighed. "Fine. Fine. I'll leave, but if something goes wrong, don't say I didn't warn you."

Christian continued staring at Azazel like he was trying to drill holes through the fallen angel's head. He watched the man walk out the door, watched the door close behind him, and then walked over and made sure to lock the door so Azazel couldn't come in. The last thing he wanted was this idiot barging in while he was doing something so gross.

It's for Lilith. It's for Lilith.

Chanting this mantra as he walked back up to the capsule containing his mate, Christian slowly slid his boxers off and prepared himself, both mentally and physically, to use the device.

For some reason, the mantra didn't help.

***

About an hour after Christian committed the most inglorious of resuscitation methods, he found himself sitting on the bed inside of his and Lilith's room inside the Watcher tower. Lilith was lying on the bed. Her skin was still pale, face still gaunt, but she wasn't dead. According to Heather, who'd come by to check on them, Lilith was still recovering from having used up nearly all of her energy.

Christian hadn't woken Lilith up yet because he was still recovering. There was something incredibly invasive about having a beaker suck semen out of his dick. He also didn't like how it had been used to essentially force feed Lilith. The whole experience had been wrong on many levels.

I just need a moment to recover from the experience, and then I can finish healing her.

He looked back at Lilith as she lay underneath the covers of the bed, her chest moving up and down as she breathed. She wasn't wearing anything underneath the blanket. In fact, she had been naked when they placed her in the capsule. Christian planned on asking Azazel who had placed her in the capsule, and who had seen her naked. If anyone but succubus like Clarissa had seen his mate naked, he was going to make them wish they were dead.

I suppose I should start.

Reaching out, Christian slowly stroked Lilith's sleeping face. She didn't respond to his touch, showing just how deep her sleep was. She almost always woke up when he caressed her cheeks like this.

Sighing, he grabbed the covers and pulled them down, revealing inch after inch of bare skin. First her collar bone became visible, and then the swell of her breasts. He stopped when the blanket uncovered all of her chest. His mouth went dry. Lilith might have looked a little malnourished because she didn't have much life energy, but breasts, large and succulent and caped with beautiful pink nipples, looked just as appealing now as they always did.

Stopping there, Christian stood up and divested himself of his clothing. He folded his pants and shirt, set them on the table, and returned to the bed. He peeled the covers back a bit more and slipped inside. Snuggling close to Lilith, Christian recalled what Heather had told him about the best method for restoring a succubus' energy.

Penile insertion was hands down the best method for a succubus to recover life energy. She had recommended that method, but Christian was not comfortable having sex with Lilith while she was unconscious, even if he knew she wouldn't mind. That being the case, the next best method was bringing her to orgasm with foreplay. It wouldn't be as good as sex, which was ten times more effective because sperm being directly deposited into the womb created the most energy. That said, it was as far as Christian was willing to go.

Kissing Lilith on the cheek, Christian snuggled against her warmth as he began caressing her body. He let his hands roam over her flat stomach, massaged her breasts, and caressed her arms and the side of her torso. As he did, Lilith's cheeks gained a healthy flush. Her breathing also picked up.

"Come on, Lilith. Wake up. I hate it when I have to do this by myself."

But Lilith wasn't waking up, causing him to sigh again.

Shifting until he was straddling Lilith, Christian leaned down and kissed her forehead. Then he kissed her eyelids, followed by her cheeks. He avoided her lips and kissed her chin, followed by trailing kisses down her neck and collarbone. Kissing his way between her breasts, he avoided her nipples and began to kiss and lick her stomach.

By this point, Lilith's body was growing warm. Her mouth was open to release gentle moans. She seemed to know what was happening at least. As he traveled further down, placing kisses on her hairless mound, she unconsciously spread her legs.

The blanket had been fully removed, and Christian looked up the expanse of Lilith's stomach to see her face carefully hidden by her breasts. Because her chest was so big, her breasts sagged to the sides a bit. They also jiggled as she breathed. While it was hard for him to get hard when Lilith wasn't, well, conscious, he couldn't deny that she was arousing to look at even like this.

Christian grabbed Lilith's legs, lifted them up, and brought them close together so her thighs and calves were touching each other. He then pushed her legs forward, until her knees were pressing into her chest. Now with her lips in full view, Christian could see that she was already wet. He watched as a small drop of her arousal leaked from her and trailed down to her butt before disappearing. Leaning down, he placed his mouth over her snatch and pushed his tongue past her lips.

The response from Lilith was almost immediate. Her thighs clenched as a loud moan escaped her mouth. Christian continued French kissing her lower lips, finding the g-spot and stimulating it with his tongue. Meanwhile, he kept her legs together with just one hand, and used his free hand to rub her clit.

Juices started from her more quickly, so much so that Christian almost had trouble lapping it all up. Her scent and taste were the same as always. It was addicting. He could almost understand what Lilith sometimes meant when she said his protein shakes were all she needed. He felt like he could subsist on her love nectar alone.

He knew Lilith had orgasmed when the juices flowing from her increased. She released a moan that sounded almost like a scream, and then her body went limp. Setting her legs down, Christian sat up and wiped off the fluids he couldn't drink from his face, his eyes focused solely on Lilith.

She was awake now. Her eyes were wide open. Even so, it didn't seem like she was looking at anything.

"Lilith," Christian called out as he crawled up the bed.

"Christian?" she murmured, her voice sounding shocked as their eyes met. She stared at him for a moment, but then tears gathered and streamed down her face. "You're okay... I... I'm so glad... that you're alright!"

Lying back down beside her, Christian pulled Lilith into a hug, entangling their legs together as he wrapped his arms around her shoulders and allowed the woman to bury her face in his chest.

"Sorry. I didn't mean to worry you, but you also worried me, you know."

Lilith sniffled. "What do you mean?"

Christian spent the next few minutes explaining everything he could to her. Truth be told, he didn't know everything that was happening himself, but he did let her know what happened immediately after she fell unconscious from a lack of energy.

"I see." Her cheeks were flushed red. "I'm sorry you had to do that."

He had just finished explaining how he had used the Masturbator to feed her sperm. It was a conversation he never wanted to have again.

"I'm the one who should apologize."

"No. I'm grateful you were willing to go so far for me. Um. Though it is a bit embarrassing to learn this."

Christian couldn't help but agree. The act of remembering what happened even caused his dick to shrivel a little, but he quickly shook the thoughts away. There were important matters at hand, and the most important one, the one consuming his mind, was that he and his mate were currently naked in bed together.

"I love you so much."

"I love you too—mph!"

Lilith released a shocked but muffled squeal when Christian kissed her with all the passion he'd kept in check while helping her regain consciousness. Despite being surprised, she gave as good as she got, kissing him back until both of them were gasping for breath. Yet even though their lungs were screaming at them to stop, they didn't. They breathed through their nose as they kept going at it like rabbits in heat.

Christian placed his hands on the small of Lilith's back, applying a light pressure that caused shivers to run down her spine. In exchange, Lilith had reached down between their bodies and was stroking him from shaft to head. An electric current rushed through his body as she toyed with him. He groaned into her mouth as he probed her with his tongue.

Rolling on top of her, Christian went from kissing her to attacking her neck. He gave it light nips and thorough licks, leaving glistening trails of saliva.

That feels sooo good!

"Did you say something?" Christian asked.

"No," Lilith sighed, and then cried when he suckled on her pulse point. "Christian!"

Christian could have played with Lilith forever, but more than that, he wanted to get to the main event. He wanted to be inside of her again.

He sat up and grabbed her left leg. Lilith was lying on her side, so when he lifted her leg and set it on his shoulder, he was still straddling her right leg. Lining himself up, Christian pressed just the tip of his head against her smooth lips, and then looked to her for permission.

She smiled at him. "Fill me up, Christian."

That was all permission he needed. Thrusting himself inside of her, Christian buried himself all the way to the hilt, bottoming out.

"Ugh... Christian... it feels like you're hitting my womb! This position! I really like it!"

"Me too. It feels like you're even tighter than usual today."

Christian needed a moment to keep himself restrained. If he didn't get a grip on these sensations, then he was going to cum before he could please Lilith.

Once he was certain he wouldn't explode from being inside of her, Christian rocked his hips back and forth. From this position, it was easy to see how his dick was stretching her lips, how inch after inch of his flesh, covered in her sexual juices, was revealed when he pulled out. Only after everything but his head was outside would he pushed himself back in, enjoying the sight of her lips sucking him in.

"Hyk! Nnn! S-soo good! It's been—hnn! Ah! Ah!—it's been too long since we've done this!"

"I-it hasn't been that long—ha... ha... but I have missed this."

"Hyk! So good! So good! Christian—ahn! Ah! Christian!"

The sound of their flesh slapping together as their bodies met mixed with the lewd noises from Christian plunging himself into Lilith's wet folds. He tried his best to alternate the timing of his thrusts based on the sounds Lilith made. It was easy since they were one as well. He could feel what she liked because of the pleasure feedback that looped through them when they were connected at this level.

"Hey, Lilith. I want to try something."

"You want... ha... what did you want to—EEK!"

Christian pulled out and turned Lilith onto her back. He placed his hands behind her back and lifted her up, until her chest was pressing against his. Sitting with his legs out in front of him, he grabbed onto Lilith's bottom, his fingers sinking into her flesh, and lowered her onto his dick.

"OOH!!!"

Lilith threw her head back, eyes going wide and tongue sticking out as her spine arced in a way that seemed almost painful. Moving his left hand up, Christian placed it on her back and pulled her back to him.

"Set your hands on my shoulders, please," Christian instructed. "And wrap your legs around my waist."

"Okay."

For some reason, Lilith became even more wet when he told her what to do. Her love nectar flowed out from around his shaft as she wrapped her legs around him and placed her hands on his shoulders. Now she was elevated slightly above him, giving Christian a perfect view of her beautiful breasts, which bounced and swayed with every rocking motion they made.

"Now whaaaAAATT!"

Lilith's scream echoed around the room as Christian took her nipple into his mouth, swirling his tongue around it. At the same time, his arms flexed as he raised her up until his head was the only thing inside of her, and then lowered her back down. He went slowly at first, but he soon picked up speed until the sound of their wet flesh slapping together mixed with the moans, groans, and grunts they released.

"Hnn! Ahn!! Ah! Ah! Christian! What is this new position?! What is it?!"

"I heard it's called the lotus position."

"Lotus! I haven't heard of that! But I—ah! Ah! Like it! You're going in so deep! I feel like I'm losing my mind!"

It was interesting how they'd begun talking during sex. He couldn't remember when they started, but during the first few times, they hadn't spoken much at all. He chalked it up to inexperience and not being used to the connection. It was still very difficult for him to figure out where his conscience ended and hers started. However, it was getting easier the longer they had sex.

"Christian! I! I—"

"Me too! I'm close. Just hold on a bit longer."

"I can't! I'm—oh! Oh! AHH!"

Christian winced when Lilith clamped down on him. Despite how tight she had become, the lubrication from her juices allowed him to keep going, lifting her up and bringing her back down. The feeling of her tight inner walls rubbing against him was the finishing blow that tipped him over the edge.

He dropped Lilith onto his dick one last time, then wrapped his arms around her waist as they rode out their shared orgasm. He could feel his warm spunk mixing with Lilith's love juices as it spilled out around his dick and drenched him and the bed. Lilith had placed her head on his shoulder and was both breathing like she'd just run a marathon and licking his skin.

He allowed himself a moment to rest, or he was going to, but then Lilith pushed him backward. As his head hit the bed, he looked up. Lilith was staring at him with a wanton look he only saw when she was starving. He guessed that going without sex for several days after using so much life energy you almost died kind of was like starving if you were a succubus.

"Christian..." Lilith panted. She didn't even give him a chance to speak before she smashed their lips together.

Christian tried his best to keep up, but her tongue had already entered his mouth, and she was rubbing her now sodden entrance against him. The sensation of her soaking wet nether lips spreading apart as they smeared his shaft in their shared juices brought him back to full mast, and Lilith did not even show a second's hesitation as she impaled herself on him. Almost before he could even enjoy the feeling, she was rocking her hips against him. She raised them. Lowered them. Raised them. Lowered them. Then she'd rock back and forth. However, as she repeated the process, her actions grew more frantic, more frenetic, and Christian found himself struggling to stop himself from cumming.

Lilith pushed him onto the bed, and Christian didn't resist. Her hips rocked against him. The bouncing of her breasts was a sight to behold, and he couldn't stop himself from reaching out. He grabbed onto her nipples and lightly pinched them. Lilith squealed as a shock of pleasure burst through her brain.

"So good! So good! Christian!"

Christian somehow found the strength for two more orgasms, but he was spent after that. His body felt like it had been hit by a steamroller. Given that he was technically still recovering as well, he upposed this act had set him back, but as Lilith cuddled into his side, e found himself not caring as much.

Lilith had already gone to sleep. Christian closed his eyes, about o follow her, but then a knock sounded at his door.

"Christian!" an annoying voice followed it. It was Tristin. "I hate o interrupt you two, but when you're done having hot, passionate, aunchy sex, get yourselves to the bridge! Azazel wants to give you and veryone else a briefing on what we're going to do about that Hell Gate."

Realizing he wouldn't be getting any sleep yet, Christian set about waking Lilith up.

There were times he wished the world would give him a break.

Chapter 18

When Christian and Lilith finished getting dressed and went up to the bridge, it was to find Azazel standing alongside Samantha, Heather, Kel (who Christian noticed only had one arm), Clarissa, and Tristin. Oddly enough, Sebastian was also present. Christian hadn't even known the crazy scientist was on the Watchtower.

The seven of them were standing around the holographic projector table. Currently, the table was displaying a three-dimensional projection of Jerusalem, which was being surrounded by a large dome-shaped barrier.

"Glad you could make it," Azazel said. "I see the princess is awake too."

"No thanks to you," Christian retorted. He was still very sore about being forced to use that device on her. Thinking back on it, he wondered if it had really been necessary at all.

"Don't be upset. I helped you out."

"Hmph."

The two of them walked up to the table. Christian took his place beside Tristin, while Lilith stood next to him with Samantha on her other side.

"It's nice to see you in good health," Samantha said to them.

"Thanks!" Lilith responded with a bright smile. The expression on her face caused the other woman to look away.

"Now that we're all here, we can get down to business." Azazel gathered everyone's attention as he gestured toward the three-dimensional construct. "Several days ago, Satan and his cohorts finally managed to create a Hell Gate on Earth. I'm sure that's an unfamiliar term to some of you, so let me explain. Hell Gates are essentially gates that bypass the barrier separating Earth from Hell. I suppose you could say they create something like a wormhole that connects these two realms together."

As he spoke, the image on the holographic projector changed. It zoomed in past the barrier, traveling through Jerusalem, until it stopped in front of a large object. The edifice was made from a dark material that seemed to absorb the light around it. It towered over the surrounding buildings. Thorns jutted from its top like a crown of spikes, while twisting spires on either side acted as supports for the massive archway situated above it. Within the middle of this gate was swirling eddies that resembled a vortex, like something out of a sci-fi movie, but the demons spewing from it every few seconds were anything but creatures of science fiction.

"You can see here that the Hell Gate is releasing a lot of demons," Azazel continued to talk. "So far, we have counted over two thousand demons exiting the gate and more are coming every second. Also, while the Seven Demon Kings have not emerged from the gate yet, it is only a matter of time before they do."

"I would have expected them to be one of the first to exit," Samantha commented as she stared hard at the gate.

"You'd think so, but they can't get out right now," Sebastian said, pushing his glasses up the bridge of his nose. "I've run some simulations and it looks like the Hell Gate is currently unstable. If one of the Demon Kings were to try and emerge from it now, their overwhelming power would cause the gate to collapse."

Christian cupped a hand to his chin. "So they're letting low-level demons come through while the gate stabilizes."

"That is correct," Azazel said. "They learned that you can't just come through a Hell Gate once it's created from their last experiment. I'm not sure if you know this, Christian, but a Hell Gate has appeared on Earth before."

"It has?"

Nodding, Azazel said, "you aren't the only one with the blood of Belial. There was another aside from you and your father, though the blood in him was thin unlike yours. Anyway, Satan used him to create a Hell Gate several years ago and sent Abaddon through it. The gate collapsed seconds after Abaddon past through."

Christian closed his eyes and took a deep breath. "I see. So that time I fought Abaddon…"

"It was part of Satan's failed experiment," Azazel confirmed. "Consequently, your battle against Abaddon was also when the Seven Demon Kings discovered you were an Executioner. I believe they decided to bide their time and make the Belial blood inside of you grow stronger, so they could create a sturdier Hell Gate, one that is strong enough to allow the Demon Kings passage into this world."

A shudder passed through Christian as he tried, and failed, not to remember his battle against Abaddon. While the fight against Asmodeus had been hard, the battle against the Destroyer had actually been the most difficult to date. The entire city had been laid to waste. Not only that, but the group he'd been a part of had gotten annihilated. Even now he could still remember the heat singing his body, how the smell of decaying and burnt flesh made him want to vomit, and the inescapable terror at seeing a high-class demon up close.

"How much time do we have before the gate is stable enough that a Demon King can pass through it?" asked Lilith.

"That's a good question."

Azazel looked at Sebastian, who adjusted his glasses some more, causing them to flash in the light.

"While we do not have a clear estimate, we can assume that the gate will be strong enough to allow high-level demons to pass through within the next week. Several mid-level demons have exited the gate within the past two hours. From my calculations, I have deduced that the gate's durability will increase at a faster rate the longer it remains active."

"Which brings me to our objective." Azazel clapped his hands together and looked at them. "Currently, two hundred Grigori have surrounded Jerusalem and erected a barrier to keep the demons from spreading beyond the city. However, once high-level demons begin emerging, it's going to be impossible for us to maintain the barrier. Our goal right now is to close the Hell Gate."

"I'm assuming you know how to do that," Clarissa said, arms crossed as she stared at the gate that continued to release all manner of demonic beings.

Christian was also staring at the holographic representation of the Hell Gate. There were a few demons coming through that he recognized, such as imps, hellhounds, and dantalions. Those were all low-level demons. However, there were also quite a few that he didn't recognize at all. There was a demon that looked like a mass of writhing tentacles, a massive behemoth that stomped out of the gate on four thick legs, and even a few demons that looked like decaying dragons.

"There is a way to close the Hell Gate," Azazel confirmed. "The Hell Gate is basically a coalescence of demonic energy that has been tied to this plane. While the first part of creating a Hell Gate involves having someone with the blood of Belial being used in a ritual to activate the gate on this side, the other involves creating an artifact that can store demonic energy and power the gate on the other side."

Azazel paused to let that sink in. Christian glanced at the others to see if they understood the implications. While some like Clarissa didn't seem to quite get it yet, others like Samantha, Sebastian, and Tristin easily understood what the fallen angel leader was implying.

"So…" Lilith scrunched up her face. "In order to close the gate, someone has to pass through the gate and close it from the other side? Wouldn't that mean whoever goes to close the gate will be trapped on the other side with no way back?"

"Yes." Azazel's expression was perfectly composed as he nodded at her. "Whoever goes through the gate and closes it will not be able to return. They will remain trapped in Hell for the rest of their lives."

A silence so poignant it made everything seem as if time was standing still spread through the bridge as, one after another, the group slowly realized what this meant. Someone was going to be sacrificed for the sake of everyone else.

"How… do we decide who should be the one to close the Hell Gate?" asked Clarissa, who looked like she had swallowed a bitter pill.

Christian was very tempted to offer himself up as the sacrificial lamb. It was his fault this gate had been created, after all, and so, logically, he should have been the one to close it. He didn't offer himself, though. It was not because he felt like he shouldn't, but because if he did, then he would also be damning Lilith. A succubus could not live without her mate, so she would either be forced to come with him or wither away on Earth without him.

"There is no need for us to decide," Azazel said. "The decision has already been made." He paused, looking at each of them in turn, and then gave them a resigned smile. "I will pass through the gate and close it."

***

The plan Azazel had come up with called for a massive gathering of armed forces. Essentially, several squadrons would travel into Jerusalem, dispose of the demons currently inhabiting it, and make their way to the Hell Gate. Once there, Azazel would travel through the Hell Gate and close it from the other side.

To that end, the Grigori had gathered all of the forces they could bring to bear, including the Executioners and succubus. Not only that, but all of the weapons they had been stockpiling were made readily available.

Christian no longer had his signature weapons. Gabriel, Phanul, Michael, and Rafael, his guns and swords, were no longer in his possession. He could only assume that Satan had either disposed of them or locked them away somewhere. In either event, he'd been forced to look at the weapons the Grigori had on hand.

All of the weapons were made from Orichalcum, which surprised Christian, but he soon learned that the Grigori were masters of alchemy, or rather, Gadreel was. He supposed it made sense. Gadreel had taught humans the art of cosmetics, and cosmetics was kind of like alchemy, in a way.

None of the weapons they had really stood out to him. Granted, he knew he was being picky, but they just didn't feel right. He had grown so used to using his other weapons that using different ones felt odd.

In the end, he'd gone with weapons that closely resembled his original ones. His guns were a pair of Desert Eagle XIX. They were .50 AE gas-operated, semi-automatic pistols with a seven-round capacity. They weighed about 72 ounces with an empty magazine, so they weren't too heavy for him. The only issue they had was that these were designed for two-handed shooting, while Gabriel and Phanul had been designed specifically for one-handed shooting.

The two swords he had chosen were called knightly swords, though they also went by the name arming sword. They were straight, double-edged weapons with a single-handed cruciform hilt and a blade length of 31 inches. Once again, the weapons felt off to him, and he felt clumsy while wielding them, but there was little he could do about that.

While the swords were easy enough to get a feel for, the guns were another story entirely. They had more recoil than Phanul and Gabriel. This meant he needed to bring more strength to bear in order to keep on target while firing one-handed. It also meant it was harder to dual-wield since his arms kept getting jerked around.

In order to compensate, Christian began working on incorporating the added recoil into his fighting style. He spent a good deal of time in the shooting range. He practiced firing at the targets, using the recoil to move his body into a spin that would help bring his other gun to bear. He had some problem with his aim at first, but it did become easier as he practiced.

Lilith also spent time in the shooting range with him. She practiced with her Glock 17, which she had grown good enough had using that she now had a 97% accuracy rate when firing at a non-moving target. He was impressed and told her so several times. Each time he complimented her made the woman smile.

When not spending time practicing, Christian and Lilith either spent time alone in their room, or they spent it in the mess hall.

The mess hall wasn't anything extravagant. It was bigger than the observation deck, and there were several bolted down tables and chairs spaced across the room. There was also a second floor. However, the second floor wasn't what he'd really call a second floor because it was more like a balcony that traveled around the room in a ring. That said, there were some smaller tables upstairs that fit four people instead of eight. Christian liked eating up there because there weren't as many people.

At the moment, Christian and Lilith were eating lunch with, of all people, Samantha and Tristin. The unlikely pair had spotted them and decided to join them. When Christian asked if they had come together, Samantha had given him a glare filled with so much vitriol it would have choked a lesser man. Tristin had merely laughed it off.

"Are you two about ready for the mission?" asked Samantha as she stirred around her pasta. It wasn't the traditional marinara pasta, but a type filled with some kind of buttery garlic sauce. The scent made Christian's nose twitch. "It begins tonight, so I hope you two are ready."

"As ready as we'll ever be," Lilith said with a shrug. Unlike Samantha, she had a simple sandwich on her plate. It was filled with meat, vegetables, and a thousand islands dressing as a spread.

"I still haven't gotten used to the new guns and sword," Christian admitted. "I don't think I'm bad at using them, but I feel like my reactions are more sluggish than normal. They don't feel like an extension of my body like my other weapons did."

Samantha nodded her understand. "After using your weapons for so long, they begin to feel like a part of you, so much so that using different weapons just feels wrong. I understand how you feel."

"I don't," Tristin replied cheerfully.

"That's because you're useless when it comes to using weapons," Samantha said.

Christian nodded as he added, "you're more liable to kill yourself than you are your enemies."

"How mean!"

"Is it really that bad using weapons you aren't used to?" asked Lilith.

Christian studied Lilith for a moment before responding. "Well imagine it like this. As humans, we are born with two arms and two legs. We grow used to these arms and legs. They're a part of us. Now imagine that one day, one of your arms is chopped off and replaced with a prosthetic limb. That's sort of how this feels."

After thinking on that for a moment, Lilith shuddered. "That doesn't sound pleasant."

"No, it doesn't."

"You'll be interested to know that all the Executioners have arrived," Tristin said, changing the topic. "I saw Sif and Leon come in just a few hours ago. It looks like the Science Division even arrived. They were carrying some pretty interesting weapons as well."

"Is that so?" Christian asked, unable to keep the fear out of his voice. The Science Division was filled with what he could only describe as mad geniuses. Every member of the division was undoubtedly talented, but they were equally insane. Samantha used to have her hands full trying to reign in their more daring experiments.

"They actually have built something fairly useful this time," Samantha admitted. "A weapon that can be charged with divine energy from a fallen angel and released as a condensed projectile. It has enough penetrating power to punch a hole straight through a greater demon. Sadly, I don't think they've made enough of that weapon to distribute it."

"They've actually begun building a lot of weapons that are powered that way," Tristin added as he looked at Christian. "Maybe you should consider finding Sebastian and asking if he has a pair of handguns you can use."

"Maybe..."

Christian was not sure he believed the Science Division would have anything useful for him, but since they had nothing but time to kill before the mission to close the Hell Gate, he and Lilith headed down to the observation deck, where the Science Division had set up a de facto lab.

He wasn't sure he could call it a lab. There were a few workbenches where members of the Science Division were building, upgrading, or modifying a piece of existing technology. Christian sought out Sebastian, who was standing off to the side, next to the only contraption that wasn't a workbench. It looked like a massive ray gun. The man in question was fiddling with a tablet that was connected to the gun via a cable.

"Ah, Christian. We meet again," the man greeted before glancing at the woman by Christian's side. "And Lilith. A pleasure as always."

"Yeah. Hello," Lilith replied quietly.

"I was wondering if you had any weapons I might be able to use," Christian said. "The handguns and swords the Grigori have are good, but they don't feel right."

"Hmm…"

The man pondered the question as he tapped on the tablet several times. A loud whirring sound emitted from the massive ray gun, which was taller than even Leo. Several blue lights appeared around the barrel as it started to spin. It looked like the gun was building up energy.

"I do have a pair of handguns that I've kept in the event you ever lost yours." Nodding to himself, Sebastian shut off the ray gun, unplugged the tablet, and gestured for them. "Follow me, please."

Christian and Lilith walked behind Sebastian as he led them to a workbench that was littered with devices. Sebastian grabbed two of the objects sitting on the workbench, a pair of guns shaped similarly to Phanul and Gabriel and handed them to Christian.

"These do not have a name, but they are based on the same design as Gabriel and Phanul. The difference is that they are specifically designed to be used against demons. See that white bar on either side of the handle? That's your power gauge. We've managed to replicate the divine power released by fallen angels and are using it to power most of our weapons. That said, the power we use is only an imitation. It isn't as strong. Even so, these guns will do more damage to a demon than anything else you've used before."

"I see." Christian handed one of the guns to Lilith, so she could look at it, while he turned the remaining gun over in his hand. It really did look like an exact replica of his previous weapons. "How many shots can it fire before I have to reload?"

"There is no reload," Sebastian said, shocking Christian. "These guns recharge by gathering energy from the surrounding environment." The scientist adjusted his glasses again. "I've heard that you're part demon. When I found out about that, I also added a little something extra. This gun is modified so that if you want to, you can inject your own energy into the guns and create bullets that way. Of course, these projectiles will be different. I don't know if they will affect a demon or not since you'd be using demonic energy instead of divine energy. However, should you find yourself in a place where your guns can't recharge, that ability should prove useful."

"So you are basically using me as a guinea pig to test whether or not these will work properly," Christian sighed as Lilith handed the gun back to him.

"Pretty much," Sebastian admitted with a shrug.

***

The time had finally come to begin the mission. Christian and Lilith were standing just outside of the barrier's perimeter along with nearly six dozen other people.

Because of how busy they had been, neither he or Lilith had seen the barrier until this moment. It was a massive dome of golden energy that surrounded the city. Members of the Grigori stood or floated around the barrier at several yard intervals, their hands outstretched, golden particles flowing from their hands and into the barrier.

Every so often, a demon would slam into the barrier to try and disrupt it, but, perhaps thanks to the barrier being fueled by so many, the demons were the ones who burst into flames, dissolving into nothing. That said, perhaps because they had been keeping this barrier up for several days, many of the fallen angels near where Christian and the others stood looked tired. Their postures were slumped, sweat ran down their bodies, and their arms kept lowering as though growing heavy.

Azazel was the only fallen angels not maintaining the barrier. That was because he would be going into Jerusalem with him.

"As you all know, Earth is currently facing a crisis unlike anything it has ever faced before," Azazel began. "A Hell Gate has opened up, and it is our job to close it. We have to be fast. So far none of the higher-level demons have invaded, but that will change once the gate stabilizes. We need to close it before that happens, and so, your mission is simple. Head in there and begin taking out the demons. Clear a path from here to the gate, and then keep the demons exiting the gate from going any further while I close it."

As Azazel began speaking, Christian glanced at his mate. Like him, she was wearing a black unitard with shoulders pads, a breastplate, and sturdy black boots. The breastplate followed the contours of her mature body. While it left little room to the imagination, it also wouldn't hamper her in combat and protected her heart. Of course, just like Christian's breastplate, it only covered her chest and not her stomach.

He also noticed that she was wearing earrings. That struck him as odd at first, but then he recognized them. They were a beautiful set of crystal earrings that glimmered in fractal patterns as prisms of light bounced inside their pentagonal forms. Those were the earrings that Titania, one of the Four Queens of Fae, had given her.

I see I wasn't the only one who brought along Titania's gift.

Christian placed a hand against his chest, where a small crystal shaped like a teardrop rested. It was the pendant that Titania had given him. He'd almost thought he had lost it, but it turned up amongst his belongings after a thorough search.

"That balance is now on the brink of breaking. Dark forces are gathering, threatening to destroy this delicate equilibrium. I have foreseen that you two will be the key to restoring the balance."

Christian remembered Titania's words, and given their situation, he could not help but feel like this moment was what she had been talking about.

"While you all have your jobs to do, there is something just as important as your job, and that is your life." Azazel was continuing his speech, so Christian focused on what the man was saying. "Everyone here is both the first and last line of defense against the demons. When I'm gone, I'll be counting on each of you to continue protecting humanity from the threat of demonic incursions. That is why I don't want anyone throwing their life away. Remember to watch each other's backs, protect each other with all your might, and make it out of this alive."

His words were quite inspiring. The Executioners and succubus who would be journeying with him into Jerusalem all gave a loud cheer. There were only a few who did not like Samantha and Sif, who were merely stoic and not the type to cheer. That said, Leon was, not surprisingly, cheering the loudest. Christian heard his voice above all the others.

Azazel nodded, satisfied with the resolve everyone had shown, and then turned to look at the two fallen angels standing by the barrier.

"Open a path," he commanded as two swords of light sprang to life in his hands.

The fallen angels nodded and took deep breaths. Christian thought he felt something shift, like the air was vibrating, but he shook it off as a small section of the barrier disappeared.

Almost as soon as it did, several demons surged out, but they were cut down by Azazel, who waded into the opening without a second of hesitation. That also appeared to be the signal for everyone else. The group surged forward and entered the barrier in twos and threes.

Christian and Lilith were at the front of the procession, and so they were some of the first to pass through the entrance. The moment they did, a dark red haze fell upon them. Perhaps it was only his imagination, but it felt like they were no longer on Earth. Everything from the buildings to the streets seemed ominous.

"Everyone!" Azazel called out as he spread his wings and created over a dozen spears of light. "To arms!"

A war cry went up as everyone readied their weapons. Christian and Lilith glanced at each other and nodded. Priming their guns, the two of them took off down the road as Azazel took to the sky.

They hoped this would be their last battle.

Chapter 19

Right from the very beginning, Christian and Lilith found themselves beset on all sides by scenes so horrible even the most corrupt of minds shouldn't have been able to conceive them. Bodies littered the streets. It looked as though the demons had enjoyed preying on the residence of Jerusalem. Painted red, the streets were filled with bloodied corpses strewn about in a haphazard manner.

It made him sick.

Of course, there was no time to feel regret or nausea at the sight, not when hundreds, or maybe even thousands, of demons were pouring in from all sides. They raced down the main road, poured out of side roads that connected to this one, and even leapt over roofs in their haste to attack. Christian could not even begin to count the number of demons they were up against. It was a horde so large most people would have lost hope at the sight.

"Lilith, can I please count on you for support?" asked Christian.

"Leave it to me!" Lilith said.

Christian nodded as he unleashed a barrage of gunfire from the two new guns in his grip. He hadn't named them. Doing so felt wrong somehow. Even so, the weapons, resembling desert eagles much like his old guns, fired off large bolts of light that slammed into the demon army without mercy. The bolts didn't just kill the demons. It destroyed them. He almost gawked as he watched demon after demon get vaporized from the bolts blitzing out of his guns without relent.

Right beside him, Lilith had unholstered her Glock 17 and was taking shots of any enemy that got too close. She wasn't as quick as him. However, her aim was pretty good. One demon, an imp, went down when she put a bullet through its head. Another squealed in pain as she shot it in the chest. The calm way she fired showed how used to this she had become. He wasn't sure that was a good thing.

Most of the demons were weak ones—imps, marionettes, molochs, and the like. Christian quickly took aim at the molochs, which were human-sized creatures that looked like muck or even sludge. They had arms with sharp claws on them, but their bodies were essentially formless blobs. Even their face could only vaguely be called a face. It was nothing but a pair of glowing red eyes and a gaping maw.

The light-based projectiles from Christian's gun pulverized them. He put a hole through one, but due to the light energies pseudo divinity, the remaining energy quickly ate the moloch. The hole widened until the demon had completely dissolved.

He and Lilith were not the only ones fighting, nor were they the only ones at the front. Samantha, Sif, and Leon were several yards away. Neither Sif nor Leon had any long-range weapons. Samantha, however, pulled the trigger on her SA Army 5.5 Colt Revolver. Each pull of the trigger caused her arm to jerk, but every shot fired was a headshot. Imps, marionettes, molochs... everything went down as their heads exploded in a shower of light particles and brain matter.

Although they had done their best to keep firing at range, it was only a matter of time before the two forces clashed. Christian and the others were doing their best to make it toward the Hell Gate. They had no choice but to press forward.

Holstering his guns, Christian unsheathed the swords he'd grabbed from the armory. They still felt strange in his hands, but as he spun around, cleaving the head from a marionette, and then thrusting his other blade into the chest of an imp, he adjusted his stance to accommodate for their weight and the shape of the blades.

Christian lost himself to the flow of battle. He invited enemies to attack, presenting openings for them to take, and then cut them down mercilessly.

Dodging a thrust to the chest, he danced around an imp, swung his sword, and watched as its head flew from its shoulder. Continuing his dance, he spun around with the sword in his left hand extended. It scraped against a marionettes ribs. The puppet-like demon went into a tailspin before it fell to the ground.

Lilith remained beside him. She had her whip in one hand and her Glock in the other. He found himself somewhat surprised as she used the whip to force demons back, and then fired a round straight into their heads. There were times when she needed to reload. During those instances, Christian covered for her, dancing around the woman as he cut down anything that came close.

A couple yards to his right, Clarissa and Heather stood side by side as they slowly waded through their own enemies.

Wielding her naginata, Clarissa spun and thrust the weapon as though it weighed less than a feather. The blade easily cleaved through flesh and bone, mowing down enemies like wheat before a scythe. Limbs flew off as the women disarmed and de-legged everything that came close. An imp tried to attack from above, but she plunged her naginata through its head, then brought the weapon down, dislodging the dead demon while slicing a marionette in half through the middle.

Heather was using her long daggers to great effect. Unlike Clarissa, who preferred keeping her enemies at a distance, she got up close and personal. Darting to and fro, she moved into the guard of her enemies and attacked with merciless strikes. In most cases, those strikes would have been instant death. The woman attacked vital organs. Unfortunately, these were not humans or any normal creatures. They were demons whose bodies defied logic. Marionettes didn't even have vital organs since they were just puppets.

That didn't stop Heather, who tore them apart with powerful slashes of her two daggers, which were long enough that every attack sliced off a limb. She darted left. After dodging an attack from a marionette with swords for hands, she swung her weapon and removed an arm at the elbow, and then darted in, ducked low, and removed a leg. As the creature fell to the ground, she swung her left dagger while standing up, cleaving off the creature's head.

As she was doing this, a moloch tried to attack her from behind. Clarissa released a war cry as she swung her naginata and sliced off the demon's arm. It released an unusual gurgle, but the arm quickly grew back. The woman narrowed her eyes as she tried to attack it again, but a moloch's body had the consistency of grease or oil. Her attacks didn't really do anything.

Seeing this, Christian sheathed one of his swords, removed his gun, and fired a blast that tore through the demon's body. It dissolved quickly.

"Molochs are basically like slime monsters," he told them, shouting to be heard over the din of battle. "To kill them, you have to either locate their core and destroy that, or you need to attack with light-based energy."

Clarissa nodded her thanks. She didn't say anything, but that was because she didn't have time. More demons were attacking… and they were losing people.

Christian grimaced as a young man screamed when his left arm was torn off by an imp. That scream quickly turned into a gurgle as another imp clawed out his throat. Blood gushed from both wounds as more imps flocked to the dying Executioner, who soon became buried underneath a pile of bodies.

Above him, Kel was doing everything he could to keep up with Azazel, who blasted through drakons—reptilian demons that resembled undead dragons. However, with only one arm, he simply didn't have what it took. Christian was forced to look away when a drakon swooped in from above and chomped down on the fallen angel, literally biting him in half. He couldn't even help because he was so busy on the ground.

"Damn, there's no end to these monsters!" a scream went up.

"We shouldn't have come here!"

"We're all going to die!"

As they lost more members, many of their group began to lose heart. Christian wouldn't say he blamed them. They were a group of not even 100 strong against an army that clearly numbered in the thousands. What's more, it wasn't like many of these people were that powerful. Their skills didn't match members of the now defunct XIII like him, Sif, Leon, and Samantha. They were casteless. Most of them had never even gone up against a demon before.

"Do not lose heart!" Samantha shouted as she cut down sixteen marionettes in less time than it took to blink. "Stick together! Watch each other's backs and keep pressing forward! That is the only way to claim victory!"

Her words had the desired effect of hardening everyone's resolve, but it was only a temporary solution. Once they began losing more people, the situation would quickly turn hopeless.

Or so Christian thought.

As they continued progressing to the Hell Gate, following Azazel as he flew overhead, both to guide them and to keep the flying demons from attacking them, a loud rumbling caused everyone to stop. Even the demons who'd been fighting them ceased fighting. Christian became shocked when, as one, the demons scattered, leaving the small force now numbering 46 alone. For a moment, he couldn't understand why they had run, but it was only for a moment.

Then it emerged.

It appeared from around a large building, a monster that walked on four limbs. Thick, corded muscles covered every inch of its body. The leathery purple skin covering those muscles seemed to stretch as it walked forward, veins bulging along its front legs, which were so massive he couldn't even judge their size. It put one paw in front of the other, though he wasn't sure those massively clawed feet could be considered paws at all. Each step it took caused the ground to shake.

Glowing red eyes were set on a muzzle that seemed slightly canine and slightly feline. A pair of massive fangs jutted from its mouth, which soon opened to reveal teeth nearly as tall as him. A black mane starting from the top of its head right between its eyes traveled down the creature's back, stopping at the long tail that added what looked like several extra yards to its overall length. And finally, a pair of ominous-looking curved horns jutted from its head.

Christian had never faced one of these monsters before, but he knew what it was.

Behemoth.

"W-what is that thing?" Lilith asked with a stutter.

"That," Christian sighed, "is trouble."

The behemoth stopped and narrowed its red eyes upon spotting them. The stare down lasted for barely a second before it unleashed a roar that chilled the bones of all who heard it. Then it stomped down at the road. Buildings were blasted apart as its tail struck them, but it didn't even seem to notice as it ran toward them at a speed that belied its great size.

Many of the fighters among them panicked and ran. Christian didn't blame them.

"Lilith, I need you to stand back."

"What?"

"I'm going to do something stupid."

"WHAT?!"

Christian hadn't relied on his demonic power very much, but that had nothing to do with reluctance. He just wasn't sure how well he ould use it. This was new territory for him. However, in the face of his monstrosity, he really had no choice.

Once more, Christian took a deep breath as he reached deep inside of himself and dredged up his most terrible memories, his most negative emotions. Then he tempered those emotions with his love for Lilith and his desire to protect her.

The world came into startling focus almost immediately after doing this. It seemed to slow down. He knew it was just his perceptions, however, and not the world that had slowed. The Eye of Belial was granting him this power, allowing him to see the world in such brilliant detail that everything appeared to be moving like molasses.

Power rushed through his body, strengthening him to beyond what he believed a human should be capable of. That knowledge just added to the self-loathing he felt. A sardonic smile appeared on his face. He may have accepted that he wasn't fully human, but it wasn't like that fact pleased him.

Holding his swords in a fierce grip, Christian rushed toward the behemoth, releasing a war cry that was in no way overpowered by the one his enemy unleashed.

He reached the monster in record time. The behemoth tried to squash him flat, but he dodged left, bending his knees to keep his balance as the earth shook. With his teeth grit, he swung the sword in his right hand, shearing through one of the behemoth's toes. Rearing back, the creature let out a roar that was more anger than agony. It glared down at him and swiped, but he leapt backward to avoid it.

Skidding along the ground, Christian bent his legs, building up kinetic energy in his thighs, which he used to launch himself forward. He darted between the behemoth's legs. With a swing of each arm, he cleaved through tendons in the demon's heel. Black ichor gushed from the wound like a fountain. Another roar, this time more agony than anger, echoed across the vast cityscape.

Its front legs were no longer able to support it. The behemoth fell forward, its chin slamming into the ground with such force that a shockwave spread across the city. Several buildings rattled and shook.

Christian would have been hit with the shockwave as well, but he had already jumped onto the demon's tail and was running up its back. He'd jabbed his two blades into the thing's tough skin. Using the demonic strength granted to him, he cleaved through the skin, sending black blood flying out behind him like a crescent wave.

The behemoth roared as it tried to stand, but its tendons had been severed, and so all it could do was struggle. Christian used that to his advantage. Once more using his demonic strength, he leapt into the air. He sheathed one of his blades, then grabbed the other with both hands and pointed it down. Descending fast, he landed on the behemoth's head and stabbed his sword straight down.

Blood splashed against his clothing as his sword penetrated the demon's skull. The behemoth roared as it lifted its head up as though ready to try and throw him off, but then it released a pained rasp. Its back arched some more, head lifting even further. Christian kept a tight grip on the blade and twisted. The behemoth moaned in agony, then, all at once, its body went slack.

As its head slumped back to the ground, Christian took several deep breaths as he let the energy he'd been using leave him. Feeling strangely exhausted, he quietly pulled his blade from the behemoth's skull and wiped it off against the creature's hide. He sheathed it, then climbed down its head and leapt onto the ground, bending his knees slightly to absorb the impact.

With a sigh, he walked back over to where Lilith, Clarissa, Heather, Samantha, Sif, Leon, and the other members of their force stood. He paused, however, when he saw how the group was staring at him. Their mouths were wide open, eyes round like dinner plates. Even Lilith looked at him like she was staring at an alien entity.

He frowned. "What's wrong?"

"Nothing," the group said and looked away as one.

***

After Christian had defeated the behemoth, Samantha reorganized their forces, which numbered 42 instead of the 46 he had assumed. With Christian acting as the spearpoint in their vanguard, the group proceeded forward once more.

The spearpoint of their formation was made of himself on point, Lilith, Clarissa, and Heather on his left, and Samantha, Sif, and Leon on his right. They acted to drive straight through the enemy formations without stopping. Meanwhile, the rest of their forces followed immediately behind them. The rearguard was the mop up crew whose jobs were to keep the vanguard from being attacked from behind.

With this formation, the group made faster progress than before. The disorganized mess of the first few minutes were an embarrassing blemish that Samantha probably wanted to erase. Christian didn't think she could be blamed for what happened. Their situation was unlike anything they had run into before. Even his battle with Abaddon could not compare to the pandemonium of their current circumstances.

They didn't need to worry about the drakons thanks to Azazel. The Grigori leader was a force to be reckoned with. He created spears of light by the hundreds, firing them off against drakons like he was showering the world with rain. Droves of flying demons were slaughtered wholesale. From his position as he waded through the hordes of demons on the ground, Christian could see the brilliant light of Azazel's spears piercing the enemies above them.

The closer they moved to the Hell Gate, the more types of demons they ran across. There were the hellhounds. They were dog demons. Most populous among this type of demon were the normal hellhounds, but there was also the orthrus variation, which had two heads. There were also the capra—half-man, half-goat demons. Large and muscled, these demons were few in number but far stronger than most of the other types they ran into. Oftentimes, they required two or even five individuals to slay, depending on who fought them.

He didn't know how long they had been fighting, but at some point, the group walked around a massive building and found their objective waiting for them.

The Hell Gate looked even more imposing in real life than it did on the holographic display. It was hard to judge the size of something without seeing it in real life. This monstrous gate, made from dark obsidian and glowing an ominous red light that pulsed like a beating heart, towered over the buildings around it. In the very center was a swirling vortex from which demons were even now pouring through.

"Clear out the demons! Push them back!" came Samantha's war cry.

Christian charged into the horde of creature's emerging from the Hell Gate alongside Lilith and the others. He could already tell that some of the demons were being affected by his mate's illusions. An imp stumbled in front of him like it was drunk. He cut it down. Spinning around he swung the blade it his left hand. Blood spurted from a wound that traveled from the left hip to the right shoulder of another demon.

The sound of gunfire echoed in his ears as Lilith shot a capra in the eye. The demon brayed as it charged blindly toward them, but she coiled her whip around one of its legs and yanked its feet out from underneath it. Christian put an end to that demon by sliding his blade along its throat.

Moving together until they stood back to back, the two of them began taking down demons in quick succession. Christian lured them in. Lilith cast an illusion to disorient them. Then he would finish them off. While Lilith still ended up killing quite a few demons, her primary purpose was support, so she tried to conserve her strength as much as possible.

Christian's body was beginning to ache as he hacked through another capra, then thrust one of his swords through the head of an imp, yanking it out and flicking the blood off.

He had long since lost track of time. Every breath caused sharp pain to sting his chest. He'd also gotten blood in his eyes, which meant he was relying mostly on his other senses. Furthermore, his limbs felt like they were being held down with lead weights.

Lilith must have been feeling the same exhaustion. Even so, neither of them gave up. Alongside Samantha, Sif, Leon, Clarissa, Heather, and the rest of their forces, he defeated the demons as they emerged from the gate.

Several screams erupted behind them, and Christian felt a grimace appear as he turned to find a large mixture of hellhounds bounding out from within the city. A young woman wielding a standard broadsword sliced through the skull of one, but then her blade became stuck. Before she could remove it, a hellhound bit down on her arm. As the woman screamed, several more bit into her legs, torso, and shoulders.

Her fellow Executioners tried to help her. However, there were far more hellhounds coming out from between buildings, and it was all they could do just to fend for themselves.

"Lilith," Christian muttered as he and his mate stood back to back, facing down a pair of capras. These were variations. Their skin was a blistering red as they towered over the pair by several feet. Bulging muscles caused their skin to stretch and veins to pop out.

The two capras weren't doing anything. They warily eyed the pair, almost as if they knew he and Lilith weren't to be underestimated, displaying far more intelligence than the rest of their kin.

"Wha... what is it?"

"How much life energy do you have left?"

"About... half a tank, more or less."

Half a tank, meaning her reserves had been depleted by half.

"Can you make an illusion of vines sprouting from the ground and grabbing all the demons around us?"

There was a poignant pause. "Not with the amount I currently have."

Christian nodded, and then called out. "Clarissa! Samantha! I need you two to protect me and Lilith for a second!"

Neither women asked for clarification as they slayed the demons they were up against, turned on their heels, and attacked the capras that had been eying him and Lilith.

As the roar of the capras mixed with the clashing of blades, Christian turned, spun Lilith around and pressed his lips to hers. It was not something one would normally do in combat. Kissing, that is. However, as Christian probed Lilith's mouth with his tongue, he could almost feel the energy gathering around his mate. Maybe it was just his imagination, or maybe he was becoming more sensitive to such things. Either way, when they pulled back, Lilith's eyes were glowing as she turned her head to gaze at the battlefield.

Illusions were a strange sight to see. They were not real, being nothing more than attacks that affected one or more of the five senses —not counting when Lilith was in her succubus form and made her illusions into reality. Only the people being affected by the illusions could even see them. That was why, as the demons suddenly fell to the ground and struggled as though something was holding them down, no one seemed able to figure out what was happening.

"What are you people waiting for?!" demanded Christian as the confused men and women stood there. "Kill them!"

Lilith's illusion had affected not just one, two, four, or even five demons. Her powers were such that she had trapped every demon within their vicinity in an illusion. There must have been at least 100 of them.

Of course, it was impossible to affect so many for a long period of time. At most, she had provided their forces with five extra seconds, but five seconds was more than enough time for everyone to get their act together and kill the demons currently struggling to stand up. While a few demons managed to break free before they were gutted, Christian and a few others had already whipped out their guns and unloaded several bolts of light energy into them. Before long, all the demons surrounding them were dead.

"Damn…" Leon muttered as he set Sandalphon on the ground and leaned against it. "I know I've said I love fighting, but this… this is just too much, even for me."

"Quit complaining," Sif muttered as she took several deep breaths. Her body was covered in small cuts and blood, both hers and not.

"I'm not complaining. I'm just saying."

"Everyone stay on guard!" Samantha commanded in a hard voice that could cut through steel. "We have no idea when more demons will come!"

Christian and Lilith leaned against each other like a pair of broken pillars unable to stand on their own. They'd been at the vanguard, fighting their hardest as they pushed through the demonic hordes arrayed against them, and they were tired.

"Christian?"

"Yeah?"

"I want to have sex."

If he didn't know Lilith, he would have assumed she was joking.

"We can't do that here. You'll have to wait until we get home."

"I know." She sighed. "But that last illusion really depleted my reserves. I've been training really hard to affect multiple people with illusions at once, but I've never tried casting one on so many before, and these demons have a strong resistance to illusions. It takes more power than normal."

"I understand that." Christian turned his head. "Will a kiss do?"

"Maybe if you give me several."

While Christian could feel the eyes of numerous people on them, he ignored that burning feeling on his back and kissed Lilith. This wasn't really a romantic kiss. Given their situation, he didn't think anything could feel romantic. Right now, he was merely providing her with more energy. There was no telling when they would have another break, and so doing what he could to "fill her up," so to speak, was merely a logical choice.

About two minutes after the battle ended, a loud cry from above made everyone look up. They were just in time to see a drakon descending toward them. The people beneath it quickly dove out of the way, allowing the creature to slam head first into the ground. Several Executioners readied their weapons, but when they realized the beast was already dead, they relaxed.

Azazel alighted next to them. "That's the last of the flying enemies, and I see you guys have secured the Hell Gate. Good job. Leave the rest to me."

"Azazel," Christian began, "are you sure about this?"

"Yup." Azazel didn't stop walking toward the Hell Gate as he replied. "I've already made my peace with all this. I'm prepared. In any case, I need you all to remain here until the gate closes. Kill any demon that emerges while I find the power source and destroy it."

With those last words, Azazel disappeared through the gate.

Everyone quickly took up defensive positions as the man disappeared inside of the red vortex. There were still demons within the city itself. Several groups would stumble upon their encampment, mostly hellhounds and marionettes, but they were quickly disposed of. Fortunately, there weren't that many big demons like the behemoth. It seemed the gate still wasn't capable of letting that many large demons through, which explained why only the behemoth, a mid-level demon, had emerged so far.

They defended the Hell Gate from demons both coming toward them from the city and exiting from the gate itself. However, two problems made themselves readily apparent as the battle continued.

The first was exhaustion, both mental and physical. While no one had any clear idea of how long they had been battling, it didn't change the fact that they had been fighting a lot. There was no telling how many demons they had killed. Their bodies were tired from the near constant stream of combat. What's more, their minds and spirits were exhausted from watching so many of their comrades perish, from seeing the corpses of so many innocent people.

The second problem came in the form of ammunition. Rather, it was a lack thereof. The longer they remained there, the more ammo they had to use to defend this position. It was only logical that they would eventually run out.

Of course, quite a few of these people were using the new guns developed by the Science Division, which meant they had been relying heavily on the destructive power of those light-based projectiles. Unfortunately, not all of them had unlimited energy. Most were the prototypes, which had a power cell. They were more powerful than Christian's gun, but they also had a limited amount of power to spare.

Without their guns having that incredible, demon-slaying power, the fighting strength of nearly half their forces dropped. When that happened, they began losing members.

Christian quickly sliced through the back of a hellhound's neck, killing it instantly. Sadly, the person he'd been trying to save already had his throat torn out and was dying. They didn't have any way to save him either.

Several feet away, Clarissa and Heather were forced to defend a group of Executioners who had looks of panic on their faces as they realized their guns no longer had any ammo. While they had swords, spears, and maces as well, they'd been relying more on their guns. The light-based bolts of energy killed demons more thoroughly than they could with melee weapons.

A little way to his left, a small group of hellhounds slammed into a pair of Executioners and tore them apart. Lilith struck the monsters with her whip, but her gun rested in its holster. He knew she was trying to conserve ammo.

Christian rushed up and slayed the hellhounds while they were busy with their meal. The two Executioners they had attacked were already dead.

"Damn it," Samantha, who was never known for swearing, finally cursed. "What is taking Azazel so long?!"

It was true that Azazel was taking an awfully long time. However it wasn't like they knew how long it took to close a Hell Gate. Closing one required finding the source of power on the other side and destroying it. That disrupted the gate and forced it closed. The problem was that they didn't know what this power source looked like, how far it was from the gate, or even whether it was guarded or not. For all they knew, Azazel had run into a Demon King and been defeated.

Christian turned his attention to the gate, frowning as he stared into the swirling vortex. No demons were coming out right now. However, they periodically appeared in droves and swarms.

"You're thinking of going inside, aren't you?" Lilith asked.

He sighed. "I'm not surprised you figured me out."

"I'm your mate." She shrugged. "I know you."

He nodded. "I was just… remembering what Titania told us. She said the balance had been broken, and that we would be the keys to restoring that balance."

"And you think this is what she was talking about?"

Another nod. "The balance of this world is clearly close to being destroyed. If we really are the keys that will restore the world, then…"

"Going in and closing the Hell Gate is our duty."

"Yes."

Lilith paused again and took a shuddering breath. "If we do this, we probably won't be able to come back."

"Probably not."

"I really don't want to go in there."

"Neither do I."

"But if we don't…" Lilith bit her lip. "If we don't… then the demons will overrun this world and Maria…"

There was no need to say anymore. If they didn't close the Hell Gate, the demons would continue to come forth, their forces would be annihilated, and Maria, Lilith's friend back in Seal Beach, along with

all the other innocent people in this world, would either die or be turned
into slaves.

Christian gripped Lilith's hand. "Even if I never return to Earth,
so long as I have you by my side, I can survive anywhere."

Lilith looked at him, tears in her eyes, but then she wiped them
away with her free hand and smiled at him. "Me too. I don't care where
we go so long as I'm with you."

Their decision had been made. Christian turned to Samantha, who
was currently giving orders to keep their eyes peeled for more enemies.

"Samantha!" he called. She turned to him, a questioning look on
her face. "Take care of things here for me."

"What are you—wait! Where are you two going?! Come back!"

Without hesitating, because they knew that if they did, then they
would lose heart, Christian and Lilith ran hand in hand through the
swirling vortex.

***

The hair on Christian's neck stood on end as he and Lilith floated
through a vortex of swirling red and black lights. Streams of energy
flowed past them on all sides. It felt like his skin was being singed by
an electric current, except there was no pain. Beside him, his mate
shared the same opinion.

"I feel like something is washing over me."

"It's probably the demonic energy of the vortex."

"I don't like it."

"Me neither."

They weren't the only ones here either. Christian occasionally
saw glimpses of demons passing through. They were traveling in the
opposite direction, meaning these demons were heading out of the gate.
He hoped Samantha and the others would be up to the task of handling
them.

"I think I see something up ahead!" Lilith pointed ahead of them,
to where a small black space had appeared. Unlike the rest of this
tunnel, which was a mixture of swirling blacks and reds, this space was
pure black and growing bigger by the second.

"Let's hope that's the exit," Christian muttered.

The darkness from that space grew larger as they moved toward
it. Like ink bleeding into parchment, it spread across the area in front of
them—or that was how it looked. Christian knew it was actually due to
them getting closer. In either event, not long after Lilith had pointed it

out did their world turn completely black, so dark they couldn't even see each other despite being close enough to hold hands.

And then they were no longer floating through a vortex; they were instead standing on an open plane of craggy rocks, jutting spires, deep trenches, and an ugly red sky. The scent of brimstone made his nose wrinkle. It was an acrid stench. Even as he complained, a loud noise erupted several yards from them, and a geyser of lava shot into the air. He could feel the heat from where he stood.

"Is this... Hell?" asked Lilith.

"I imagine so," Christian said. "Come on. Let's not linger here. We need to find Azazel and that core."

Lilith nodded her assent and they quickly left the Hell Gate behind, traveling between several craggy spires that looked almost like horns protruding from the ground. It was a good thing they had left so quickly. The instant they moved, several low-class demons rushed up to the gate. A group of hellhounds stopped for a moment, sniffing the air as though they could smell the two of them, but Christian and Lilith breathed a sigh of relief when the demons just went through the vortex.

"Where do you think we'll find Azazel and the core?" asked Lilith.

"I have no idea," Christian admitted.

"We didn't think about this very well, did we?"

"It was a rash decision, but it's not like we could have done anything else."

They kept their conversation light as they wandered between spires, past chasms, and across natural bridge formations that hovered over pits of lava. Sweat broke out on their skin from the sweltering heat. It caused their clothing to stick to them. Christian gasped for air as he debated discarding his clothes, but these outfits also offered them protection, so he decided to tough it out.

As they climbed up a steep incline, a loud rumbling caused them to pause. At first, they thought it was distant thunder, or something similar to that, but then everything rumbled again, and they realized what it truly was.

Laughter.

Someone was laughing.

Christian and Lilith glanced at each other, and then climbed the rest of the incline to find themselves standing on the edge of a steep cliff. The source of the laugh came from down below. When they peeked over, the two of them froze as they found someone who they'd never expected to see again standing there.

His ash gray body was covered in several hundred cracks that spread across his flesh like a spider's web. He had a torso that was shaped similar enough to a human's and his head was humanish. That said, he was bald, had no ears, and arrayed around his head like a crown were nearly a dozen horns. Strange outcroppings jutted from his elbows. Each hand only possessed three fingers, which were reminiscent of talons. While his upper half seemed human enough, his lower body was like that of a goat. Even his feet were hoofed, though they were also clawed. Behind his body, waving back and forth, was a long, spaded, tri-tipped tail.

The two of them ducked back down.

"Asmodeus…" Lilith whispered as a shudder coursed through her body. She wrapped her arms around herself as though to stop her body from shaking. "I can't believe he's here."

"He must be the guarding the core. You saw it, right?"

Lilith shook her head. "I was too busy staring at him."

Christian leaned back over the edge and peeked back down. Asmodeus was standing with his back to them. He hadn't changed size like some of the other Demon Kings, leading him to believe this was his true size. Several yards from where he stood were two things that stood out to Christian.

The first was the massive black orb, which at first glance appeared to be obsidian, but a closer inspection revealed that it was actually made of energy. Unstable and crackling, the orb fizzled and hissed as its shape threatened to break. The entire thing was surrounded by a red barrier that kept it from getting destroyed. No. Christian shook his head and looked at it with the eye of Belial. That thing wasn't a barrier. It was Asmodeus' energy being absorbed into the sphere. He could see the tethered thread between it and Asmodeus.

He must be the energy source to keep the gate open. This must be his punishment for being defeated by me and Lilith.

What grabbed Christian's attention after that was Azazel. The fallen angel was hovering above the ground, but it wasn't under his own power. His twelve wings had been ripped off and were lying scattered on the ground. Blood covered much of his face and dripped down his back, while his head and legs dangled limply. His arms would have probably done the same, but several red manacles had wrapped around his wrists and pulled them wide.

"Did you really think a fallen such as yourself could best a Demon King on his own turf?" asked Asmodeus. **"Even with a good**

portion of my power being used to stabilize this blasted gate, I am still more than a match for any one angel."

So I was right. Asmodeus is being used to stabilize the core, which means only one thing...

"We're going to have to defeat him if we want to destroy the core and close the gate," Christian said with a sigh as he leaned back and looked at Lilith, who had closed her eyes and was taking deep breaths. "Are you up for it?"

Lilith took several deeper breaths, centering herself, and then she opened her eyes and gazed at him. There was still fear present in her gaze. However, that fear was tempered by determination.

"I am." She smiled. It was a surprisingly sardonic expression. "It's not like we can turn back now."

"No, it's not." He smiled back.

They didn't have any great plan for dealing with Asmodeus, nor did they try to come up with one. A Demon King was such an overwhelmingly powerful entity that any plan they made would crumble once the battle began. In that case, if no plan if work, then it would be better to go in without a plan to keep themselves flexible.

"On the count of three," Christian said.

"One," Lilith began.

"Two," Christian counted off.

"Three," they said at the same time just before leaping over the edge of the cliff.

As they descended, Christian and Lilith unholstered their guns and unloaded them onto Asmodeus. While Lilith's bullets merely pinged off the demon's skin, Christian's weapons, which he had to power with his own energy now that they were in Hell, left black scorch marks.

The sudden attack caused Asmodeus to look up at them. He glared at the two, but then his eyes widened as he realized who they were.

"You two!!"

Those were the only words he was able to get out, mostly because Christian aimed his two guns and fired bolts of dark red energy that struck his eyes. Even if Asmodeus was a powerful Demon King, he still had weaknesses, and the eyes were a weakness every being had.

Asmodeus stumbled back and screamed as he brought his hands to his eyes. In the next instant, Christian had holstered his guns, unsheathed his swords, and infused them with his demonic energy.

Ethereal red flames covered his blades as he swung them at Asmodeus, who had enough sense to move back. That didn't stop his attack from hitting. Christian was pleasantly surprised when, after a moment of resistance, his blade sliced straight through the Demon King. Another scream. Black blood oozed from the two cuts on Asmodeus' chest.

"Curse you!!"

The demon swiped a hand toward Christian. It was too far to reach him, but Christian moved out of the way regardless, and it was a great decision. A wave of energy slammed into cliff face they had been standing on. It gouged a mighty chunk through the rock, which caused cracks to spread before, like a house of cards falling down, the cliff crumbled, sending a wave of dust outward to create an expanding cloud.

While Christian distracted Asmodeus with a frontal assault, Lilith, after landing on the ground, went over to Azazel and tried to figure out a way to dispel those restraints.

"Lilith…" Azazel said in a raspy voice. "What are you doing… here?"

"You were taking too long to close the gate, so Christian and I came to help," Lilith said.

Azazel closed his eyes as though pained by her response. "I'm sorry."

"You don't have to apologize. It was our decision." At that moment, the cloud of dust obscured their vision. However, Lilith had already seen everything she needed to. "Christian! I can't remove these without entering my succubus form!"

"Got it! I'm there!"

Christian followed the source of her voice and raced through the dust cloud. He could hear Asmodeus screaming in rage somewhere to his left, but he ignored that and darted quickly to where Azazel and Lilith were. The moment he saw them, Christian infused more energy into his swords and brought them down on the manacles shackling Azazel's wrists. His sword sliced through them. The fallen angel fell to the ground in a heap.

"Thanks for that…" the fallen angel muttered as he staggered to his feet.

He was in worse shape than Christian thought. Not only were his wings gone, but his face was swollen with numerous bruises and contusions. Furthermore, his robes were gone, revealing a multitude of cuts leaking blood down his body.

"Can you still fight?" asked Christian.

"If you can give me a moment to recover my energy, I should be good for another round or two," Azazel said, then grimaced. "But I have to recover first. I used up all my energy fighting Asmodeus... and my energy isn't recovering as quickly here." He smiled sardonically. "That said, it is recovering. I guess it's a good thing I'm a fallen and not an angel."

"I guess so."

At that exact moment, a massive shockwave permeated from within the dust cloud, blowing the makeshift smokescreen away and revealing Asmodeus, dark energy wafting off his body as bloodlust radiated from him.

"We'll buy you what time we can," Christian said.

"Sorry to ask this of you," Azazel responded.

Christian and Lilith didn't bother telling him not to apologize. There was no time.

Heading the assault, Christian raced across the ground, his body moving faster than it ever had before. Perhaps because he was part demon, he felt a lot stronger in this place. In fact, the more he used his powers, the more powerful he felt himself becoming.

Asmodeus roared as he shot several beams from his eyes. Christian hopped left to avoid one beam, which sliced straight through the ground, and then hoped right to avoid the next one. Seeing his attack miss, Asmodeus glared at Christian with unbridled hatred in his eyes. No doubt he was remembering the indignity he suffered at Christian's hands.

Unlike this time, the Eye of Belial offered no hint as to any weak point on Asmodeus' body, though that made sense. This was his true body. There was no symbol to mark a human being possessed.

That said, his eye did offer more insight. As he stared at Asmodeus, he saw a vision overlapping the demon, showing Christian what his enemy would do next. This allowed him to avoid the next several beams sent his way. He even foresaw Asmodeus sweeping his arm in a horizontal slash to create a blade of energy, which he leapt over to avoid.

"Damn brat! I'm not going to play with you like I did back then!"

"I'm not playing around either!"

At that moment, Christian had reached Asmodeus, who brought down his hand in a powerful punch that caused the ground to crack. However, Christian wasn't there anymore. He was behind Asmodeus.

"What?!"

The demon seemed confused as he whirled around, but Christian wasn't about to tell Asmodeus that he'd been tricked by one of Lilith's illusion. With energy wreathing his swords, Christian brought them down in a slice that created an X-pattern on the Demon King's chest, blood spurting out, black and thick.

"Grrraaa!!"

Asmodeus stumbled back. Using his unbalanced position to her advantage, Lilith coiled her whip around his leg and yanked. With an indignant cry, Asmodeus crashed face first into the ground, a loud crunching noise echoing around them.

Christian leapt up to finish the demon off by impaling him through the neck, but Asmodeus waved a hand, sending a blast of energy that caught him in the chest. He released a strangled cry as his ribs snapped and he was sent backward. However, a moment after they broke, he felt them reforming.

Landing on the ground, he skidded across the surface. Christian sheathed his swords and brought out his guns. Firing in rapid succession, hundreds of black bolts struck Asmodeus, who had to raise his arms to protect his face. It seemed he had learned his lesson.

However, at that exact moment, a pair of trees suddenly sprouted from the ground, and then the branches of those trees grabbed Asmodeus' wrists and pulled them apart. Now unimpeded, Christian's projectiles slammed into the demon's face and chest. Black burns began appearing. Christian narrowed his eyes and focused on shooting on specific spot, the center of Asmodeus' chest, over and over again. The black mark became even darker. Cracks appeared. Then blood leaked out. Just a little more. Just a little.

"GGGRAAAAA!!!"

A powerful shockwave of energy caused the trees to disperse, blasted away. The shockwave spread out, cracking the ground, and then hit both him and Lilith, flinging them away.

While Christian landed on the ground and stumbled backward, Lilith flapped her wings, now fully transformed into her succubus form, and took to the skies. Using her ability to turn illusion into the reality, she created several dozen spheres of incandescent light, which burned brighter than a thousand suns. With a wave of her hand, she sent them toward Asmodeus.

The spheres struck with spectacular results. A series of massive explosions went up as each sphere struck Asmodeus like a nuclear warhead. Christian had to cover his face with his hands as a wave of heat washed over him, and he crouched low when the resulting force of the explosion tried to send him sailing again. He couldn't even look now it was so bright.

When the light died down, he glanced into the cloud of smoke that clogged his vision. Was Asmodeus dead? He didn't know if even an attack like that would be powerful enough to do this monster in.

As if giving credence to his hypothesis, Asmodeus burst from the black smoke seconds later, having leapt high into the air. It was easy to see that he had suffered. His skin was mostly black. His wings had several holes in them. What's more, he was bleeding from numerous places and even had several third degree burns on his body. Even so, he glared balefully at Lilith, who was breathing heavily as sweat ran down her forehead. That last illusion must have consumed too much energy.

"Fucking cunt," Asmodeus snarled. **"I'm going to make you regret meeting with me again."**

"I already regret seeing you again," Lilith retorted as she fired off several more spheres.

These ones must have lacked the power of her first attack. Asmodeus swatted them away as he closed the distance between them. Lilith tried to fly away, but he was too fast, and his fist slammed into Lilith's back.

Christian's eyes went wide as he raced across the ground, pumping so much energy into his legs that the rocks beneath him cracked. He skidded to a halt just beneath Lilith and tried to catch her. However, her speed was such that when she slammed into him, they were both sent to the ground.

A pained gasp escaped his mouth as he felt something pierce his lung—a rib. However, just like before, his ribs and lung quickly mended. Even that was painful.

Lilith had changed back into her human form. She must have used all her energy in that last attack. Fortunately, she was still conscious.

"You okay?" he asked.

"Not really. I think my leg is broken."

He grimaced. That was going to seriously hamper her fighting capability.

Before he had time to truly lament, Asmodeus appeared before them, a black spear glowing with an ominous energy now in his hand.

"I'd normally take my time playing with you, but I've run out of patience. Do me a favor and die."

Asmodeus thrust his spear at the two of them. It was so fast neither of them could even track it with their eyes. However, just before the spear struck, a figure moved in the way.

"Gkkkk!"

Christian and Lilith stared in shock as Azazel stood before them, his back to them, and the dark tip of a blood-covered spear sticking out of his back.

"Wha—Azazel?!"

"H-hey… it looked like you needed a hand." Azazel was gripping the spear in both hands, though his limbs were shaking. "I… I don't have much strength left, so I thought I'd use what strength I do have to give you guys this chance. D-do me a favor and don't waste it."

Christian and Lilith were unable to do anything as Azazel, gathering the last of his strength, pushed forward against the surprised Asmodeus. His fist slammed into the demon's face, burning it with divine energy. As the King of Lust stumbled back and screamed, Azazel continued racing forward despite the spear impaling him, wrapped his arms around the demon, and leapt into the air. The two of them only had a moment to wonder what was going to happen when a bright sphere of powerful divine energy flared into life. It was as if a star had been born.

Unable to look at it, Christian and Lilith looked away. Seconds later, two loud thuds reached their ears, causing them to look back up.

Azazel and Asmodeus were lying on the ground several yards away, and it was clear from how Azazel's chest was not rising and falling that he was quite dead. Asmodeus, on the other hand, was slowly rising to his feet, and though his body was covered in burns and bruises, though he was missing his left arm, he still stood up.

"Damn that fallen…" he growled. **"What kind of fool uses their life force as an attack? Fucking suicidal cunt."**

"He gave his life to save us," Lilith mumbled.

Christian felt a surge of guilt, but he pushed it back and stood to his feet. "Since he did that, we can't waste his sacrifice by wallowing. Let's make Asmodeus pay."

"Right."

The two of them had recovered enough to stand up. Christian once more grabbed his swords and charged at Asmodeus, who didn't seem to realize what was happening until he was already on top of the demon.

An attack from the left created a deep gash from Asmodeus' right shoulder to left hip. The demon stumbled back, then regained his

balance and attacked with his spear, which materialized in his hand
However, Christian used the sword in his left hand to deflect the spear
to the side, and then moved in close again. This time he thrust his blade
straight into Asmodeus' chest.

"GGGGAAAAAA!!!!"

Christian was unable to pull his blade out as Asmodeus swiped at
him, so he left the blade in the demon's chest and leapt back. He pulled
out his gun. Now wielding a gun in one hand and a sword in the other,
Christian fired off several rounds that struck the spot around his sword
widening the wound. Meanwhile, he used his other hand to fend off the
demon's spear.

On Asmodeus' next swing, the demon found himself unable to
attack as Lilith wrapped her whip around his spear. However, with a
powerful yank, he tore Lilith's feet from the ground and sent her
hurtling through the air. Even so, the succubus didn't allow herself to
fall. Wings sprouted from her back, a partial transformation, and she
used them to land safely. Her whip was still coiled around the spear.

Christian darted forward. He grabbed the handle of his sword, still
impaled in Asmodeus' chest, and yanked it out. Without pausing to
assess the situation, he spun around and slashed at the hand holding the
spear, still outstretched thanks to Lilith. The scream that erupted from
Asmodeus' mouth as the hand was severed made Christian smile. Just a
little. However, before he could celebrate, something powerful
slammed into his face, and he was sent flying.

"Christian!"

He landed hard on the ground, air leaving his lungs, and then
tumbled across the rocky floor before slamming into an outcropping
some yards away. As he shook his head to clear it, Lilith landed next to
him.

"Are you okay?!"

"Yeah. I'm fine." Christian shook his head again, and then
glanced past Lilith. "More importantly, Asmodeus is coming."

Asmodeus' hand had already been reattached. He ran at the two of
them. Lilith tried to create several illusions, but they weren't working.
Christian guessed Asmodeus wouldn't be affected by anything other
than the illusions Lilith made when she was in her succubus form.
Realizing this, she stood up and moved in front of him.

"Lilith. You need to get out of the way."

"No."

"He'll kill you!"

"It doesn't matter. I can't live without you, so it's death to me either way."

Christian would have argued with her, but there was no time anymore, for Asmodeus had reached them. He thrust his spear at Lilith. Christian couldn't see her face, but he could imagine the expression she wore, determination mixed with fear. And yet, just before the spear penetrated Lilith's chest, a bright light suddenly erupted in front of her. The spear struck the light, and then Asmodeus was blasted off his feet.

"What the—"

Asmodeus crashed into a large spire several feet away, destroying the entire thing. As the spire collapsed on top of him, Christian stood up and looked at the massive golden wall that had sprung into existence in front of Lilith. He thought it was something his mate had created at first, but then he saw that her earrings were glowing.

"This must be the protection Titania talked about."

"Christian, your pendant is glowing."

Christian looked down to see that his pendant was, indeed, glowing. He clasped the pendant in his hand and yanked it off his chest, breaking the chains of his necklace. In the next instant, his pendant had changed from a small gem into a sword—one he'd never seen before.

The blade was made of a substance that resembled silver. It was bright and shone with a light that made it seem like something not of this world. The curved guard was gold, while the handle was blue. Several strange, archaic symbols from a language he didn't understand were engraved into the sword's blade, and they glowed with a faint silver light.

Rubble from the broken spire exploded in all directions, reminding Christian that their battle was not finished. Asmodeus burst from the rubble. His face was covered in more cuts, but his eyes were not showing pain. They revealed nothing but hatred.

"I think we should finish this," Christian said.

"Me too. I'm not sure I have the strength to fight for much longer."

"Can you still transform."

"Of course."

Lilith transformed into her succubus form, which he found every bit as alluring as her human form. She pressed herself against his back, her breasts pushing into his chest, but he ignored his baser instincts as he held the sword in a two-handed grip while she wrapped her arms around his waist.

Taking off into the air, Lilith nimbly spun and danced in a series of aerial maneuvers to avoid several crackling beams of energy that were fired at them. Asmodeus didn't try to fly anymore, which Christian realized was because his wings had been ruined. Several of those beams struck them, but the golden wall defended them. However, they could see cracks beginning to form. This protection wouldn't last very long.

"Take us down, please."

"Way ahead of you."

Lilith quickly moved into a dive that would take them straight to Asmodeus. The demon's baleful glare met them as he raised both hands and sent a powerful blast of demonic energy their way. It slammed into the shield. More cracks formed. The shield broke apart seconds later, but Asmodeus' attack had also run out of energy at the same time.

Using what remained of her power, Lilith created a massive wall that appeared behind Asmodeus, and then made arms sprout from the wall and wrap around the demon. The King of Lust released an enraged scream as he tried to break free, but Lilith yelled out her own war cry as she struggled to maintain her illusion. Christian felt something wet leak onto his neck.

And then they were there. Christian extended the sword, which slid almost too smoothly into Asmodeus' flesh. He did feel a moment of resistance when it hit something hard, but even that only lasted for a second, and then the blade continued moving until the hilt rested against Asmodeus' chest.

Asmodeus stared down at the blade like he could not believe what he was seeing. His eyes were wide in shock as dark blood spread across his body. What made the spectacle even more fascinating was how white lines were traveling from where the sword had impaled him to the rest of his body. Christian couldn't make heads or tails of it.

Raising his head, Asmodeus stared at them for but a single second, and then his body released a silent shudder and his head dropped again.

"Is he... dead?" asked Lilith.

"I think so." Christian stared at the now sightless eyes of the demon king, one of the Kings of Hell, a creature that, by all rights, only archangels and other divine creatures should have been capable of killing. "I can't believe it."

"Believe it or not, I don't think we should remain here. Let's hurry up and destroy that core."

Christian nodded and pulled on the sword, which slowly slid from the demon's body. At the same time, Lilith's illusion faded away, and Asmodeus, with nothing left to hold him, fell to the ground in a heap.

The two of them made their way over to the core. They were exhausted, leaning on each other as they stumbled across the destroyed space of their battle, which had cracks, craters, and destroyed edifices all around them. Oddly enough, the glowing black core, no longer covered in red energy, remained unharmed.

"So... how do we destroy this thing?" asked Lilith.

"I don't know." Christian raised the sword that had slayed Asmodeus to his eyes. "I guess... we could just stab it?"

"If you did that, the backlash would kill you both," a voice said behind them.

The two stumbled around in shock, both fearing another enemy. They did not have the strength to continue fighting. Yet as they looked at who stood behind them, their eyes widened, and then narrowed.

"Kokabiel!"

Indeed, the one standing behind them was none other than Kokabiel, the fallen angel who had kidnapped Christian and brought him to Satan, allowing the King of Wrath to create a Hell Gate on Earth.

The man glanced at Azazel's body, sighed, and then turned to the pair of them.

"I only caught the tail end of your battle against Asmodeus, but I was very impressed. I did not think a succubus and someone who can barely be considered a demon would be capable of defeating one of Hell's seven kings."

"What are you doing here?" asked Christian.

"That should be obvious," the man replied as he walked up to them with calm, collected footsteps. "My entire reason for delivering you to Satan was so he would open a Hell Gate. I couldn't do it myself, so I had him do it for me."

"Why?" asked Lilith.

"So I can die in glorious combat," Kokabiel replied. By now, he had stopped to stand beside them and was staring at the core. "I have lived a long time, and in that time, I have realized that I no longer care for anything besides battle. Fighting is all I crave. I thought that if Satan could open a Hell Gate, then I could enter Hell and finally battle to my heart's content. I'll fight against everything within this accursed world, and then I'll eventually be slain."

He glanced at Lilith and Christian, his eyes sparkling as he stared at their disgusted expressions.

"You think I am insane. That is fine. I care not for what you think of me." He looked back at the core. "Anyway, you two should leave. I will destroy the core for you. However, I'm only going to give you five minutes, so you had best hurry. Any longer than that, and I fear another demon king will come to take Asmodeus' place."

The two of them glanced at each other, needing only a moment to make a decision.

"We're not going to thank you," Christian said.

Kokabiel's reply was mild. "I do not expect thanks. I am doing this for myself, not you."

Christian nodded as he and Lilith limped off. They tried to move as quickly as they could, but both of them were exhausted from their battle. Even so, as they continued, Christian did feel more energy flowing into him. Undoubtedly, the demonic blood in his veins was being empowered by this place. He hated that, but right now, it was thanks to his demon side that he gained enough strength to lift Lilith into a bridal carry and begin running toward the Hell Gate.

Several demons stood in their way, but Christian hopped along the spires and blasted across the air to avoid them, making it to the Hell Gate in record time. However...

"The gate is closing!" Lilith shouted as she clutched the sword, careful not to let it slice her skin. The gate was indeed closing. The swirling vortex shrank as the seconds ticked by.

"Tch!"

Putting on a burst of speed, Christian narrowed his eyes and gritted his teeth. Closer. Closer. He pushed his body as hard as he could, felt the muscles in his calves and thighs constantly tear and regenerate, all to reach the shrinking vortex before it closed. Two yards. One. Christian slammed his left foot into the ground and shot forward, crashing into the vortex seconds before it closed up.

The world around the flitted by. Swirling reds and blacks surrounded them as they shot through the tunnel. Seconds after entering the vortex, the two of them tumbled out and landed on the ground, sprawled out in a tangle of limbs.

It took Christian several seconds to regain his bearings. However, as the ringing in his ears stopped, Christian realized that someone was calling their names. Several someones.

"Christian! Lilith! Are you two okay?!"

The pair of them looked up to find several familiar faces standing above them. Clarissa, Heather, Samantha, Sif, and Leon. Christian looked around and realized that they were back in Jerusalem. The barrier was still up. He could see the golden light from above. However, the dark red atmosphere, caused by the miasma being released from the Hell Gate, was clearing up.

"We're fine," Lilith mumbled as the two of them sat up. "I just... never want to do that again."

The group of individuals hovering around them looked at each other and grinned.

"You had us pretty worried there," Leon admitted. "When you went into that Hell Gate... man, that sure was something. I'm impressed, but at the same time, it took everything Sif and I had to keep Samantha from following you."

"T-that's only because I thought they would need help."

Christian was tempted to rub his eyes as Samantha blushed. It was the first time he'd ever seen her do that.

"It looks like the Hell Gate has been closed," Clarissa said, and then added, "You two did a good job."

As if her words were prophetic, a loud rumbling made everyone turn around. They were just in time to see cracks spread along the black gate. Chunks of the strange material broke off and struck the ground, shattering, and as more cracks spread and more chunks fell, the whole structure ended up collapsing.

Christian and Lilith stared at the gate, now a pile of rubble, and then turned back to each other. The others were talking, though neither of them could tell if they were talking to each other or the two of them. They only had eyes for the other just then.

"Christian?"

"Yeah?"

"I want to go home."

He took a moment to ponder those words and realize what she truly meant when she said, "go home."

"Me too." He nodded and grabbed her hand. "Lilith. Let's go home."

Epilogue

Lilith sat in front of a computer in the school newspaper room, staring at the screen as she manipulated the formatting on some of the typography for the school's newspaper. The quiet hum of the air conditioner and the sound of fingers hitting the keyboard were the only sounds currently present.

California State University was a big campus. There were about 500,000 students enrolled in the university, though this included all 23 campuses and the eight off-campus centers. Still, with so many students enrolled, it was only natural that the newspaper club, whose job was to properly report on issues that dealt with important matters regarding the school, would be swamped with work.

Feeling her shoulders stiffen, Lilith stretched her arms above her head, offering a satisfied groan as her sore muscles loosened.

"Stiff shoulders?" asked someone to her left. It was a young woman with short brown hair, brown eyes, and glasses.

"Yeah…" Lilith smiled. "I think I've been sitting here too long."

"Maybe you should take a break," the girl offered.

"I could always give you a massage if you want," offered the young man on Lilith's right. He was a fairly average boy, neither andsome nor ugly. His brown hair was short. He wasn't in bad shape, though he didn't have any muscle definition either.

She smiled at him. "If you lay one hand on me, I will break your fingers, and then we'll be even more behind schedule because one of our club members can't type."

"R-right." The boy shuddered. "I got it. Forget I offered."

Justin Jansen, her fellow club member and the man responsible for printing the newspapers, was not a bad person by any means, but he was still a man. Lilith could feel the salacious desires behind his words.

Of course, she had yet to meet a single man who didn't have lecherous desires for her, so the chances of someone other than her mate being allowed to touch her were zero.

"You should know better than to say something like that, Justin," the young woman on Lilith's left sighed. "Do you not remember what happened the last time a male touched her?"

"Ah ha... how could I forget?" Justin wiped some sweat from his forehead. "I don't think anyone will ever forget what happened to him."

Last week, a male student on the varsity football team had asked if she wanted to join him at a party his friend was hosting. Of course, Lilith had declined. She had no desire to party with someone whose intentions were so obvious. However, the varsity player had not been willing to take no for an answer... and so Lilith had been forced to take extreme actions.

"Two broken ribs, one broken arm, a hairline skull fracture, and brain trauma," the woman said, adjusting her glasses as she listed the injuries the varsity student received. "I suppose it could have been worse."

"Can anything be worse than that?" asked Justin.

"Yes," the girl answered. "You're new, so you didn't see what Lilith did to the other people who've tried getting into her pants."

At those words, Justin blinked and began asking about what sort of things Lilith had done to the other men who hit on her.

Lilith stopped paying attention by this point. She really wanted to finish formatting the layout for next week's newspaper. All of their writers had finished their articles, so all that was left was for her to format it, Miranda—the girl on her left and the club president—to give it her approval, and Justin to print it and send it to the distributor. Of course, they also had digital copies that they sent out, but someone else was in charge of making those.

It took another hour before Lilith finally finished, and after having Miranda check it over and sign off on it, she picked up her bag and smiled at the others.

"I'm heading out now."

"Bye." Miranda waved her off.

"See you." Justin turned to look at her, only to look away.

Lilith sighed when she saw where his eyes strayed, but she didn't let it bother her and, exiting through the door, began walking down the hallway toward the exit.

Several people greeted her on the way. A few were women she'd become friends with, like the quiet girl on the varsity cheer squad, Christine, and the nice woman who ran the library committee, Hallee. However, there were also quite a few men who made comments at her. She ignored them, and fortunately, everyone already knew about what she did to men who were too forward, so no one actually tried anything.

The campus in Los Angeles was quite large, spanning upwards of two or three square miles as it sat nestled against the Long Beach Freeway and San Bernardino Freeway.

After crossing a street, Lilith wandered through a campus park filled with several benches and tables situated underneath a series of gazebos. There were quite a few trees as well. She didn't know what type, but they offered shade to people who wanted to sit underneath a tree and read, which quite a few students were doing. She also saw several people who had set out blankets and were having picnics.

Ignoring the park for now, Lilith wandered past a set of buildings before reaching a large structure that acted as something of a landmark for her. It wasn't much. Just a red bricked building called The Golden Eagle. A tin structure shaped like a curved V supported by several dozen iron bars moved around it and was very easy to recognize. Lilith searched the area for a bit, and then found who she was looking for and made a beeline to them.

Christian was sitting at a round table near The Golden Eagle building, completely oblivious to the admiring looks of the female students near him. She didn't blame them. The black shirt he wore stretched across his broad chest and shoulders, and his powerfully built arms were on full display. His chiseled face was intently focused on what he was reading as well. The intensity in his red and green eyes as he scanned the page no doubt was the cause of the swooning directed at him.

"Hey! I'm sorry for taking so long. There was more work to do than usual."

Upon hearing her voice, Christian looked up and a smile lit his face. He set the tablet on the table and stood. Reaching out a hand, he pulled her close and gave her a very welcome "hello" kiss.

Lilith ignored the disappointed groans from basically everyone present as she threaded her hands through his hair and enjoyed the soft feel of his lips. A thrill traveled through her body, down her spine, and to her loins. She felt a rush of energy give her more strength than any energy drink could hope to.

Making sure to break the saliva connecting their tongues before it could become a problem, Lilith leaned back and smiled.

"Thanks for always picking me up."

"Why wouldn't I pick you up?" asked Christian, smiling. "Coming to take you back home just means I get to see you that much earlier."

"I guess." Lilith giggled. "Thanks anyway."

A lot of whispers followed them as Christian grabbed his tablet and they left the area, their fingers entwined, but neither of them cared to listen to what was being said.

"What were you reading?" she asked.

"A new series that just came out called I'd Defeat A Demon Lord If It was For My Daughter."

"Oh! I've heard of that. How is it?"

"Not bad so far, though the writing could use a bit of work. I'm giving it some leeway since this is just the first volume and Chirolu is obviously a new author."

As they talked about the current story Christian was reading, they walked toward a parking garage, traveled up to the second floor, and wandered the semi-dark garage until they reached Christian's car. It was a brand new Toyota Prius. The red paint gave it a kinda sporty look, but it was too cute to really look sporty.

"So you'd say it's worth reading?" Lilith asked as Christian opened the door for her. "Thank you."

"Hmm… yeah, I'd say it is." Christian shut the door after she sat down, traveled around to the other side, and got in the driver's seat. As he buckled up and turned on the car, he continued. "After you finish volume one, we can read volume two together."

"Sounds good to me." Lilith nodded her agreement to the idea.

Christian pulled out of the parking lot and soon merged onto Paseo Rancho Castilla road. He eased into the traffic without missing a beat, and then began driving toward the freeway.

"I got a call from Samantha," he said casually. "She said she has a job for us."

"Oh?" Lilith perked up.

After the Executioners officially disbanded, Samantha D'Arc founded a new group known as the Supernatural Investigations Bureau. Unlike the Executioners, this group was funded by the US government. It was more or less the same as before. That said, there were several key differences between her new group and this one.

"It seems a fight broke out between a group of vampires and werewolves in Orange County. She asked us to mediate between the two groups." He paused, a smile curling at his lips. "And don't worry. She paid up front."

While Christian had said he wasn't interested in becoming an Executione again, that didn't mean he had no desire to help others. Lilith figured the desire to protect people had become ingrained into his psyche. That was why he worked part-time as a Supernatural Mediator for Samantha's new group.

His job didn't always involve combat. In fact, his job normally involved mediating between groups, though it sometimes did require him to fight, such as a recent case where a Nachzehrer went on a killing spree in Nevada. Christian had tracked that one down and was forced to kill it when it attacked him. Fortunately, most of his tasks these days involved talking instead of killing.

It wasn't like wanting to help people was his only reason for doing this. His job was currently their only source of income, and he made quite a lot doing it. Thanks to his job, Lilith's college was paid for, they had bought their own house, and Christian could afford this car.

"Will it take long?" Lilith asked.

Christian shook his head. "No. We should make it back in time to see the movie with Maria."

"That's good." She sighed in relief. "The last thing I want to do is listen to Maria speculate about why we ditched her again. Some of the scenarios that girl came up with were…"

"Accurate?"

"Well… yes, sort of." Lilith scratched her cheek. "But when she gets like that, she makes it sound like all we do is have sex."

"You can't blame her for thinking that way."

"I know that."

After she and Christian had been caught having sex in the living room of their new house when Maria barged in, she had taken away the woman's key for more than a month. However, even doing that hadn't stopped her friend from teasing them.

"Anyway, are you ready?" Christian asked. "I doubt things will get rough, but you never know."

Placing her hand on Christian's shoulder, she offered him her brightest smile. "I'm always ready, so long as I'm with you."

"Yeah." Christian removed one hand from the steering wheel and placed it on Lilith's hand. "Me too."

~Fin

Afterword

It's the final book of *The Executioner Series* and rather than lament on how I am unsatisfied with my writing for this series as a whole, I want to take this afterword to thank everyone who read this series.

The Executioner Series was my attempt at writing something different from what I normally do—a purely western urban fantasy series that didn't rely on anime/manga tropes to tell a story. While I do not believe I succeeded in this regard, I do feel like I learned a lot by writing this. Partially, I just learned that I should probably stick with my harem anime-esque storytelling, but I also learned that I might be able to incorporate some pure western concepts with anime tropes to improve my storytelling. I'd like to try creating stories that are a better fusion between western tropes and anime tropes.

You ladies and gentlemen who stuck through with me on this series are all amazing. I really, truly appreciate your encouragement and support as I tried to do something different.

I don't think I'm going to write anymore purely western novels. It's not my style. I'm the anime guy. My stories use Japanese tropes found in anime and manga—particular harem anime and manga—to create something that, while not unique, is a little different from the standard Western reading fare.

On top of thanking all of you who read this story to the end, I would also like to thank Dominique Goodall for editing my series and Lawrence Mann for creating the book covers. They both did an excellent job. I was truly blessed to have such great people working on this with me.

I'm not sure what project I am going to publish next... mostly because I am working on several different projects at the same time and I don't know which one I will finish first. I can tell ou that I'm currently working on a somewhat Wuxia-style light novel series. For those who don't know what Wuxia is, it stands for Chinese martial arts fantasy, so this will be a blending of Japanese, Western, and Chinese fantasy tropes turned into a somewhat mishmash of a story that I hope will prove to be entertaining.

Currently, this project is only available to read on my Patreon (https://www.patreon.com/BrandonVarnell), but it will become available in paperback and ebook at some point. If anyone feels like supporting me, please go there. I also provide goodies like SFW and NSFW artwork, signed paperback copies, and extra chapters. If you'd like to catch a glimpse of my wuxia series, *WIEDERGEBURT: Legend of the Reincarnated Warrior,* you can read the first chapter on the next page of this novel after the afterword!

That is all for this afterword. I know *The Executioner Series* was not the best work I've ever produced, but I do hope you all enjoyed it. Thank you so much for reading this series, thank you everyone who decides to leave a review on whatever site you bought it, and thank you for continuing to support me. It means a lot.

I hope you'll join me on my next project!

~Brandon Varnell

WIDEREBURT: Legend of the Reincarnated Warrior

Chapter 1: The Final Battle

The air burst all around me. Flames seared the hair off my arms and caused my skin to crack and burn. Blood seeped from my skin, looking almost like lava leaking from crack in the earth's crust.

Though I quickly circulated my Spiritual Power, channeling the water element through my body to heal my wounds, I did no allow myself to sigh in relief. More explosions were detonating al around me, forcing me to swerve in every direction. What's more by channeling the water element and using it to heal myself, I had been forced to split my attention two ways.

The lightning covering my body had grown weaker as a result of my split attention. In that moment, seven figures appeared above me. I glared up at the winged beasts flying over my head. They were naughty but shadows. However, those shadows were currently surrounded by intense Spiritual Auras that crashed into me like tidal waves rolling over a small village.

One of those great beasts released an avian cry before it swooped down, and the moment it did, the blazing heat surrounding my body grew even more fierce. Sweat broke out on my skin. It quickly dried up under this unfathomable heat. I could feel my skin getting singed once more, and I knew that I could no longer afford to run.

Since this creature was using fire, I decided to use water.

Dissipating the lightning in my body, I took a deep breath, and then circulated my Spiritual Power again. Instead of the sensation of static crawling across my skin, something soft and almost gel like covered my body. One step further. Grimacing as the heat from the creature closing in caused steam to rise from my body, I channeled more Spiritual Power into myself and transformed my entire body into water.

The great beast was finally upon me. What had appeared was an avian of such immense size that even the dragons living in the Misty Mountain Range could not compare to it. Wings of orange and red fire flapped, causing heat waves to distort the air. Colorful designs ran along its body. It was a mixture of red, orange, yellow, and blue. Its plumage was a brilliant white that burned like an illuminating flame. Red and yellow tails trailed behind it as though simulating the ends of a shooting star. Intense crimson eyes glared at me with a hatred that I knew was mutual.

Gnashing my teeth together, I turned around, tucked my fist into my torso, and put all of my Spiritual Power into my next attack.

The beast drew near. I waited until the last second. Then I quickly spun around, dodging the beast by a hair's breadth. It was so close that my body, currently composed entirely of water, was beginning to boil. However, I did not let myself get distracted. Thrusting out my fist, I channeled my Spiritual Power through it and created a massive spike of water that extended from my arm.

Even though the intense heat from the flames surrounding this creature was immense, I was no weakling myself. Water evaporated and created waves of billowing steam. Even so, the spear held firm, refusing to dissipate, and it soon penetrated the beast's chest. Rather than spewing blood, what emerged from the creature was a bright white flame.

As the beast cried in pain, I immediately retracted myself and prepared to attack again.

That was when one of the other beasts swooped down. I saw the shadow and sensed the intent to kill me and quickly moved away. Once I had reached what I deemed a safe distance from the firebird, I released my control over water and transformed into lightning again. Everything around me immediately sped up, allowing me to safely jump several dozen meters in less time than it took to blink.

The bird that had swooped past me was just as massive as the firebird, but instead of being coated in flames, this one had green and white feathers. Its soft feathers gave it a very gentle appearance. However, I knew from the thousands of razor sharp cuts I'd received during my earlier engagement that I couldn't underestimate its deceptively soft appearance. A long tail moved behind it like a tassel. If I looked closely, I could see the atmosphere around it being cut by thousands of wind blades.

A loud crash caused me to cast my gaze toward the ground. Flames spewed from the ground down below as the fire bird crashed into the forest. I felt a sense of grim satisfaction as the creature shrieked in agony. Brilliant white flames, the lifeblood of that great beast, were spewing from its chest like a fountain.

I did not have much time to admire my handiwork, for the green bird released a sharp cry before charging at me. Knowing that my element was weak against this creature that could control the wind, I used Flash Step Version 3: Lightning Step to move away as quickly as I could, but the beast remained stuck on my tail, creating a vacuum that cut through the atmosphere to increase its speed.

Frowning, I once more split my attention. I didn't do much this time. Channeling the light element into my finger, I took careful aim and sent a condensed beam of light at the wind bird. What I got in return was a satisfied shriek as my attack sheared through one of its wings. Greenish white blood spewed from the area where the limb had been severed. Without both wings, it was unable to maintain flight and fell to the ground below.

However, just like before, I was given no time to celebrate my success. Five other birds had just descended. Each one was just as big as the previous two. Each one possessed the ability to control a different element.

A powerful beam of light slammed into me without mercy, burning my back as it sent me sailing toward the ground. My scream was lost to the wind. My body felt like it was being thrown into the Sun. Everything hurt. However, I did my best to shunt aside the pain, increased the flow of lightning through my body, and rolled out from underneath the powerful beam of light.

The beam continued on. It struck the side of a mountain several kilometers below. An explosion so massive that the wind buffeted me despite its distance went up, sending plumes of smoke and rubble into the sky. When the attack died down, the mountain was gone. In its place was a crater so large I was sure it would be visible even if I moved beyond this planet's atmosphere.

"Damn..."

I looked at the result of that attack, and then turned back to glare at the beast who'd caused it. The massive bird flapped its wings as it glared back. This creature looked like it was made of pure light, a combination of white and yellow feathers that appeared both soft and translucent. Yellow eyes glowed with a power that seemed almost divine.

While the bird and I entered a glaring contest, an intense killing intent slammed into me, forcing me to swerve from the spot where I'd been floating.

Six spheres made of water flew past the spot where I'd been. They slammed into the ground far below. Each sphere created a crater that easily spanned ten or fifteen meters across.

I could not admire this attack, for the moment I dodged it, I was forced to move again. This time, seven blades of darkness cut through the air. They were nothing more than black ripples. I swerved over one of them, and then flew down to avoid another. Twisting my body, I managed to avoid two more, but the last one had been aimed at where I would be rather than where I was.

"HA!"

Channeling light into my palm, I slammed it into the blade of darkness, causing the air around me to crackle as arcs of light and dark Spiritual Power raced across the sky. Gritting my teeth as the dark blade pushed me back, I released a furious cry and poured even more Spiritual Power into my palm. The dark blade exploded as I finally tore through it.

The creature that had released this was a bird made from darkness so pure it was like a black hole. Sharp wings covered its body. The only part of it that wasn't black was its eyes, which were pure white and contained no pupil. Alongside it was a bird with blue feathers, one with yellow feathers, another with brown feathers, and the light bird that had attacked me earlier.

I took a heavy breath as sweat poured from my brow. However, I knew I couldn't stop. Without even trying to recover, I released the restraints on my Spiritual Power. My body became energized as though the last several hours had never happened. I could feel the Spiritual Power coursing through me like a tempest. Light mixed with water and lightning inside of me, some of which leaked out because my body simply couldn't withstand the power output.

"Dammit... I had been hoping to save this for your boss," I muttered in a bitter voice.

Whether or not the five elemental birds heard me, they certainly knew that my threat level had suddenly increased. All five of them screeched as they gathered their own Spiritual Power. It congealed around their mouths, forming spheres of condensed energy. Barely a second had passed before they launched their attacks. Five beams of water, lightning, light, darkness, and earth flew toward me.

I did not meet their attacks head on. I wasn't stupid.

Using the power of light, I immediately vanished from the spot where I'd been standing. Their attack went through my after image. I didn't give them a chance to be surprised. Reappearing several meters above the most troublesome of the five, I turned myself into a streak of light and descended before it realized what I was doing. I barely felt any resistance as my body blew a whole clean through the black bird.

Landing on the ground at almost the exact same instant I had moved from point A, I looked up to see that my attack had done what I intended. The black bird with powers over darkness now had a large hole in its chest. What's more, the edges were frayed and refused to heal. While darkness was the antithesis of light, the same was equally true.

"Kari, I still have no real grasp over your affinity, but it is only thanks to you that this was possible," I said to myself as I watched the massive bird slowly break into particles of darkness.

My attack enraged the four remaining birds, who quickly descended toward me. I didn't even need to use Spiritual Perception to feel their intent to kill me. Almost before I could even move, they had each launched their own attack. The four elements of water, light, lightning, and earth swirled around each other to create mixed beam of power so large it could engulf a small city.

But I was no longer there.

As their attacks slammed into the forest floor and caused even more damage to the environment, I was already in front of the water bird. I reached out with my hand and touched its head. The bird's eyes were crossed as it stared at me, but I just smiled at it. I'm sure my smile was quite cold.

The water bird lit up as I shoved as much lightning into it as I could. With a shriek so loud it was nearly inaudible, the bird lit up like fireworks during the Summer Solstice. Smoke soon rose from its body. However, it was too slow. This attack would kill it, but the other birds would get to me first.

Clicking my tongue, I raised my hand, which had turned into a five meter blade of lightning, and then I brought it down. My attack created a seam of light within the bird, a small line that appeared from its beak to its tail feathers. The bird peeled apart at the seam, the two halves almost gently falling away from each other before the elemental beast turned into water that rained upon the ground.

Barely a second had past before something sharp pierced my back. I couldn't even cry out in pain as the air was stolen from my ings. The ground beneath and the sky above blurred past me in full streaks. Gritting my teeth, I turned my head and found the enraged eyes of the light bird glaring at me. It had pierced my back with its beak.

"Don't think…" I struggled to raise my hand. "Don't think…" Light, lightning, and water swirled around my arm as I channeled all three elements. "Don't think this will be enough to do me in!!!"

With a roar of defiance, I crashed my fist into the light bird's beak. A loud cracking sound echoed from the beak as an incision line appeared. One incision became two, then two became three, four, eight, sixteen. It quickly multiplied before cracking underneath the power of my fist.

The bird immediately stopped flying as it thrashed and screeched in pain. However, the forward momentum it had generated was enough that I was not able to stop from flying until I generated enough force with my own Spiritual Power to stop myself.

Reaching behind my back after I had stopped moving, I pulled out what remained of the beak from my back and tossed it away. Warm blood spilled down my back. I ignored it as I eyed the three remaining elemental birds. The lightning bird, the wind bird, and the now injured light bird.

"Ha… ha… ha…"

My shoulders heaved as I glared at the birds. However, I didn't think my glare was very effective just then. The Spiritual Power flowing through me was fluctuating. The aura covering my body flickered in and out. I didn't reveal my thoughts, but I was swearing up a storm internally as my Spiritual Power started running dry.

This technique I was using wasn't complete yet. If I'd had time to finish it, then maybe I could have already ended this battle, but luck had not been on my side.

It looked like the birds were just about to renew their attack, and I myself was prepared to re-initiate hostilities, but all of us suddenly froze in place as an intense Spiritual Pressure filled the air. My breathing quickly grew heavier as sweat formed on my brow. It was a cold sweat. I tried to take in a breath, but the pressure was causing my lungs to struggle with the simple act of taking in oxygen. It felt like something was crushing them.

A figure had suddenly appeared in front of me. He was a luminous being more beautiful than the Sun, a creature of such incomparable beauty that even in my hatred, I could not deny there was not a single flaw to be found. Pure white robes covered his body. Long and silver hair flowed freely like a waterfall down his head all the way to his bare feet. His long, pointed ears were the clearest signs that he wasn't human.

He did not have a very muscular body. Indeed, I would have said his body was quite feminine. He was slender and willowy. However, I didn't let that fool me, and even if he had been a woman, I wouldn't have underestimated him like some people would have done.

Despite his beauty, there was something odd about this man. Every part of him seemed bright and divine—every part except his blood red eyes. They were a dark crimson that seemed tainted somehow. Furthermore, that dark aura surrounding him seemed to present a direct contradiction to his vibrant, almost divine appearance.

The man took a deep breath as he looked at the three birds. He surveyed them with a slight frown, and then quickly glanced at where I had killed the others. I wanted to move, to attack this man with everything I had, but some invisible force kept me in place.

Finally, he looked at me.

"**To think a half-blood like you was able to defeat four of my seven slaves,**" he murmured. "**You know I had enslaved these monsters specifically to kill you? Your powers are indeed great. Given enough time, you might even pose a threat to me. It seems trying to send enslaved Demon Beasts after you was a mistake. I should have just come myself.**"

"Great Overlord of the Seventh Plain…" My fists shook with barely restrained hatred as I stared at the being before me. "You took everything from me. My wife. My child. Everything. I have waited for this day, waited for the day I would finally face you again, for the day I would finally kill you."

The being before me, the one I called the Great Overlord of the Seventh Plain, chuckled as though I had said something amusing. It was a grating laugh, not at all like something I'd expect from such a feminine figure. His laugh caused the hair on my neck to prickle.

"**Had your wife not shielded you from me, she would not have died. She only has herself to blame.**" He paused, his head tilting as he stared impassively into my rage filled eyes. "**As for your daughter… I could not allow a human who possesses such divine blood to live. Had I not killed her, she would have become a threat.**"

"A threat?" I whispered. "We were just living peacefully when you attacked us unprovoked and without warning. We were no threat to you. You laid waste to our home, destroyed our civilization, and killed my family without even a hint of mercy or provocation."

The Great Overlord of the Seventh Plain snorted. **"You may not understand it now, but you are indeed a grave threat to me —no, you are perhaps the greatest threat to ever exist. What I did was necessary."**

I didn't think the blood flowing through my veins could have run any colder than it already was, but I was wrong. It was like my blood had frozen over. Only a chilling coldness that seeped through my entire being remained.

"Necessary, you say?"

"Yes. Necessary."

"Necessary… for what?"

"To keep you from being able to interfere with my plans." The Great Overlord of the Seventh Plain spread his arms wide and chuckled again. **"Just look at what you have done. A half-blood who hasn't even learned to control even a tenth of his abilities has defeated four of my seven slaves, Divine-rank Demon Beasts capable of annihilating entire cities with a single attack, and you would have defeated all of them had I not intervened. I'd say this level of destruction warrants intervention."**

I had no idea what this monster was talking about, but I was done listening. He had attacked my family for a reason as dumb as protecting himself? From what? It was true that I had been the one who awakened him, but I had never harmed him nor had any intention to. Had he never appeared attacked my city, never attempted to kill me, never murdered my daughter, we would have left him alone.

My hatred surged, allowing me to overcome the intense pressure that had been pushing down on me. I compressed the last remaining Spiritual Power in my body. The aura that had been covering me vanished. To the average eye, it would have looked like my power had disappeared.

The Great Overlord of the Seventh Plain narrowed his eyes.

Then I vanished.

It happened in a flash. I appeared directly behind my foe, thrusting out my fist in a punch that caused the air to burst. However, without even looking behind him, the Great Overlord of the Seventh Plain placed his hand in the direction of my punch, catching it. A shockwave erupted from the contact.

I was already moving.

Appearing on his left in a manner that was almost like teleportation, I launched a powerful kick. This was also blocked. I was undeterred. I appeared again and again, moving all around him at speeds so fast I left multiple afterimages in my wake. One. Two. Four. Sixteen. Yet no matter how many punches and kicks I threw, no matter how fast I pushed myself, this monster blocked each and every one of them as though it was easier than breathing.

Meanwhile, I was running on empty.

With the last of my strength, I released a vicious scream and channeled all my energy into my fist. A bright glow erupted from it. The air around it distorted. Ripples spread through the sky as though the fabrics of reality itself were being torn apart.

The Great Overlord's eyes finally widened. With something resembling panic, he threw out his own punch, which glowed in the same manner as mine but with a dark energy that seemed vile. The air exploded between us as one fought to overpower the other. I gritted my teeth and pushed as hard as I could, wrecking my body. Blood exploded from my arms as my capillaries burst, my muscles tore apart like they were made of soggy parchment, and could feel my very life being drained.

I didn't care. It didn't matter if I died so long as I killed this man.

Perhaps it was because I was so focused that I didn't see the attack coming at me until it was too late. However, when a fist appeared out of nowhere, all I could do was swear. The attack hit me. Pain overrode my ability to see, causing a white film to cover my eyes.

I think I must have passed out. When I came to, I was lying on my back, in the middle of a massive crater so large I couldn't even judge its size. The Great Overlord of the Seventh Plain was above me, a sword made of pure darkness grasped firmly within his right hand. He raised the sword and brought it down.

In a last ditch effort, I unleashed all of the Spiritual Power I had left, channeled it into my right hand, and met the blade with a punch. Our attacks struck each other. Light bent. Air warped. Lightning crackled. The area around our mutual attacks became distorted as strange cracks appeared in the atmosphere like the gaping maw to a bottomless abyss.

An explosion suddenly rent the air as the world around me was torn apart. The last thing I saw before darkness engulfed me was the Great Overlord's surprised crimson eyes.

Hey, did you know?
Brandon Varnell has started a Patreon
You can get all kinds of awesome exclusives
Like:

1. The chance to read his stories before anyone else!
2. Free ebooks!
3. exclusive SFW and NSFW artwork!
4. Signed paperback copies!
5. His undying love!
Er... maybe we don't want that last one, but the rest is pretty cool, right?

To get this awesome exlusive conent go to:
https://www.patreon.com/BrandonVarnell
and sigh up today!

Have you been turned on to Brandon's Light Novels Yet?

Wait. That sounded kind of wrong.

Try out Brandon's first original English light novel series!

All Alex wanted was to
become a hero...

Instead, he picked up a harem
of beautiful women!

Follow Caspian's Journey to become a Sorceress's Knight in Arcadia's Ignoble Knight vol. 1-4!

He was their best Executioner

BRANDON VARNELL
SUCCUBUS

BRANDON VARNELL
ESCAPE

BRANDON VARNELL
ENCLAVE

BRANDON VARNELL
GRIGORI

Story by
Brandon Varnell

Illustrations by
Aisoretto

Summoned to another world...
  ...Betrayed by the kingdom he saved
Now he seeks a way to return home...
  ...By going on a Journeying with
The daughter of the dark lord he slaid...

Get Journey of a Betrayed Hero, volume 1 now

Want to learn when a new book comes out?
Follow me on Social Media!

 @AmericanKitsune

 +BrandonVarnell

 @BrandonBVarnell

 http://bvarnell1101.tumblr.com/

 Brandon Varnell

 BrandonbVarnell

 https://www.patreon.com/
BrandonVarnell

CPSIA information can be obtained
at www.ICGtesting.com
Printed in the USA
FFHW020519300519
52712666-58232FF